FINAL DESIGN

Also by Noreen Gilpatrick

THE PIANO MAN

FINAL DESIGN

NOREEN GILPATRICK

THE MYSTERIOUS PRESS

Published by Warner Books

A Time Warner Company

1 - 5334

Mysterious Press books are published by Warner Books, Inc., 1271
Avenue of the Americas, New York, NY 10020.

W A Time Warner Company

The Mysterious Press name and logo are registered trademarks of Warner Books, Inc.

Printed in the United States of America

First printing: October 1993

10 9 8 7 6 5 4 3 2 1

Library of Congress Cataloging-in-Publication Data

Gilpatrick, Noreen.
    Final design / Noreen Gilpatrick.
        p.   cm.
    ISBN 0-89296-514-2
    1. Police—United States—Fiction. I. Title.
    PS3557.I4638F56   1993
813'.54—dc20   92-50658
                                                                    CIP

For Deb
Who gives such a good lecture

ACKNOWLEDGMENTS

Much expert help, assistance and input from others went into the development and execution of the book, and any errors that may be there are solely mine. My deepest thanks go to the following people:

For technical and procedural help:
Hubert W Holton, Commander, Third District, City of Chicago Department of Police, Chicago, Illinois
Michael H. Bowman, Police Officer, San Jose Police Department, San Jose, California

For research help and fact checking:
Gloria Bickley, Kirkland, Washington
Kay Conrad, Research Librarian, Fond du Lac City Library, Fond du Lac, Wisconsin
Betsey Greenbaum, Bellevue, Washington
Ann Henderson, Manager, Book World, Fond du Lac, Wisconsin

For readings and proofings of the early drafts:
Shirley Brusius, Van Dyne, Wisconsin

And, as always, for their love, support, counsel and encouragement:
My husband, my children, and my friends.

The characters and events delineated in this book are fictional, as is the Eastside Police Force. The EPD was invented strictly to allow the use of the entire eastside geographical landscape as a background to the telling of the tale without regard to jurisdictional boundaries. I have also placed a pharmacy in a town that currently has none.

The towns used as settings in the book are real, however, and have been depicted as accurately as I could portray them.

FINAL DESIGN

1

There wasn't much give in the mid-morning traffic, and the disagreeable weather blowing in from the Olympics did nothing to help. A stormy sheet of sky spread over the whole of Puget Sound and the March wind came in a biting fury from the northwest. It drove a fine, icy mist onto road surfaces and windshields, and cars were forced to feel their way along the crowded city streets of Bellevue.

Kate MacLean crept forward in traffic along with everyone else. Her partner, Sam Morrison, had taken the departmental car checked out to them and she lacked the red light and siren to force her own car quickly through the slowdowns. She finally broke through the last of the traffic snarls and made a quick left onto a side street. A second quick left led into the parking lot behind an old office building.

The uniformed patrolman standing next to his squad car didn't know her, and she had to show her I.D. "MacLean. Homicide." He nodded and she gunned past him.

Two more cruisers, light bars still flaring, were parked to either side of the back entrances to the building and more patrolmen guarded the door against the curious. A couple of dozen spectators, huddled deep into heavy coats, milled about on the lee side of the building out of the wind, talking and peering around, not sure what they were supposed to be seeing. Since Kate was in plain clothes and driving her own car, they dismissed her as just another onlooker and went back to their peering. An ambulance was backed up to the back door, empty and waiting.

Kate had been sure she'd dressed warm enough for the weather that morning, in a wool suit and long-sleeved sweater, with a lined all-weather coat belted tightly around her. But as she climbed out of her car, the raw March wind caught her full-force. Her shoulder-length hair blew in wings straight past her cheeks and the hem of her coat flapped like a canvas sail in a gale force. She kept her face turned away from the icy edge of the brutal wind as she made her way to the building.

Just inside the doorway, safely out of the weather, the two ambulance whites lounged against a wall, talking quietly between themselves. They shook their heads at her as she entered the small hallway. There was nothing they could do.

The building was a dilapidated four-story frame structure, built in the old part of Bellevue early in the century, with the small windows and dusky lighting common to the day. It was one of the very few old buildings left in the city. It, too, was scheduled to be razed, but some holdup in the permit process had given a few starving businesses their last chance at cheap rent.

To the right of the entranceway, a poorly lit stairwell wound up into shadow. The wooden steps were bare, steep and badly worn. She had to watch her footing as she climbed. At the top, there was a dark, uncarpeted hallway that ran down half the length of the building, with a couple of closed doors lining one grimy wall. At the end of the gloomy tunnel, a door leading into the back half of the upper floor stood open, and she paused in front of it to assess the scene.

The dead woman was slumped over a desk against one long wall. The medical examiner and police photographer were already at work over the body, and a patrolman stood to one side, watching them. The M.E. was intent on directing the photographer's angles. Both of them looked up at Kate's entrance, then ignored her. At the far end of the room, next to a large window looking out onto the gray world, a young woman—a girl, almost—sat weeping at a drawing board.

The room was cavernous, Kate noted. She surmised from the open beams running crosswise to the ridgepole that it had been an attic in its previous incarnation. At some point the walls had been whitewashed, some cheap linoleum had been laid and a pair of plastic skylights installed. Scarred desks ran at right angles along the two side walls. Set below the large single window at the gabled end, next to the girl's drawing board, was an old bookcase topped with an array of art supplies. Against the front, next to the doorway, stood a bank of files and a coffee center set up on a dented typing stand. A couple of large, battered worktables spread with brightly colored artwork filled some of the cavernous middle space. The white walls, the bright artwork, and the poor furniture all spelled a brave poverty. A cash-starved graphics business, Kate judged.

The dead woman had her head resting on her left forearm braced on the desk, her face turned to one side. There were no obvious wounds that Kate could see, no blood anywhere. Her eyes were closed and the peaceful look on her face gave a first impression of sleep. Her right hand was loosely curled next to a coffee mug and a discarded tea bag sat in a puddle of its own juices in an ashtray.

Even in death, the woman was stunning. A thick mane of glossy black hair sprang away from the cheek and forehead into a swirl of tight curls hugging head and neck. Long black thick eyelashes rested on high cheekbones. Her face was a perfect oval, her nose straight and classic, her mouth full, a perfectly shaped bow. Though her skin was smooth and clear as a young girl's, there was an air of maturity embedded in her features. Late thirties, Kate judged. Or early forties. She had on a simple brown skirt, a white blouse of no particular style, and a pair of plain, low-heeled walking shoes. A tan blazer hung over the back of her desk chair.

George Leffick, the responding officer, moved her way, his face impassive. "Morning, Katie." He looked back at the dead woman. "Damned shame, isn't it."

She nodded. "It always is," she said gravely. George expected respect for the dead. She pulled her notebook from her shoulder bag and opened it to a fresh section. "What do we know so far?"

"The dead woman's Catherine Fletcher, part owner of the studio here. The artist is Ginger Burklund, also a part owner. She's the one who found her. According to the artist, there are two other partners in the business that aren't here yet. The artist said she was late coming to work and claims she found the Fletcher woman just the way you see her. Says she called nine-one-one, then sat on her stool and waited. She hasn't budged since. She's pretty shook up. I can't get much out of her, and I was afraid to push it. Afraid she'd lose it if I did."

Kate watched the dapper little man still directing the photographer. "Has the M.E. come up with anything yet?"

"He's not saying."

"Any visible wounds on the body?"

"Not that I saw. There's no blood anywhere. Looks like she just felt a little tired, laid her head down and just went to sleep."

"How about drugs?" Kate asked. "Any sign of use by either of them?"

"I couldn't tell on the dead woman. The artist seems a bit zoned out. That could be natural, though, seeing she's the one who found her."

"Okay, thanks, George."

He nodded and turned back to watch the M.E. and the photographer.

While she waited for the M.E. to finish, Kate stood against one wall, drawing a simple outline of the room in her notebook, using rectangles for the furniture and marking the locations of the body and the artist with black circles. It was obvious the artist was in a mild state of shock. She hadn't moved since Kate had first arrived. She still stared at the same blank spot on the wall. Kate's heart stirred in sympathy. Walking in on death was a tough thing for a civilian to handle. Civilian, hell, she thought. It was damned tough for the pros, too. That's why George always made some formal comment about it. It was his way of dignifying death.

The M.E. finally finished with the photographer. He straightened up, studied the body one last time, then came over to where Kate stood. "Where's Sam?" he asked bluntly.

Kate refused to feel slighted by the question. Sam headed the team; the M.E. was used to dealing with him. "He'll be here. He's finishing up a booking at the jail, so I took the call. What'd you find?"

"Enough for you to bring the lab boys in," he said in a gruff tone of voice. "She didn't leave earth today 'cause God called her home."

"Suicide?"

"Or murder. You're looking at an overdose of something. I'm gonna say morphine, to get you started. Her pupils are like needle points. But that's only an interim guess, Katie," he warned, "don't make book on it. We'll have to wait for toxicology to know for sure."

"How long ago?"

"Not long. Body temp's down a couple of degrees. Lividity's just starting in the legs. Mucous membranes are dry now, but there's no rigor yet. At a guess, I'd say maybe an hour, hour and a half. Not much longer than that."

Kate glanced at her watch. A couple of minutes past eleven. Time of death, nine-thirty to ten. She indicated the girl at the drawing board. "How about our friend there; is she in any condition to talk?"

"Should be. I offered her a happy pill to calm her down, but she turned me down flat. Said that pills aren't good for you, she only does pot."

Kate half-smiled at that and turned to the patrolman. "Patch through to the station and have them send out a lab crew, George. Then play guardian at the door and direct them up here when they arrive."

"Make sure they take the tea, Katie," the M.E. said. "Bag, cup, canister, everything."

"You think that's how she got the morphine?" Kate asked him.

"Maybe," he said. "You know me, I don't know anything until I write up the final report and read what it says. I'm always surprising myself." With a curt nod, he walked out.

Kate watched him leave. He'd be sending the stretcher up for the body soon and she'd have to get the artist out of the way, but until then, she had just a bit of time. She glanced over at the drawing board. The girl was still staring into space, taking no notice of anything going on around her. She'd be okay for a couple of minutes more, Kate decided. She moved to the side of the body and began a detailed visual examination of it.

She noticed for the first time the woman was wearing no makeup. Although, really, the eyes didn't need any. Her lashes were black, long, and naturally thick. But there was no eyeshadow and no liner. She wasn't wearing any lipstick either. And the cherry-red fingernail polish was showing its age with a shade too much white circling the cuticles. Kate absorbed this for a moment. Wouldn't someone planning suicide make herself up as attractively as possible?

She stood well away from the jacket hung over the back of the chair and eyeballed it from a distance, then moved back in and fingered the material. To any casual onlooker, the skirt and blazer would've looked appropriately businesslike. But the quality was poor, and inside the jacket the lining was frayed. The low walking shoes were run over at the outside of each heel, as if she'd walked with a heavy, uneven gait. Except for an inexpensive cubic zirconia ring on her right hand and a cheap digital watch on her left wrist, she wore no jewelry. It was apparent Catherine Fletcher had suffered from money problems. Serious enough for her to decide to take her own life?

Kate backed away again, this time viewing the desk and body from the front. The time element was bothersome. Morphine or its sister drugs weren't akin to cyanide, where death was near instantaneous. To die from an overdose of morphine, even a monstrous overdose of morphine, you'd have to allow at least some time for the drug to do its fatal work. Yet even a business as out of the way as this one would be liable to interruptions. If you were going to commit suicide in your own office with morphine in your teacup, she thought, would you wait until a workday morning to do it, when the phone could ring or a salesman could walk through the door? Or would you come in the night before, when all is quiet, and there's a long stretch of undisturbed hours ahead of you? Unless she'd wanted someone to stop her. To find her and get her help and not let her die. If that was her goal, Kate thought, it hadn't quite worked out that way.

And that same time problem would plague a killer. How could you guarantee uninterrupted time while the drug did its deadly little job?

Her gaze moved to the desktop itself. There was a simple gooseneck desk lamp at the center back, pouring out a slightly stronger light than the ineffectual dusky daylight coming in through the panes of the skylight and windows. The light caught the last dregs of brackish liquid in the mug that was only a mere shade lighter than coffee. Catherine obviously liked her tea strong, Kate thought. There was no way of telling from the residue that was left whether it had been laced with more than tea leaves or not.

A plain business-card file was set off to Catherine's right and a phone sat to her left within easy dialing reach. Some loose sheets of plain white paper were overlapped in an untidy heap near where her head lay, as if she'd been looking them over, then felt too sleepy to sit up straight any longer, and had pushed them back to rest her head on her forearm for just a quick second or two. An address book lay closed next to the card file, and a cheap black vinyl pouch-purse was propped up against the desk on one side. Cash-starved business, cash-starved lady, Kate thought.

Her focus broadened now to take in the rest of the room. Her gaze went from desk to desk, table to table, wall to wall. Though surfaces were untidy with artwork, nothing seemed out of order. What was scattered around looked like bits and pieces of various graphics projects. In particular, she eyed the coffee setup at the front of the room. The coffeepot was an old drip pot, stained with brown where coffee had been spilled at one time or another. A stack of Styrofoam cups was propped upright against the wall. A dented and scratched canister, presumably holding tea bags, was standing next to a small jar of instant coffee. Evidently, they ran plain water through, then let the unit's hot plate keep it warm, ready for either coffee or tea. An assortment of mugs rested upside down on a rumpled pad of paper towels. In all, it was just an impersonal array of coffee-break items, no different from the ones on her own floor at headquarters.

She backed into the center of the room and gave one final glance around. There was nothing out of the ordinary that she could see, nothing that would account for the sudden end of a woman's life. The entire room contributed to the sense that Catherine Fletcher had been peacefully drinking a cup of tea and had simply slipped away into death.

Her gaze narrowed in, then, on the artist still staring off into space.

2

Sam Morrison finally came in, bundled up in a heavy overcoat. Sam was almost forty, a few years older than Kate, six foot, broad-shouldered with a good, solid body, a leathery face crisscrossed with deep creases, and mild brown eyes that looked upon the world with a doglike calm. Like an old mutt, Kate thought. Then she smiled inside. Better not share that thought with him. Those mild brown eyes were deceptive in their gentleness. In his own quiet way, he was one of the toughest cops on the force. Yet that's what he reminded her of—the old family Lab.

He'd arrived just as Kate was leading Ginger into a shabby little conference room she'd found behind one of the closed doors lining the gloomy hall. She conferred with him briefly, filling him in on the little she knew, then stayed with the artist while he did his own examination of the scene.

As Kate sat on one side of the rickety table across from the artist, her notebook open, Ginger gave a vague look around, as if she couldn't quite remember why they were here. Then memory returned and her eyes overflowed again. She grabbed a tissue from the opened box Kate had found and set on the table.

In other circumstances, Ginger Burklund would have been a very pretty woman. Dressed in an old pair of jeans, a paint-smeared sweatshirt and scruffy tennis shoes, she had an apple-cheeked face with a gently rounded chin, and her hair was long and silky, falling in a light-brown veil to her shoulders. Even through the tears, there was a vague, soft look about her that spoke of daily hours spent lost in daydreams and private visions. But at the moment her appearance was blotched by eyes badly swollen from crying and her face was heavily patched with grief.

Kate probed her features, trying to judge her emotional strength. Usually weepers were all right, they wouldn't go hysterical on you. It was as if they had a terrible well of sadness inside that filled up and spilled over in a regular, tidal-like rhythm. It wasn't like the tremendous roiling of volatile grief that led to uncontrollable outbursts. Except for the tears rolling down her cheek, Ginger sat at the table, head bowed, staring down at the tissue she was twisting now into tight coils. She showed no curiosity about Kate, or why she was sitting there, or of what was going to happen next.

When Sam joined them, minus his overcoat, he slid into the chair at the head of the table, in position to watch Ginger, but out of her direct line of sight. Taking out his notebook, he lounged comfortably in the chair and nodded at Kate. This would be her session.

Raising her head up, Ginger looked at each of them timidly.

Kate smiled a bit to ease the girl's anxiety. "Ginger—may I call you Ginger?" she asked softly.

Sniffing behind the tissue, the artist nodded.

"Ginger, we need your help," Kate said in an easy tone of voice. She waited patiently for a second nod of agreement. "Our job is to figure out what happened to Catherine. I'd like you to start by telling us what happened this morning when you got here."

"There—there isn't anything to tell." Her voice was soft and tear-choked, barely a whisper. "I came in and found her like that. That's all." She began twisting the tissue again between her fingers.

The girl's eyes were filled with the horror of it. She'd have bad dreams about this day for years to come, Kate thought with sympathy. "Was anyone around? Anyone in the hall, or on the stairway?"

"No, she was alone."

"Had Catherine seem depressed lately? Down in the dumps at all? Moody, having up-and-down mood swings of any kind?"

Ginger shook her head. "No. In fact, everything was going really good for her. She was divorced, but she'd met someone special last fall, about Thanksgiving-time, and they were planning to get married this summer. She was really up about that." Her eyes teared again and she grabbed a fresh tissue and dabbed at them. The first lay in a crumpled ball on the table in front of her.

"What about family?" Kate asked. "Does she have any children?"

"Just a daughter, Rebecca."

Kate made note of the name. "How old?"

"I don't know—nineteen, maybe?" Ginger said, vaguely. "Twenty? And Rebecca has a little boy, Mark. He's about three now, I think."

"Do they get along all right?"

Ginger nodded. "Catherine was real close to Rebecca. And she's—she *was*—plain nuts about Mark. She'd tell us all the cute things he did. Like learning to walk, and tasting his first ice-cream cone. Things like that." Her fingers worked the fresh tissue over, twisting it into shreds, her eyes downcast, watching her own fingers twine and play among the folds.

Kate assessed the nervous twitches of Ginger's hands. The girl didn't seem to be using the playing with the tissue as an excuse for avoiding her questions, or evading answering. Generally, her whole attitude was cooperative. Submissive, almost. She didn't even seem to be trying to determine the importance of the questions, wasn't trying to anticipate where each question led. She took them as they came. Kate asked, she answered. The tissue twining was merely an attempt to hold at bay the shock and grief that kept threatening to overwhelm her, Kate decided. It was as simple as that. At least, on the surface.

Kate continued on. "And the ex-husband? Where is he now, do you know?"

Ginger simply shook her head.

"Is he still in the area at all?"

"I guess so, I don't know. Since Catherine met Jack, she hasn't said anything much about Vern."

"Jack's the new one, Vern's the ex-husband?"

Ginger nodded. "Jack Turner. Vern Riley."

Kate noted down the names, then asked, "What do you know about the new guy?"

"Nothing much. I've never met him. Catherine kept her private life pretty much private."

"She didn't talk about this new guy at all?"

"Not a lot. All she told us is that he owns his own company and has a lot of money, I guess. I don't remember her saying much beyond that."

"What about Catherine's health? Was she in good health?"

"Sure, she was okay," she said. Then she thought a moment. "Well, she had some arthritis, and it was kind of bothering her neck lately, that's all. It wasn't very serious."

"Did she take any painkillers for it? Prescription drugs of any kind?"

"I don't think so." Ginger sounded doubtful. "She always carried a small bottle of aspirin around with her. I think that's all she took for it."

"You're sure she wasn't taking any prescribed medication for the pain?" Kate persisted. "No codeine, or anything like that?"

The artist shook her head. "I don't think so."

Kate paused to think a minute. Wouldn't morphine be an overkill for arthritis anyway? She made another note to check it out. So far, the dead woman's life seemed normal. A divorce, yes, but a good relationship with her daughter, and a new man in her life. Not exactly the stuff suicides are made of. Unless the new romance had suddenly foundered. She led into the subject of the graphics studio. "How did you come to start the business together?" she asked.

They'd formed it the previous spring, the four of them, Ginger said. She and Catherine had been friends for years and had ended up at one point working together at a small publishing house, where they'd met Suzie. The three of them decided to go out on their own, but they needed a fourth, one more sales rep. Suzie introduced them to Phyllis, everyone seemed to click, and the business was started.

"How did the four of you get along? Any dissension, feuds, disagreements, squabbles, spats or down-and-dirty fights?" Kate asked lightly. "I mean, four ladies working together. . ." She let a broad gesture of the hand and a humorous glint in her eyes finish the sentence for her.

She was rewarded by a first smile from Ginger. It was only the merest hint of a smile, the slightest up-curving of the corners of her lips, but it helped lighten the deadly air of heavy sorrow that had been swamping her. She shook her head. "No," she said softly. "We all got along fine."

"Was Catherine usually the first one here in the morning?"

Ginger shook her head. "No, I am. Catherine's sales. She thought that sitting at a desk was a waste of time."

"So when did she normally get in?"

"Not until late morning, usually. She'd be out on calls all morning, and then come in about eleven, eleven-thirty, to use the phone to make afternoon appointments."

"And your other two partners? When do they generally come in?"

"They're sales, too, like Catherine, but they work the opposite of her. They come in early, make their appointments, and then run out to keep them."

"Then they've been here this morning already?" Kate said.

"Well, no, not today," Ginger said, shaking her head. "We've been trying to land our first Boeing contract, and they had a big presentation down there this morning. Suzie's presenting the designs and Phyllis is doing the numbers and costs and things."

Kate frowned, mentally picturing the schedule. "So today was unusual in that Catherine normally was out, but she was in. And the rest of you, normally in, were out. So Catherine was alone all morning. Do I have it right?" At the girl's nod, Kate asked thoughtfully, "Who else would've known about this switch in schedule?"

"No one, really," Ginger said, vaguely. "Our families, I guess."

"Why were you so late in getting here today?"

"The Boeing job. It was simply spec work, and the mock-ups and art boards for it had to be done nights after my regular work. I knew I wouldn't finish up until after midnight last night, so I asked Catherine to cover for me so I could get some sleep."

"What time did you get through last night?"

"Not until four-thirty this morning. It took a lot longer than I thought it would."

"What about the door, Ginger? When you got in this morning, was it unlocked, or did you need to use your key?"

"It was open," she said between sniffs. "Once we're in for the day, it's open all the time. Except when we go to lunch."

"Is the office ever unattended with the door unlocked? Bathroom breaks? A quick errand?"

Ginger had to think about that one. "Sure, I guess so. If it's just a run to the restroom, then we don't bother locking it."

"And what about the tea? Who else drinks tea here?"

Ginger didn't have to think about that one. "No one," she said promptly. "It's Catherine's."

Kate raised an eyebrow. "No one?"

Ginger shook her head. "No, no one. Only Catherine drinks tea."

Kate fell silent, letting the import of that bit of news sink into her mind.

They were interrupted by the arrival of the M.E.'s crew. The little room was stuffy and they'd left the door open to let some air circulate. Several metallic thumps echoed up the stairwell, feet pounded up the bare flight of stairs, then attendants rolled a gurney past the doorway toward the studio. An empty body bag, obscenely black, had been tossed on the top.

Puzzled, Ginger stared out into the hallway, listening to the sounds carefully, trying to make sense of the noise. When she saw the gurney roll by, grim knowledge hit. Kate took one look at her face and went and closed the door.

In spite of the closed door, the soft grunts of the attendants contending with dead body weight and the almost mystical thump of the body landing on the stretcher still echoed through the walls. The sounds drew Ginger's gaze in the direction of the studio. She stared at the blank wall as if her gaze could penetrate the Sheetrock and she could clearly see the grim work being done. She had managed to get through the interview much more calmly than Kate had anticipated. But now, when the sounds of the gurney being rolled back down the hallway filtered in, the girl broke down completely. Her head sank down onto forearms folded on the table and she sobbed like a child overwhelmed by hopeless pain.

Instinctively, Kate reached across the table and squeezed the sweatshirt-covered arm, just so the girl could feel some human contact. Sam lounged back in the chair, watching her, his face devoid of expression, his eyes in neutral. Kate knew damned well what he was thinking. Mother MacLean. Earth Mother to the world. A cupcake.

After a minute, Ginger looked up at them both through flooding eyes. "I'm sorry," she whispered, her voice half-choked. "I can't seem to stop crying. I know it's a nuisance for you, but I just can't seem to stop."

Kate nodded understanding. "Is there someone we can call? Your husband, perhaps?"

Ginger shook her head, struggling for control. "No, I'll be fine. Besides, he's out of town anyway."

"What does he do?"

"He's a dentist." She was struggling to bring herself under control, and she grabbed another tissue from the box and blew her nose. "He's at a convention in Phoenix. If you called, he'd be too busy to come home anyway."

Kate grinned suddenly. "Somehow the image of any dentist being just a normal guy with a wife and home doesn't compute. Not the way *I* feel about dentists. Do you have children?"

Ginger nodded. "Three girls."

While Sam looked on, slouched and relaxed in his chair, the picture of unlimited patience, Kate got Ginger talking about her daughters, all in elementary school, a year apart in age and grades. She watched as Ginger's face softened, the tears dried up and her breathing calmed to normal.

Then Kate began all over again, starting over at the beginning, asking Ginger the same questions in different forms. The answers were the same. Catherine was fine, the business was fine, they all got along well, and there wasn't anything more than that to tell.

The other two partners arrived around noon.

Suzie was the first one through the door. She was a petite, slightly built girl, with a flaring head of unruly black hair. Short coat flapping around a full skirt, she raced down the hallway, headed for the studio at full speed, obviously full of excitement, but as she caught a glimpse of Ginger through the doorway of the little conference room, she applied some quick brakes and burst into the room like a whirlwind. "*We did it!*" she squealed. "Ginger, *we did it! We got Boeing! Signed, sealed and delivered!*"

Slowly, she took in Ginger's tear-streaked face, then the presence of the two detectives. Her whirlwind skip slowed to a halt. "Well, practically signed." Her voice quieted somewhat, grew more uncertain as fresh tears spilled down Ginger's cheeks. "And it was your artwork that sold them, Ginger. They loved the concept." Her voice faltered and her eyes grew huge and waiflike. "Ginger. . . ?"

The girl wouldn't have had much warning of anything wrong, Kate knew. The ambulance was long gone, the tenants of the building would be back in their offices and the squad cars would've gone back on patrol—except for George and his partner waiting outside to direct the lab crew up to the crime scene. But the two blues wouldn't do more than check people entering the building to make sure they had necessary reasons for being there and weren't a member of the media trying to pull a fast one. They'd duck any questions about their presence with vague banalities and assurances. They were experts at that. So no one entering the office building would be expecting anything more than business as usual.

As Sam watched the newcomer with interest, Kate spoke up. "We're police officers. I'm Detective Katie MacLean, and this is my partner, Sam Morrison. You must be one of the partners."

The girl nodded hesitantly. "Suzie Plummer. And Phyl's right behind me. Phyllis Walsh. She's parking the car. She'll be here in a minute." Large brown eyes fixed themselves on Kate, asking questions she couldn't voice.

"There's been a death—" Kate had just begun when the sound of high heels tapping up the last flight of stairs brought her to silence. The echoing taps intensified, and a moment later a second woman appeared in the doorway.

Phyllis Walsh was tall and slender and attractive, with a calm, poised manner about her. She was in her thirties, dressed in a sleek wool suit and white blouse, carrying a full-length wool coat over one arm. The dark-brown hair was cut to neck length, and she was smoothing it back into a disciplined wave that cupped her ears when she walked in. She looked professional and competent— very much a woman in charge. One step past the doorway, she stopped dead at the sight of the two detectives, then took in Ginger's teary sniffles. "What's happening? What's going on?" She frowned. "Why are there police downstairs?"

Before Kate could answer, Suzie pointed to her and Sam. "They're police, too. They said there's a death . . . ?" Her voice faltered.

Phyllis looked at Kate with shocked astonishment. "My God, who?" She looked again at Ginger, noted the tears, then, clearly worried now, turned to Kate. "Who? Surely not her husband, or . . . ?" Her eyes finished the statement, the bleak: *Or her children?*

"No," Kate answered. "I'm sorry, it was Catherine Fletcher."

Phyllis drew in a sharp breath and swallowed. Hard.

Suzie went dead-white. "Catherine?" she gasped. "*Our* Catherine?" At Kate's confirming nod, she collapsed into the empty chair next to Ginger and shrank back as deep as she could go. Now that her wild, extravagant motions had stopped, she shriveled to the size of an elf.

Ginger had started weeping again. Through her tears, she looked up at Phyllis. "I found her," she whispered.

Phyllis simply stared at her for a moment. Then she gathered some inner strength, and said to Kate, "What does Ginger mean, she found her? Where?"

"Here," Kate answered. "In the studio. At her desk."

Suzie sat bolt upright. "*Here?*" Her voice came out somewhere between a squawk and a gasp. "You mean, *here!?* She died *up here!!? In our office!!!?"* She looked around wildly for a moment, as if a shrouded specter hovered over her with his scythe at the ready.

Phyllis was still absorbing the shock. "How? I mean, what happened? Did she have an attack or something, like a heart attack?"

Kate ducked a direct answer. "We're not sure yet what caused her death. That's what we're trying to find out. And we need your help. We need to ask a few questions."

At that point, Phyllis' legs turned weak. She leaned suddenly on the table, supporting herself along its edge until she came to the empty chair at its foot, opposite Sam, and slowly sank into it. "My God," she whispered. "Catherine." Her gaze lost its focus and she stared ahead into empty space.

Kate studied both women. Phyllis' lips were pinched together, as if she were fighting the need to vomit. Suzie was gnawing a knuckle, her chair pushed way back from the table, staring at the floor as she blinked rapidly, forcing back tears.

Kate gave them a couple of moments to absorb it a little, then repeated, "We need to ask a few questions."

Phyllis gave a distracted nod. Then her gaze sharpened. "Questions? About what, Catherine?"

"Partly."

"Why?" Then full intelligence returned to her eyes, and she leaned forward to confront Kate straight-on, "Wasn't it a natural death?"

Up until now, Sam had been content to sit back and let Kate handle it. But at the challenge from Phyllis, Kate sensed him shifting in his chair, tensing up, ready to step in and take over. Without letting go of Phyllis' gaze, she willed him to be still.

"It's standard routine," she said in an easy tone. "We're required to look into all cases of unexpected death. Let me ask you, Mrs. Walsh, had Catherine been ill lately that you know about?"

Phyllis was still absorbing this and responded in a distracted manner. "Just arthritis," she said slowly. "And a touch of flu now and then, like we all get. Nothing, I mean nothing, that would cause—this."

"Was she taking anything for the arthritis?"

"Aspirin, I think."

"No prescription drugs?" Kate asked. "No painkillers of any kind?"

"Not that I know of." She suddenly caught the implication. "Is that how she died, an overdose of some kind?"

"It's one of the things we'll be looking at," Kate said smoothly. She moved on before Phyllis could respond. "As I understand it, Catherine was a full partner in the graphics studio. One-quarter ownership. Is that right?"

Phyllis nodded.

"What happens to her share of the business now?"

"It's split evenly among the three of us," said Phyllis. "We've all made out our wills and they're on deposit at our attorney's. We did that when we had our corporate papers drawn up."

Suzie had been following the conversation, her eyes hopping from speaker to speaker, nodding to back Phyllis up at every point. Now she spoke up. "Plus the insurance," Suzie reminded her.

"Yes," Phyllis said. "We each carry a hundred thousand dollars in life insurance. The company's the beneficiary. It's to be used to hire a replacement if anything happens to any one of us."

"Does the business pay the premiums?" Kate asked.

"Yes. Although it's simple term life anyone can get."

"Who's the executor of Catherine's estate?"

Phyllis instantly saw the implications of that question. "We are," she said reluctantly. "The three of us. All her personal stuff goes to her daughter, Rebecca. At least that's how she drew up her will last spring. She showed us a copy of it then."

"Do you have any reason to think she might've changed it?"

"Well, yes, frankly, I do," Phyllis said. "Catherine became engaged last Christmas. It wouldn't surprise me if she'd redrawn her will after that and named Jack Turner as executor."

"Have any of you met Jack Turner?" Kate asked.

All three shook their heads. Then Suzie popped up with a sudden elfin grin. "She said he was a hunk, though."

Kate had to grin. Suzie was one of those irrepressible souls that nothing could keep down. No disaster was strong enough to suppress her spirit for long. Not even death. One would expect to see Suzie dancing on her own grave long after she was dead and buried.

Then Kate's amusement faded. A hundred thousand bucks. Kate suddenly grew very interested in the business. "How was Catherine to work with?" Kate asked.

Phyllis was silent a moment. "All right," she said finally.

The answer and the way it was given intrigued Kate. There was none of the shy, hesitant, vague artist in this woman as there was in Ginger. She was intelligent, quick, assertive, and definitely in charge. Now she was turning cautious. And Suzie was suddenly back looking at the floor, the shrunken elf once more. Interesting. "You don't sound too sure," Kate said in a quiet voice.

Phyllis stayed silent.

Kate pushed it a little. "Wasn't she holding up her end of things?"

Phyllis looked more uncomfortable. She glanced quickly at the other two, but Ginger had her gaze glued to the tissue ball rapidly forming in her fingers, and Suzie had found some water stain on the floor that positively captivated her. Sam was watching all three with a keen gaze, examining first one face, then the next.

Kate let the silence build for a moment or two. She had hold of something, she could sense it, and she wasn't about to let it go. She waited until the tension forced even the vague Ginger to shift slightly in her chair, then she said again, "Wasn't she holding up her end of the business, Phyllis?"

Phyllis gave a resigned sigh. "I'm not so sure," she said reluctantly. "She scheduled her own hours, so she was never in the office much before noon. Supposedly, she spent the morning making cold calls and keeping appointments."

"Supposedly?" Kate said softly.

Phyllis looked even more uncomfortable. "A lot of times I'd wonder about it, whether she really had or not."

Suzie's head snapped up at that. "You shouldn't say things like that!" Her voice was a horrified whisper. "She's dead now! You shouldn't talk about her that way."

"But it's true, Suzie," Phyllis said in a weary tone. "It isn't going to help to hide it. A lot of times I suspected she'd just gotten up, that she'd slept in late."

"How come?" asked Kate.

"She'd come in close to noon, and her hair would still be damp from the shower. Little curls of it, around her neck. But she was supposed to have been out on calls for the previous three hours. Wouldn't it have dried by then?"

"Did you ever ask her about it?"

"No." Phyllis started to say more, then stopped.

Kate waited, giving her the chance to add to the abrupt answer. But Phyllis' jaw was set at a stubborn angle, and it was obvious she wouldn't say anything more. Kate made a note of it, then let it slide. Each of these ladies would have to give a formal statement at headquarters. Time then to probe deeper. "But she was supposed to be selling, wasn't she? If she was sleeping in instead of doing her calls, wouldn't that noticeably affect her sales?"

"That's just it. She wasn't making any sales. She hadn't sold a job in months."

"But this is the slow quarter," Suzie protested. "None of us have done much."

Ginger sat quietly, her eyes fixed on the shredded tissue. She said nothing and her face was expressionless, but Kate felt she was listening closely to what was being said. And why, Kate wondered, was the story turning vastly different from the one she'd told? Were the discrepancies merely due to the artist's vague otherworldliness? Or was it much more? Again she made a note to be followed up in a more private interview, then moved on. "Just how was business?" Kate asked Phyllis.

"Fair," Phyllis said cautiously. "Like Suzie said, first quarter's always tough. Most of our clients are small retailers, and they don't do much after the holidays. That's why we've been concentrating on getting some corporate accounts. To help smooth out the lows and highs."

"Were you able to pay yourselves?"

"Not a whole lot."

That fit the cheap clothes Catherine had been wearing, Kate thought. "And how did Catherine take that?"

"Not well. Not well at all. She'd get real upset about it. She was always complaining about being short of money. On the other hand, to be fair, the three of us have husbands, Catherine didn't. She had to count on what she earned here for rent and food money. We didn't. Plus, she was supporting Rebecca and Mark. And while Mark's only three or so, he had some serious medical problems that drained Catherine of every spare dime she did get ahold of. So all in all, she had some dreadful financial problems." Phyllis stared off into the distance a moment, thinking about it, then returned to Kate, sighing. "She probably shouldn't have gone into business for herself. She needed a regular income, and we're just too new and rocky to provide that."

"So a new marriage to a wealthy man would've solved a lot of problems for her," Kate said softly.

"Absolutely," Phyllis said firmly. "Difficulties with Catherine would've eased up for all of us if she married Jack Turner."

"Why haven't you met him?" Kate asked. "Why didn't she introduce you? After all, you were her business partners. Weren't you all friends as well?"

"Oh, sure," Suzie said. "You bet we were."

The heavy silence returned. Kate gave Suzie a hard, skeptical stare and waited.

Suzie hung her head with a guilty look, scuffed her shoes together a few seconds, then sighed and looked back up at Kate. "I guess Catherine didn't like Phyl all that much," she finally admitted. "She felt Phyl acted too much like a boss, always questioning where she'd been, who'd she'd seen that day, what the results of her calls had been, where she'd be the next day, that sort of stuff. Catherine hated anybody questioning her. She was strong on trust, and I guess she felt Phyl didn't trust her."

Kate turned to Phyllis. "Did you trust her?"

The other woman gave a long sigh. "No," she said quietly, "I didn't trust her. I didn't trust her at all."

"Why not?"

Phyl thought a minute, then said slowly, "Well, she was always pulling stuff. Pulling stunts. Behind-your-back type of stuff. Something always seemed to be going out of kilter somewhere. You never quite knew what Catherine was going to do next. You just never knew. It was a weird feeling. An unpleasant one. You could never quite relax around her, wondering what she'd been doing behind your back."

"Give me a specific incident," Kate said.

"Sure. Last week was typical. We were short of money for bills—and we had a printer's bill coming due. Suzie and I hustled up a few new contracts, so we had some contract deposits to help out with cash flow. And even though Ginger isn't in sales, she called a few old customers for us and got a couple of orders, too. Between the three of us, we managed to cover what we owed. So we agreed to delay any kind of payday for ourselves for a few days until the bank account was healthier.

"Catherine was livid. She claimed she needed her money and turned on me and said I could damn well hustle up some more contracts to cover the bills, that she was taking what she needed regardless. At that point, I started asking why, if *she* needed money so bad, *she* hadn't brought any new business in. That made her even madder, and she started cross-examining me on what I was doing all day every day, demanding to know how come I only managed to bring in the few contracts I had. She was great at taking the offense when she was challenged."

"What was the outcome of your argument?"

"She took what she wanted and the creditors waited. She had Ginger countersign a check for two thousand dollars."

Kate was surprised by the amount. Two thousand seemed an awful lot of money from a cash poor business like this one. She eyed Phyllis. "How did you feel about that?"

"Pretty damned upset. I felt it was poor business tactics. We had agreed to finance the business out of cash flow and not take a dime for ourselves from any project until the costs of that project were completely paid. And then we would share in the excess equally. This arrangement went against our whole policy."

"Did you have words with Ginger over signing the check?"

At the mention of the artist, Phyllis' anger collapsed and she gave a small, sad smile. "No. There wasn't much Ginger could do about it. Catherine cornered her into it. Literally."

Kate glanced Ginger's way, but the girl had her head bowed over a new tissue ball. Her long hair veiled her face and it was impossible to see her expression. But Kate was sure she was listening. "Ginger?" Kate said gently.

Slowly Ginger raised her eyes to the detective. "She needed the money," she said softly. Her words weren't stubborn or defiant, just matter-of-fact. "She said she really needed the money. And that she'd do the same for me, wouldn't she? She kept asking me that. 'You know I'd do the same for you, don't you?' I had to agree. And once I agreed, she pushed the check at me and I had to sign."

"Did the creditors get paid?" Kate asked Phyllis.

"Finally. We have a lot of receivables that are past due. Suzie and Ginger and I went out on collections and brought in enough during the rest of the week to pay everything up."

"What was Catherine's reaction to that?"

"She just blinked her long eyelashes at me, smiled and said, 'See, I knew it would work out.' Frankly, I could've crowned her."

Ah, Kate thought, and did you, symbolically speaking? She turned to Suzie. "What did you think about it, Suzie . . . Catherine taking money the business really needed?"

Suzie shriveled again. "I knew that Catherine really needed the money. And I knew we really needed to pay the bills, so I stayed out of it. I didn't want to tangle with either one of them."

A clear picture of the partnership had been drawn, Kate thought. Catherine and Phyllis, two strong women, battling for supremacy and control. Ginger, the gentle, easily manipulated artist. And Suzie, the whirlwind pixie who had learned to protect herself by avoiding confrontation.

"Was this the only time she'd helped herself to money from the company when she wanted to?" Kate asked Phyllis.

"No," Phyllis said wearily. "I wish it were. As I said, a lot of Catherine's problem with money was Rebecca and Mark. That's why it was always so hard for Ginger to say no to her. Often it came down to rent and food money for them, and we"—she indicated the three of them—"we just don't have that problem to face every month. Not like she did. She really was hard up financially."

"What about her ex-husband, Vern Riley? Couldn't he have helped?"

Phyllis shook her head. "I can't see him doing that. But it's hard to tell. From the things she said, I got the feeling Vern's a strange kind of guy. Couldn't hold a job, played around a lot when he did have money. . . But help Catherine out? No, I don't think so. She was pretty much on her own."

"Would her money problems be reason enough to take her own life?" Kate asked softly.

Suzie looked shocked by the question. Ginger teared up again and her hand spasmed, smashing the tissue she had carefully wound into a balanced coil.

Phyllis frowned in thought, considering the idea. "Suicide? No, I don't think so," she said slowly. "You see, you have to understand Catherine. She was an angry lady. Inside, underneath everything, she was a very angry lady. Things kept going wrong for her. But you see, nothing that went wrong was ever her fault. It was always someone else's fault. It was always everyone else who created problems for her, everyone else who caused her grief. It was never Catherine who was creating her own messes. And since she never took any share of the responsibility at all, her solution was to strike out at everyone else."

She paused for a moment, thought over what she'd said, then looked at Kate. "To put it baldly, Catherine would kill someone else before she'd kill herself."

3

King County covered more than two thousand square miles; Seattle only owned eight-four of them. The majority of the county covered the land east of the twenty-mile-long Lake Washington. Ringing the city of Bellevue like satellites sprinkled around a rising sun, a dozen or so smaller cities and towns stretched from the lake eastward up into foothills of the Cascades, making up the area commonly known as the Eastside.

During the past decade, growth had exploded across the green countryside, eating up the rural lands by the tens of thousands of acres as the computer giant, Microsoft, attracted thousands of subsidiary high-tech firms praying that the Bill Gates magic would somehow burnish their bottom lines, too. The tremendous influx of population moving up from California, with their trendy, pricey life-styles, had turned the once-lush, pastoral Sammamish Valley into Silicon Valley North, an amorphous sprawl of industrial parks, housing developments, and strip shopping malls.

Seattle, the city, was also Seattle, the county seat, and in spite of the explosive growth on the Eastside, it continued to dominate the county. Though occupying less than five percent of the total King County land area, Seattle, it seemed to the besieged fathers of the Eastside towns, received ninety-nine percent of the county's focus and attention. For years now, the no-longer little towns and cities of the Eastside had smarted under their poor-country-cousin status in relation to its big sister across the lake. Hence, there had been much talk about forming their own regional government to deal with issues traversing town lines that were drowning the Eastside. The talk was more a venting of the spleen, however, than a call to action. Nothing had been done about it.

Until recently. Along with the newcomers had come the usual low-life types that follow cash cows everywhere, no matter the pasture. Suddenly the patchwork quilt of a dozen different police jurisdictions was no longer effective. Crooks would do their crooking in one jurisdiction, cross the town line and escape to the next. Sure, there was reciprocity. With all the goodwill in the world, the towns cooperated with one another. But more often than not, the timing was off, and the lowlifes could run across a neighboring city limit, thumbing their noses at pursuers halted by an arbitrary line drawn on a map. In self-defense, the towns got together, pooled their monies, and created one regional police department, with jurisdiction over all of the Eastside. A police commission was established, a budget developed and manpower hired. The Eastside Police Department was born.

Central Headquarters for the EPD had been built along a deep, wooded ravine on the northeastern edge of Bellevue. The build ing, an enormous ugly concrete rectangle, burrowed deep into the bottom of the ravine, rose several stories up to road level, and continued on for another few stories above that. Though skillfully tucked into stands of evergreens, no amount of trees or landscaping could disguise the brute strength of the building, and with its thick walls and rows of castle arrow slits for windows, it had been christened The Fortress by the first cynic to catch sight of it.

Kate pulled into the upper-level parking area just off the main road fronting the building, encircled by a grove of the tall, stately firs. The front entrance opened onto a spacious marble foyer that a luxury hotel would envy. A set of electronically-controlled security doors led into a rabbit warren of administrative offices to the left of the foyer. Off to the right were the public-access elevators and stairs. The entire back half of the building at the lobby level was the detective division.

Kate flashed her I.D. in the direction of the rear security window, punched in her personal number into a numbered panel next to the door, and waited for the green light and accompanying click of the lock release that would allow her through. The number she punched in was assigned solely to her, and it automatically logged the number into a mainframe buried somewhere in the building. Since she had to punch back out in order to leave, the process provided anyone with authority—or creative hacking ability—a computerized record of her ins and outs at headquarters. Big brother was watching, she thought.

The bull pen was enormous, one large open area that spanned the width of the building. In the original blueprints, the various divisions were to be separated by movable walls, with each detective having an individual cubicle. But the marble foyer and other esoteric construction cost overruns had made themselves felt before the building was completed. And since detectives needed filing cabinets anyway, it was rationalized by the powers-that-be, they could also act as hallways and partitions. So the room was one vast arena of hulking, gray steel boxes standing elbow to elbow, meandering in a convoluted maze that would defeat a bright rat.

From the doorway, Kate headed north along the maze, circled around Robbery on the outer rim of the pen, curved eastward around the center bulge that was Arson, curved north again around Vice, then finally turned south on a straight stretch running along offices and interrogation rooms lining the rear wall of the building until she could turn west into Homicide. It was a hike no one in his right mind would want to make more than once a day, if ever, and every detective did it a dozen times a shift, or more. The grumbling occasionally grew belligerent.

Budget compromises had also affected the furnishings and equipment provided the rank and file. Chairs and desks had been bought wholesale through a government-surplus agency, and instead of a computer on every desk, as promised, there were second-hand typewriters, one for every four desks, bought for a dime on the dollar. The one good aspect of the whole setup was that there was, predictably, also a shortage in the manpower budget and the various divisions had more real estate than people. She'd been able to carve out a generous ten-by-ten space for her desk, and had angled it in front of a couple of filing cabinets that by virtue of squatter's rights became hers. So she did have a measure of privacy. The nearest desk was Sam's, and it was a good twelve feet from hers.

With his departmental car, lights and siren, he'd beaten her into headquarters and was already at work when she arrived. He looked up and grinned. "Slowpoke."

"Yeah, well, don't get me started on gridlock," she muttered. "You know me and my soapbox."

She slid off her heavy coat and slung it on top of the nearest filing cabinet. Among other minuscule shortcomings in the plans, the wondrous architects had never designed a coatroom for the detectives. They'd assumed—wrongly—that all personnel would enter from the parking garage built on the back side of the ravine and enter the building at basement level like the beat cops did, and the designers had placed all the coatrooms there. Somehow it had never occurred to them that detectives run in and out all day, and that between the pokey elevators and the bull pen maze of walkways, each one would lose half a shift just getting to his desk and back out again if they followed the route laid out for them. The Brass' solution to the problem was simple: coatracks in their offices. And tops of whatever was handiest or the backs of their chairs for those in the bull pen.

Kate slung her shoulder bag over the back corner of her chair and walked over to Sam's desk. "Is that the paperwork on the Fletcher case already?"

"Nope, I'm still six cases behind." He looked up. "Captain's after you."

She frowned. Being interviewed by the Captain was not among her favorite amusements. "Me? What for?" Her frown deepened into a worried knot. What the hell had she done wrong?

"Actually, he wants to see both of us. For a briefing on the Fletcher case." Sam grinned, shoved back his chair and rose. "Had you going for a minute, didn't I? Come on, let's go face down the old gorilla."

She grabbed her notebook and followed him, happy for once to have him lead the way.

Captain Ed Hatch, Homicide, was a big man with a massive stomach shaped like the mounds of mashed potatoes that had caused it. Dark and swarthy, he had dark-brown eyes that could freeze over like an icy mud pond, or warm to a spaniel-like gentleness. He stood well over six feet tall, and between his height, girth and the huge nose mashed down in the center of his face, he looked tough.

He was tough. A survivor of the streets, he'd never make chief; he was too war-battered and nonpolitical. His broad face wore a secretive, weary look that came from the sad knowledge of how life really worked. But he was also shrewd. He had a whole range of emotional reactions and used them all. He could go from icy intimidation to bellowing rage in a single breath, while covering an operatic range of emotions in between. He scared the hell out of Kate.

Hatch glanced up as she and Sam entered. "Shut the door and sit." He waited until they were seated, then, ignoring her, he asked Sam, "So?"

Sam crossed his legs and tilted his head in Kate's direction. "She caught the call."

Hatch leaned back in his desk chair and scrutinized Kate intently. She hadn't been with the department long, eighteen months, and her interviews with the Captain to date had all been brief. A giving of a report and a receiving of a response. She knew little about him personally except that he lived alone, a victim of a failed marriage, and rumor was he'd made no attempt to try again. At times, he'd use a tone of voice that made her feel like a kid in kindergarten. Yet, at other times, he could be understanding in his deeply weary way. Mostly, though, she found him intimidating.

"Okay, tell me about the case," he said.

She did her best. Her briefing was short and to the point. The finding of the dead woman, her background, and a summary of the business, and the resulting money problems it caused both for the studio and for Catherine Fletcher.

He listened without interruption, his elbows resting on the chair arms, head bowed and supported on two steepled fingertips, the weary eyes fixed on hers. He took a few moments to reflect, then lowered his hands. "So what's been done so far?"

She ticked off the list. "The M.E.'s come and gone and the body's on its way to him for autopsy. The lab crew's going over the place now. The tea bag, the cup and the tea canister are already on their way to the lab for analysis. And all three surviving partners have been interviewed, but no formal statements have been taken yet."

"Do you feel they're needed?"

Kate considered it. "Yes. As a precaution. We don't know yet whether it was murder or suicide."

"What else needs to be done?"

"Notify the daughter, first. Then locate the new fiancé. Trace the ex-husband. Talk to everyone she'd seen recently. Search her place for some trace of morphine—we probably should get a warrant for that, in case the daughter puts up a fuss, or the fiancé has moved in with her. Track down her bank accounts and see exactly what her money situation was. Check out the partners. The business comes into a hundred thousand dollars from a life insurance policy they took out on Catherine. That's a lot of money that a starving business could sure make use of. We need to check into the finances of those partners."

"Then your focus would be murder?"

She thought a minute. "Well, there was definitely some animosity between the one partner and the victim. But whether it ran deep enough to prompt a bit of murder isn't clear yet. As for suicide, the recent engagement would argue against it. However, we really don't know the dead lady yet, either. Maybe she suffered from depression. Maybe her daughter was more than she could handle. Maybe her lover jilted her last night and she couldn't face life without him. It's really too early to tell."

He sat quietly a long moment, his hard gaze playing over her features, making judgments in the silence that strung out. The hard stare, combined with the sheer bulk of the man behind the desk—even when he was sitting down—was intimidating. The whole effect was one of a ten-foot grizzly about to pounce. She resisted the impulse to glance at Sam for support and sat as still and composed as she could.

With an abrupt motion, Hatch shot upright in his chair, yanked a sheaf of papers in front of him and made some notes. "Okay, MacLean, I'm making you D.I.C. Congratulations, you've got your first murder case. Seems like a nice ladylike one to get broken in on."

She sat shocked a moment. Detective in charge. Her own case. She struggled to hold back a stirring of excitement.

"Investigate both premises," Hatch continued, "suicide and murder. Keep tuned to other possibilities—a generic poisoner on the loose, for one—but it doesn't look like you've picked up an echo of that so far. If it was murder, right now it looks like she was the specific target. I want written briefings daily and a full one weekly. And more than that when things start to break. And I'm available to you anytime. Any questions?"

"How much help do I get?"

"The lab for anything you need. And Sam. Until I can't spare him anymore."

Dismay knifed through her. There were people to question and histories to research and morphine to trace and bank accounts to examine and . . .

She started to protest, but he forestalled her by holding two fingers up in the air. Without saying anything more, he bent his head over the pile of paperwork in front of him, dismissing them. The implication was clear. One victim, a nice, ladylike murder. . . why would anyone need more than two people to solve such a simple crime?

Sam disappeared, returning a few minutes later with a bag of burgers and a couple of Cokes. She looked at the food with surprise. She'd been concentrating on the names and addresses of Catherine's nearest and dearest that Phyllis Walsh had provided them before they left, and had forgotten about eating.

That was typical of Sam, though. Part thoughtfulness, part self-preservation.

For the last twelve months, he'd been her mentor—her tutor in the knotted world of Homicide. Her first partner had been a detective named Goddard. Goddard was tall, blond, good-looking, arrogant and belligerent. He was one year younger than she, but had six years on her, Homicide-wise. She hadn't been assigned to him to rile him deliberately; his partner had been transferred to Vice, and it was the only slot open when she joined the squad. Goddard didn't like working with a woman, and he didn't like her. He felt she was too soft, bled too easily, wasn't tough enough to be the kind of backup he deserved, and he did what he could to cut her out of the action. But he also knew, since she was female, he'd get his ass in a sling if he complained, so he put up with her. He treated her, though, in an autocratic and imperious way purposely designed to provoke her, while staying just this side of departmental charges.

But Kate was usually good at getting people to soften up and open up with her, and things between them might have worked out, except one day shortly after she'd started with Homicide, another new hire wandered through the bull pen when both she and Goddard happened to be in. He was big, mouthy and brutal. He stopped at her desk where she'd been typing up a report, and within easy earshot of a dozen detectives or better, said in an aggressive challenge, "You're Kate MacLean, aren't you."

Startled by the tone of his voice, she looked up from the typewriter and merely nodded.

"Thought so. Seen you around SFPD a time or two," he said, and turned away.

That was all he said, but his disgust was clear. For the life of her, she couldn't place him.

Soon she saw him in deep conversation with a couple of other detectives, who listened intently, looking her way before drifting on to other groups, who listened in their turn intently, looking her way. Within a short time, the new hire had spread the word about how she'd walked out on her partner and the whole SFPD. He'd put the worst possible interpretation on her actions, but she instinctively knew it would be futile to try and counter it. It would sound weak and defensive, and be greeted with silence—or worse, ridicule. By the end of the shift she was the pariah of the division. No one wanted a cop next to him who couldn't be trusted.

Once he heard about it, Goddard felt he was completely

vindicated in his dislike of her. From then on, as senior partner of their team, he assigned her grunt work that kept her chained to her desk. She became his secretary, file clerk, records clerk and janitor. If there was drudgery to be done, she did it. The only time she saw the street was driving to and from the station house.

She gritted her teeth and took it. It was a psychological battle between the two of them. Battle, hell! It was out-and-out war! Goddard was intent on wearing her down, forcing her out, and she was intent on surviving. So she swallowed back the resentment and frustration and anger that built up in her gut like bile from the liver, and took every bit of shit he handed out, and when he was through with that bit, she firmed her jaw up and readied herself for more. She was damned if he was going to get to her; she was damned if she was going to break.

The Captain saw what was happening. Everyone did. It was pretty hard to ignore the fact that when the whole shift was out on the street, she'd be the only one left behind in the bull pen, bent over her desk, stuck once again with the grunt work. It was pretty hard to ignore the fact that she was never present at the odd party or off-duty gatherings or the after-work drinks common to the squad. It was pretty hard to ignore the fact that conversations shut off like a water faucet at her approach. She was an outcast in her own division, more welcome in Narcotics than among her own squad, and Narc didn't like *anyone* from outside their exclusive club. The Captain saw all this, she knew, but he himself was a survivor of the streets, a firm believer of sink or swim.

After four months of it, four months of absolute hell, she began to detect a lessening of Goddard's animosity. The deskwork didn't ease, but the verbal garbage did. He became impersonal in his treatment of her, as if she were now a no-account he didn't have to bother about. She'd become a habit, a repository of everything he chose not to do, and he saw there were advantages in that. It was like having your own personal slave, and he began to treat her as simply a desk on which he could get rid of a pile of unwanted work. She became his personal out-basket. But she took the slight change in treatment as a positive sign and began to cautiously drop a comment here and there about one case or another. Each time, he seemed surprised, as if the human desk had suddenly developed the ability to talk, but he simply dusted her off like a bad case of dandruff and ignored her. Still, he didn't fight with her about it, and she took that as another positive sign.

Then came the day she solved a case at her desk. Ninety-nine percent of all homicides were no-brainers. Husband kills wife; wife kills husband. Kid kills parents; parents kill kid. Jealous boyfriend goes after the other man; jealous girlfriend castrates the boyfriend. Lust, greed, jealousy, turf. No-brainers.

This case was different, though. Late one night, a transient biker had been killed out back of a local-area tavern. A thick wad of twenties he'd been flashing inside the tavern was missing. His body had been found at dawn by a pair of officers on routine patrol and Goddard had caught the call.

There were five main suspects: the bartender and four customers. By then, they were all home and in bed. With borrowed backup, Goddard woke each of them up and took their statements. No one knew anything, of course; no one saw anything. One guy had spent the hour playing the video games that were lined up against a far wall of the tavern. The second had been practicing pool shots at the table on the other side of the bar. A third had watched a late movie on the TV tucked high up in the back corner of the bar. The fourth had brooded quietly into his drink a few barstools away from the television watcher. Even the bartender was no help. He'd taken advantage of a quiet night to restock his coolers. No one had paid any attention to anything anyone else was doing.

The bartender admitted making trip after trip down the rear hall to the storeroom next to the back door. Each guy admitted making a trip to the john next to the back door. But no one admitted to following the biker out the back door, and no one of the four could point to the fifth and say, yes, he saw him leave right after the biker had.

According to the bartender, the regulars had cashed two fives, a ten and a fifty to pay for their beers. Without a search warrant, Goddard could do little except take statements and ask for a voluntary peek into each man's wallet. There were no twenties in any of them. Since there were no twenties in any of the wallets, but there was a stack of them in the cash-register till, Goddard focused on the bartender.

It was the twenties, of course, that pointed the finger at the guilty one. Kate spotted it right away when she was typing up the report from Goddard's notes. Sam Morrison was within earshot when she approached Goddard about it. "There's a discrepancy here between what the bartender reported and the money in the pool player's wallet," she pointed out to Goddard.

Goddard was on the verge of brushing her off once again, when Sam fixed a pair of thoughtful brown eyes on her and said quietly, "What is it?"

"The bartender claims the pool player cashed a fifty, bought a beer, got five bucks' worth of quarters for the table, then bought a second beer. All told, that's seven bucks he spent. The pool player should've had forty-three dollars in his wallet. Yet he only showed Goddard three singles. Where are the other two twenties?"

That was it, of course. A search warrant was issued based on the probable cause she'd found, and a search of the pool player's rooms turned up the wad of twenties stashed behind a bunch of clothes in an overloaded closet. In an effort to make himself appear innocent, he'd stashed all the twenties, overlooking the fact that he should've held two of them back.

Goddard booked the pool player on Murder One, then, steaming that she'd found what he'd missed, threw the final paperwork at her to finish up. Sam looked on, his eyes still thoughtful, and later on, when he had a chance to catch her alone, invited her out for a drink.

He didn't take her to any of the cops' hangouts, of course. She wouldn't have been welcome there. Instead, he took her to a quiet bar where they could talk undisturbed at a small table in the rear and, after their drinks had been ordered, he asked her point-blank about San Francisco.

And point-blank, she told him. She told him about the streets. She told him about the gangs. She told him about the brutality that owned the projects, the nine- and ten-year-olds as hard as lifers, about the kid who shot and killed another kid just because he crossed his path. She told him about the projects and the broken, stinking johns full of shit and the plumbing pulled out of the walls. She told him about the smells—the urine, the vomit, the blood, the filth. She told him about the poverty and the hopelessness and the defeat that scarred a person's eyes by thirteen. She told him about the kids found dead in the alleys. Little kids. Shot. Whipped. Knifed. Broken. Gutted. She told him of the dark, seamy underside of the glittering city pictured in the glossy magazines and how it worked on her. How it wore her down. How the despair and the hopelessness was catching, like the plague come to call. And how she began to think she couldn't make a difference after all. That no one could make a difference. That violence won the battle fought every minute of every day.

Then she told him about the houseboat in Sausalito and the man she lived with, a gentle visionary of an artist who couldn't begin to fathom the sights that filled her days and nights on shift. Who traipsed without care through the violent city streets, seeking, always seeking—the perfect light, the perfect angle, the perfect scene—giving his all to his art, wrapped in a secure blanket of oblivion to the dangers that preyed on innocents such as he. She told him how extreme her reactions to the artist became, how she veered from fierce protectiveness to a near-violent rage that he could so willfully refuse to listen to her warnings about the dangers out there, and how he'd still go about his wanderings with some kind of foolhardy belief in his own immortality. She told him how her job was tearing them apart, ripping their relationship to shreds, another victim of the terrible destruction that seemed to be overtaking her.

And she told him about her last night on the job. About the four-year-old kid they found chained to a radiator pipe by his mother while she spent the night out drinking, the kid crouched at home like a wild thing, his eyeballs white with fear. She told about the dead little two-year-old, its tiny broken body flung again and again against a cement wall by a father wired on coke who couldn't tolerate any crying. And then she told him about the call that came halfway through the night.

A night cleaning woman had come home from work and had

tired at last of the horrible stench coming from the apartment across the hall and had finally called the cops about it. The responding squad car broke the door down, took one look and called Juvie. Inside a bedroom, a girl about twelve lay dead in a bed of blood, a filthy nightgown pulled up over her breasts, a newborn baby lying dead between her thighs, the dried-up placenta lying like a dead, shriveled liver in a pool of black-crusted blood. A few days before, the neighbor said, the girl's mother had met a new man and had gone off with him, leaving the pregnant girl to have her baby alone, without food, without money, and without a phone to call for help if she needed it.

"That's when I broke," she said to Sam, her eyes bleak. "It wasn't fear," she said to him. "Please understand that. It wasn't fear that drove me off. It was worse than that. It was an all-pervading sense of uselessness. At that moment, I realized that I was never going to make a difference. The neglect and the brutality and the violence were going to continue. The beatings and the whippings and the rapes and the killings were all going to happen, whether I was there or not. The street was too strong to defeat. You took an inch and it took a mile of your soul in retaliation. I was at the breaking point and didn't know it when we found that young girl. I simply turned away from the bedside and picked my way through the filth that was strewn all over the place and walked out into the hallway, that stinking filthy hallway, and I leaned against one of the walls out there and I broke. I simply broke."

She was terribly tired now. It was a hard story to tell. "My partner was beside himself with worry, of course. He called in another team and took me back to the station to see the Lieutenant. They tried to give me a leave of absence. Two weeks, a month, six months. Whatever I needed. But I knew it was over. That I was through. That I couldn't handle it anymore, no matter how much rest I got. I turned in my badge on the spot, and by dawn I'd packed up my car and as the sun came up, I headed north, out of the city forever."

"What did you do after that?"

"I wandered all over Northern California and Oregon the next couple of years, waitressing when I needed money, moving on when I'd save some up. Until it dawned on me that I wasn't helping anyone by doing that, either. That maybe the world didn't really need another waitress. That maybe I had some good honest skills that could be put to use in other areas of police work. I began thinking of Homicide. If I couldn't prevent the killings from happening, then maybe there'd be satisfaction in bringing the killers to justice. Legal vengeance on behalf of all victims everywhere. By the time I'd worked all this out, I'd already arrived in Seattle. I fell in love with the area and decided to see if there wasn't some kind of an opening in one of the forces around. Seattle PD didn't have an opening in Homicide, but Eastside was just forming, and they did. And after a lot of hesitation on a lot of the brass' part, I was finally given a chance. Strictly affirmative action, I'm afraid. But still, it was a job."

His eyes were thoughtful as he studied her. "Does the Captain know your story?"

She nodded. "He's the one who persuaded the brass to give me a chance."

He smiled then, that warm kind smile of his. "Good. You've got him on your side, and that's important."

She stared at her drink then. "It doesn't feel like he's on my side."

Sam chuckled. "His management techniques are unique." He seemed to have reached some internal decision about her, for he relaxed back in his chair now and asked softly, "Have you ever been back to San Francisco?"

She shook her head. "No."

"Do you want to go?"

She thought about it. "Maybe. Someday, maybe."

He nodded, accepting that. He signaled the cocktail waitress for refills, then changed the subject. From that time on, neither of them mentioned the San Francisco story again.

Over the second drink, they began the tentative exploration process of two people getting to know each other. He was thirty-eight, divorced, and lived in a cheap apartment because he didn't care about fancy anymore. He'd come to accept the fact that the dedication he brought to his job would kill any marriage, and though she didn't think he was happy about the prospect, he was resigned to being single. He didn't mention anything about what he did for relaxation in his off-hours, but when he ordered a third drink and she covered her glass with her hand to indicate a pass, she suspected a good portion of his free time was spent in the company of a bottle.

She didn't care. His was the first kindness and friendliness directed her way since the mouthy bruiser from San Francisco had played town crier and bugled her story around the bull pen, and she was grateful. At the end of the evening, she left Sam at the bar feeling that she'd made a friend. Or had begun to make one, anyway.

Nothing was said the next day at the station house, but at one point Sam disappeared into the Captain's office, and when he came out, Goddard was called in. Shortly afterward, there was a minor shuffling of duty assignments, a swap was made and she was teamed up with Sam Morrison and her tutoring in homicide began.

They each contributed to the success of their partnership. He brought experience and wisdom and street smarts, while she provided a natural empathy for those caught in the machinations of crime, which encouraged people to open up with her. She also contributed the patience for detail, research and analysis she'd developed, thanks to Goddard. While Sam could spot a perp at fifty feet, she could spot a discrepancy at a hundred. Between them, they had broken a couple of real puzzlers, and had begun to garner a reputation as a dynamic twosome. There were even occasional glances of respect aimed their way. But always, Sam had headed up their team.

And now she'd been put in charge of the Fletcher murder and he would be the one responding to her authority, and she wondered if it would make a difference between them.

They ate at his desk and, between bites, organized their approach.

They needed to start with those closest to the victim and spread out. Catherine's address book had not listed any personal addresses. They'd have to check the daughter's name through DMV. Same for Riley and the fiancé, Jack Turner. Once they had spoken to those three, they needed to go over to Catherine's place and get it sealed and searched. Supposedly, from what Phyllis had said when she gave Kate the address, it was in a shabby section of Redmond. Once they had the more personal things under control, they'd start backtracking the people Catherine had seen recently.

Kate shoved the last bite of cheeseburger in and crumpled the wrapper. "As the man once said, we've got miles to go before we sleep. Are you ready?"

Sam grinned and indicated his second cheeseburger. "You don't mind if I get enough nourishment in me to sustain me for a few hours, do you? If you're going to become a slave driver, it might be a month before I eat again."

She laughed at her own zeal. "Sorry. I'll just start my calling while you finish up." She grabbed one of his french fries. "Just to help you out."

4

Rebecca Wilson, the dead woman's daughter, lived well east of Carnation, on a winding wooded lane meandering through heavy forests spread over the foothills of the Cascades. The developers hadn't moved into that area yet to clear away the forests and litter the hilltops with cookie-cutter houses. They would soon, Kate thought, but for now, the road was lined by a series of old homesteads of varying ages and conditions, and it held a charm for her. She didn't bother saying anything to Sam; they'd been through the conservation-versus-growth arguments before. He simply didn't feel as passionate against the sterilizing of the land as she did. So she kept quiet and concentrated on checking house numbers on the rural mailboxes while he drove.

The house they sought was a tiny old cottage set in the center of a circular clearing edged in tall firs. It had been touched by time and weather; the siding had weathered to a mottled gray and the roofline was not quite straight. But a few cheerful daffodils sprouted here and there and a handful of tulips not yet open were fighting the stormy wind. Smoke drifted out of a tin stovepipe that pierced the old sloping roof, giving a promise of warmth against the foul March day. It looked old and worn and comfortable.

The gusty wind eased a moment as Sam parked next to a

battered old Volkswagen bug, and in the momentary stillness, the first thing that struck Kate's senses as she climbed out of the car was the heavy, tangy scent of pine. Then the wind freshened and returned to its assault as she climbed the creaking wooden porch steps.

The house was a simple frame structure of perhaps four rooms, with a veranda spreading across the whole of the front. The porch had been swept clean and a battered rocker sat next to a large clay flowerpot not yet planted for the season. More than likely the rocker had been either a hand-me-down or a rummage-sale find and the clay pot looked as if it had seen better days. But its sides were scrubbed clean and the dirt was freshly turned over. Someone took pride in living here, Kate thought, as she knocked on the door.

Rebecca Wilson was a too-pale, too-thin girl in her late teens, twenty at the most. She wore faded jeans, a man's flannel shirt with the shirttail flapping, and clean but ragged tennis shoes. A small boy, neatly dressed in his own set of faded jeans and flapping shirttail, two or three years old, clung to her leg.

The two detectives showed their I.D.'s. "We're police officers," Kate said. "May we come in a minute?"

"Sure, I guess so."

The girl led the way into the front room warmed by a wood stove snapping and crackling in one corner. She indicated an old couch for them to sit on, took a wooden rocker for herself, only slightly better than the one outside, and pulled the boy onto her lap. A knitting basket next to her rocker spilled over red yarn and a half-completed child's sweater. An old floor lamp, its brass plating long worn through, tried to chase away some of the gray March gloom and failed miserably in its attempt. A small black-and-white TV stood on an old table in the corner opposite the stove. There were no pictures on the wall, only plaster scrubbed bare. A large thick oval braided rug on the faded linoleum gave the room its one bit of color, and as Kate examined it, the girl noticed and said in her soft voice, "That came from my dad. His mom made it a long time ago, and he gave it to me when the baby started to crawl, so he wouldn't get cold."

"It's beautiful. Did she make it herself?"

"Yes. And I've got some doilies and a lace tablecloth she did, too. Someday I'll have a nice dining room and be able to use them." She looked down at the boy. "Won't we, Bunny? You and me, we'll have a real nice house someday." The boy nodded serious agreement and the girl pulled him close in a tight hug. She smiled shyly up at the two detectives. "We talk a lot together." The rocker creaked as she set it in easy motion.

Kate looked over at Sam. He caught her eye, shook his head sadly and gestured her way. It would be up to her. She took a deep breath. "We have some bad news, I'm afraid. About your mother." She paused to give the girl time to absorb that much, then continued on. "She was at work and collapsed at her desk. I'm sorry, but she's dead."

The rocker paused in its movement. The girl had a small, pointed face, very thin and white, with the same large, waiflike eyes her child had. Quick tears sprang up along the lower lids and she hugged the child closer to her and began rocking him gently. Her chin quivered with an effort at control. "How?" she whispered. "Why?"

"We don't know that yet."

The girl fell silent again. She held the child close to her, as if he were the one who needed comforting, and not herself. Kate had the impression that the rocking chair provided the only stability and security in the girl's life. "We're going to have to ask you some questions," she said quietly.

"Why are you here? The police, I mean. Wasn't it just—" The girl hunted for the right word. "Wasn't it just ordinary?"

"We're checking that out now. Did your mother have any health problems that you know of?"

"I don't know. I haven't seen my mother in three years. Since before Mark was born. I don't even know where she was living now. Dad said she has a beautiful condo on Lake Sammamish, but I don't know."

"Three years?" Kate asked in surprise. She and Sam exchanged puzzled glances.

"Just about. Why?"

"We were told you were very close to your mother."

"That's not true. My mother couldn't stand me."

"Why was that?"

She nodded toward the child in her lap. "Mark."

"You're not married?"

"No."

"What about Mark's father? Does he support you? How do you live?"

"I'm on Aid to Dependent Children right now." The chin went up defiantly. "But I'm taking classes in bookkeeping. I'm getting off just as soon as I can get a job."

"And Mark's father?"

"He has nothing to say about it. About anything. Mark and I are making it on our own." There was a quiet firmness in her voice. "I trade baby-sitting with a girlfriend so I can go to school."

"Do you have anyone special now? A boyfriend? Someone who can come stay with you awhile?"

"No. I don't need anyone. I'm sorry about my mother, but maybe it's for the best. She had a lot of problems."

Suddenly Kate felt out of her depth. She was looking at a child holding a child, but listening to words that might've come from a weary old granny of ninety. She probed the girl's face, trying to fathom the emotion behind the composure, but all she saw in that too-pale, too-thin face was an implacable calm. Even the initial tears had dried without falling. "Your mother had a lot of problems? Such as?"

"Well, money, for one. She was always out of money. She got most everything my dad had through the divorce. Even part of his business. He had his own clothing store, you know," she said with quiet pride. But then the sadness came again "The divorce made him go broke. And she went through everything he'd given her. Supporting me, she said. But it really wasn't me. It was her. Expensive houses, jewelry, clothes—lots of clothes—and she went out a lot. Some weeks every night."

"Didn't she work?"

"Not until the money ran out. Then she had to work. But she kept losing jobs, one after another."

"How come?"

"I'm not sure." The girl gave it some thought. "It always

started off great. It'd be fine for a couple of months. But then the boss would start to pick on her and pretty soon she'd be fired. She drank a lot, too."

Kate frowned. No one had mentioned a drinking problem. Why not?

"I figure that had something to do with it," Rebecca continued. "Drinking always made her tired. Too tired to get up and go to work sometimes. And when she did, she was usually pretty late. She said that no one cared. She'd just tell them she had early-morning appointments, and they wouldn't care." She shrugged. "Maybe it's true they didn't care. I don't know. All I know is she kept getting fired."

"What did she usually drink?"

"Wine. White wine. Lots of it. Almost a big bottle of it a night. And more than that when she wasn't working."

"If she wasn't earning money, how did you live?"

"Well, that depended on whether Vern was with us or not. Vern Riley? My mother's husband?"

What a curious way to phrase that, Kate thought. Not my father, but my mother's husband. Sam nodded, as if he'd picked up on it, too. "Hold on a minute, Rebecca," Kate said thoughtfully. "You mentioned your dad before, and now your mother's husband. Isn't Vern Riley your father?"

"Gosh, no!" The girl looked shocked. "Thank *God!* My dad and mom were divorced when I was nine."

"Then who's your dad?"

"Bob Wilson. Robert L. Wilson? He lives in Redmond."

"So Vern Riley's your mom's second husband?"

"Yes."

Kate paused to think a minute. Would this new information make a difference? It might. "About Vern Riley and money for your mom . . . You were saying . . . ?"

"Well, if Vern was there, he'd pay the bills. But half the time he was out of work, too. And when he was out of work, he was out of the house. He had to bring in money if he wanted to stay with my mother. And if he wasn't there, then we'd fall behind in the rent and stay until the eviction notice came; then my mother would take Vern back, he'd get us another place, and we'd move on. I went to five different junior highs 'cause we kept changing school districts. Money was always a problem."

"If Vern couldn't hold a job, why did your mother marry him to begin with?"

"When she first met him, she thought he was rich. He had his own business and a big house on Lake Washington and drove a Cadillac and took her on fancy trips and bought her tons of clothes—expensive clothes, including a fur coat. And jewelry. Lots of jewelry. Especially diamonds. She loved diamonds. So she really thought he was rich. They got married, and a few months later he had to file for bankruptcy. He'd bought everything on credit."

Becky stared into the memories, absently rocking the boy back and forth. "Oh, she was mad. He told her he could save the house and the car and all her clothes and jewels, because the courts wouldn't take stuff like that away from anyone. But something went wrong. The court sold it all, including the furniture. Something to do with the bills he'd run up in his business. Anyway, supposedly he was lucky to get off without going to jail. And my mother was furious. She had to go to work and support all three of us. Or try to, 'cause like I said, she couldn't hold a job too long. And Vern couldn't either. He'd get them easy enough, but there was never enough money in any of them for him to stick around long. He used to say it took just as much work to make the big bucks as it did the little bucks, so why waste his time."

"Were you still at home then?"

"Yes. This all happened in high school. We managed to stay in one school district, though we switched houses a lot. Vern saw to that much, at least. Then I left during my senior year and went to live with my dad."

"You were pregnant then?"

"Yes."

"Did you finish school?"

"No. I dropped out. But I took my equivalency exam and passed it a few months ago. That's how I got into the bookkeeping classes. My dad helped me study for it. So I have my diploma now."

"What about Vern? Did your mother ever divorce him?"

"I don't know. I think she kept hoping he'd strike it rich someday. He was always coming up with some scheme or another. Nothing ever came of them, but I think she thought something would. I guess in her way, she really loved him. I don't know why. He was an awful man."

There was such a final tone of conviction in the girl's last statement that Kate had a sudden suspicion. "Rebecca—"

"Becky, please. The only one who ever called me Rebecca was my mother."

"All right. Becky, who is Mark's father?"

A tear suddenly quivered, but the chin firmed into a stubborn point. "That's all over with. It's not important."

"But a lot of high school girls get pregnant. I can understand your mother being upset. But to simply cut you out of her life? Wasn't that a bit extreme?"

"You'd have to know my mother to understand. She said some pretty bad things, called me some pretty awful names. Not just once, but all the time. She couldn't even stand looking at me. Finally, she just kicked me out. I called my dad and asked if I could stay with him. He said of course I could, so I did. That was the last I ever saw of her."

"Did you try making up with her?"

"A few times. My dad made me go to the doctor for regular checkups to make sure the baby and I were all right, and I'd call her to tell her what the doctor said. But she didn't care. She told me that . . . that she just didn't care. When I called her from the hospital to tell her I was in labor, she didn't care about that, either. And when I called afterward to tell her it was a boy and he was okay and so was I, she said she didn't care about that. She didn't even want to see the baby. Or me. That I'd really done it to myself now. She said I'd proved to the world what I really was, and after that, I never called her again." She hugged the child closer. "She never saw Mark. And if she's dead like you say, she never will, now. That's too bad, 'cause he's a little sweetheart. Aren't you, Bunny?" Mark pulled away from her chest to grin up at his mom, then settled back down again, gnawing on a knuckle, large deep-blue eyes fixed on the two detectives.

Kate kept a tight rein on the anger beginning to well up. She'd seen girls in worse shape than this one. Hell, she'd seen them dead. But no matter what form it took, parental cruelty was never easy to bear. She had to wait until she could trust herself to speak calmly. "We need to explain the procedures to you. In cases of unexpected death like this, there's an autopsy performed to determine the cause of death. That'll be done as soon as possible. By morning, certainly. When it's finished, the body'll be released to a funeral home for the final arrangements. If your mother was still married to Vern Riley—and if we can find him—then he'd be the one to take charge. If she wasn't, or we can't find him—is there any other family about? Besides your dad, I mean."

The girl shook her head.

"Then you'd be responsible for the arrangements."

The girl's face whitened. "But how? I don't have any money. And I don't know what's supposed to be done."

"The funeral home can help you there," Kate said gently. "They know what needs to be done. And as far as money goes, supposedly your mother left all her personal possessions to you. Car and furniture, and things like that. Although, from what we understand, there isn't much there. Still, it'll be a little something for you. By the way, Becky, are you aware that your mother was part owner of a company?"

"No, I'm not. I have no idea what she's been doing at all."

"Apparently, the business carried life insurance on her. It's strictly to benefit the company, according to what we've been told. But funeral expenses can sometimes be subtracted from the estate before final disposition's made. We'll get the name of the attorney to you. And we'll give you the names of her business partners. There are three of them, and one of her partners in particular seems to have been close to your mother. She'd probably be willing to help you. And there's your dad. He could guide you, too. You won't have to go through this alone, Becky. In fact, if you want to, we'd be willing to call your dad now. You really should have someone here with you."

Becky suddenly looked heavily weighted down. "I guess so. There's going to be more to this than I thought." She recited her father's work number from memory and Sam rose to make the call.

Mark watched Sam disappear into the kitchen and looked questioningly up at his mother. "Man hungry?"

"No, Bunny. He's just going to make a phone call. I'll bet you're getting hungry, though. I'll fix you some lunch pretty soon now." She settled him back down and resumed rocking him.

Kate eyed the scene with a cynicism born of experience. Mother rocking child in front of cops. Oh, sure. The stuff of sappy home videos. But as much as her eye probed behind the facade for the horror story behind the image, she couldn't find it. The boy had total trust in his mother. He leaned comfortably back against her breast, his head cushioned against the softness there, and his body was relaxed, his eyes dreamy as he stared off into space. He looked the picture of a contented child, secure and well-loved.

Seeing Kate's stare, but misreading it completely, Becky gave a quiet smile of pride, smoothing the boy's blond hair. "He's such a miracle to me. How he's so perfect. You know, fingers and toes, and a sturdy little body. When he was first born, I'd rock him and rock him—just feeling his warmth against me. He's such a love."

Kate studied the young girl's face. Where does a twenty-year-old get such good sense? she wondered. She wasn't even really out of childhood herself in some ways. "Do you ever get out?"

"Sure. I've got a girlfriend, Dana, and she's got a little boy, too. Petey. She's the one who takes care of Mark while I go to class at night. And most Friday nights we go out to the movies, or for pizza, or something. Dad comes over and baby-sits for us both. Then Dad takes Mark and me to all kinds of stuff. Out for hamburgers a lot. Or to the circus. Or maybe to something down at the Kingdome. And we go to the rodeo when it's here. And the State Fair in Puyallup. We do lots of stuff. So I get out a lot."

"But no guys."

A faint tinge of blush warmed her cheeks. "Well . . . there is this guy in my bookkeeping class. He's got his own floor-finishing company he's just started. Works for a lot of housing contractors. We've gone out for coffee a couple of times. He's

kind of nice. Kind of quiet. Like my dad. Which is great, 'cause
I don't like guys who're loud and noisy. They're a pain. But this
one seems okay. And he knows about Mark and seems okay about
that. He's got a buddy we're going to introduce to Dana. We'll
see. I don't count on much but what I've already got. So we'll
see." But her eyes were soft and sparkling in spite of the casual
shrug she gave.

Don't count your chickens before they're hatched, Kate thought,
but, oh, doesn't it feel good to have a few fertile eggs in the nest.
She grinned at the girl, acknowledging both the promise of a
new romance and the self-protection and casualness that were so
necessary. At that instant, they were two single women sharing
the same moment in time without regard to age differences or
circumstances.

Sam came back from the phone. "Your dad's on his way. Do
you want us to stay until he gets here?"

After a moment's hesitation, the girl shook her head. "No, I'll
be all right."

Somehow Kate believed it. But for how long? How many years
would it be before the girl's own lack of mothering would surface
in one way or another? She might be able to handle a two-year-
old content to sit and be rocked, but those days wouldn't last
much longer. The demands upon her parenting skills would grow
and grow and grow. What would she do then?

Kate, she warned herself sternly, you *cannot*—simply *cannot*—
take the whole of the world on your shoulders.

She bit back a sigh and rose. There was nothing left to
accomplish here. They left the girl rocking her child, holding
him tight. Or holding *on* to him tight. Kate wasn't sure which.

Outside, the sky had blackened and the wind had gone to a
gusty gale force. A beaut of a storm was brewing. As they got to
the car, Sam made some comment, but the wind tore his words
away and flung them to the skies. Kate shook her head, ducked
against the cutting edge of cold that sliced through her, and
climbed into the passenger seat.

Before starting the engine, Sam turned and repeated his
comment, looking at her with some concern. "The kid got to
you, didn't she, Katie."

She dropped her gaze to hide her eyes from his probe. She had to admit, she did feel like scooping up both Becky and Mark and taking them home and spoiling them a little, she thought morosely. She turned away from the hard-cop look he was giving her and watched the trees struggle and bend beneath the merciless wind. "Sort of."

5

The condominium complex where Catherine Fletcher had lived sprawled along several hundred feet of waterfront on Lake Sammamish in Redmond. Curved paths wound through beds of manicured evergreens to low cedar buildings clustered in secluded groupings. Lush lawns spread from the brick terraces attached to each unit down to the waterfront. From there, an interconnected series of wooden walkways led to a private marina filled with gleaming speedboats and sleek cabin cruisers. Black clouds roiled low and ominous over the storm tossed lake, obscuring the whole of the Cascade Mountain range, but on sunny days, the high, glaciated peaks would glisten white against a deep-blue sky and the view would be breathtaking, Kate knew.

Only one word came to mind. Expensive. She exhaled a breath of disbelief.

His eyes thoughtful, Sam stood silent next to her, taking it all in.

Catherine's unit was an end one, with carved double doors and sidelights of frosted beveled glass. Soft Westminster chimes sounded when they pushed the doorbell. They waited a minute to make sure no one was home, then used the key they'd picked up at headquarters from Catherine's things, along with the signed search warrant waiting for them.

Inside, a broad, tiled foyer led to a huge, sunken living room, dominated by a massive fieldstone fireplace rising two stories to a beamed cathedral ceiling. Plush white carpeting ran wall to wall and a bank of floor-to-ceiling windows at the rear opened onto the terrace, with a panoramic view of the white-capped lake and the dark, ominous sky.

The furnishings were elegant. A pair of deep-cushioned floral couches flanked the fireplace, with an oriental carpet and an ultra-modern cube of glass between. A lustrous rosewood wall unit held a stereo television, a state-of-the-art sound system and a collection of heavy lead crystal—Baccarat, Kate guessed, eyeing the weight and breadth of them. What appeared to be an original oil hung over the hearth.

Kate stared at the crystal, then up at the painting. This was the lady who needed money so badly? She glanced at Sam. As if reading her mind, he nodded in agreement.

To their right, a sweep of open stairs led up to a second-floor balcony overlooking the living room, and a movement in the shadows up there caught Kate's eye. A man wearing a lush terry-cloth robe moved to the wrought-iron railing and peered down at them. "*Hey!* Who the hell are you?"

Instinctively Kate and Sam drifted apart so as not to offer a single target, their right hands hovering near the openings of their loosened jackets. Moving to the foot of the stairs, Kate squinted up at him, keeping close watch on the hands jammed in the robe pockets. "Police. Come down and identify yourself."

"Slowly," Sam warned from several feet away. "Keep it slow and easy."

The man at the rail stayed put long enough to show he wasn't about to be ordered about, then when he'd felt he'd made his point, he shrugged and started down the stairs.

He was a small man, not quite five-eight, with a slight, wiry build. Black stubble covered his chin and curly dark hair stuck out all over his head in sleep-created clumps. Combed and shaved, he might've been an attractive man, Kate thought, particularly with his coloring, a striking combination of near-black hair and pale-blue eyes. But the blue of his eyes was weak and watery, his face was set in sullen lines verging on the rebellious, and he looked like a spoiled child about to throw a tantrum. There was also a bit of a swagger to his movements that she found distasteful. She backed away from him as he came down, keeping a wary distance between them.

He reached the bottom of the stairs and moved across the room to perch on an arm of one of the sofas. Scowling, hands shoved deep into the robe pockets, he addressed himself to Sam. "Answer my question. What the hell're you doing here? How'd you get in here anyway?"

Kate fielded the question. "We have a search warrant. Now take your hands out of your pockets," she said firmly. "Slow and easy, like the man said."

Turning her way, he looked her up and down with a deliberate slow disdain. His glance clearly derided her dull-gray, straight-cut suit and low-heeled shoes. Then his eyes lingered on the two mounds of firm breast swelling up beneath her sweater, visible through the opened jacket, and his face turned from narrow disparagement to a pursed-lipped approval.

She waited until he was through with his inventory, then said again, "Hands out of your pockets. Slowly."

The man raised his eyes toward the ceiling and considered it. Kate waited him out. Finally, his hands slid up and out, a cigarette pack dangling from between two fingers. He grinned as if to say, Fooled you.

"Now identify yourself."

Taking his time, he extracted a cigarette from the package, and with a sly look her way, used a single forefinger to fish a lighter up from the pocket. He lit up, inhaled deeply, then dropped his gaze back to her breasts for another long look. Another glance up at her, and another smirk, then he blew a cloud of smoke in her face. "Vern Riley."

Ignoring his adolescent act, Kate withdrew her notebook from her purse and slowly turned the pages until she came to the one she sought. "Where do you live, Mr. Riley?"

"Right where you see me."

"DMV has you listed at an address in Renton." She read it off.

He smirked. "Behind in their record keeping, aren't they?"

"And how long have you lived here?"

"Since Sunday night. At my wife's request." The smirk broadened into a little-boy grin and he shrugged, as if to say it wasn't strange a woman couldn't stay away from him. He crossed his arms, the cigarette dangling between two fingers. "You say you're police? What's this all about anyway? And why do you have a search warrant?"

"Just part of an investigation," Kate said easily. "We simply have to ask you a few questions." She wasn't about to tell him about Catherine if she could help it. Not yet. She held her pen over her notebook, ostentatious in her readiness to take notes. "And just where do you work, Mr. Riley?"

Riley seemed to accept her explanation. "I'm on vacation. I start with a big investment firm on Monday."

"Which company?"

"MORE, Inc. Metropolitan Operational Real Estate, Incorporated." He emphasized each syllable as if talking to someone who had to lick the pencil lead before making a mark on paper.

"Offices?"

"In Bellevue." He gave the address.

Kate was writing it all down. She looked up. "Now, you said you moved in here at your wife's request. That would be Catherine Fletcher, right?" At his nod, she said, "We understood she was your ex-wife."

"Estranged. My sometimes estranged wife. She has her moods." He stubbed out the cigarette that was only half gone into an oversized lead-crystal ashtray.

"How would you describe your relationship with your wife?"

"On-again, off-again. Like I say, she has her moods. For now it's on-again, so it's all lovey-dovey of course." The smirk was back. His moods changed colors like a chameleon.

"And when will it become not so lovey-dovey?"

"Oh, it'll stay that way this time. I'll be bringing in the bucks. Some real bucks. Long as I do that, it stays good between us." He grinned suddenly. "But, hey, don't get me wrong. She's a neat lady. We've been married for seven years or better. Or worse." He chuckled at his own wit. "And here we are, still together. Says something about us, right?"

"Does she usually instigate the reconciliations?"

"Naw. Usually I just give her some space, time to remember what it's like out there in Singleland. Time to get lonely. Then I start dropping around. Just to check on how she's doing, understand. Never make a play the first time around. Keep it on the up-and-up. But I'll start working her around . . . behave myself . . . cater to her a bit . . . that sort of thing. Then pretty soon I'll say, 'Well, might as well stay the night.' Then I gradually move my stuff back in and there we are, all lovey-dovey again." He shrugged again. "Simple when you know how to do it. Gotta work the angles, see?"

"And this time?" she asked. "The reconciliation followed the same pattern?"

He looked at her with some surprise, as if he hadn't expected such a shrewd question. "This time she called me. Called and invited me to supper on Sunday. So I came." He eyed her breasts again, then grinned up at her. "Better believe I came."

She ignored the innuendo. "Why did she ask you back, Mr. Riley?"

"She got lonesome for me, of course. She said she wanted to make it work this time. That she'd been doing some thinking, and the problem was that nothing had ever broken my way. But that was all past now. That all I needed was the right situation. Well, I'd just gotten offered this job at MORE. Strictly commission, but lots of bucks there. Big bucks, too, let me tell you. So she said I'd have to pay rent and food somewhere, so it might as well be here. She'd only charge me what I was paying anyway in Renton—so what the hell? Nothing to lose in that setup. And free nooky to boot. She even went with me to pack my stuff. Said she wanted it permanent right away. Lovey-dovey, like I said."

"Did you have to give her any money?"

"You betcha. She's no dummy. I had to fork it over Sunday, before we left here to pack."

"How much?"

"Fifteen hundred bucks. I gave her a check. All I had. I held back the cash in my wallet." He shrugged. "I'll be on an expense account, and I can finagle that real fast, so I don't care. And there'll be a draw. The company understands I gotta live. So I gave her the money for the next three months like she wanted.

Hell, in three months, I'll be rolling in the bucks. Big bucks. Real big."

Kate made a note to check out Catherine's bank accounts. Two thousand from the business, fifteen hundred from Riley. Not bad for a weekend's haul. "So Sunday night you moved back in? Did she go to work yesterday at all?"

"Yeah. And it really surprised me. Big reconciliation, you know. Lots of passion built up to let loose. We went at it most of the night. Thought sure after that she'd be too worn out to work. But she bounced out at nine. Said she had lots to do, lots of people to see. Me, I just rolled over and recuperated, if you know what I mean."

"She left about what time?"

"Well, about nine-thirty, quarter to ten. Catherine was never a ball of fire in the mornings. She took her time. Did her hair. That sort of thing." He looked then at Kate's hair with disapproval. Her style was pretty much wash-and-go.

"And what time did she get back in yesterday?" Kate asked.

"The usual. Four-thirty, five. Somewhere like that."

"And how'd you spend the evening?"

"The evening? Or the night?" He tossed out another bragging look, eyeing Kate's breasts for a second, then lit another cigarette. "Last night was the same as the night before. Said she was going to make me yell Uncle. Well, I got her to yell first, believe you me. Never met a broad yet who could best me. Still, she kept up with me a lot longer than I figured she would. She could be real dynamite when she got going, whew, let me tell you. And during the evening? She wanted to go to the Fountain Court. To celebrate our happy reconciliation. A hundred-buck evening, but hey, it was worth it. Especially later, she made it *real* worth it."

Kate ignored the verbal drooling he was doing. "If you gave her all your money, who paid for dinner?"

"Me. You don't take a lady like Catherine out unless you're ready to foot the bill. I just put it on the old plastic. Got a walletful of them."

But hadn't Becky said he'd had to declare bankruptcy? Kate

made a note to check that out. "And this morning? What time did she leave for work?"

"Early. Again. Surprised me again, too."

"Anything different this morning from yesterday?"

"I'll say. She didn't want to go. No way. Was all worn out, too tired to go. She griped about the other broads down there. Said they weren't carrying their weight, that she had to do it all. That the business would cave in without her, and who were they to tell her what to do. She went on and on—she was in a state, believe you me. Threw a shoe at the wall, had a regular fit. Said they'd told her she had to be there by seven for the phones in case there was a hitch with the Boeing job and said she'd be goddamned if she'd be ordered around like some goddamned flunky when she owned the goddamned business and was the only one doing a goddamned thing around there—I want to tell you she could carry on when she got going. Me, I just ducked it all, glad it wasn't something I'd done. I just sat back and watched, enjoying the whole thing. But she'll be a tiger at work today, I can tell you, and a bitch on wheels when she comes home tonight. Anyway, she finally got out of here about seven-fifteen, cursing all the way."

"Does Catherine drink much?"

"Naw, just mostly wine. She loves the wine. Any kind, but white wine the best. Goes through cases of it. Me, I love the Scotch. Wine's kind of tasteless to me. Too finicky, know what I mean? Scotch is a man's drink, and that's what I like, a man's drink."

"Do you think she has a problem with alcohol?"

"Nope, she just loves the stuff is all. Always says it makes her feel sexier. It does, too, let me tell you. She can be hot stuff when she gets in the mood. Course I have to watch my own drinking so I can perform adequately. If you know what I mean."

Kate was tempted to say, No, I don't know what you mean, you're much too subtle. But he'd probably take her literally and explain in explicit detail. She kept a straight face and let it go. "You have a problem with alcohol?"

"Nope. I'm like her. I just enjoy it."

"Aside from booze, what else does she usually drink? Coffee? Milk? Juice?"

"Tea. Just tea. Hot tea, iced tea. It's the only thing she likes besides her wine. She drinks tea like other people drink coffee."

"Loose tea?"

"Tea bags. She can't be bothered with the loose stuff. Brought some home to her once. She never used it after the first time."

"Have you ever been in her office?"

"Sure. Sunday night. It's really sleazeville. Slummy, know what I mean? I wasn't impressed. But, hey, if it suits them . . ."

"You were in her office Sunday night?" Kate asked slowly.

"Yeah. She had to copy some papers or something or other. For Monday, she said."

Kate tried to put that piece of information into the context of a time frame. "She drink anything there that night?"

"Just some wine. Had a bottle locked up in her desk. Said she couldn't trust the others not to get into it. We polished it off. I'm a Scotch man, but booze is booze, right? Anyway, we took the empty with us, so if the other broads got there ahead of the trashman, they wouldn't realize what she was doing. Catherine's sharp that way. She wasn't in anyone's back seat when the brainpower was handed out. Then we went to Renton for my clothes and dumped the bottle there."

"What'd you do while she was doing the copying?"

"Hell, I don't remember. Wandered around, I guess. Looked at some of the junk Ginger was working on. I don't know what I did. Mostly waited for her to finish."

"Junk?"

"Yeah, junk. Catherine's real unhappy with the work Ginger's turning out. Calls her an artist of the last rank." He grinned. "She has a sharp way of turning a phrase like that to stick the needle in. Stuff looked okay to me, though. Nothing great. Ginger doesn't have much of any kind of talent, but it's okay."

"How'd Catherine get along with her partners?"

"Shit, she doesn't like any of them. Says Suzie's like a little kid, always needing to be told what to do. Thinks Ginger's spoiled rotten by that husband of hers. And like I say, she can't stand the crap she turns out. But I guess she gets along okay

with those two. The one she hates, though, is Phyllis. Says she's
trying to take over the business, trying to force Catherine out."
"What was she doing about that?"
"Who cares. I know she's taking some steps to make sure
Phyllis doesn't get hold of it all for herself. Catherine's a sharp
lady, she'll protect herself."
"Do you know any of her partners yourself?"
"Not really. Ginger I've seen a time or two. She's kind of dull,
like Catherine says. And I only met Suzie once. She's a royal pain
in the ass. Yaps constantly. Won't shut up and let anyone else
talk. Never have met Phyllis yet. Catherine says she's not worth
meeting. She's pretty sharp about people, so I'll take her word for
it."
   There was a certain momentum and rhythm to the questions
Kate had asked, and that momentum had carried Riley through
his initial suspicions and questions and beyond, into a steady flow
of information. Once the rebellion had been overcome, he'd
proven to be a man who liked to hear himself talk. But as the
preening had eased off, the suspicions flowed back into conscious-
ness and he looked over at Sam, who'd been silent, taking his
own notes, throughout the interchange. "Something's happened,
hasn't it," he said to Sam. "To Catherine, I mean. You keep
referring to her in the past tense. She's dead, isn't she."
   Sam glanced at Kate, who was weighing one more attempt at
more information before giving the news that might just turn the
whole fountain off. Finally she gave Sam a nod, and he turned
back to Riley. "I'm afraid so. She died this morning."
   Riley was shocked into silence. His face lost color and he
looked bleak and lost. "Oh, shit," he whispered. It was such a
drastic change, and seemingly so real, it occurred to Kate with
some surprise that just possibly, underneath the preening and the
posturing and the bragging, there might be some real emotion
there.
   His voice when he spoke again carried a defeated undertone. "I
always knew someday—the amount she drove—it's just the odds
of it, you know? Christ, I hope she kept the insurance paid up."
His face tightened with a beginning anger. "I hope those sons of

bitches that hit her have insurance! They'd goddamned well better! This is going to cost them lots of bucks! *Big* bucks!"

"It wasn't a car accident," Sam said quietly. "She had a cup of tea at work, and it was laced with an overdose of pain killer."

"Tea?" It took a minute to sink in. "You mean *murder!*" He appeared to be honestly shocked and it silenced him for a minute. "Someone doped up her tea? *Killed* her?! . . . Jesus. Catherine." Another moment's silence. "Jesus . . ."

"I gather you don't think it was suicide," Kate said.

"Suicide! That broad? Not on your life. Kill someone else? You bet. Kill herself? No way." Then he thought of the alternative. "Jesus," he said simply. His face reflected the emotional struggle going on inside him. Then the pale-blue eyes grew bright with anger again as his gaze jumped from Sam to Kate to Sam again. "Hey, now! You're not trying to pin this thing on me! No way, man! No fucking way! Crazy as it seems, I loved the woman! Really loved her! I mean, man, I *cared!*"

"We're not going to 'pin' this one on anyone," Sam said easily. "We're just trying to find out what happened. At the moment, we're simply gathering information."

"Yeah, well, thinking back on it, I don't care much for your questions. Pretty cagey, playing me like that. You act like I'm missing a few bees in my hive. Well now, I guess I'd just better phone my attorney. Shoulda done it when you first got here. Really pisses me off you didn't say nothing till now. Really pisses me off, I can tell you."

"You're certainly free to call a lawyer if you feel the need," Sam said. "But we're not interrogating you, we're simply running an investigation right now."

"Yeah, that sounds great, but we ain't talking need here, we're talking self-protection. That's what we're talking—self-protection." He was tight-lipped with fury. "Fucking bitch. Just like her to go and get herself killed."

Sam's face showed a sudden intense distaste. Kate hoped hers was unreadable. She managed to keep her voice expressionless, at least. "Let me ask one more question," she said, "then you can decide if you need an attorney to answer it. Did you kill her?"

"I don't need no fucking lawyer to answer that! I did not! Plain and simple. I didn't do it!"

"Do you know anyone who'd want her dead?"

"You bet your ass I do. That Phyllis broad. Catherine's all that stood between her and taking over the whole shebang. Fucking bitch." The news hit him anew and he collapsed onto the seat of the couch, his anger collapsing with him. "Jesus. Catherine dead. She was alive this morning—and last night—Last night! Oh shit, oh Jesus, oh shit." He buried his head in his hands. "Oh shit," he muttered again through them.

He was like a child, she thought. Whatever emotion was uppermost was the one that surfaced. Adulthood seemed to have escaped him completely. She waited until he'd regained control of himself again. "Do you have children, Mr. Riley?"

He lit a cigarette, glowering at her. "Not that I recognize legally."

"And Catherine had just the one? A daughter?"

He nodded. "Rebecca."

"How was their relationship?"

"It wasn't." His eyes narrowed in sudden thought. "Hey, that might be the answer. The kid hated her mother."

"Enough to kill her?"

"It was strong. Real strong. Yeah, I'd say so."

"Why?"

"The kid got herself knocked up in high school. Things here broke down at that point and she went to live with her father. Guess he took the kid's part and turned her against her mother."

"Here?" Kate indicated the condo.

"Nah, not this place. Catherine didn't have it then. We were living in a house then. A cheap house, but it was a house."

"Did Catherine ever try to set things right with her daughter?"

"Let me tell you she did!" he exploded. "I know! I paid the goddamned bills! Catherine sent her buckets of clothes. Outfitted the baby completely. I mean, crib, clothes, quilts, stroller, high chair—the whole nine yards. From Nordstrom's, no less. I finally had to bring it to a halt. Cost me a couple of grand. And for what? Catherine'd call and the kid'd hang up on her. I finally couldn't take it no more. I told Catherine, just leave it alone. Let the kid want you, make her come to you. First rule of salesmanship. Just dangle the bait and the fish'll jump. Works every time. Come on too eager, you turn them off. Yep, I'd tell her, make the kid come to you. She finally listened when I threatened to chop off the credit. Said maybe I was right. Goddamned right I was right!"

"Did Rebecca ever call?"

"Couple of times, maybe. Before the kid arrived. I passed on the message to Catherine. Nothing ever came of it, though. Evidently the kid just called to lambaste her mother. Catherine'd tell me about it, really upset over it. Give it time, I'd tell her. The kid's still young. Give it time."

"And how was your relationship with Rebecca?"

"Oh, we got along okay. Up and down. Like with any teenager. They're generally a pain in the ass in the best of times."

"Mr. Riley, who was the father of the baby?"

He shrugged, intent on stubbing out his cigarette. "Some kid she shacked up with, I guess. She never would say. Hey, how much longer you gonna be, anyhow? I got things to do."

Kate studied him. He'd been pushed just about as far as he was going to allow. "Just one more question. How could Catherine, with a new business and all, afford this place? Did you help her out, moneywise?"

"Shit, no. She did this on her own. I don't know how. But she was one sharp lady. She had ways of getting money if she wanted it bad enough. Lately, she's been selling jobs on the side. You know, keeping the sale for herself, then going and having the work done someplace else. That gave her all the profit for herself. She was sharp that way. She didn't see why she should have to split the profit four ways when the others weren't doing diddly-shit to make any money. You couldn't blame her for that. She had a right to look after number one. She always said, you don't look out for number one, no one else will. So she had her ways to get her hands on the bucks if she needed them."

His voice faded away and he sat deflated and still, staring into space, drawing absently on the cigarette. His face had gone white, his lips were downturned, and there was an air of sullen shock about him. Obnoxious? Totally. Killer? Kate wondered.

He'd talked freely, his feelings transparent, as if his skin was made of glass and whatever was going on beneath was plain to see. He'd be easily manipulated, mainly because he thought he was smarter than everyone else, skilled at the con, able to outsmart everyone. Yet he was easily used, as Catherine had so flagrantly proven time and again. Had he any idea of how he gave himself away? Oh, not the swagger and the leering and the other physical posturing he did out of form or habit or ego necessity. But the way every word out of his mouth built up the picture of total depravity. He was so easily read.

Or was he?

She gazed around the living room again, once more aware of the luxury surrounding her. How did all of this square with the cheap clothes Catherine had worn to work? Riley was still lost in his deep funk, and she said to Sam in an undertone, "Keep him occupied, will you? I'm going upstairs and check out Catherine's closets."

She managed to ease her way upstairs without attracting Riley's attention. The first door off the hallway led into a guest room that was larger than her own at home, and better furnished. But it was the master bedroom farther down the hall that brought her to a complete halt.

The room was straight from Hollywood. An enormous bed sat on a platform against a long, spacious wall, satin sheets and comforter tossed back into thick, inviting clumps of softness. Obviously, Riley had just gotten up. On the far wall beyond the bed, windows swept from corner to corner and the wind-tossed lake played across the view like a movie unreeling on a panoramic screen.

The master bath was nearly as big as the bedroom, with a sunken tub, a walk-in shower large enough for a dinner party, and twin vanities that took up one entire wall alone, all done in a creamy-white marble. The clothes closets were off a separate dressing area beyond the soaking tub. One of the closets held enough mens' suits and shirts to stock a clothing store. Riley's. The con artist's tools, she thought. But at least it proved out his story. He'd obviously moved back in. Unless this was just his overnight wardrobe.

She tried the closet next door, and paused in the doorway in amazement. The room was jammed with clothes. Dinner dresses, rich wool suits, silk blouses, slacks, skirts, sweaters, satin lounging pajamas, long gowns were jammed onto row after row of hangers. Shoes and leather purses crowded every inch of a twelve-foot section of shelves. Scarves in every color and design and a large assortment of leather belts hung from a decorative chain suspended from the ceiling. And a large plate-glass mirror at one end reflected it all back. Kate just stood in the doorway, stunned. It took a moment to comprehend it all.

She didn't need to finger any of it to know that these were the highest-quality clothes available outside of New York or Rodeo Drive. Somehow, though, the sight sickened her, rather than inspiring envy. There was *too* much of everything, too much there. It screamed of greed, an avaricious, insatiable lust, a sick soul lost in some unholy gluttony.

She turned away and carefully closed the door. Then she stood in thought. Her intentions had been to run a quick search of the medicine cabinets for any morphine tablets. Now, though, she decided against it. She wanted this case pure and clean. She wanted the chain of evidence unbroken and unsullied by any premature snooping on her part. She wanted this woman exposed. For what she was. For who she was. As she was. Without any doubt or question of impropriety on the part of the cops.

But a new thought did enter. She retraced her steps through the sumptuous bedroom, made her way down the hall to the guest room and crossed the room in long, purposeful strides to slide the wall-closet door open. There, on half a dozen hangers, were the cheap discount clothes Catherine had used for her other life. A couple of shabby vinyl purses tilted against the end of the closet shelf. A pair of shoes from an outlet store with worn heels and frayed soles were tossed onto the floor. Kate nodded. This was where the double life began each morning. This was where the image of the hard-up, cash-starved, poor-little-me female that Catherine chose to present to the world began.

A tremendous anger was building in Kate. Anger on behalf of a young girl barely surviving from day to day, trying to do her best by a little boy dependent upon her. Anger on behalf of three women who worked all hours of the day and night to get a company up and running, who'd entered into a mutual contract with trust and good faith. Anger on behalf of every other victim of every other grasping, conniving parasite that fed off the good and the honest and the decent. Oh, yes, there was a terrible anger building inside her. And it was a good thing Catherine was already dead. Otherwise, the temptation to do her in herself might be too great to resist.

Her arrival down the grand sweep of stairs coincided with the arrival of the lab crew. She let them in, murmured some instructions, then moved into the living room and sat on the couch opposite from Riley. "The crime lab's here," she said calmly to Sam.

Her tone of voice was fine, but her eyes were glittering with repressed anger, and he looked sharply at her.

She ignored him and turned to Riley. "They'll be sealing the place up."

Riley reared back at that. "What the hell does that mean, sealing the place up?"

"It means you'll have to find someplace else to stay."

"Find another place to stay! How in the goddamned hell am I supposed to find another place to stay? I gave her all my money!"

"What about your apartment in Renton?"

He turned suddenly quiet. "Yeah, well, that's not such a good idea."

Kate was suddenly just as interested, her anger forgotten. "Why not?" she asked casually.

"Yeah, well, the goddamned manger down there . . ." He lit a cigarette, his hand shaking. "Who's got Catherine's things? You gotta have Catherine's things, right? Like her purse and other stuff? Sure, you gotta have them. Well, hell, you can give me my money back, then, can't you!"

"You said you gave her a check."

Hope collapsed. "Shit, you're right. No point in even trying to put a stop-payment on it. She's—She *was*—*Jesus!*—was too sharp a lady to take a check and not clear it the next day. What about her purse? Any bucks in there? Any at all?"

"Sorry. Her purse is locked up until the case is over. About the apartment manager—he's not a good friend of yours, I take it."

"Oh, he's a real jerk-off. Just 'cause I was a day late now and then . . . Jesus, you'd a thought it was his money, the way he carried on." Riley lit another cigarette and gloomily contemplated the tip. Another thought occurred. "Hey, we're still married, you know! She never picked up the final papers. That makes this place half mine. Which means you can't just toss me out like this, you just fucking well can't." His chin was bunched up in a stubborn clump like a rebellious child's.

"Am I hearing you right?" Kate asked slowly. "You're claiming the marriage is still valid?" She directed a meaningful, take-note-of-this glance to Sam.

Riley thought he'd won a point. "Goddamned right I am."

Kate pretended to seriously consider the situation. "Well, it's not actually the scene of the crime . . ." She glanced at Sam. "You agree?"

He didn't know where she was going with this, and for a moment she saw him struggle with doubt. Then he let her have her head. God bless him. "Absolutely," he said firmly, as if he'd had no doubt at all.

Kate leaned forward toward Riley, having apparently reached a decision. She smiled gently. "I'll tell you what, Mr. Riley; I'll make you a deal." He loved a deal. It was written all over him. His face came alert, his eyes came alive, his head tilted slightly so as not to miss a word. "The lab crew *does* have to search the place," she went on. "They'll be going through Catherine's things very carefully. You find a place to stay tonight, then I'll personally see to it that the key's released to you tomorrow and you can move back in. That is, of course, if you truly were still married to Catherine."

A grin of delight spread over his face. The change from truculence to charm was fascinating to watch—if you liked little boys instead of grown-up men. He held up his right hand in solemn oath. "Absolutely, I was. I swear. She never picked up the final papers, and now she can't, so I'm her husband forever."

"Good, that's settled then." She rose. "One of the lab men will escort you upstairs so you can pack an overnight bag."

She moved toward the door, followed by a still-puzzled Sam. "Oh. One more thing." She turned to Riley as if an afterthought had occurred to her. "Since, as her husband, you're Catherine's closest kin, you'll naturally be responsible for her final arrangements."

His jaw dropped. "You mean the funeral and all that?"

She smiled. "Yes, that's exactly what I mean."

"Jesus Christ, I'd have to pay for the goddamned thing, right?"

Kate stood silent.

The struggle was plain to see. Claim the marriage and pay for the funeral, or end up homeless. Trapped.

Finally, he spread his hands in helplessness. "Shit. Fucking bitch."

Sam chuckled softly while Kate grinned all the way to the car. Becky was off the hook.

6

The Kohl Business Park was in a light-industrial section of the Eastside, in a series of long, low buildings surrounded by parking lots. The fronts were offices, the backs were warehouses with loading docks. Turner Bearing Company, Inc. took up one whole building for itself.

The inside of the office was plain. Brown utilitarian carpeting, portable walls, and acoustical tile on the ceilings to help cut down the noise level were as far as the decorating had gone. Jack Turner's office was at the end of a long, narrow hallway, an interior room with no windows. It was furnished with simple metal storage shelves, a wall of locking file cabinets and an old battered desk. Books, papers and files spilled over all the surfaces. Kate felt right at home. It was on a decorating par with headquarters.

The man himself was as casual as his office. A suit jacket hung over the back of one straight chair. His tie was loosened, collar button opened and shirt sleeves rolled up. He was an attractive man in his early forties, about six feet tall, with a full head of dark-brown hair and strong blue eyes beneath strong eyebrows that had a bit of an arch to them. Deep lines ran down to a strong jaw, yet his face fell naturally into a pleasant expression that left Kate with the impression of someone with nothing left to prove, an achiever who'd fulfilled all his goals. Attractive, she thought. Very attractive. And suddenly she wished she'd worn something besides the drab gray suit that had earned Vern Riley's scorn.

After they were settled into the side chairs he'd indicated, Turner said in a friendly tone, "My secretary said you insisted on seeing me today. What exactly can I do for you?"

"We're here about Catherine Fletcher," Kate said.

His face closed down immediately. He blanked out all expression and pulled a yellow pad free from one of the paper piles and dated the top page. "I see. Your names again? Kate MacLean? How do you spell it?"

She spelled it for him.

"And Sam Morrison?"

"Two r's," Sam said.

"Now what is it you need of me?"

"We understand you two were engaged," Kate said.

Turner shook his head. "Nope. Not true." It was a quiet statement, leaving no room for doubt.

"Exactly what was your relationship with her then?"

"Exactly what is your interest?" he shot right back at her

Kate studied him, weighing alternatives. He was no Vern Riley. They could waltz around the block and back, and he would give no more information than he chose to. And he made it plainly obvious he'd choose not to until he knew why they were there.

Sam gave her an almost imperceptible nod, and she knew he'd reached the same conclusion. "Catherine Fletcher was found dead in her office today," she said, "shortly before noon."

"I see," he said again. There was no reaction to be read from his face. He made some more notes on the yellow pad. "Cause of death?"

"An overdose of painkiller."

"Self-inflicted?"

Kate was getting amused by the way he'd taken control of the interview. He was beginning to sound like a cop. "Would she have any reason to commit suicide that you know about, Mr. Turner?"

"I have no idea. I never knew the lady that well. Are you sure the overdose was intended for her?"

"She was drinking tea, and she was the only tea drinker working there."

"And now you want to find out what I know about her death."

Kate nodded.

"Nothing. Absolutely nothing."

"My original question still stands. What was your relationship with her?"

"Brief. We met in November, kept company for a week or two, then parted ways."

"Where did you meet?"

"At a restaurant in Bellevue. I'm not even sure which one now. It was a long time ago."

"Did you just pick her up there?"

His eyes took on a humorous glint. "You sound rather disapproving, Miss MacLean. In a way, yes. In another way, no, not the way you mean. She'd been left stranded there, and I helped her out with a bit of taxi money so she could get home. A day or so later I called to make sure she was all right, and ended up inviting her out for dinner."

"Stranded?"

"Yes. The—uh, *gentleman* who'd taken her to dinner had simply walked out on her. I gather it was a fairly typical occurrence with this particular fellow. But this time, it happened to catch her short of money. So I merely helped her out."

"And then what?"

"As I said, I called the next day to make sure she was all right, and I ended up inviting her out for dinner. She was a most attractive woman, and seemed like an interesting person."

"Was she? An interesting person?"

He considered it. "At first, yes, I suppose she was. She was part owner of a business, and that gave us something in common. At least, in common enough for me to ask her out a couple of times more."

"And then?"

"And then nothing. She grew less interesting."

"In what way?"

"Some basic differences quickly surfaced and it came to a natural end."

"And those differences were?"

He held up his hand to stop her. "No, Miss MacLean," he said, shaking his head firmly. "That's all I have to say. If you need to ask any more questions, my secretary will provide you with the name and phone number of my attorney. If you have suspicions to discuss, discuss them with him. I've helped you all I can and I have nothing more to say on the subject of Catherine Fletcher. She was not a nice lady." He stood up behind his desk. "Now I'll say good day."

When they didn't move, he swung from behind the desk and simply walked out on them.

Sam was steaming. She could tell by the way he jerked the car around the parking lot and into the street traffic. Surprisingly, she wasn't. She glanced down at the name the secretary had given her. A call to Turner's attorney would be fruitless. He'd be under orders not to tell them anything more. But there were ways around that. She slid the paper into a notebook pocket more out of respect for detail than from hope that it would prove useful. Then she turned to a fresh page, wrote down Turner's name and began to make a list under it. Bank accounts to be discovered and examined; newspaper files to be surveyed; state licensing records to explore; friends to be found and interviewed. It all made her work more complicated. And intriguing.

Sam's head of steam began to collapse and the jerky motions of the car smoothed out. He let out a sigh. "High-handed son of a bitch." And then he was over it

That was one of the things she liked about Sam. He was quicker to react than she was, but he was also quicker to get over it. While she was slow to anger, once she got mad, it lasted and she didn't care about anyone or anything until it wore itself out. Consequently, through the years, she'd learned to prevent the anger from forming in the first place. Which made her the better person of the two to handle Jack Turner, if he had to be dealt with again. Jack Turner. An intriguing man. Very intriguing.

*　*　*

Before she entered her own bull pen, she got some evil-looking coffee for both herself and Sam from Narcotics. Sam had settled down at his desk to make some calls when they'd first come in, and he was still at it. She shoved the coffee into the cave he formed slumped over his desk pad, phone glued to his ear, and carried the other cup to her own desk, beginning to sort out priorities. There was a lot to be done, and it all needed doing this minute. And already it was after five. The business day was over. Most of the questions she had would have to wait for the next day. But there were a few things that still could be done.

She placed a call to a contact she had at the Seattle *Times*. Tony Throckmorton was grumbly and curt, had never heard of Jack Turner, he said, and finally agreed to run the name through his computer. There was silence while he waited for the computer to divulge its information, then he was back on the line. "Okay," he said finally, "got him. Nope, nothing much, Kate. A routine notice of forming the company, Turner Bearing Company, Inc. Incorporation: Delaware. Purpose: distributor of stainless-steel bearings, mainly aircraft. Sole stockholder: Turner. That's it."

"Anything personal on him at all?"

"Zilch. Just the single graph, bald statement of fact."

"What about financial status? Supposedly he's rich."

"Nada. You'll have to snoop in his checkbook for that, Kate. Want me to send a hard copy over?"

"Please. Thanks, Tony, I appreciate the help."

The noisy rhythm of the station house washed around her unnoticed as she sat in thought. An image of Turner in shirt sleeves came to mind. He'd seemed like such an ordinary, comfortable guy. He certainly didn't look rich, or act rich. Had Catherine pretended he was more than he was, maybe to impress her partners? Or, looking at it in the context of the luxurious condo that Catherine had lived in, maybe Turner did have some dough, and he was the one who owned it, and had bought her all those clothes, and he'd been lying through his teeth about bringing the relationship to an end. But if he had lied, and had been still seeing Catherine, how did her supposed reconciliation with Vern Riley fit in?

She let her mind wander over various combinations of possible answers before relegating it to her subconscious to let it all simmer. The questions concerning Turner really came down to the man himself. How he'd met Catherine Fletcher, why they'd started seeing each other, and why they'd stopped. It all boiled down to the man himself.

The phone on her desk rang. "MacLean."

"This is Phyllis Walsh, one of Catherine Fletcher's business partners? Thank God I've caught you. When your people left today, they must've taken the key to Catherine's desk with them. There are some papers the attorney needs and they must be in one of her drawers. Could you have someone bring the key over so I can go through her stuff? They can watch while I photocopy what I need, if they want to."

"Hold on a minute, Mrs. Walsh." Kate pushed the hold button and called across to Sam. "It's Phyllis Walsh, Sam. She needs a key to Catherine's desk that we've taken into evidence. I'd like to talk to her alone while I've got the chance, but I'm supposed to meet with the crime lab in an hour. If I take Walsh the key, can you cover the meeting in case I don't make it back in time?" He nodded and she punched back into the line. "Sure, Mrs. Walsh. I can bring it over. But I need to make one quick call first. About half an hour?"

"Yes. Thanks. Thanks a lot."

Kate disconnected, sought out Rebecca Wilson's phone number and called her. She identified herself, then said, "I'm sorry to bother you, Becky, but I have another question or two. Did your mother send you any baby things for Mark? Furniture, a crib, some clothes, anything like that?"

"No. Not even a card."

"How about maternity clothes? Or clothes for you after you had the baby?"

"Nothing."

"Phone calls? Did she ever call you?"

"No, never. I called her a few times, like I told you. Then I quit."

"When you called her, did you ever reach your stepfather?"

"Vern? Yeah, I guess. A couple of times, maybe."

"What did you talk about with him?"

"Nothing. I have nothing to say to him. I just asked him to have my mother call."

"Did she? Return your call?"

"No. She never called me at all. Why?"

"Just making sure I wasn't confused about who did what calling, that's all. Don't let it worry you. By the way, it's turned out your mother never picked up her final divorce papers from your stepfather, so he'll be responsible for the funeral. Is that all right with you?"

"Sure. I didn't know what to do anyway."

Her voice was low, a hopeless, sad sound. Kate's hand tightened on the receiver. She was so young . . . "How are you doing?"

"Me?" Becky sounded surprised. "I'm okay, I guess." Then her voice perked up. "Thanks for asking."

"How about if I check in with you tomorrow, just to see how you're doing?"

"Sure. That'd be fine. I'd appreciate it."

"Okay. Until tomorrow then."

Sam was standing over her desk when she hung up and she avoided his thoughtful look. "Yeah, I know," she said, "Mother MacLean."

"She is a suspect, you know."

"Right. Well, off I go." She gathered her stuff, stopped to pick up Catherine Fletcher's key ring they'd put back in Inventory, and fled.

7

The day had darkened to a false dusk as a legion of menacing black clouds moved in from the northwest. The first thunder rolled as Kate negotiated downtown Bellevue's going-home gridlock, and lightning sparked over the lake, making her shiver slightly. A perfect night for a murder. Kate swung into the parking lot behind the old four-story building that rose like a tired crate against the storm-ridden sky.

Most of the offices had closed for the night. The sound of a metal drawer slamming home echoed down the dusky stairwell from the top floor. The empty building and the dark and lonely staircase made her cautious. She crept up the stairs and moved soundlessly to the studio door, her suit jacket loosened, her hand hovering in the vicinity of her shoulder holster.

Phyllis sat cross-legged on the floor in front of a tall filing cabinet, the bottom drawer pulled open in front of her. While locked out of the office by the crime lab crew that afternoon, she'd obviously gone home and changed clothes, and was now dressed in jeans and a sweatshirt. Her hair was rumpled from running her hand through the normally smooth style, and she wore no makeup. As Kate watched, she pulled a folder free, examined each paper it contained, closed it again and replaced it, plucking out the next file in line.

Kate relaxed and knocked on the doorway. "You look hard at work."

Phyllis raised a tired face and managed a tight smile. "I'm more frustrated than hardworking. I just cannot figure out what she's done with it."

"Who and what?"

"Catherine. Her stock certificate. For the company here." Phyllis closed the folder, replaced it and pulled the next. "I went to the attorney this afternoon to get things started, and Catherine's stock certificate is gone. She took it from his office over a month ago and I can't find it anywhere." She plucked out the last folder, looked at the single sheet inside, then put back the folder and slammed the drawer shut. "I'd already looked through them all, but I was hoping . . ." She rose to her feet and brushed dust off her hands. "A forlorn hope, obviously. Did you manage to get the desk key?"

"Yep." Katie searched her purse, pulled it free and handed it over.

"I really appreciate this." Phyllis unlocked the center drawer of Catherine's desk and pulled open a file drawer on the side. She began as she had with the ones in the filing cabinet—pulling one folder free from its hanging file, opening it, then putting it back and taking up the next. But after the first few, she simply raised each one, peered in and let it fall back. "Did you guys take her papers, too?"

"No. What's wrong?"

"They're empty. Every single one of them's empty." Finished with that drawer, she turned to the file drawer on the other side. It took only a minute to determine that those folders were empty, too. Phyllis sank back in the desk chair. "Cleaned out. Someone's cleaned out every single one of her files." Her eyes were bleak. "Damn it anyway. We'll have absolutely no idea where she stands with any of her clients. Or even who they are."

"Don't you keep duplicates?"

"Only after they're signed contracts. Up till then, it's just our work notes."

"Would Catherine have taken them home with her? To work on, maybe?"

Phyllis shook her head slowly. "I can't envision her doing that. She never took work home with her."

"Well then, the keys. Who had keys to the office?"

"The four of us. Plus the landlord. And the janitor."

"That's six. Anyone else?"

"No. That's it."

"Husbands?"

"Nope. At least, not mine. I don't know about Ginger's and Suzie's. But I don't think so. You have Catherine's key and I've got mine, so that's four left."

"Out of those four, who had keys to the desks?"

"That's it." Phyllis indicated the key still stuck in the center drawer. "We each had one to our own desk. No duplicates."

"And you locked your desks every night before going home?"

"The rest of us didn't. Just Catherine. She'd lock hers every time she left the office. She was concerned about privacy. Said that bosses used to go through her stuff at night and it drove her nuts." Phyllis focused on a couple of old filing cabinets against the far wall and shoved her chair back. "Maybe she stuck her papers over there." With intense concentration, Phyllis fell silent as she searched the first of the file drawers.

For a moment, Kate watched her, then she began wandering around the large pair of worktables in the center of the room, looking at the various projects grouped there. They were in all stages of progress, from uncut strips of typesetting to completed paste-ups. Black-and-white photos and colored slides were stacked near whatever art board they belonged to. One small brochure looked ready for the printer, but she couldn't see how the photos would fit, they were too big for the picture holes left in the paste-up. She asked Phyllis about it.

Phyllis slammed home a searched file drawer and came over to look. She pointed out the crop marks on the borders of the photos and the percentages written on each for reduction. "Shrink and cut," she explained. "The print world's black magic." Noticing Kate's curiosity at last, she took her on a tour of the art table, explaining half-tones, printer's proofs, and ad slicks. Then she went to a set of flat, shallow storage drawers and began pulling out completed projects from the past few months.

Brochures, flyers, flexis, direct-mail pieces, newspaper supplements, mail-order catalogs, more ad slicks—Kate was astounded by the assortment of work the studio did. Not only the assortment, but the quality, too. She commented about it.

"It takes a lot of attention to detail," Phyllis explained, "to get it that way. Print's an unforgiving medium. In radio and television, you see what you've got as you go. You can edit the ads again and again until you get them right. Tape's fluid that way. But with print, you don't know what you have until it rolls off the presses, and then it's too late to correct."

Phyllis picked up an ad slick. "For example, this was sent to the *Times*. Camera-ready. All they had to do at the newspaper was strip it into the made-up page and go to press. You'd think it was foolproof, right? But for whatever reason—page oversold, some story running too long, whatever— they had to trim back the length a bit." She dug around and came up with a copy of the printed ad. "Look them both over a minute. Do you see where their paste-up department made the cut?"

Kate compared ad slick to ad. It was a small one, a couple of columns wide, about three inches long, she guessed, announcing the appearance of a visiting sculptor from the Midwest at a local pewter collector's shop. The sculptor's name meant nothing to her, but she assumed it would to collectors. Date and time were there, she noted. Also a brief bio of the sculptor. It all seemed complete. Then she hit the store name at the bottom and made a soundless "Oh." At the bottom of the ad there was simply the name of the shop. No address. No phone number.

Phyllis nodded. "Exactly." Then she brought out a slick full-colored brochure for a small shop. "Here's another one." She pointed to the face of one of the models pictured there. "See how orange her flesh looks? And over here, that dress should've been a cool, icy blue, and look how it came out, almost a muddy purple, and now the model's face is too red."

"But how would you prevent that?" Kate asked.

"You run what's called a press check. When the first sheets roll off the press, the account exec stands right there and does a color check with the pressman. Then final color adjustments are made to the ink flow, and the presses begin their run." Phyllis smiled.

"It's really kind of an exciting moment. Some of those big presses hum and throb like huge semitrailers, and suddenly what can be weeks of work comes roaring down the line, and there you have it—your finished product."

Kate studied the blotched brochure. "Who was the account exec on this one?"

"Catherine." Phyllis's voice betrayed no emotion.

Kate gave her a curious look. "I thought she wasn't making any sales."

"That was last summer, when she was still doing some work." Phyllis put away the print samples she'd taken from the storage drawers and returned to her search of the filing cabinets.

Kate wandered over to the drawing board and perched on a stool. Streaks of lightning shot past the skylight and the dusky corners of the room flared into view, then died away again. After each flare, the loft seemed darker and gloomier than before. Wind gusts rattled the large square of windowpane at Kate's elbow, and rivulets of icy cold fingered their way through the loose wooden frame. The loft itself, with its skeleton structure of rafters and sharp angles, was gaunt. Not a cozy place to be in a storm.

Without appearing to do so, she watched Phyllis closely as file folder after file folder was examined with quick, deft motions, trying to get a read on her character. She was an attractive woman, with a calm, almost grave expression in her eyes. Though strain and tension showed through in the slightly drawn cast to the thin face, she seemed composed enough, going about things in a logical order simply because they had to be done. She struck Kate as well-organized, competent, in control.

Kate shifted a little on the hard stool to get more comfortable. "Tell me a little about Catherine as a woman," she said quietly. "Not as a business partner, but what you sensed about her simply as a woman."

Phyllis had been working on a lower file drawer, bending over it. At the question, she straightened up and leaned against the cabinet, rubbing her lower back. "That's a pretty broad question you're asking there," she said slowly.

"Try," Kate said, encouraging her. "Anything that comes to mind. I'm trying to get a sense of her as a person."

Phyllis thought a moment. "Catherine. How to describe Catherine . . . Well, she was a strikingly beautiful woman. Black hair, high cheekbones, deep-violet eyes with long, thick black lashes—the kind a movie star would kill for. And when she was at her best, she had charming little ways, a bit naughty in a way that was funny and cute and contagious. You just couldn't help laughing with her sometimes, even if she was being outrageous. For instance, when Vern was around, I guess she'd really put the needle to him. Like one time he asked her to get him some new undershorts because his old ones were full of holes, and she asked him how come they were full of holes, he never got big enough to take a poke at anything. She'd repeat these stories to us, with a giggle and a flick of the eyelashes, and we couldn't help but laugh. She was outrageous, but funny."

"Have you ever met Vern?"

"No, but Suzie had. She said he was a real jerk."

"A jerk how?"

"I guess he got drunk that night, and then came on like some superstud to the gals in the bar. He had a reputation for being quite a womanizer. And he had a habit of sticking other people with the bill. At the end of the evening, at pay-up time, he'd head for the men's room, then just disappear. Just walk out. And the time Suzie was with them, she got stuck with the bill." Phyllis paused a moment, thinking. "I guess Catherine really did have her hands full with him. She couldn't rely on him for much of anything. Especially money. He'd go broke and she'd get mad and make him leave, then after a while, he'd get some money again and she'd take him back. I don't know why she put up with it. I guess he had a way of ingratiating himself with her. Either that, or he was irresistible in bed. I don't know, really. I don't understand that kind of relationship. To me, the money alone wouldn't be worth it."

Kate thought of the expensive condo and the secret clothes closet. Money seemed to govern everything Catherine did. "Did she have some kind of a financial cushion built up to fall back on?"

Phyllis gave her a sharp look. "Not that I know of. Why?"

"Just curious," Kate said easily. "I can't seem to get it straight in my mind. If she had no savings to fall back on, or anything, how could she start a business of her own?"

"The underground economy," Phyllis said with a slight smile. "Basically, we bartered our way into business. We traded services for furniture, services for letterheads, services for supplies, and services for the first month's rent. By the end of thirty days, we'd landed a couple of monthly accounts that brought in enough to cover our basic expenses at least. The summer was good, and Christmas was better. The retail season really picked up this past year and we worked overtime to take care of the demand and keep the work flowing out. We actually split some profit for the fourth quarter. Then the first-quarter slump hit." Phyllis made a wry face. "So far, since the first of the year, we've only brought in about forty thousand gross."

"Isn't that a lot?" Kate asked, somewhat surprised at the amount.

Phyllis shook her head. "We're still the new kids on the block. Until we've built up a reputation for quality work, we have to keep our prices low enough to entice the business through the door. Plus, there've been some cost overruns that we've had to swallow. Right now, profit's running less than ten percent. Spread over three months and among four people, it barely keeps our cars going."

Ten percent. Four thousand dollars. A thousand each. For three months' work? That wouldn't pay for the first outfit in Catherine's closet, Kate thought. Never mind food and rent. Especially for that condo. "You said Catherine hadn't sold any jobs in months. Could she have been keeping the sales to herself and having the work done someplace else?"

Phyllis looked shocked at the idea. "No, of course she wasn't," she said sharply. "Why would she? We can do the work right here. Why pay some other graphics house—" The light bulb clicked on. "Oh. To keep the profit all for herself." She stared out the window a moment, then gave Kate a speculative look. "Has someone said something that would lead you to think that?"

"It was just a thought that occurred to me," Kate said. "I'm trying to figure out how she lived. Did she have some kind of basic draw to help cover her normal monthly expenses?"

Phyllis nodded. "We set that up in the beginning. At first, it was just a thousand a month. Barely food, gas and rent money. But then, when business flowed so well, we upped her to fifteen hundred. Plus commissions and profits, of course. That gave her some relief for a while. But the last of her commissions were paid to her in December, and she started complaining again about the lack of money. She was pushing us to increase her draw to twenty-five hundred a month. But we just couldn't do it. Not without some sales from her to justify it. Not in this kind of business climate."

"So her solution was to just help herself," Kate said quietly.

"I guess." Phyllis sighed. "Just in the last three weeks, she'd taken four thousand dollars out of the business."

"*Four* thousand." The number startled Kate. "I thought you said *two* thousand when we talked earlier today."

Phyllis gave a weary nod. "That was just last week's haul. A couple of weeks before that, it was another two thousand dollars."

"But that was your whole profit for the quarter."

"That's just my point. She was draining the company of every extra dime she could get hold of."

"And Ginger countersigned all the checks?"

"Yes, she couldn't say no to a purse snatcher." Phyllis looked a bit bleak.

"Sounds like her name should be taken off as a signatory."

"It was. Yesterday. Suzie and I are the only ones who can sign now."

"Does Ginger know her signature's off the bank account?"

Phyllis nodded. "We told her as soon as we got back from the bank. She just said, 'Thank God,' and went back to her drawing board."

"And Catherine? Did you tell her, too?"

"Yep. When I finally ran into her." Phyllis paused a moment, a puzzled frown on her face. "But her reaction was weird. Really weird. She never said a word. She just blinked those long lashes of hers and smiled at me, and never said a word. It was like it didn't matter anymore." Phyllis stared off into space again.

"Maybe that's it. Maybe she just really didn't care anymore. And that's what went wrong."

"There's been some talk of a possible drinking problem," Katie said. "Do *you* think she had a drinking problem?"

"I don't know. I've kind of wondered now and then." Phyllis paused, thinking it over. "Especially since she was never here in the mornings. Heavy drinking night after night might explain some of that." She paused, her face bleak. "I don't know, there were so many things going on, it's hard to pin any one of them down to a single cause. What you've suggested about her making sales on the side really bothers me now. It would tie in with a few other things."

"Like what?" Kate asked.

"Her appointments, for one. She'd put down phony sales calls, then would take the day off. I caught her at it. Twice."

"How'd you discover this? Were you checking up on her?"

Phyllis shook her head. "No, it was all accidental. One day last summer, on a Friday, she supposedly had appointments scheduled in downtown Seattle. We were filling out itineraries then, so any one of us could track another down if we needed something. So on this particular Friday, she checked in here first thing in the morning, and then left. She'd said that she probably wouldn't be back before we closed that night, that the weekend getaway traffic from the city would probably trap her on the bridge. I didn't think anything of it at the time. We'd all been stuck for hours on one of the bridges or another. But then, later that morning, a client of mine in downtown Seattle phoned and needed some copy picked up for a last-minute ad. I called Catherine's two-o'clock in the city to leave a message for her to call me, thinking I'd have her pick up the copy since she was already on that side of the bridge. But the guy I called didn't have an appointment scheduled with her for any time that day. So I called her three-o'clock. Same story. No appointment. So then I called all the other names on her schedule and, lo and behold, *no* one had an appointment scheduled with her that day. The itinerary was phony. The whole thing."

"What did you do?" Kate asked.

"Well, I didn't really know what to do," Phyllis said. "I didn't really know what was going on. There could've been a reasonable explanation for the whole thing. Nothing more than a change in schedule. Though a whole day's change seemed stretching it a bit. And then on Monday, Catherine didn't say anything about any problem or conflicts or anything, and I was busy with my own accounts, so I just sort of let it drop.

"But the next Friday it was the same thing all over again. She was scheduled for downtown Seattle again, and went through the same song and dance about not making it by closing because of the bridge, and I suddenly got suspicious. So after she left, I called the names on her new itinerary. Same thing. A bunch of phony appointments. Now I figured there was something really out of whack. So first thing on Monday, I asked how her Friday appointments had gone."

The anger at the memory was clear in Phyllis' eyes. "I guess I expected some kind of a laughing confession that she hadn't really made any calls and had played hooky instead. But her response was unbelievable. She looked me square in the eye and described the interviews just as if they'd really happened. I mean, clear down to actually repeating conversations that were supposed to have taken place! It was unreal. That woman lied through her teeth with the clearest, most innocent look on her face I've ever seen!"

"So how'd you handle it?" Kate asked.

"I kept my mouth shut. I honestly didn't know what to do, so I just let it go. I ended up not saying anything about it at all. I was just so—*paralyzed* by it, I guess."

Kate nodded her understanding.

"She knew something was wrong, of course. Maybe by the shock I showed. I don't know. Anyway, she didn't say anything directly to me, but from that day on, she never gave us another itinerary again. Said it was a matter of trust. But I'm sure she'd caught on to what had happened."

"What about Ginger and Suzie? Did you tell them?"

"No." Phyllis got a distasteful look on her face. "Catherine had this little act she'd put on in front of other people. If anyone accused her of anything, she'd get this wide-eyed, innocent, terribly hurt look on her face. She could even produce a single tear that would tremble on her lower lashes, just so. So if I'd tried to tell Ginger and Suzie what she was doing, she'd have simply gone into this act of hers, and I'd have been the one who ended up looking like a troublemaker."

Phyllis' voice had been even-toned through all of this, but anger flared in her eyes. A lot of passion was backed up in that slender frame, Kate thought. A hell of a lot. Enough to kill? "What about this new Boeing project; was she involved in that at all?"

"No. In fact, she ridiculed it. She thought it was ludicrous to put in that much time on something that was simply spec and had little or no chance of succeeding."

"Exactly how much time have you put into it, Phyllis?"

"A lot." Phyllis sighed. "Every night last week, all day Saturday—the three of us. Ginger, Suzie and myself. The whole project ate up the hours like crazy, and it was brutal, trying to fit it in around our normal work day."

"You worked on it every night last week?"

Phyllis nodded. "Except Friday night. We all took Friday night off. And Sunday."

"What did Catherine do while the rest of you were so busy?"

"I don't know. I only saw her three or four times all last week. And I didn't see her at all over the weekend."

"She didn't come in Saturday to help you?"

"Catherine didn't believe in pitching in to help," Phyllis said dryly.

"What about yesterday? When did you see her yesterday?"

"Let's see . . . I saw her just before quitting time last night. That's when I told her about the bank account. That was about a quarter to five. Then she left. Oh, yes, I saw her briefly at noon. I came in for lunch and passed her as she was on her way out. Time's been tight, so we've all been bringing lunch with us so we could work through the noon hour."

"Including Catherine?"

"No. Supposedly, she was skipping lunch and keeping on with her calls."

"You sound skeptical."

"She was so damned deceitful. You couldn't trust her at all."

Kate let it pass. "What about the other two? What were their schedules like yesterday?"

"Well, Suzie and I met at the bank to change the account first thing in the morning, then we went in separate directions on appointments. And Ginger spent the day putting together a double spread of newspaper ads for one of our regular clients. She left to get them approved about four and got back shortly after five. Then the three of us went out for a quick supper. Afterward we came back here, Ginger to finish up the artwork for Boeing, Suzie and I to work out the last hitches in our presentation. We finished our part about nine, and left. I don't know how late Ginger stayed, I didn't have a chance to ask her today, what with everything that happened."

"Who was here to cover the office when Ginger took the newspaper ads for approval?"

"Suzie was. I came in about four-fifteen. Ginger was gone by then. Suzie said she'd left at four. Then Suzie had a four-thirty appointment and she left a couple of minutes after I got here, and I baby-sat the office. Catherine came in about a quarter to five. I told her about the bank, she just smiled that weird smile, picked up her stuff and left. She wasn't here longer than a minute or two."

"How long was that before Ginger came back?"

"Maybe fifteen, twenty minutes."

"So at some point yesterday, each of the three of you were alone here."

She looked unhappy with that summary. "So it would seem."

"Who else would be liable to come into your office? Outsiders, I mean."

"That kind of varied. Printers' reps for Ginger. Typesetting pickup and deliveries. Newspaper messengers for display ads or proofs. Occasional deliveries, office supplies, art supplies. Mailmen. The bookkeeper now and then to pick up bills. Salesmen. No clients, though. We usually steered them away from here. It's not very fancy."

"Any of them tea drinkers?"

"Coffee to the last."

"So Catherine was the only tea drinker?"

"Yes."

"What about Vern Riley? Or Jack Turner? Did she ever bring either of them around here, to show them the studio?"

"Not that I know of. I don't think she was that proud of it." Phyllis fell silent for a moment. Then she asked in a quiet voice, "Exactly how did Catherine die?"

There was no point in ducking it any longer. "We're pretty sure it was an overdose of painkiller," Kate said, watching her closely for her reaction. "Probably in her tea."

For a long moment, Phyllis stared at Kate, then her gaze drifted off into space. Her body was tense, her spine stiff, as she struggled with a dozen different emotions.

Thunder rumbled overhead and a streak of lightning flared like a flash cube in the night sky. The first slash of rain hit the plastic skylights, a hollow drumming sound like shower spray hitting a bathtub curtain.

Phyllis shivered and looked up. She watched the water bead and run on the skylight overhead for a moment before speaking again. "I've been thinking about it all afternoon," she said slowly. "Catherine's death, I mean. Somehow I knew it wasn't just her heart suddenly giving out, or a blood vessel popping in her brain. I did think of suicide, but that didn't fit either. Catherine just wasn't the type. She was the kind to strike back at people, like a rattlesnake, a diamondback. Suicide wouldn't have fit her character. Which means, of course, that murder is the only explanation."

Then she swung a pair of deeply troubled eyes onto Kate. "But who would do something like that?"

Kate waited to see if Phyllis would attempt to answer her own question. Suspects were often anxious to provide the cops with theories. Particularly guilty suspects. But Phyllis didn't. Instead, when Kate didn't answer the unanswerable, the other woman wrapped her arms around herself as if she were unmercifully cold, and fell into a sad, contemplative silence.

8

Bellevue had once been a charming small town built on narrow streets originally designed for leisurely rural traffic. But then, in the very core of downtown Bellevue, several blocks from the freeway, a two-block area had been roofed over and enclosed, forming Bellevue Square, the Pacific Northwest's largest regional shopping center. Soon, the dozen blocks or so around the mall were crammed with freshly-erected tall, slender, space-age office buildings, and the dozen blocks around *them* were filled with apartment and condominium complexes. All of it, shopping center, office buildings, apartments and condos dumped thousands of cars each day onto the old, narrow streets. With short blocks, traffic lights at every other corner and no maneuvering room, traffic backups and gridlock raged through the city like a disease. Heavy rain just made it worse.

Stalled in line behind the third fender-bender in four blocks, Kate cursed the storm, the Gods, and the City Council. She wondered again, as she did several times a day, every day, why she stayed and put up with it. She always thought longingly of the wide open spaces of Montana whenever she was trapped like this. Day or night, it seemed, traffic grew worse and drivers grew ruder. And all because of a handful of shortsighted, power-hungry grow-at-any-cost city councils. If she had her way, she'd sentence every one of them to twenty years in California.

Then, as always, she began to find excuses for her irritation. It had been a long day and she was just tired. There was still a lot to do, and she was just impatient. She wanted to get to her meeting in progress and find out what the lab boys had to say, and she was just in a hurry. There was a killer out there somewhere, who may or may not be through with his or her program, and she had to get him—her?—found. It was her, that's all. Just her.

Then she looked around, up at the tall buildings surrounding her on the impossibly narrow street, at the trendy restaurants that came and went like a rain squall, at the cars jammed around her on streets too inadequate to handle their numbers, and she thought, No, it wasn't just her.

The tow truck cleared away one of the cars, opening up a lane for the backed-up traffic. She inched her way forward, waited her turn to funnel into the single line of cars allowed through and finally broke free of the whole tangle. She drove faster than she should have, considering the heavy rain, as much in a hurry as any of the drivers she'd just condemned, she noted wryly, and finally pulled into the station parking lot

Sam was just checking out for the night when she burst through the door, shedding raindrops everywhere. "I'd about given you up," he said.

"Typical stormy-night traffic." She shook what water she could from the umbrella and closed it up. "I missed the meeting, right?"

"Right. But I took more notes than we'll ever need."

"Thanks." She grinned at him. "Guess I owe you one."

"A big one. Look, I want to hear what Walsh had to say, but I'm starved. How about grabbing some dinner?"

Kate thought a minute. "The only person I still want to see tonight would be Bob Wilson, Catherine's ex. I thought I'd give him a call—"

Sam shook his head. "Don't bother, I've already tried. He's out, and so is his daughter. No one answers at either place."

Kate shrugged. "Then tomorrow will have to do." Weariness

crept in around the edges, and she could feel her energy level begin to sag. Time to call it a night and give it a rest. Her subconscious would perk along just fine if she gave it a chance. "Okay, dinner it is."

Sam grinned then. "Mexican?"

Sam had been born to the wrong country, she'd long ago decided. His taste buds belonged south of the border. Come to think about it, his dark and swarthy features did, too. Sometimes, when the light was just right, and the set of his muscles was just so, an Indian-like flint settled over the lean planes of the deeply-lined face, and she could suddenly see generations of conquistadores in the depths of his eyes. Spanish eyes, she often thought. Deep, dark, sometimes liquid with softness, other times hard and cold. The eyes of a complex man. Not easily read.

Normally she was up for Mexican anytime, too. But it didn't appeal to her. Not tonight. "I'm in the mood for some pool. I need to work some of the tension out. Let's go to Smokie Jo's and order in pizza from George's."

"Sure, since you're buying."

"You're really going to hold me up for supper, huh? Just for one lowly, little, no-account meeting?"

"Lowly? Little? No-account?" he said slowly. "Do you realize how tedious scientific types can be? How humorless, how sincere?"

"Okay, then, I'll toss you for dinner, double or nothing."

"Not on your life." His dark eyes flashed amusement as he shook his head. "Nice try, though."

Smokie Jo's, in downtown Kirkland, was as quiet as the street outside. It was typical of many of the old-style taverns scattered throughout Puget Sound, with a large horseshoe bar, dark wainscotting and the obligatory neon beer signs. The after-work regulars had come and gone, and the place had settled down for the evening. A couple of Kate's tavern buddies had a pool game going on one of the tables by the front door. In front of the shuttered street window, a young couple talked quietly at a table for two by the jukebox, which was blessedly silent. Just another quiet night at Smokie Jo's. A good place to unwind.

Smokie Jo wasn't on tonight, Pearl was, perched on a stool

behind the bar, a cribbage board and cards spread between herself and another customer. Both women looked up and waved at her as Kate entered, then Pearl left the crib game to set a glass of rosé on the bar for Kate. "I'll catch you later," she called out, and returned to her card game.

Sam had beaten her there and was already seated at one of the three high counters angling from a side wall. On her way to join him, Kate paused by the two pool players. "You two practice real hard," she said to them, " 'cause later on I'm going to clean your clock."

One of the guys turned to the other. "We're in deep trouble here."

"I hope to tell you," the other replied. "Those clanking sounds you hear are my knees knocking with fright."

Kate grinned and picked up her glass, calling out her thanks to Pearl, then slid onto the stool across from Sam at the high table and took a long sip of the wine. It was icy and she could trace the progress of the first swallow all the way down to her stomach. The coldness of it made her shiver for a second, then a warmth began to spread out in pleasant ripples. "This almost makes the whole day worth it," she murmured.

Sam merely nodded. He was drawing idle circles in a sweat puddle on the tabletop with his beer glass. He looked beyond tired, well into weary, his face crosshatched with lines like old leather. The hours, the tension, the psychological demands were catching up to him. And him not yet forty, she thought. But the job did that to you. It went with the territory. Take heed, Katie, my girl, she warned herself.

She took a second sip of wine, then swiveled around partway on her stool to rest her back against the wall and turned her head Sam's way so she could talk directly to him. "So what did the lab come up with?"

"All prelim stuff," he said. He, too, swiveled and leaned back, looking old and weary, still drawing his beer-sweat circles. "And they're backlogged as usual. We won't get a report for weeks. But Saint Homer played a hunch and hit the jackpot. It *was* morphine. Definitely. Crushed in with the tea in the tea bags. He said there was enough dope in them to send a herd of elephants to their happy hunting grounds."

Saint Homer had earned his nickname long ago. The police crime lab inched ahead with typical bureaucratic inefficiency. Things would be done in the order they arrived, and not before their order arrived, and if the cops had to cool their goddamned heels waiting for solid information, then they'd just have to cool their goddamned heels. Patience was a virtue, after all. But after joining the lab a couple of years ago, Homer had quickly shown an instinct for winnowing out the important from the trivia and would take the odd moment or two to follow his hunches. If his hunches proved worthy, he'd actually pick up the phone and convey the results to the investigators involved. It still didn't speed up the appearance of the final report, but it did give the cops a slender route for accessing critical information when they needed it. As a result, he'd been instantly canonized by grateful cops everywhere.

"In the tea bags," Kate echoed. "Who'd have guessed. Were all of them doctored?"

"Nope, only three. Two mixed in with the rest in the canister, and the one in the teacup. The others were okay."

"How was the morphine inserted?"

"Cleverly. Very cleverly." His voice began to perk up, his spirits buoyed up a bit by talking about the case. He quit playing with his beer glass and illustrated his words with hand motions. "Each bag is basically one long tube, folded in half so the two ends meet. Then they're stapled together with the string tab that you dangle over the edge of a cup. In the case of the tampered bags, the original staple had been removed, the morphine tablets were ground to powder and poured in, and the whole thing was restapled. The staples were the giveaway, Homer said. The ones the manufacturer used were small, made specifically for that purpose. The ones on the doctored tea bags were larger. Just your common, everyday, plain old office number ones. He showed us samples of both, and after he'd explained it, it was easy to tell the difference. But it *wasn't* noticeable if you weren't on the lookout for it. A very clever person, our little morphine friend."

"Where were the doctored tea bags in the canister in relation to the rest of them that were okay?"

"The good ones were all jammed together at the bottom. The two doctored ones were just lying on top, as if they were the only two left out of the top layer."

Katie gave a silent whistle. "So they'd almost certainly be the next ones used."

"Right."

"Is there any way of telling when they were put into the canister?"

"Not to the minute, no. But we know now it was after this last Friday night." He paused to swallow some beer. "Let me jump ahead a little. After the meeting, I tracked down the name of the janitor through the landlord and spoke to him on the phone. He has a schedule for cleaning those offices every other night. Tuesday, Thursday, and once during the weekend, usually Sundays. But this past weekend, he and his family were headed out of town on a camping trip, so he cleaned the offices on Friday evening instead of Sunday, so he wouldn't have to worry about doing it after they got back. When I quizzed him on how thoroughly he cleaned the studio, he said he never moved any papers or artwork, but he lifted everything in the coffee area each time and wiped it down completely. Including the canister. And—surprise!—guess what? The only prints on there were Catherine Fletcher's. Somebody had wiped it clean after he'd come and gone."

Kate took a sip of wine, mulling it over. The time element was a break for them. "So the bags weren't a time bomb placed there months ago," she said softly. "We're looking at someone with access to the studio during this past weekend, or on Monday. Did he see anyone in the building that night?"

Sam shook his head. "Nope. He was done with the whole building before ten. During that time, he said, he was completely alone."

"That fits. Phyllis Walsh said they all took Friday night off. What did Homer say about the morphine? Anything more there?"

"No, and there won't be. Not unless we find the tablets. He

can't reconstruct the specific compound used just from the crushed powder found in the tea bags. Morphine's morphine. It's the holding compound that varies from company to company. But without a whole tablet to work with, he can't identify the holding components, and until he knows those, he can't identify which pharmaceutical company made it. We're out of luck on that score, I'm afraid."

"Damn," Kate said. "I was really hoping he could help."

"Cop's law number ninety-seven. Nothing's ever easy." Sam got Pearl's attention and held up two fingers for refills. "Why don't I go next door and order our pizza? Then you can fill me in on Phyllis Walsh. What do you want on your half?"

"Sausage and onions. And I'm hungry. Really hungry."

"I'll order a large."

Kate started to reach for her purse.

He held up a hand. "You take care of the booze. I'll handle the pizza."

She looked at him with suspicion. "I thought I owed you one. Or three. Or whatever."

"Yeah, but pizza's cheaper than Mexican. I'll wait and collect some other night. Besides, I know how much pizza you leave. This way, I own the leftovers."

She sighed. "Oh, Sam, sometimes I worry about you. You'll probably eat it cold,too. For breakfast." He grinned and ducked out.

When he came back, she went over her interview with Phyllis. Sam hunched over his beer as he listened. When she'd finished talking, he asked a few questions to clarify points in his own mind, then said, "So, Mother MacLean, what does your coldly brilliant mind make of all this?"

She ignored the earth mother reference and swirled the remainder of her wine. "Well, I've been trying to sort fact from fiction. I've also been playing around with motives. For instance, the only fact we know for sure is that Catherine was taking money she shouldn't have been out of the company. We haven't seen the canceled checks yet, granted, but all three partners confirm that. We also know it was hurting the business. So Catherine's death accomplishes two things—the business gets rid of a serious threat to its survival and, at the same time, it gets a large injection of much-needed cash from the insurance policy. That's one large-sized motive right there. Opportunity? Even given the time parameters of Friday night to this morning, each of the partners had plenty of chances to plant the tea bags. So opportunity exists for all three as well."

Sam thought a moment, then nodded. "Okay. Top of the suspect list—the partners. Who's next?"

"Catherine's daughter, I guess. There are some discrepancies there, Sam. Three people—Riley, Ginger, and Phyllis—have stated that Catherine supposedly did all she could to help her daughter. Two of them, Ginger and Phyllis, said the relationship between the two was close. But Riley said it wasn't, that the daughter was abusive to her mother. Discrepancy number one. Was the relationship close or wasn't it? Then there's the daughter's claim her mother had turned her off like a water faucet over three years ago, when the girl got pregnant, and has done absolutely nothing for her since. Yet Riley claims he paid a couple of thousand dollars' worth of bills for baby clothes and furniture. Discrepancy number two. So who's lying?" she mused. "Is Riley lying when he said the girl was abusive to her mother? Is the girl lying about her mother's rejection of her? Or was Catherine lying when she claimed to all and sundry that she was helping her daughter? An examination of Catherine's bank account and a look at those Nordstrom's charge slips will prove a lot. Unless, of course, Catherine handed her daughter cash, or Riley lied about the purchases and there were no bills at all."

"That'd be a dumb thing for him to do," Sam pointed out. "He must realize those records can be checked."

"Maybe he just didn't carry it far enough forward in his mind."

"If one can call a sewer a mind," Sam said.

Kate wrinkled her nose. "He is disgusting, isn't he."

"Disgusting's an understatement. Try obnoxious. Repugnant. Repellent. Not to mention repulsive." He shook his head. "I don't know, Katie, this appears to be a pretty well-calculated murder. No witnesses, plenty of suspects and no source yet for the drug. Some bright mind's behind it. And somehow Riley just doesn't fit the bill."

"True. He didn't strike me as the brightest man I've ever met."

Their pizza arrived, and as they ate, they tossed out one wacky theory after another, trying out each person involved in the role of poisoner. It was far too early yet in the investigation to narrow in on any one person. Or even two. It was more like an open casting call for a new play. You gave each aspirant some lines to say and let him have his few moments on stage, taking note of the fit between actor and role.

Finally, Sam pushed the box away from him. Kate, as hungry as she'd been, had eaten only one slice, and he had almost half a pizza to take home with him. He stared at it moodily for a moment, then returned to the subject of Catherine's daughter. "I'm intrigued by the mother/daughter relationship," he said to Kate. "What's your thinking about young Becky?"

She stared unseeingly at the pool game in progress. "Let's take it both ways. Let's suppose the daughter's lying, that Catherine really was helping her. Why kill the golden goose? And why lie about the help her mother had given her? But if what the daughter said was true, a complete rejection of the girl by Catherine, then a motive certainly exists for striking out at her mother, wanting to hurt her back. But why now, after three years?"

"Brooding on it?" Sam suggested.

"Possibly. But what about opportunity? There's none that I can see. She lives in her little place on the other side of Carnation, and the office is a good twenty miles away, in downtown Bellevue. She claims she didn't know anything about what her mother was doing these days, so how would she know about the office? And even if she did know, how would she get in? I went over the key situation thoroughly with Phyllis. They keep the place locked up except when at least one of the partners is in, and except for the landlord and janitor, they are the only ones with keys."

"Unless the office happened to be left unlocked this weekend and the girl happened to have chosen the same weekend to plant spiked tea bags."

Kate just looked at him. "That's a lot of happen-tos, isn't it?"

"Doesn't make much sense, no," he admitted.

"Plus, would she know her mother only drank tea at work? And was the *only* one to drink tea?" Kate gave it another moment's thought, then shook her head. "I don't know, Sam, that one's pretty iffy." She continued down her mental checklist of people. "We haven't heard her dad's story yet. Maybe that'll clear up some of the confusion."

"We haven't heard Jack Turner's, either. Not really." Sam's voice was carefully neutral, his gaze impassive on Kate. "We only have his word for it that his relationship with Catherine was over months ago."

"Not quite," Kate said quietly. "There's Catherine's reconciliation with Vern Riley, don't forget. That would tend to confirm that the romance with Turner was over."

"Ah, but once again, we only have Riley's word for that. Besides, all three partners are claiming that Catherine and Turner were planning to get married soon. If the relationship had ended, why would she continue the pretense, knowing she couldn't produce the groom?"

"Well, to give the man his due," Kate said carefully, "Catherine seems to be somewhat unreliable in the area of truth-telling. Maybe she was maintaining the pretense of a relationship until it just sort of died a natural death in everyone else's mind."

"You mean to save face?" He shrugged. "You're the female, not me. You tell me. Do women do those kinds of things these days?"

Kate fell silent a moment. "The women I know don't," she finally admitted.

"Point made."

She thought about it, focusing on the tavern now as she did so. The young couple had left; the cribbage game had turned into a marathon. And so had the pool game. The world turned on while they sat probing people's psyches for murderous impulses. Insane. Obscene and insane. She sighed. "Okay, try this one. Suppose Riley found Catherine alone at the studio this morning, distracted her attention so he could slip the spiked tea bags into the canister and wipe it clean, then went on to move into her condo, knowing she was dead."

"Same objection as the daughter," Sam answered. "How could he know that she would be alone in the office this morning? It wasn't her usual pattern. And how did he know that she only drank tea while she was there?"

"Ah, but he's had more of an ongoing relationship with Catherine than the daughter has. He was with her last summer when the business was still young and getting off the ground. That'd give him the chance to know about the tea drinking. And the chance to make a duplicate key of the office, for that matter."

"And motive?" Sam asked.

"Well, Catherine had kicked him out, then afterward met Jack Turner. Maybe Riley learned of the new romance and jealousy reared its ugly little head, and he decided if he, Vern, couldn't have her, no one could."

"Then Turner still lied about it being over."

"Maybe not. Maybe Riley didn't know it had come to an end."

"Or maybe it wasn't over," he said softly, "but Turner wanted it to be, and found he couldn't get out of it for some reason or another. Maybe she found out something that allowed her to dig her nails in and keep him on the hook and he could see no other way out. If they were as involved as she's told everyone they were, then somewhere along the way, he'd have plenty of chances to swipe her office key long enough to have a duplicate made. Also, being such a recent romance, there's a hell of a good chance he'd know about the tea quirk."

Kate raised a quizzical eyebrow. "You make a good case against him. It wouldn't be personal now, would it?"

"Just because he's a grade-A, number-one asshole doesn't influence my judgment one degree." Sam's eyes were as dark as night as they stayed fixed on hers.

Under his strong gaze, she shifted uncomfortably. Finally, she dropped her eyes to her wine and became fascinated with the interplay of wine colors and bar lights. He was usually right about people. He held back and sized them up, and his perceptions were ninety-nine percent accurate. Except about her, of course. This Mother MacLean business had worn itself out long ago, yet he persisted in it. But otherwise his judgment was sound.

She peered up at him a second and tried to read his expression, but he was staring down now at his own near-empty glass, his face closed off. She had to content herself with trying to guess what he was thinking, and she was too tired to bother. She'd have to wait and see what emerged.

They both switched to coffee, but their talk was wearing down. They'd done as much speculating as they could. They made a list of things that needed to be done the next day, and split the list between them. Sam would start a money trace, tracking down various bank accounts to find out who had paid whom, and exactly how much. Kate would start taking formal statements from everyone involved. Then they'd hitch up again, and tackle the next items on the list.

That decided, Sam looked at his watch, looked at her watching the pool game, then looked at his watch again. "It's getting late," he said at last. "You ready to go?"

She shook her head. "Nope." She indicated the pool players. "I've promised to clean their clock, and I'm going to polish it to a fare-thee-well."

He didn't like it, she could tell. His eyes darkened into an unreadable murk, and he ostentatiously glanced at his watch again. "Well, it's off for me," he said, tossing a couple of bills on the table as a tip. He gathered up the pizza box, paused once to give her one more chance to change her mind, and when she didn't, gave her a curt, parting nod and headed toward the door.

"Thanks for the pizza, Sam," Kate called after him.

He merely shrugged and kept walking.

As soon as the door closed behind him, Kate put her quarter on the pool table to rotate her way into the game. Although clearly Sam didn't approve, he also didn't dare disapprove. It was one of the problems a female cop faced. A male partner often tended to act like a brother/husband/father. Sam was semi-okay in the role. He treated her like an equal. Mostly. And when he disapproved of something she did, he kept it to himself. Mostly. She wouldn't call him her best friend, like some of the teams were. But she would call him a friend. Sometimes. Well, occasionally. Still, it was working out okay. Mostly. Except when he got that look on his face that he didn't quite approve. Like when the subject of her pool-playing came up.

But once he'd left, she chalked up her cue and enjoyed herself thoroughly, laughing and joking with the guys. As she'd promised, she not only cleaned their clocks, she stripped their damned gears. By the time she'd won enough games to chase them home, the tensions of the day were gone. The tavern was empty now and she hung up her stick and moved to the bar to visit with Pearl awhile.

Pearl was in her late sixties, slim, attractive and youthful, with tightly crimped, brown-tinted hair and perfectly-applied makeup. She had the energy of a teenager, the illusions of a young romantic, the humor of a realist and the compassion of an octogenarian who's seen it all. She was a deep favorite of Kate's, one of the good people who always had time for other people's troubles and a shoulder to cry on.

Even though Pearl was a good generation older than herself, they had much in common—including being single—and the conversation gradually drifted toward a favorite topic of theirs . . . men. When they got through dissecting Pearl's latest gentleman friend, they began on Sam. Pearl's considered opinion was that he was waiting around for Katie to wake up to his virtues.

Kate scoffed at the notion. Not Sam. He'd never hang around like some moonstruck teenager, waiting for some female to notice him. If he was interested in someone, he'd pursue her. If he didn't pursue her, he wasn't interested. It was that simple. Sam was as romantic as an old shoe.

Pearl gave her a wise grin. "Okay, Katie, be so smart. But you mark my words, he's ready to settle down. He wants a home and a wife. He wants you."

Kate just snorted.

It was almost eleven before she called it a night and left for home. Home was a seventy-year-old cottage, less than five minutes away, a few blocks west of Market Street and two blocks up from the lake. With no view. Which was what had made it affordable. That, and the decrepit condition it was in when she'd bought it. She'd gotten it at a steep discount from the original owner, an elderly widow whose arthritic joints had stopped keeping up with the demands of maintaining the place twenty years before she'd been willing to admit it.

The cottage was at the far end of a long block, with a detached garage sitting well back from the house. She pulled in, grateful the day was done. Wearily, she climbed out and, ignoring the back door to the house, walked around to the front to gather her mail, as she always did coming in from work. Catalogs and junk mail. Throw-aways. She climbed the porch steps, house key in hand, and let herself in.

The cottage had a simple layout. To the right off the small foyer was the living room, with dining room and kitchen behind it. To the left were the two corner bedrooms, front and back, with a bath between. Through the time-honored magic of elbow grease and paint, she'd created a light, airy haven of comfort for herself. The pale-peach wash she'd put on the walls of the living room . . . the warm florals of the rummage-sale furniture she'd had slip-covered . . . the clean lines of the white brick fireplace running up the end wall with white-painted built-in bookshelves filling in the space to the corner. . . . It made her breath catch every time she entered.

She loved this world she'd created for herself. Loved it deeply and fiercely. To her, it represented warmth and welcome, and implied a certain order to things. It balanced her soul against the chaos of her work, and put her in touch with decency. It added just a little bit of the beauty of the world. It was her sanctuary against the casual cruelties and perversions of her daytime life.

She'd taken the largest bedroom for herself. She'd painted it a deeper peach than she'd used in the living room and had turned the woodwork from a dark, drab brown to a soft white. The room was simply furnished—a white makeup table, a low dresser, a slipper chair and, against the rear wall, a large brass bed covered with a plump eyelet comforter in a soft creamy-white, with big fat eyelet-covered pillows propped up against the headboard.

She stripped her jacket off, hung it up in the closet, then removed her shoulder harness. The heavy service revolver was an obscenity in the room. It was too hard, too metallic, too strong, too real for the tranquil mood she'd created. She quickly stowed it out of sight on a closet shelf, restoring the pristine aura surrounding her. The night was chill and she pulled on a flannel nightgown and warm robe and slippers. The robe, a blue-striped terry cloth, was wearing out, she suddenly noticed. The colors were faded, the edges of the cuffs were wearing thin, and the belt was dangling rivers of unraveling thread. One of these days, she'd have to take some time to shop for a new one.

She glanced through the throw-aways in the mail, then dumped them unread into the kitchen trash, and checked her answering machine signaling a message. The properly cool, socially correct New England tones of her mother announced she was just calling to chat a bit. Next time, dear. The message was a shade hurried, as if her mother didn't quite trust the machine to get the whole of her brief words in the time allotted. Smiling, Kate glanced at the kitchen clock. Eleven, her time. Two A.M., Connecticut time. Too late to return the call.

She poured herself a glass of rosé, put on an old Charlie Byrd tape, picked up the latest issue of *Time* magazine from the sofa table and curled up on the couch, settling in to read awhile. But her mind kept drifting back to her case. *Her* case. As she recalled the day and began trying to put the bits and pieces together in rational order, she couldn't help but feel a tickle of satisfaction. *Her* case. Finally. God, it felt good.

9

By six the next morning, Kate was seated in her regular booth at the Kirkland Denny's just off the 520. The newsstand out front provided her with the morning's *P-I* and *J-A*, and the previous night's *Times*. As she ate her bacon and eggs, she scanned the two Seattle papers first. There was no mention of Catherine Fletcher's death in either. She turned to the *J-A* and found the two-paragraph article buried in a back section. It was simple and straightforward. A woman had collapsed and died at her place of business; heart failure was suspected; no name was given pending notification of the family. Though it did mention that an autopsy was being conducted, there was not enough information there to attract the interest of the reporters from the other two dailies. At most, maybe a routine query. Satisfied, Kate drank the last of her coffee and left for the station.

Sam was already in. He was on his phone, hunched over as if protecting the receiver from prying eyes. He waved a greeting at Kate, hunched further over and continued on.

She would be taking formal statements and spent the early-morning hours on her own phone making arrangements for each of them to come in. Ginger wanted to come down immediately and get it over with, so she could take advantage of their office being closed to catch up on some design work. Phyllis begged off for the morning; Boeing had put in an urgent call for her; there was some hiccup in the new contract. But she'd stop in later before returning to the office, where she also intended to take advantage of the quiet to organize the next phase of business, necessary now that Catherine was gone. Suzie's phone didn't answer.

As for the rest, Becky Wilson said her car had broken down, so she would have her father drive her over, and they could take turns watching Mark while they each gave their statements. Vern Riley sounded cheerful for a recently reconciled, now freshly bereaved husband, and stated he'd certainly look forward to *seeing* her again. Kate's nose wrinkled with revulsion at the obvious innuendo in the voice. That reminded her of his claims of purchasing baby things to the tune of two thousand bucks, and she called Nordstrom's and got a promise they'd pull the records on Riley's account for the past three years and send over copies.

Only one call remained. Kate hesitated. She grabbed her cup and headed over to Narcotics, where they kept their own pot of vile black liquid going. They didn't mind freeloaders as long as they chipped in a coffee bean every so often. She had about half a pound left to go before her turn came due again.

Most of the narcs were either out or busy, but a couple were hanging around the pot. Rosie, a tall, cadaverous undercover cop, grinned at her. "Yo, Mother MacLean! Hear you got yourself a *gen-teel* little caper going." Brillo, big, black, and stolid, watched impassively.

"Gives a whole new meaning to the term 'herbal tea,' doesn't it?" Kate said, grinning.

But back in her own section, she banged the full cup of coffee down onto her desk a little harder than necessary. It was all good-humored bantering. On the surface. Below, it was something else. Mother MacLean was *not* a sign of affection from anyone in the bull pen, like most of the nicknames were. She knew it and they knew she knew it. But she was damned if she was ever going to give them the satisfaction of letting them see just how much it grated on her. She kept up her end of the bantering, oozing good humor and joviality from every pore, hating every minute of it. It was like what she imagined a fraternity hazing would be. And it grew tiresome real fast.

Her irritation feeding her resolve, she made up her mind about the last call and reached in her notebook for the name and phone number of Jack Turner's attorney. The firm was one of the big, prestigious Seattle law offices, with half a dozen names in the title, and another few dozen junior partners waiting for the chance to lengthen it further. The man she wanted was a senior partner, but that didn't faze her in the least. No one was going to intimidate her this morning. No one. Not the bull pen, not the narcs, not Rosie, and especially not Jack Turner and his high-falutin' lawyer.

When the senior partner came on the line, his voice was low-keyed and pleasant. She quickly outlined the situation concerning Catherine Fletcher's death and what she needed— Jack Turner's statement. Voluntary, of course. "The victim declared to all and sundry," she explained, "that she was engaged to Mr. Turner and they'd be getting married this spring. If you could persuade your client to voluntarily come in and give us his statement, he could probably clear this up. He might even be able to shed some light on the case."

"And if he won't?"

"But you could advise him to, couldn't you." Kate made it a quiet statement of fact.

His voice took on a strong tone of amusement. She could just envision a quirked eyebrow and a slight smile. "Miss MacLean, I've spent my whole career giving clients advice. I've learned never to be surprised when they ignore it, which an intolerable number of them do. How far up the list of suspects is he?"

"He's not a suspect. At the moment, he's not even a material witness. Though I suppose that could change."

"I see. Do you intend to Mirandize him?"

"No. It's strictly voluntary. He will be asked to sign his statement, though."

The attorney was silent a moment. She could almost hear him drumming his fingertips as he pondered the situation. "Jack can be a tough nut. Let me get back to you."

"You will urge him to cooperate?"

"I'll get back to you, Miss MacLean. That's all I can say at this point."

Damned lawyers, she thought as she hung up. Even the ones that sounded nice could make a cop's life hell. She crossed mental fingers that he'd come through for her.

The interrogation room was small and ugly, just large enough for a rectangular table, with three wooden chairs on each side, and one at each end. The walls were covered with cheap, unadorned panels clothed in a drab brown. Functional, neutral, efficient and boring. Which was the idea. She signed one up for the day, checked out a couple of tape recorders, then set about organizing the sessions. She arranged for a transcriber to be available so that statements could be typed up immediately for signatures, then began compiling a series of questions that she wanted to ask. When she was through, as an afterthought, she set out a fresh box of Kleenex. Ginger would be first, and she anticipated a tearful session.

When she arrived, the artist was a nervous mixture of anxiety, grief and apprehension. Kate greeted her warmly, as she would an acquaintance who had the potential of becoming a friend, and led her through the maze of filing cabinets that snaked through the bull pen to the rear offices. The artist in Ginger surfaced for a split second as they entered the interrogation room, but after a single glance at the cheap, dull, synthetic panels, she lost her alertness again. Kate invited her to sit and began the session with simple questions, merely asking her to account for her time and movements, starting with Friday evening.

Ginger was hesitant at first, her voice barely audible, but as she recounted her actions, some of it related to her home life and therefore nonthreatening, her voice strengthened and the words came easier. Nothing new of importance emerged. Her husband had left on his business trip to Phoenix early Friday morning, and she'd taken her three daughters out for hamburgers at McDonald's that evening, then they all went to bed for an early night. On Saturday a baby-sitter had come in and she, Suzie and Phyllis had worked at the studio on the Boeing project until mid-afternoon. The three of them had left the office then, about four. Yes, she was sure Phyllis had locked the door. She remembered her testing the doorknob to make sure it was locked. Catherine hadn't come in anytime during the day.

Saturday night and Sunday had been spent with her girls. On Monday, she was the third one into the studio; Phyllis and Suzie were already there. They were in and out on calls all day while Ginger stayed put at her drawing board. No, there were no deliveries or pickups that day. No one except the partners came into the studio all day long. And Ginger had seen Catherine only once on Monday, shortly before noon. She'd been out getting client approval on a display ad when Catherine had checked back in before quitting time. Noontime was the last time she'd seen her alive.

There was a welling-up of tears at that point, and Kate reached across the table and patted her arm. Ginger managed to regain her composure and continue on.

She'd begun the final work on the Boeing project after the day's normal work was done and finished up around four-thirty in the morning. She'd gone straight home and to bed. No, no one could verify it. Her husband was still in Phoenix, he wouldn't be home until the coming weekend, and her girls had stayed overnight at the baby-sitter's place, so she'd gone home to an empty house. And yes, she'd locked the studio door behind her when she left. She knew she had, because when Phyllis and Suzie had left her about nine Monday evening, she'd locked herself in and had to unlock the door to leave, and, with key in hand, she'd turned the lock once more and raced out of there. Empty buildings at night made her nervous. At home, she'd slept a few hours, then arrived at the studio mid-morning to relieve Catherine, only to find her dead.

The flow of words stumbled to a halt and the flow of tears began. Silently, Kate pushed the box of Kleenex her way.

Ginger broke then, as if the Kleenex gave her permission to cry. Her face fell forward into hands cupped to receive it, and she wept and wept, the tears pouring like water from a spout.

Kate detached herself from her own feelings of empathetic pain and watched her clinically, making assessments. Was the grief real? Was it staged? Was it from an overwhelming sense of loss, or an overwhelming sense of fear? Was it for Catherine, her life cut short, or was it for herself, left behind, truly bereft? Or was it strictly for police view, to throw them off the scent?

Finally, Ginger slowly straightened, raising her head and wiping her cheeks and eyes with the tissue. "I'm sorry," she whispered, "I just can't seem to stop crying."

"I'm not surprised. This is tough going." Kate watched her as the other woman dried her face and eyes and recovered a shaky composure. She'd been going to hold to the end any questions about Catherine's relationship with the artist, afraid of just such a breakdown as had just occurred. But the woman seemed drained for the moment, and vulnerable, and open, and Kate adjusted the sequence. "Tell me about your friendship with Catherine."

Sighing a little, Ginger hunched over her hands, her fingers twisting the Kleenex into a long taut spiral. Her voice was tear-ravaged and strained. "I don't know. . . ." She cleared her throat and tried again, but she couldn't find the words and ended up shrugging.

Kate rephrased the question. "What was Catherine like as a friend? From what I hear, she was a very different kind of person than you are."

Staring down at the spiraled Kleenex, Ginger nodded. "She was," she said slowly. "She was everything I wasn't. She was sharp, and bright, and funny and quick . . . And restless. She always wanted to do things, to go places . . . She hated being tied down, being in one place for a long time. I kind of like that, being in one place. I like having my things around me, and just being quiet for hours at a time. I didn't think of it as being tied down. But she did. It made her feel trapped, and she hated that feeling. That's why she was so unhappy with the other two. They wanted to trap her to a regular schedule, a regular routine, and she couldn't accept that. There was no reason for it, not in her eyes. So I'd try and help her out. I'd do things for her, like some of the paperwork that absolutely had to be done. It didn't bother me any to do it. I was happy to do it for her. And she was always so appreciative."

"What kind of paperwork, Ginger?"

"Expense-account sheets . . . We did get reimbursed for out-of-pocket expenses, even if we couldn't afford salaries that week. We all felt that at least it shouldn't be costing us anything except our time. So we'd take a little gas money, and if we took a client out to lunch, we'd get reimbursed. Or if I bought some art supplies on my way home, nickle-and-dime stuff that wasn't charged to the business, I'd just turn in the receipt and get reimbursed for it. Things like that. But that kind of stuff drove Catherine crazy, so I'd do it for her."

"What kind of expenses did she turn in these recent months? Say, from New Year's on through."

Ginger started to answer, then paused, frowning. "You know, that's kind of strange. Now that I think of it, it was only lunch tabs and mileage. She was spending a lot of time in downtown Seattle, she said, trying to develop accounts there. She wasn't producing any hard sales, but she said she was laying a lot of groundwork."

"What bothers you about that, Ginger?"

"Well, before—before the holidays, I mean—there'd be parking-lot stubs and receipts for materials she'd pick up on her rounds. And she'd want me to work up an idea or two, do some quick sketches. Maybe get a few brochure costs for her. But after the holidays, there wasn't any of it. There was just the lunch tab and mileage. No parking-lot stubs. If she drove to Seattle every day, where did she park her car?"

Good question, Kate thought, and made a note of it.

Ginger had straightened up now, forgetting the Kleenex and her grief. "Another thing—the meal receipts all last year always had names of the clients she was seeing written on them and the reason for the meeting. Since New Year's, all they had was an amount, with the tip noted. No names. Dates, yes, but no names."

"Did she explain why?"

"Well, I never asked her," Ginger said with some amazement. "It never occurred to me until just now. I merely added them up, made out a check, put my signature on it and turned it over to her; then she could sign it and cash it."

"How much did they amount to?"

"Oh, maybe fifty, sixty dollars a week. Not much."

"What happened to the receipts?"

"They were turned over to the bookkeeper."

"Did Phyllis and Suzie ever see them, or ask to look at them?"

"No, it went in the envelope with mine. I'm not sure they even knew. By fall, Phyllis was keeping a pretty close eye on everything Catherine did and everything she spent, so Catherine simply turned the stuff over to me and I took it from there. Catherine hated being spied on, and refused to let Phyllis know what she was doing. And Phyllis never asked, so I never mentioned it. I mean, it was harmless, wasn't it? Catherine was going to be reimbursed anyway, wasn't she? So when she explained it to me that way, I said, sure, I'd do it for her. And she was so grateful to be rid of the paperwork . . . As I said, she hated it."

More ways to drain money out of the firm, Kate noted. The woman had certainly been inventive. "It seems like you were a good friend to her. What did she do for you in return?"

Ginger looked at her quizzically. "I don't understand. What do you mean, do for me?"

"Well, you did her some favors. What kind of favors did she do for you?"

"Oh. Well, none, I guess. I mean, I didn't really need any, did I."

"Didn't you ever get behind in your work and have to ask for help?"

"Sure, once in a while I'd get behind. Especially with this Boeing project as big as it was. And it all had to be done after hours. But no one could do it for me. I was the only artist we had."

"But couldn't Catherine have helped with the paperwork? By doing her own for a couple of weeks, and maybe yours, too?"

"Oh, I see what you're saying. Well, I suppose she could've, but she didn't think of it and neither did I. I mean, it was such a habit that it sort of became part of my job."

"But you did ask her help in covering the office phones Tuesday morning."

"Well, yes, but I had to. The other two would be gone all morning—they couldn't help that—and I *had* to get some sleep, at least a couple of hours."

"And when did you arrange for Catherine to cover the office on Tuesday morning?"

"On Monday, after I became aware of how much work was still left to do on the Boeing project. I knew I'd be working terribly late that night. That's when I arranged the baby-sitting for the girls, too."

"What was Catherine's reaction?"

Ginger dropped her gaze to the Kleenex and started twisting again. She was silent a minute and reluctant when she did speak. "Well, actually, not all that good," she said softly. "She had her own schedule, you see."

"What did she say?"

"She asked me why I was always so disorganized about my work, why I couldn't ever arrange my time better." This time the tears were of hurt. They welled without spilling. "I'd been planning to take the whole day off, but when she finally got through, I agreed to just take the morning off to get some sleep, and to get there before noon so she could go to lunch. She was also pretty upset that both Phyllis and Suzie were doing the presentation. She didn't understand why it took two of them, and why one of them couldn't just stay back and cover the phones."

"Why *did* it take both of them?"

"Suzie's pretty good with production data, and Phyllis knows the figures and has the costs down to such a degree that she could answer questions Suzie couldn't, so they each complemented the other when it came to a presentation. And Boeing was so important to us that they wanted to make sure they had all their bases covered."

"I gather Catherine didn't get along very well with the other two."

Ginger looked down at her hands and wove the spiraled Kleenex through her fingers. "She treated them well enough." Her voice was low and rather off-hand.

Kate pushed it. "But what did she really think of them?"

For the first time, Ginger looked really uncomfortable. She glanced over at the tape recorder running and shifted a couple of times in her chair. When it became clear that Kate was merely going to wait until she had an answer to her question, she formed a reluctant sentence. "I guess she didn't much care for either of them."

"What exactly did she say about them?"

"She told me she was getting a lot of complaints about them from our accounts. That Suzie didn't do what she was promising people she'd do. And that Phyl was rude and too aggressive. She said I was the only one she could really count on, really could trust. She was always strong on trust, and she said she simply couldn't trust the other two. She even said she had proof that they were selling on the side, that they were making sales and getting other graphics studios to do the work so they could keep the profits. She said they were cheating us right and left."

"Did she ever show you the proof?"

"No."

"So do you think they were? Selling on the side?"

"I don't know. It's hard to imagine them doing anything like that. Phyl's so honest about everything. And Suzie gets so—so *up* whenever she makes a sale. I don't see how she could hide it from us. Besides, they were the only ones making any sales at all."

"Did you say all that to Catherine?"

"No, I didn't argue with her much. She mostly just needed someone to listen, that's all. It's kind of like my girls. Sometimes they just get upset and need to spout off a little. That was Catherine. That's all she was doing."

Kate studied the gentle artist for a moment. The long, slender fingers shredding the Kleenex, the softly rounded face, the cloud of silky brown hair that hung down past her shoulders. Where was the truth? As Catherine had claimed? As Suzie and Phyllis saw it? Or somewhere in the middle? Though there didn't seem to be much middle ground here.

Something else was nagging at Kate, too. Something deep in her mind, something she should be asking. She tried to let the image take form, but nothing came. After a moment, she gave up. It'd come to her sooner or later.

She moved on to the topics of depression and health, then wound up with questions about Jack Turner.

Ginger was straightforward in her answers. Catherine, in her opinion, was not the suicidal type. No, she couldn't exactly explain why she thought that, but she was definite about it, Catherine would not have committed suicide. And no, she'd never seen Catherine take any prescription medicine. As far as Catherine's health went, she'd had a touch of flu a few weeks ago, but that was it. And no, Ginger didn't use any prescription drugs herself. And wouldn't. She believed in herbal remedies.

As for Jack Turner, all she knew was what Catherine had said. He was rich, good-looking, and they would be married in the spring.

Kate brought the session to an end and led Ginger to an outer waiting room while the stenographer transcribed the tape for her signature. Ginger's shoulders dropped a dozen inches as she left the interrogation room, Kate noted, but that was normal. It wasn't the most pleasant experience to know every word you say would be written down for the police to examine later, and in Kate's opinion she'd done just fine.

While she waited for the transcription, she went to her desk and made another try at reaching Suzie. Still no answer. It was simply amazing, she thought as she slowly replaced the receiver, that in this day and age people still figured they could function without an answering machine. They could be a nuisance, true. Messages could inadvertently be erased, true. And people could hide behind them if they chose to do so, true. But a caller could at least reach *something* and leave a message, and then move on with the day.

When the typed statement was ready, Kate carried it to Ginger and had her read it over. As Ginger read it through, she grew more and more distressed. She swallowed hard several times.

Kate was puzzled. "If there are inaccuracies in there," Kate explained, "we can correct them."

The tears welled again and Ginger tossed her head back and looked up at the ceiling to prevent them from spilling. "It's not that," she gulped. "It's . . . it's this whole thing . . ." She looked at Kate through a blur of tears. "I can't seem to stop crying about it. *I just can't seem to stop!*"

Kate took the chair next to her and took both her hands in her own. "Ginger, maybe you should have your husband come home early. Maybe you should ask him to cut his business trip short."

Ginger shook her head in a strong rejection of the idea. "No." Eyes still flooding, she drew in a couple of shaky breaths, refusing to break down into actual weeping. "You've been so kind . . ." she whispered. With a trembling hand she took the pen and scribbled her signature on the statement and handed it back. Then she stood up, sighing shakily, emotions finally under some control. "Really, you have been . . . so kind, I mean . . ."

The trust in her eyes almost undid Kate. God, please don't let it be her, she thought. Please don't let it be her.

As she escorted Ginger through the security gates into the foyer, a small part of her echoed derisively, Mother MacLean.

10

Kate had the feeling that if Bob Wilson had had a hat in hand,
he would have twirled it like some respectful beggar come to
call, fearful he'd be booted out if he didn't behave properly. He
was a balding, paunchy man in his mid-forties. He seemed a
pleasant, decent sort, but he walked in a kind of shuffle, his
shoulders slumped. He had the air of a defeated man. Life had *not*
been kind to him, she judged.

She was going to take Becky's statement first, so she led
grandfather and grandson to a reception area beyond the security
check-in foyer and offered the older Wilson coffee while he
waited, which he gratefully accepted. On the way back to him
with a Styrofoam cup, she scrounged a toy police car and left
Mark happily playing with it under his grandfather's chair legs.

In the interrogation room, Becky seemed more wide-eyed and
curious than nervous and she watched Kate as she inserted a tape
and started the recorder. She had Becky give the standard "One,
two, three," then played it back to check the volume level, while
the girl's eyes widened and a grin spread across her face. She was
so young yet, Kate thought while taking her own seat, young
enough to still take a childlike delight in electronic wizardry.
Childlike, yet already a mother of a two-year-old. Mentally

shaking her head with sadness, she led Becky into the opening portions of her statement.

Becky's account of her relationship with her mother didn't differ from the one she'd given the day before. She hadn't seen or heard from Catherine since she'd been kicked out when she got pregnant. There'd been no call, no clothes, no furniture, no nothing when the baby was born. No, she didn't know where Catherine had lived or worked these last few years, didn't even know she had her own business until the cops told her. Yes, she was terribly relieved that Vern Riley had to handle the funeral arrangements; she didn't want anything to do with her mother, dead or alive. And no, she had no intention of attending her mother's funeral. She spoke in a quiet voice, her chin firm.

As for Becky's schedule the last five days, her weekend had been quiet. A movie with her girlfriend, Dana, on Friday evening while her father baby-sat. She'd spent Saturday with Mark, except for a couple of hours when his grandfather had taken the boy with him to run a few errands so Becky could get some homework done. Sunday she'd cooked dinner for all three of them. Monday night had been her bookkeeping class; she'd gone by bus since her car was acting up. Tuesday her mother had died.

This was all said dry-eyed, in a calm, unwavering voice. Either the hurt was so deeply buried that Becky didn't realize it was there, or she was so detached from her mother by now that the thought of her had lost all power to wound. Whichever it was, the girl was open and straightforward about the lack of feelings she had toward her mother and her mother's death. Kate understood. Becky had been a victim, too, a victim of the victim, and even the finality of death wasn't strong enough to erase the fact—or even to gloss it over. Death could not retroactively excuse the severe cruelty that had been inflicted on a young girl of seventeen.

Kate moved on with her questions. "What's wrong with your car?" she asked. "And when did it start having trouble?"

"Last week sometime. Wednesday, I think it was. Dad thinks it's the alternator or the regulator. Anyway, it's something that makes the whole thing shut down. And it's a fairly new battery, so it shouldn't be always dead like that. Dad has a friend who'll look at it for me, but he's been away the last couple of weeks, and neither of us can afford to take it down to the repair shop to be fixed. So we just have to wait."

"How'd you get to the movies Friday night?"

"Dana. She's got an old Chevy. It eats up the gas like crazy and is as big as a house, but it'll run forever." She looked rueful. "Mine's the old VW bug, which is real cheap to run. But it never works two weeks in a row."

Kate took her over the birth of Mark, and Catherine's total ostracizing of them both, in a couple of different ways, but each version agreed with the one before. And she quizzed her extensively on the car and its problems. There were no discrepancies there, either. Finally, Kate shut off the tape recorder and relaxed. The girl looked fairly well in the clear. Unless she'd used a bus to carry doped tea bags across half the county. She pressed the button for the stenographer to come get the tape.

"You know," Kate said while they waited, "I used to own a VW bug. A bile-green one. Dreadful color, but at the time I thought it was the most beautiful thing on earth. I loved it dearly. Even though it was more temperamental than a rock star."

Becky giggled. "When was that?"

"Oh, when I was young and silly. I was living on a houseboat then."

Becky's eyes grew round. "You used to live on a houseboat!?"

"Sure did. In my early twenties. For a few years. I loved it."

"That's what I've always wanted to do! Get a houseboat on Lake Union! I've always thought that'd be so neat. Everyone seems so friendly."

"Houseboat people usually are. Why don't you, if you want to?"

" 'Cause stuff like that's not meant for people like us."

Kate's heart wrenched suddenly. She didn't say anything more.

She switched Becky for her father. Mark was making siren noises as he rolled the toy cruiser in and out of chair legs. He glanced up to grin at his mom, then went right back to his roadwork. Becky sat in a chair where she could watch him, obviously fascinated by her young son so intent on his play.

Bob Wilson, cowed and apprehensive, followed Kate back to

the interrogation room. She offered him a seat, then slumped into her own chair and stretched her legs out, acting as easy and relaxed as she could manage. In a quiet voice, she said, "Tell me about yourself."

He shrugged. "Not much to tell. I'm a shoe salesman in Redmond, that's all."

"Have you always sold shoes?"

"No. I used to sell men's clothing."

"Did you have your own store?"

"For a while."

"What happened?"

His eyes fell and there was a long moment's silence. "It went under," he said finally.

"While you were married to Catherine?"

"No. Just after." He shifted in his chair, obviously discomfited.

"Why don't you tell me what happened," she said quietly.

"Oh, it would take so long," he murmured.

"We have as long as you need."

"Becky's waiting."

"She'll be fine."

"It was all so long ago. It doesn't have anything to do with this."

"Any background would be helpful."

There was no way out of it. With her quiet implacability, she'd left him no out. She could see him mentally hemming and hawing, his glance darting this way and that. She waited in silence, steady gaze on his, and finally the last of his resistance collapsed.

His shoulders slumped in defeat, he leaned forward, his forearms on the table, his hands clenched tight. He stared down at them and began to speak.

He went back a quarter of a century, to when he was twenty-two. He'd been a management trainee at Nordstrom's in downtown Seattle, working in the men's clothing department, when his parents had been killed in a car crash. An only child, he inherited the house he'd grown up in, a small lakefront cottage in the not yet fashionable Medina section of Bellevue on the shores of Lake Washington. He'd also received a generous—for the times—insurance settlement from the other driver's insurance company, plus some life insurance his father had carried on both himself and his wife. At that time, Bellevue was a sleepy little town serving the rural farming communities around it, but already its potential for growth could be seen. With the broad width of Lake Washington spanned by first one bridge then a second, it wouldn't be long before the residents of Seattle overflowed into its surrounds. So he moved into the cottage, took the insurance money, leased some store space in downtown Bellevue, and opened an exclusive men's clothing shop.

In the beginning, he ran it alone, putting in sixteen-hour-or-better days, with barely enough coming in to meet his overhead. But slowly his store caught on, and he was able to hire a top tailor from the area. Next he lured a top salesman from Nordstrom's, who brought his following with him. And with some steady business to fund it, he began a heavy advertising campaign on the radio and in the newspapers. One of the newspaper reps who called on him was a young woman named Catherine Fletcher.

Catherine had been born in a small town in eastern Oregon, and had escaped to Seattle to make, as she put it to him, her fortune. She was twenty when they met, selling ads for a little weekly, and barely surviving. She also was the most beautiful girl he'd ever seen, with a wild mane of black hair, a slender, pointed face and these deep, deep lavender-blue eyes. An Elizabeth Taylor twin. He'd pursued her with the same dedication he'd brought to his business, and within six months they were married. Nine months to the day later, Becky was born. At Catherine's urging, he expanded his store space into first one neighboring retail space, then another, brought in new lines, took on more salesmen and added a second tailor. His business thrived and flourished. Again at Catherine's urging, he tore down the cottage and built a big sprawling house on his lakefront property, complete with dock and motorboat. At today's prices the place would be conservatively worth two to three million dollars, he said. Life had been rich and good, really good.

Until, on a cold gray November day when Becky was almost ten, he came home to find his world gone. The house had been stripped bare in a single day, his bank accounts were cleaned out, and his wife and daughter were gone. Even the boat had been sold. The buyer came to the store the next day, demanding the title slip; he'd already paid Catherine the money.

Worse was yet to come. The day after the moving van had come, Catherine's attorney filed liens—lis pendens—against the house and the store. Legally, it tied his home and his business into knots. Within hours, the bank was calling. He had trusted Catherine with all his money, expecting her to pay any bills due, and now the mortgage was more than six months in arrears, the bank told him, and all his accounts were overdrawn. They also had been informed of the freshly filed liens. They demanded immediate payment in full of everything that was owed and, because of the liens, absolutely refused to give him any extension or leeway. The line of business credit he'd had with them for more than a decade was withdrawn without notice or ceremony. His life, economically and emotionally, lay in shambles all about him, strewn like timbers from a shipwreck.

It had, of course, all been carefully planned and executed by Catherine. Yet, even knowing by then what she had done, even with the advantage of hindsight, he could not recall a single instant when she had given even the faintest clue of her intentions. Her lips were always smiling. Her eyes were wide and innocent. Her voice was soft and tender. They'd even made love the night before the moving vans arrived. Nothing, no word, no deed, no wayward glance had contained the slightest trace of the terrible destruction she'd so carefully wrought.

On the same day the bank called, Catherine's attorney reached him. He stated that Catherine wanted to meet with him the next morning at the law firm's offices. It was not a request; it was a command. Having little choice in the matter, he agreed. In spite of the tremendous shock, or maybe because of it, he still, in his heart, believed that somehow his world would right itself. That some miracle would make the horror all go away. That he'd wake up from the terrors of a nightmarish march through hell to find his home, his business and his family intact.

In the attorney's office, however, he met a new and different Catherine. She was cold, cruel and hostile. She'd had a settlement already drawn up for him to sign. She demanded the house. Free and clear of the mortgage, of course. She demanded the furniture—already moved out of the state and out of his reach anyway. She demanded sole custody of Becky, also stashed away out of state somewhere, like the furniture. And in lieu of alimony, she demanded half the value of his business in cash. In return, the liens would be lifted, he'd receive an uncontested divorce and he'd be given generous visitation rights with Becky. He argued, he begged, he pleaded, but Catherine was cold, uninterested and immovable.

In the end, his choice was simple; if he wanted to keep part of his business and see Becky again, he'd have to sign. If he didn't sign, he'd lose it all. Everything. He signed.

She had also had the attorney prepare a disclaimer, stating that he'd refused their offer of independent counsel and that he'd signed the settlement agreement of his own free will. No offer of independent counsel had been made, of course, but it seemed a moot point by then. Through a contact of the attorney, they had already paved the way for a loan from the bank so he could cash out Catherine's half of the business, with enough extra to clear the mortgage. They had a quitclaim deed ready to sign. Within forty-eight hours, he'd gone from a prosperous businessman with a lovely home and a beautiful family to an indigent without a roof over his head and ninety percent of his business owed to the bank.

Still he might have made it. But a month later, when he placed his main order for spring merchandise from his largest supplier, he was politely informed they'd ship it immediately. . . C.O.D. Then a second supplier placed him on C.O.D. Then a third. Like a prairie fire, it spread from one to another until he found his lines of credit cancelled everywhere he turned. Rumors had spread that the store was going under, and there was a collective bailing-out by his suppliers. His number-one salesman quit instantly. So did his top tailor and a second salesman. Inventory became depleted, service suffered and his customers shopped elsewhere. He had to lay off the other tailor. The bank refused to lend any more money. He tried to find an investor to buy into his store. No luck. He tried to sell the store outright.

But Bellevue Square was already built and open, and no one was interested in a failing business three blocks away.

Finally, hat in his hand, he went to Catherine to negotiate a loan. She'd sold the house as soon as the deed had been recorded and had gotten rid of all the furniture at an auction in Portland. With the money from everything she'd gotten—house, boat, furniture, his business—she'd leased a big, expensive furnished house down the lake from his old place, and had bought herself clothes, furs, jewelry and a couple of exotic cars. The omens weren't exactly in his favor, but as a last resort he humbled himself and went to her anyway.

Her response was to laugh at him. She laughed and laughed and laughed. But she laughed at him with such a tremendous enjoyment that a sudden suspicion struck him. He accused her of starting the rumors and, surprisingly—or maybe *not* so surprisingly— she admitted it openly. Of course she had, she said to him in an amused tone of voice. That's why she'd taken the cash settlement in lieu of alimony, she told him; she'd *planned* on making him fail. When he demanded to know why, she simply blinked her beautiful, wide, innocent eyes and said, Because I felt like it.

He came to a halt and couldn't go on. His voice faded away into silence. The interrogation room stifled but did not eliminate the sounds of the bull pen just outside the door. From what seemed like a very far distance came the muffled sounds of phones ringing, the constricted buzz of conversations, the odd strangled laugh, the arrhythmic clack of typewriters and printers. It was the discordant fugue of a station house at work.

Ever so slowly, he came back from his sojourn in time. Slowly he turned his eyes to Kate and said, "I closed the store and filed for bankruptcy. I had no other option. If ever I was going to kill her, it would've been then."

Kate sat, vaguely aware of the distant noise, transfixed by the story. She'd been there with him; she'd shared his shock, his hopelessness, his helplessness, his despair. She'd seen what he'd seen, felt what he'd felt, suffered what he'd suffered. Now she simply sat and stared at him. Why didn't you! she wanted to demand of him. Why didn't you just knock her off then and there, and save us all from today! Quivering inside from the strength of her own emotion, she drew in a long, slow breath, exhaled deeply, then drew in a second one. By the time she'd exhaled again, she'd regained control of herself and her thoughts and could function once again as a cop. "What did you do next, Mr. Wilson?" she asked, even-toned.

"Oh, various things." His voice was vague and hesitant again, as it had been when he walked in. The intensity with which he'd unburdened himself was gone. Only defeat was left.

"Such as?"

"Oh, I sold cars for a while. Used ones. Tried my hand at selling boats. That didn't work. Worked for Sears for a while. Right now I'm working in a shoe outlet in Redmond."

"And Catherine? What did she do?"

"Well, she ran through her money pretty fast, and after a while she just plain ran out. She took a series of jobs, but none of them lasted very long. She moved from one cheap place to another. Finally, she married Vern Riley, thinking he was rich. But actually he was poorer than she was. About that time, I tried to get her to let Becky live with me—I had an apartment by then. It wasn't much, pretty small, but still, it was mine. But Catherine wouldn't hear of it. I did see a lawyer about it, but he discouraged me from trying anything legally. Custody fights were expensive, he said, and almost guaranteed failures. It wasn't too long afterward that Becky got herself in a bit of a predicament, and she called me up one night to come get her, her mother had thrown her out. I was mighty glad to take her in. She's all I have. She means a lot to me."

"What's her relationship been with her mother since Mark was born?"

"Nonexistent. Catherine cut her off when Becky got pregnant. Without a backward glance. Just like she did me. That's the way Catherine was with people. She'd use them and use them, then out they'd go."

"What's Mark's physical condition? Does he have any health problems of any kind?"

The grandfather in him came to the fore and a softness came into his eyes. "Not that one," he said with pride. "He's about as strong and sturdy as they come. He's just a neat little guy, a delight, both to his mother and to his old grampa here."

"And he has no physical problems? No handicaps, disabilities, or any medical condition that you know of that would be any kind of a problem to him or require him to have ongoing medical care?"

He shook his head firmly. "Nope."

So much for Catherine's claim of poverty because of Mark's medical bills, Kate thought. Chalk another fairy tale up in her column. "Mr. Wilson, who's the father of Becky's child?"

"I don't know. She never would tell me. All she'd say is that it would never happen again. I felt pretty badly for her. Losing her own childhood so young."

"But you have your suspicions as to who it was, don't you?"

His chin rose with a touch of stubbornness, the first Kate had seen. "Like I say, I don't know."

She backed off. She'd gotten a lot, a tremendous lot from him, and there was no point in pushing him now into a corner. "Becky said you knew that Catherine was living in a condo on Lake Sammamish. Did you ever go to see her there?"

"No, I only sort of knew she lived there. And that was accidental."

"Accidental how?"

"I ate dinner at the Sea Galley in Overlake one night a few months back. When I was leaving, Catherine was just coming out of Uwajimaya's next door. She didn't notice me. She got in her car and was just ahead of me leaving the parking lot. Both of us were headed toward Redmond. After we'd gone a few miles on Lake Sammamish Road, she turned into a condo development. One of the fancy, expensive lakefront ones. And I just kept on driving home. I don't even know which unit she lived in."

"How do you know she lived there at all? Maybe she was just visiting a friend?"

"Well, she was pushing a grocery cart with a couple of sacks in it from Uwajimaya's. It was late, about nine, too late for visiting—at least, for me. So I guessed she was headed home."

"That was a few months back, you say?"

"Yes. Before the holidays. Late November, early December, I think. Somewhere in there."

"But you didn't know where she worked."

"No. I didn't care to know. It wouldn't have helped Becky at all. Her mother had no time for her, no interest in her. She wasn't normal, that woman. Not normal at all."

"How did Becky manage with Mark? What did she do for baby furniture and baby clothes?"

"Oh, I kind of helped out a little. I bought the crib and high chair and stroller and things like that from secondhand ads in the newspapers, and most of the baby clothes came from thrift shops."

"Catherine never helped?"

"Not a dime."

"Why did Becky move out on her own from your place?"

"My apartment's pretty small for three, for one thing. And there wasn't a good place for Mark to play, either, when he got old enough. No yard, no playground. Nothing. Then it turned out a girl she knew at work—she was working at McDonald's then—had to give up the little house she'd been renting, and Becky wanted to try it out on her own, so I agreed. But I keep an eye on the two of them. I see that they get out a little and have a bit of fun. And I'll take a few groceries over now and then."

"What about Becky's car? How did she get that?"

"A fellow I knew was selling it cheap, so I bought it for her. She has to have some way of getting around, taking the baby to the doctors, getting to school, buying groceries, that sort of thing. But the way it's acting up, it wasn't such a good buy."

"What's its condition now?"

"The electrical system's shot. I haven't said much to Becky, but if it's as bad as I think it is, we'll have to pronounce it dead and see that it has a proper burial. But I won't do anything until a fellow I know looks it over, and he's out of town on a job just now."

"How long has it been down?"

"A week or more this time. Last time, it was the carburetor. That took a few days to fix."

"What about your car?"

"It's old, but it'll last awhile."

"It's running?"

"Yes. That's what I drove down here in today."

"And what was your weekend like? Tell me what you did."

"This last weekend? Not much. I baby-sat Mark Friday night so Becky could get out for a while. Then on Saturday—let's see—I had to run some errands . . . groceries, things like that . . . and I took Mark with me. Sunday I watched a pre-season game with the Mariners on TV, went to Becky's for dinner, then wandered over to the Workshop for a beer before I headed home. I guess that's about it. Nothing special."

The picture of a lonely life, Kate thought. "You mentioned taking Mark to the doctor. But you said he's a very healthy child."

"That's just for normal checkups. That kid's a sturdy little rascal. Full of fire and brimstone." He smiled. A pleasant smile. A fond smile. A *grandfatherly* smile.

"And Becky? Does she have any health problems? Is she taking any prescription medication that you know about?"

"Nope, she's strong and sturdy, too." Kate could feel the affection pouring out of him for his daughter and grandson.

"And yourself?"

His smile was tinged with sadness. "Not as strong, perhaps. Certainly not as sturdy. But I'm okay, too." Then his face turned somber. "You know, I said earlier the only time I'd have killed Catherine was when she laughed at me when I was losing my store. That's not true. If I'd have thought of it, I'd have been mighty tempted to tear her apart when she kicked Becky out. I don't know which got to me more. My own hurt, or Becky's. Catherine tried so hard to destroy us. And all we ever did was love her," he said, his gaze fixed on one spot of the grimy table. "That's all we ever did, was love her."

11

Vern Riley hadn't arrived yet. Neither had Phyllis Walsh. Kate tried again to reach Suzie, but there was still no answer at her house. She called the graphics studio and left a message for her with the answering service, then idly tapped her pen against her lip.

Her instincts told her to forget the Wilsons. Bob Wilson was right; the time to have killed Catherine was when she'd left him, or when she'd kicked Becky out. Unless she'd done something new to them? But neither had admitted any recent contact with her. Kate played with that idea for a moment. Vern Riley might be able to help there.

Her thoughts moved on to the type of person she was seeking. A poisoner was a cold-blooded person. Beatings, knifings, shootings, stranglings, suffocations required personal involvement with the victim at the time of death and often were true crimes of passion. But poisoning? The killer had to get it, plan it, dispense it, then sit back and wait. That required a powerful amount of self-control. Certainly it wasn't a crime that could be blamed on temporary insanity, or the full of the moon. Who on her list was cold-blooded enough to plan and execute it? Of the business partners, Phyllis would be the most likely. Vern Riley? Too hotheaded and impatient. Poison would be too slow for him. Jack Turner?

Turner. She swung around and headed for the front of the

building. "Did the *Times* deliver a packet for me?" she asked the clerk at the front desk.

"Yep, came in a couple of minutes ago."

The packet was ominously thin. Obviously no media hound, Jack Turner.

She had the flap slit open at her desk when Reception called to announce Vern Riley's arrival. She was tempted to make him wait while she scanned the Turner articles, but she wanted the time to absorb the contents. Reluctantly, she set the packet aside and went to meet him.

Riley was dressed in a dark suit and sober tie, his hair slicked down with some greasy hair tonic. "Funeral parlor," he explained, indicating his clothes. His face looked as if he'd put in a tough night. His eyes were watery, red-rimmed and bloodshot. His lips were pulled downward into a thin line, and the truculence had strengthened since the previous day. He also was in a hot rage which burst out as soon as she'd shut the door to the interrogation room. He was even too steamed to notice her switching the tape recorder on. He'd already launched into his tirade before she'd finished entering the date, time and his name onto the tape.

"*That fucking funeral's going to run over three grand!*" he exploded. "*Outrageous!* That's what I told that asshole! *Goddamned outrageous!*" He plopped into a chair and started drumming a rhythm with his fingers against the edge of the table. "They got charges for this and charges for that, and by the time he got all through, it added up to over three grand! And me with a hundred bucks to my name! The estate'll pay, I says to him, the estate'll pay. No way, he says, no way. Had to fucking well sign my life away! What a bunch of assholes. What a bunch of *shitty assholes!* And speaking of assholes, when the hell are they going to release the goddamned body anyway!"

"They'll notify the funeral home," Kate said. "Which one is it?" She made a note of the name, then began the chore of leading him into some kind of a rational and coherent statement.

It was a grueling hour. He rambled, he bragged, he leered, he crowed, he complained. Through it all, he was in constant motion—shifting, jerking, twitching, scratching, drumming. He'd straighten, then he'd slouch. He'd cross his legs; he'd uncross them. He tapped his foot, drummed his fingers, then crossed one foot over the opposite knee and drummed a rhythm on his ankle with his two forefingers. He was so wired he made her own nerves jump, but she managed to sit quietly through the tales that came pouring out, piecing together a version of his whereabouts the past weekend, and his overall relationship with Catherine.

On Friday night, he'd picked up a meat-market broad—no, no one special—and had taken her to his place until he shoved her out early Saturday morning. Handball in the afternoon, then a repeat of the previous evening, only with a different broad. Again, no one special. He didn't even know her name. Wasn't interested enough. Meat-market broads. Not worth the time to even take names. He'd sent the second one home early the next morning, too; said he didn't like the looks or the smell of them the morning after. Spent the morning with the Sunday papers. Alone. Then back to the bar for a couple of drinks with the guys. No, no one special. Just a bunch of yakkers. Then back home shortly before Catherine called. He still stood by his story that she'd taken him back. No, he hadn't killed her. Sure, he knew who'd done it—those business partners of hers. Catherine was just too sharp for them. They were all a bunch of assholes, and they knew she knew it, so they had to get rid of her. Simple. Any asshole could see that.

It was when she led him into the tale of his history with Catherine that the hour she endured became worth it.

They'd met while Catherine was still married to Bob Wilson, years before the divorce. Riley was in real estate then and Catherine had walked into his office from the street to find out what their new lakeside house was worth on the open market. "You gotta understand," he told Kate, "that this was one gorgeous broad. Deep-blue eyes, long thick black lashes. And stacked. She hadn't thickened up yet. One smile could melt your heart. Mine sure did. And man, she was a plum ripe for the plucking. She was married to this asshole in love with his store. So I escort her to this absolute gem of a house they owned and plucked the plum. She was panting for it. And right in the asshole's own bed, too."

The two of them clicked from the beginning. They were quick on their feet, diamond-sharp, and they viewed the world as one giant buck to be pocketed. Daytimes, when the asshole thought she was out shopping or lunching with the girls, she was taking lessons in real estate and passion. And little old Vern was her teacher. To provide her with some pocket change to play with, he suggested that Catherine start a "shopping service" for women she knew. When someone wanted to buy furniture, clothes, jewelry or anything expensive, she'd guarantee them a better price than any store could give them. All the buyer had to do was to select the items and have them set aside. Then Catherine would go to the store and charge the purchases to that asshole of a husband of hers, charge the customer fifty or a hundred bucks less, and pocket the cash while her husband paid the bill.

"Them rich folks," Riley said, "they're always after a bargain. They don't make all that money by spending anything they don't have to, no sirree! And the asshole, he didn't pay attention to what the bills were for. He just forked over the dough to pay them. Trusting jerk. She must've pocketed two, three, sometimes five grand a month."

Meanwhile, Catherine had put in her hours in a formal real estate class, passed the state exam, joined a real estate company and hit the streets running. A listing agent received a portion of every commission, and since she didn't like wasting her time showing dozens of houses to people who couldn't make up their minds about diddly-shit, she left the sales to others and went for the listings. This also gave her first chance if any good buys came along. And there were. She'd tell the assholes their place was worth fifteen, twenty grand less than it was, and buy it on the cheap, using the money from her shopping service. To hide the real estate, she'd formed her own company, so most of the time the trusting jerks who listed with her never even realized she was the buyer. For sure, the asshole she was married to didn't. By the mid-seventies, she had quite a sizable real estate empire built.

When the asshole finally started questioning some of the bills, it was divorce time. Riley introduced her to an attorney who specialized in helping husbands beat the property settlement and alimony raps and the three of them planned the clean-out and the squeeze. The kid, Becky, was shipped to some people Riley knew in Idaho, the movers were called in to pack and ship all in one day, the bank accounts were cleaned out while the movers were there, and the liens were filed the moment everything and everyone was out of sight.

But romance was never meant to be smooth, Riley said philosophically. Having succeeded so successfully in building up her empire, getting the lakefront house for herself free and clear, and grabbing half of the asshole's business, Catherine decided she didn't need Riley any longer. "So I let her go," Riley said. "I just opened my hands, and I said, 'Hey, Baby, you're right, you don't need me anymore,' and I let her go. It's the only way to treat a broad like that. And I sat back and waited."

He waited a long time, a couple of years, he said, through Catherine's extravagant high living and a couple of rich boyfriends. "Yeah, she dated those assholes. Thought the country-club life was for her. Later on, she admitted they screwed like their peckers hurt."

By the early eighties, she'd gone through all the divorce and house money, sold off all her investment real estate, gone through those profits, too, and was broke. Meanwhile, the real estate boom of the middle eighties was just beginning, and Riley couldn't take in the dough fast enough. He had his own lakefront house by then, a couple of expensive cars, and a forty-foot cruiser moored at Shilshoe Bay. All mortgaged up the yin yang, but what the hey, wasn't that what the fucking banks were for?

In the end, Catherine called him. And since no one had known of their relationship earlier, or even suspected that they knew each other, they put on like they'd just met and it was a brand-new romance. Only this time he made sure he did it right. He made sure the ring went on the finger, that it was all legal. And then the really high living began. There were parties and trips and clothes and diamonds. They wore handmade shoes and silk nightclothes and custom-made suits and dresses. And when they tired of what they were wearing, they'd fly to Hong Kong and have new wardrobes made. "Hey," he said to Kate, "some guys when they got it are too cheap to enjoy it. I know how to spend the bucks and have a good time. One night we went out to dinner and decided to go to Vegas instead. We caught the next flight out, no clothes, no toothbrush, no nothing. We bought what we needed down there. I dropped a few grand—maybe fifteen, all told—at the crap table, and that wasn't no big deal. Hell, in those days, I lived on commissions that weren't even born yet."

But during the boom, a lot of people were buying houses who shouldn't have been. Sales began to fall through and commissions dried up. "Now we're talking a few lousy bucks here," he complained to Kate in a lightning-quick change of mood. "A couple of big deals going through would've solved everything. And I had them in the works. But could those assholes at the bank understand that? That it was temporary? Hell no. All they cared about was their monthly pittance. They refused to look at the big picture, the overall scene. Well, screw them all anyway!"

The first thing to go was the cruiser. The bank sold it for less than he owed and suddenly he was left with a debt of fifteen grand. He'd fallen behind on mortgage payments on the house, and that was the next to go. When foreclosure hit, no asshole of a bank would touch him. Within six months, he was bankrupt and the high life was over. Furious with him, Catherine, who'd sworn she'd never work again, hit the streets. They needed food money, and it took too long to sell real estate and then close on it to get your bucks out of it, so she took up her old job as an ad rep. As soon as she had some dough again, she kicked Vern out the first time he asked her to buy his booze. And that began the on-again, off-again marriage.

"See, I understood Catherine," he said to Kate. "I knew her clear through. She always said I was the only one who did, too. All the assholes in the world, they'd see this gorgeous broad with a cute grin and those big, wide, beautiful eyes and they'd think she was so warm, so sweet, such a nice person. *Shi-it*. What a bunch of shitheads. Hell, her blood was money-green. That's what turned her on. Not some good-looking guy or a pair of cute buns. Mo-ney. M-o-n-e-y. That was her aphro-watchamacallit— you know, what makes you get your rocks off? So anyway, every time she'd kick me out she'd feel sorry about it, but she'd say, 'If I don't look out for number one, who will?' Oh, I'd fight and curse and bellow, you bet I would, but in the end I'd leave and go find a new pitch and wait until I made some more bucks, then I'd start hanging around again. You see, she really loved me. In spite of everything, in spite of all the times I was flat busted, or seeing some broad on the side, in spite of that, she really cared. But she was a sharp lady, Catherine was. She wasn't gonna let anyone get hold of her pennies, not even me. She always looked out for number one first. And not a single one of those trusting assholes out there knew that about her. Just me. I was the only one who knew. Just me. And that's why I didn't kill her. Because I knew her, and she knew me, and we was just plain good together."

It went on and on until he wound down at last and Kate was able to get away from him. After he'd signed the statement, she took herself off to lunch. Alone. Sam was just coming up the steps as she was leaving headquarters and she simply shook her head at him without saying a word and kept plowing on to her car.

She drove up to the Sea Galley. Not for the food, but for the quiet. The quiet, the dim lights, the isolated booths. She postponed ordering lunch and asked for a large Bloody Mary. It was a mistake. When it came, she just stared at it. The blood-red color made her sick to the stomach. Her head was a painful jangling of images and impressions. She made no attempt to sort through them. She merely endured them.

Gradually, the soft muted sounds of the restaurant, the low-keyed hum of conversations, the discreet attention by soft-voiced waitresses seeped in, and as she began to unwind, rational thoughts began to form.

She had no doubt that Vern Riley was telling things pretty much the way they'd happened. He and Catherine had been two amoral sociopaths engaged in an unholy alliance against everything decent in the world. And unapologetic about it as well. If anything, he overestimated his own importance and underestimated Catherine's. The fact that she had so quickly and skillfully absorbed and executed the lessons of amorality only indicated that of the two, she'd had the greater-warped soul.

How did that tie into the killings?

She reviewed the list of suspects.

Becky Wilson. Now Kate could fathom how Catherine could chop off a child in trouble. The woman had no more feelings for the girl than a barnyard hen. She was just the chicken who'd hatched the egg. And Becky, capable of deep caring—witnessed by her relationships with her father and son—was the victim. She wasn't experienced enough yet in life to understand that her mother was an empty shell with nothing human inside. She was certainly a victim, yes. But murderer? No. Becky, like her father, wasn't cold-blooded enough to conceive and execute a poisoning. If Becky had been going to lash out at her mother, it would've been years ago.

The same with Bob Wilson. He'd followed all the edicts of normal society. Work hard, play fair, earn your way, respect right and wrong, love your family—and life would be rich and good. In fact, he'd used those very words. Rich and good. Another trusting soul who wouldn't recognize the kind of evil that Catherine encompassed until he'd experienced it himself. Then he'd have lashed out at the time, as his daughter would've, and it would've been done in the heat of the moment.

The Wilsons were past history, their hurts inflicted years before. What she was looking for now was a present-day victim. She moved on to the business partners.

Ginger. Trusting, naive, an innocent. Taken in and boldly used by Catherine. Had she finally realized that? Had it finally dawned on her that Catherine was all take, take, take? Kate doubted it. Ginger was too transparent to have successfully carried off an *act* of innocence. No, Ginger *was* an innocent. An unknowing victim, not a knowing one.

Suzie. What about Suzie? She'd been perceptive enough about the business needing Phyllis' steady hand, no matter what Catherine said to the contrary. So some instinct was operating there. But she shrank from confrontation in the verbal world, thus probably shrank from confrontation of the psyche, where Catherine waged her best wars, thus she'd probably chosen not to perceive Catherine for what she was, and would simply hope it all would work out for the best. Kate was eager to get her alone and do some probing. But for the moment, Suzie looked doubtful.

Phyllis. Ah. Kate sat back over the remains of her lunch, sipping some coffee, her Bloody Mary still untouched. Phyllis was sharp. No question about it. And had consistently sensed something was wrong, but hadn't quite put the pieces together. Or had she? Had all the myriad of perceptions, impressions and clues finally coalesced into a grim realization of what Catherine really was? Possibly.

And what would Phyllis do if she had tumbled to the true picture? Was she capable of planning and executing such a cold-blooded murder? Yes, Kate thought, she was. The question then became one of motivation. Was her motivation strong enough? The business was threatened with destruction by Catherine. Phyllis would have some powerful feelings about that. She would have some formidable protective instincts that would feed a need to do something, to rid the business—her child, if you will—of a potentially fatal threat. But wouldn't confrontation be more her style? Kate thought it would be. But that didn't necessarily rule out murder. If confrontation didn't work, if there were no legal means for removing Catherine from the business, if all methods led to dead ends, what then? She certainly was bright enough and organized enough to plan a murder, and once such a decision had been made, she'd do it in a way that would minimize her chances of getting caught. So intellectually, Kate had to agree that Phyllis was a top suspect.

But instincts argued against it. Phyllis was straightforward, not devious. She was honest, not deceitful. She was open with people, not one overly concerned with herself. Could a person like that *hide* the fact she'd committed a crime, even if she was capable of planning it? Kate had her doubts.

Still, Phyllis was the most likely suspect yet.

Unfortunately, she had to put Vern Riley at the bottom of the list. First of all, he was the *only* person so far who had *not* been a victim of Catherine's. Even when she dumped him after her divorce, he'd treated it like a poker hand and waited for a new deal. And he was so damned open about the scams they'd pulled. There were no apologies, no shame, no awareness of wrongdoing. He assumed that if he was this way, and Catherine was this way, then everyone was this way, and if they weren't, then they were the sheep for the plucking. Even his happy reconciliation with Catherine, being brought back into her world for her final days of life, worked in his favor. If all he'd said proved out. And Kate saw no reason it wouldn't; he certainly hadn't bothered to cover up any of his other activities. But if it did all prove out, then Riley wouldn't have had the opportunity to plant the tea bags. Not unless he'd carried around some doctored tea bags for some reason or another, then planted them in the canister on Sunday evening when Catherine had stopped by the empty studio with him.

No, Kate didn't see him doing that at all. Damn. It would've been such a tidy ending . . . One con artist killing another.

That left only Jack Turner to be considered. Kate flagged the waitress for more coffee. Jack Turner. Mr. Unknown. Had he seen Catherine for what she was? Kate had no way of estimating that. Why had he broken off with her after only a couple of weeks? By all accounts, Catherine was a beautiful woman. Had he seen through the facade to the empty core inside? And if he had, would he have the cold-bloodedness to kill her?

She thought back over the aborted interview of the day before and how skillfully he'd controlled the entire session. Yes, she thought, he would. He was tough. Not blustery-tough, like a bully, but strong-tough. A man used to making hard decisions. If he decided to kill, he'd kill. But was a two-week involvement with a previously unknown woman be enough to generate the kind of emotion it took to *want* to kill someone? Possibly. He had given away nothing of himself during that brief encounter except control and toughness. It was imperative she talk to him again.

So that was her list. Jack Turner. Phyllis Walsh. And possibly, but not likely, Suzie. Ginger, Bob Wilson, and Becky, down at the bottom. As was Vern Riley. If only there was a Fairy Godmother of Cops in the world, she'd turn out to be wrong, and Vern Riley would be It. But at least now she had a focus. Turner, Walsh, and Suzie. She motioned for her check.

12

Phyllis Walsh was dressed in a sleek gray suit and a pale-blue blouse, wearing a simple strand of pearls. A navy shoulder bag was slung over one shoulder. Her makeup was faultless. She looked neat, trim and professional. But beneath the image, her shoulders were squared into tense blocks, her face was pale and drawn, and her mouth was compressed into a worried line. "I'm sorry for the delay. A business problem."

"I can imagine all the things you've got to do." Kate escorted her to the interrogation room and indicated a chair at the table.

"You're disarming, you know that?" Phyllis gave a strained smile. "I keep wanting to forget that you're a detective. Have you come up with any answers yet?"

"We're still looking into things. For now, I need you to go over your activities from Friday night through Tuesday. Where you were, what you did, who you were with. Then we'll explore what you might know about Catherine. What she did her last few days. It's not a complicated procedure at all. We'll simply record your recollections on tape, type it up and you can sign it before you go."

"This tape recording. Does that mean I'm under suspicion? Should I have an attorney here?"

"You can if you'd like. It's a pretty standard procedure,

though. Sometimes we interview people in their own homes, and sometimes we ask them to come on down here. In this case, the people involved are so scattered geographically, I felt it would save time for everyone to come to me. All we're doing at this point is investigating the situation. We're not interrogating you. Ginger was in earlier and gave her statement. And we're taking one from everyone connected to the case. By the way, I've been trying to reach Suzie. Do you happen to know what her plans were for today?"

"No, I'm sorry, I don't." Phyllis was calm, but she still looked worried. "Officially, the office is closed today. She's too hyper to just laze around, though, so she could be anywhere. But I'm going to have to reach her soon myself. She needs to know what happened this morning. I can pass on a message then if you like." Her tone was polite, but her attention was far away, apparently caught up in whatever was troubling her.

Kate watched her for a couple of moments. "Is something wrong, Phyllis? I mean, aside from having to be here?"

Phyllis shifted her gaze to Kate, her eyes filled with a puzzled despair. "We lost the contract with Boeing this morning."

Kate looked at her sharply. "Why? What happened?"

"Our credit didn't check out." Abruptly, she pushed the chair back and began to pace along the wall on her side of the table, her arms crossed tightly in front of her. "They were kind about it. They gave me a chance to straighten it out. They even made a phone available to me. But the long and the short of it is that our suppliers have put us on a C.O.D. basis. All of a sudden, we don't have a dime of credit. And not one of them would tell me why. After leaving Boeing, I stopped at five different vendors and I couldn't get an answer from any of them. They were sorry, but that's the way it had to be."

Kate's mind was flying. Bob Wilson's story jumped to mind. Had Catherine been setting up her partners for the same downfall? But that didn't make sense. Why would she, as partner, cut her own economic throat like that? Unless she'd started another business on the side, and it was already up and running. That would explain a lot, Kate realized. The lack of effort at work, the attempt to drain every penny out of the company she could, the statement Riley had made that she was making sales on the side. Yes. That could explain a lot. "Were you behind with any of your suppliers?" she asked.

Phyllis shook her head. "We only have the usual ongoing monthly accounts that come due on regular dates. Other than that, all we have is one outstanding printing bill. And that job just came off the presses a few days ago. In fact, except for one time, we've been able to take advantage of most of the discounts offered for timely payments. Sometimes it amounted to only a few bucks. But a few bucks is a few bucks. The time we missed, we missed only by a day or two. The Christmas mails had slowed it up." She shook her head again. "I just don't understand it."

"But didn't you say at one point you were having trouble paying creditors because Catherine kept cashing checks against the business?"

Phyllis nodded. "Yes. But that wasn't a clear expression of what was going on. What actually was happening was that the other three of us weren't able to take *any* money out—not even for expenses—so that the bills *could* be paid. No, we didn't skip paying the bills. We had to skip paying us."

"Because Catherine kept helping herself."

"Yes."

"And these creditors, you couldn't get any reason for this sudden about-face from them at all? No hint? No clue?"

"None. They were polite. They'd be happy to do business with us, but it was cash up-front or nothing. But Boeing doesn't pay out any up-front money at all. Not until the job's done. Even then, they take anywhere from ninety to a hundred and eighty days to pay their accounts payable. That makes credit an absolute necessity. That's why they ran the credit check before they actually handed us the job."

She turned in her pacing to give Kate another deeply puzzled look. "The odd thing is, when we put out this project for bid a few weeks ago to come up with our pricing, I explained to most of our suppliers who the client was and why the necessity for the credit terms I was asking for, and because of our prompt payment record, there wasn't a problem at all. First no problem, now no credit. I don't understand it. I just don't." She sighed, then gave

Kate a wry grin. "Well, I feel a little better for having told someone about it. Though you're probably the last person in the world I should be sharing this with."

"Don't worry about it for now. I just wish I could help. What about banks? Or using other printers?"

"The bank won't give us any credit until we've been in business two years. And what credit references do we have now for another printer? A month ago, every printer in the Northwest was after our business. Now no one will want it." She sank into her chair, looking morose all over again. "This is going to break Ginger's heart. Suzie and I did our share to land this account, but it's really Ginger who put in the hours on it. Hundreds of hours. And all for nothing."

"So what do you do now?"

A puckish grin broke through the gloom. "If there's one thing the graphics industry loves better than its food and drink, it's gossip. There are going to be a lot of happy sales reps wined and dined the next few days. Sooner or later, I'll get wind of what's going on. You can bank on it. But enough about that. I really do feel better. We still have all our other clients, and they do put down contract deposits, so we can keep operating. It's not the end of the world, it just feels like it. Now what can I do to help you?"

Phyllis' statement was thorough and exacting, complete with addresses and phone numbers looked up in a purse-sized appointment book as each name came up in turn. Friday night had been pizza with her husband, Richard, and a gang of friends. Saturday was spent at the office with Ginger and Suzie until four, then grocery shopping on her way home. Another couple in for drinks, dinner and cards that night. Sunday was spent alone with Richard, a simple lazing around with the papers in the morning and a drive to Camano Island in the afternoon to look at some property they were thinking of buying. A Chinese dinner at the Seven Seas in the International District, then an early night. Monday... At this point, Phyllis referred to her appointment book and read off the list of everyone she'd seen that day, all clients. A quick dinner with Ginger and Suzie that night, then back to the office to finish the work on the Boeing presentation until nine or so, then home to bed. She'd only seen Catherine briefly twice that day—just before lunch, and at the end of the afternoon. She'd only been alone in the office once on Monday, and that was after Catherine had left for the night and before Ginger returned from getting ad approval from a client. Suzie had been still out on her last appointment of the day, and both she and Ginger had returned to the office around five, within minutes of each other. Suzie had gotten in first, as she recalled.

"What about bathroom breaks? Lunches? You worked all day Saturday; what did you do for lunch?"

"Let me think . . . Okay, Ginger and I went out together to get some sandwiches and brought them back at noon. Ginger needed to take a break from the drawing board and stretch her legs."

"So Suzie was alone in the studio then."

A look of alarm crossed Phyllis's face. "Yes, but—"

Kate forestalled the defense about to come. "I'm simply trying to get it fixed in my mind is all. I'm not accusing anyone of anything."

Phyllis relaxed a little, but she still threw a distrustful look at the tape recorder running relentlessly on. Absently, she ran her fingers through the smooth cap of brown hair. "Yes, she was alone then. Later, some spring sunshine had broken through the clouds, and since Suzie doesn't have a lot of sit-still in her anyway, she grabbed Ginger and they went out for a walk. I was there alone for a while, too. And Ginger was alone off and on all day Monday. So each of us had a chance to do whatever evil deeds we were planning to do, if we had been planning to do them. Which we weren't."

Kate nodded her understanding. Message received. Phyllis refused to believe that any of them had anything to do with Catherine's death. She dropped the subject and moved on. "Tell me about your relationship with Catherine."

Phyllis repeated in succinct form most of what she'd told Kate the previous day. She was honest about the problems the partners had been having with Catherine, but she toned down a lot of her personal opinion for the tape recorder, Kate noticed. On the whole, though, it was complete.

"Phyllis, how did Boeing reach you to tell you there was a problem?"

"I'd given them my home number for emergencies. They're on a deadline and have to get this contract awarded. But they wanted to give us a chance to straighten the credit problem out. They really were kind about it. They'd left messages with our answering service yesterday afternoon, but I never thought to check—"

"Answering service," Kate interrupted. "That's what was nagging me when I was interviewing Ginger. Your office phone never rang once while we were there yesterday. Who put it on the answering service?"

"I don't know," Phyllis answered slowly. "I guess Ginger did. I mean, Catherine was there to cover the phones yesterday morning. That was the whole point of her being there. So she wouldn't have had the answering service take the calls. Ginger must've done it after she found Catherine."

"Can you check with your answering service and see?"

"Sure. Do you have a phone I can use? I'll call now."

Kate led her into the bull pen and pointed to a desk and phone that were free. Phyllis spoke briefly, hung up and gave Kate a puzzled look. "They handled the calls all day yesterday. Catherine never took them off. Why would she do that? That's what she was there for, to cover the phones. It doesn't make sense."

"Yesterday, Ginger said the office door was open when she got there. I wonder if the lights were on."

"I don't know. Why?"

Kate didn't answer her. "Where are you headed when you're done here?"

"First some lunch, then to the office. There's too much to do to just take off for a few days. Even if the office is formally closed. Clients are always facing a deadline of some form or another. Why?" she asked again.

"Ginger said she was going back there to get some design work done. If you run into her, would you ask her to give me a call? Suzie, too, if you see her. I'll keep trying to reach her at home in the meantime." She escorted Phyllis back to the tape recorder. "Just a few more questions and we'll be through. I want to ask you about Catherine's health. Was she on any prescription drugs you knew about?"

Phyllis was hesitant, then realized it and apologized for it. "I'm sorry, you're really asking two different questions. About the prescription drugs, I never saw any. But about Catherine's health . . . You know, on thinking about it, I don't think she was really all that great. She was tired so much of the time . . . And a lot of the time she acted like she just plain didn't feel good. You know, when you've got a bug or something, and you feel kind of rotten, but you haven't really come down with it yet? That kind of thing."

"Ginger said she thought she'd had flu back in January sometime."

"Yes, I remember that. She was out a few days with it. Maybe a week, or slightly more."

"Do you think she just didn't quite get over it?"

"You mean, it might've hung on and on and on, like it sometimes does? Yes, I guess that's a possibility. I don't know, though, I sure wouldn't want to make that a definite statement." She looked again at the tape recorder.

"Last night we talked about the possibility of a drinking problem. If Catherine did have one, would that account for the way she felt?"

Phyllis shifted positions. She obviously was uncomfortable. Frowning, she stared into space, thinking, then reached a decision. She nodded to herself once, then turned to face Kate squarely, leaned forward with her elbows on the table, her gaze on Kate steady and grave. "You know, it's one thing to speculate about all of this, like we were doing yesterday. It's quite another to have it all recorded for the world to hear. So I'm going to phrase this very carefully, Detective MacLean. Yes, I *do* think Catherine drank too much. But I seldom drink at all, and so what would be normal for one person might just *seem* too much to me. I'm not qualified to term her an alcoholic, or even to firmly state she did have a problem or a dependency. I simply don't know. I seldom saw her in off-hours outside of the business, and was not privy to the details of her social life. That was her business, not mine. All I can tell you is that she acted at times like she didn't feel well, and she seemed to be terribly tired far more often than a healthy person would be. That's all I know. I don't know any more than that."

With that, she stood up and looked down at Kate in the same way that Jack Turner had looked at her. "Now, if there's nothing more, I'll wait for this to be typed and be on my way."

Whew, thought Kate, as she buzzed for the transcriber and escorted Phyllis to the waiting area. A lady of steel.

Phyllis was definitely at the head of the list.

Sam was gone again when she got back to her desk. A terse note simply said, "Am still cracking bank vaults. Catch up with you later."

Grinning, Kate settled down to some desk work.

She made a call to the partners' business attorney to check on the structure of the company, its stock and Catherine's will. Unlike Turner's lawyer, this man was open and forthright with her. Each partner inherited the others' shares on an equal percentage basis, plus any life-insurance benefits the business carried on each. Since the business portion of Catherine's estate was handled through the partnership papers, her will contained only personal bequests. Vern Riley had been left one dollar. Everything else she owned, including cars, furniture, clothes, and jewelry were to be sold and the proceeds of the sale—plus any monies in her bank accounts—were to be donated to an arthritis-research foundation. There was no provision for her daughter or grandson. They were specifically excluded from the will, and if they contested it in any way, they each were to be given one dollar and no more.

As for the missing stock certificate that Phyllis had been hunting for, the attorney knew nothing beyond the fact that Catherine had taken it from his office late in January or early in February with a promise to return it in a few days. Which she never did. No, he didn't know the reason she took it. It was hers; if she'd wanted it for any reason, she had the right to it without a lot of cross-examination over it. Kate thanked him for his help and hung up.

Paperwork stared her in the face. She stretched her legs

underneath the desk and rubbed the small of her back as she read through her own file from the beginning. She matched every detail with the statements. The words were sometimes different, but the facts jibed. So did her memory. She closed the file and stared into space. At the moment, her conclusions made at lunch held up. Still, she went over them one more time, notebook in front of her. Follow-up actions needed to be organized.

The Wilsons, father and daughter. Motive, absolutely. Opportunity, questionable. Just to be sure, though, she made a note to get pictures of each of them and circulate them among the partners and other tenants of the building. Just in case one or the other of them had taken to hanging about the area.

Riley. Motive? Unknown. Opportunity? Possibly... Patience to use poison? Nothing slower than strychnine. Still... Get photo and circulate. Maybe he'd been hanging around the office building, too. And check for a source of morphine.

Partners. Motive and opportunity, without a doubt. Photos not needed at this point. Again, check for source of morphine.

Where the hell was that lab report anyway? she thought suddenly. Homer hadn't called. No report from the M.E., either. She picked up the phone again.

The calls produced no results. Homer was tied up. The coroner was in a meeting. Suzie's home still didn't answer. Neither did Ginger's. And the studio's answering service was still intercepting calls. Just to be thorough, she tried Phyllis's home and was surprised to hear her voice.

"No," Phyllis explained, her voice sounding tired. "I didn't go to the studio after all. At lunch, all of the past two days hit me. I guess it sort of just penetrated what's happened. So I came home and soaked in a hot tub instead."

"Then you didn't see Ginger to ask her to call?"

"No, I'm sorry, I didn't. I'll try her at home tonight for you, if you'd like. Or I'll see her tomorrow morning. I'll be going in then."

"That'll be soon enough, I guess. Thanks." Kate hung up, frowning. She could run over to the studio now. It wasn't that far. She glanced at her watch. It was after four already. Nope, she decided, talking to Ginger would have to wait. She had the daily report to do.

While waiting for her the previous evening, Sam had completed a rough preliminary report. She redid it, adding in summaries of the present day to this point, and attached copies of all the statements and placed them in her out-box for delivery to the Captain. Sam would also receive a complete copy of the report and statements. By the end of the case, they each would have a complete file. It was their way of closing some of the cracks that occurred when two people worked the same case, but in different areas. Also, fresh eyes brought to paper often would raise questions overlooked by the other. Assumptions and too-easy acceptance of what they were told were common enemies of detecting.

That finished, she turned to the final name on her list. Jack Turner. She picked up the *Times* envelope. It contained only the one clipping. It was as Throckmorton had said. A simple announcement of the formation of Turner Bearing Company three years ago.

She paper-clipped the article to the envelope and inserted them in Turner's file, then sat back in her chair and idly swiveled. All she'd learned was that his proper name was John E. Turner. That was it. The sum total of her knowledge. She wondered what the middle letter stood for. Elliot? Emery? Eugene? Edward? Mr. John Edward Turner? She tapped her pen on paper. If, as he claimed, he really had quit seeing Catherine after a mere two weeks, then why? Not having his story was becoming a damned nuisance.

She played around with several ideas. Legal steps? There wasn't a shooting chance in hell of getting anything issued.

Seek his cooperation by asking him if he wouldn't like to voluntarily give his statement so she could eliminate him as a suspect? She could hear him laugh at that.

Appeal to his better nature?

Did he have one?

Civic pride? Citizenship? Responsibility to mankind?

Or none of the above. She sighed and placed a call to his

attorney. The message from him was brief and terse: Mr. Turner had nothing to say.

Oh, really? She pushed away from her desk and rose. She'd see about that.

After leaving a note for Sam, she checked out for the night. She used her own car so she wouldn't have to return later to the station, and headed for Redmond.

Mr. John E. Turner.

Catherine's fiancé, or casual acquaintance?

13

When the receptionist called back to his office, Jack Turner ambled down the hall and greeted Kate with a cool politeness. "Did we have an appointment?"

"No," she said, just as coolly. "I'll wait."

He quirked an eyebrow. "I see. I still have nothing pertinent to tell you."

"You don't know what I'm here to ask."

He studied her a moment, then seemed to make up his mind about her and indicated a chair near the receptionist's desk. "We have a crisis we're settling. It may be a while."

She nodded and took a seat.

There may have been a crisis, but to a nervous system exposed daily to the constant ruckus of the bull pen, it was blissfully calm. Promptly at five, the receptionist stamped the last envelope in the pile, covered her typewriter, aimed a general good-night in all directions and left. People, alone or in twos and threes, drifted from back offices and disappeared through the front door. Some nodded her way, some looked curious but walked on past with no acknowledgment, the rest passed her by as if she were a chair cushion.

By six, silence had descended. By six-thirty, her rump was numb. By six forty-five, she figured he'd gotten away from her.

At seven, he appeared, raincoat slung over one arm.

He seemed a little surprised to see her still there, but came over without pausing. "I have one hard-and-fast rule. No matter what the schedule, I always eat a good dinner, preceded by a cold Scotch and water. Sometimes even two. If you want to talk to me, you'll have to join me. Or you can skip it. The choice is yours."

It was a no-brainer. "I'll join you."

The wayward black eyebrow moved again. He took her arm and guided her to her car. "Since I seem to be a murder suspect, you'd better follow me in your own car. That way you'll be safe."

The Cutlery East was located on a side street in downtown Redmond across from a feed-and-grain store. Turner pulled into a parking lot next door to the restaurant, leaving the first available parking slot for her. He may have been proclaimed rich by Catherine Fletcher, but he drove a tan Chevy Caprice, three years old. Nothing flashy, and certainly not rich. She swung her old Honda Civic into place, climbed out and waited for him to join her.

The restaurant took up the front two-thirds of the building. The cocktail lounge was in one rear corner, back by the kitchen. They moved down a center aisle of the restaurant to the hostess' desk, where Jack stopped to reserve a table, then he guided Kate into the small dim lounge, to a table at the rear. The atmosphere was subdued and soothing. Three businessmen sat well apart from each other at the long bar running along one wall, each walled off into a compound of his own thoughts. A few couples occupied other tables, the jukebox played a quiet song that was pleasant and not nerve-jangling, and the drinks were strong and good. She felt the warmth of the Manhattan she'd ordered hit her stomach and spread through her body. A contented sigh escaped her.

"That kind of day, eh?" Turner was studying her again.

She just smiled and nodded, studying him in turn. He was attractive, she had to give him that. Long, lean face, body to match. A shock of dark hair and those strong blue eyes beneath the damnably mobile black eyebrows. His mouth was broad and generous, his chin strong and firm. Six-one, one ninety, fortyish, more or less. Away from his office, his manner was easygoing and relaxed, his long legs stretched out before him.

His eyes were intent on her, doing his own summing up.

She let him look until he shifted his attention back to his drink, then she asked, "What was the crisis?"

A bit of a grin flickered around the broad mouth. "A derailed freight train and a boxcar of bearings spilled over half the countryside of Montana. Reports coming in indicate a high number of unhappy cows."

She grinned.

"You're pretty when you smile," he said quietly, his eyes playing lightly over her features.

Her heart began its dog race again and she raised her glass to give her mind something else to think about besides him. "Thank you. So what do you do about it? The unhappy cows, I mean."

"Well, that's kind of the railroad's territory, but I'd guess they'd buy a garden rake or two and get busy. As for my customer, he's had such an upsurge in business, his inventory's depleted, so I'll use the old borrow-from-Peter-to-supply-Paul trick to keep his production line moving. We've shaved a portion of other shipments back and are air-freighting a supply of bearings to him tonight."

"Does this kind of thing happen often, a foul-up of deliveries like this?"

He openly grinned now. "My favorite is the trucker who wandered around St. Louis hunting for an address that was in San Francisco. Somehow he mistook the 'S.F.' for 'S.L.' and off he headed for Missouri."

"Interesting work. How'd you get into it to begin with?"

"Are you on- or off-duty?"

She thought about it. "Neutral, I guess. I'm interested, that's all."

He raised his hands to signal another round. "I had an engineering degree from U.C. Berkeley, took a job with Hewlett-Packard down the San Francisco peninsula, and thought I was settled in for life. Only a couple of realities rose up real fast. In any new project, there are three stages: creating it, producing it, maintaining it. The first balloon that popped was the idea I'd create something strong and powerful for the universe. I simply wasn't a creator. The second balloon that self-destructed was the idea that I was a maintainer. It bored me out of my mind. And the corporate power games struck me as asinine and juvenile. Where I really got excited, though, was in the production end, taking someone else's new idea and running with it. Bringing it into being. There were lots of bright, timely ideas out there, but they were suffering from the lack of someone like me. Not all the people bright enough to create something have the common sense or the know-how to make it commercially successful. I parted company with H-P and headed out to find my first genius. A couple of decades later, here I am."

Kate laughed at that. "I have a feeling that 'a couple of decades' skips over a whale of an interesting story."

"All in good time." He grinned. "Never give away all your mystique the first time out. Now it's your turn. Why a cop?"

"The market in candles failed."

He gave her a quizzical look. "Why don't I understand that remark?"

"It's part of my mystique."

He burst out laughing. "Okay, message received. You still haven't answered my question, though. How did you come to be what you are? A police science degree?"

"No. Though I've got some post-grad courses in it. I was in the San Francisco area, too. After a good New England upbringing and education, I headed west, to live on a houseboat and make candles for the rest of my life."

Sudden understanding lit his eyes. "Ah, the candle-market dive."

"Yep. And in Sausalito, houseboats cost a lot of money, and after a while, I couldn't even pay for my next meal, so eventually I had to go to work."

"Obviously, you don't get hired and start on a police force all on the same morning. So what kind of a glorious career position did you take to feed your starving self in the meantime?"

"Waitress, what else? If you're hungry, go where the food is. No waiting for payday that way."

"And then?" he said softly.

She hesitated, tempted to end it there with the light comment. But their second drinks had arrived and he was exuding interest and the lights were low, the lounge quiet around them, and it encouraged the exchange of confidences. "I was drifting, I guess. And I drifted until I got tired of drifting. I woke up one morning and it was as if my New England heritage had washed in overnight, like the tide. All of it, clear down to the Puritan work ethic. And I was pretty disgusted at that moment with what I saw, with myself and with my life. There were a lot of affirmative-action programs being put into effect just then, so I applied for juvenile cop, passed the tests and got accepted for training."

She paused to sip her drink.

"Juvenile cop? Why not a social worker or—"

She exhaled an exasperated sigh. "Tell me, is it something written in blood on my forehead? Do I only imagine I'm wearing a suit and blouse and it's really sackcloth and ashes instead? What *is* it about me that shouts to the world that I'm a major cupcake?"

Her outburst didn't faze him in the least. He examined her thoroughly, then said softly, "It's everything about you. It's the warm look in your eyes, it's the instinctive way your face reflects sympathy and understanding, it's the sincerity you project . . . It's the way your carry yourself, the way you listen, the half-smile of interest even when you're just people-watching . . . I don't know you well—hell, I don't know you at all—yet in some ways I know you through and through. You're kind, concerned and compassionate. You could no more hide it than you could your head of brown hair."

"Chestnut," she murmured, her cheeks flaming.

"Beg your pardon?"

"My mother always told me to say my hair was chestnut. She had gorgeous black hair, you see, raven black, and she thought brown was too plain."

His face lit up with sudden humor. "You're a fascinating woman, Miss MacLean."

She smiled slightly in response. "Now it's your turn. What does the *E* stand for?"

"A long-dead uncle. And a good thing, too. If he'd still been alive, I'd have wrung his neck."

She grinned. "Come on, give."

"Not on your life. *No* one knows me that well."

"Edward."

"Too trite."

"Emilio."

"Too Spanish."

"Frank, and you're just pretending it starts with an *E.*"

They both laughed at that.

Their table became available and the hostess led them to it. The restaurant was divided by a center aisle that stretched from the front door to the hostess' desk. Screened from the aisle by filigreed paneling on either side were double rows of high-backed booths. The privacy was almost total.

The food was superb. Salad served family style with three homemade dressings served on the side, freshly made rolls still warm from the oven, and steak that was fork-tender. Jack ordered a bottle of wine for them and kept their glasses full as they ate. They talked easily, of this and that, exploring common interests. She discovered he was as appalled at the California-like takeover of the Seattle area as she was, but he thought a twenty-year sentence of all the city councils to Silicon Valley was much too short. "Three lifetimes at least," he said, "that's what they need to spend down there, so they'll *really* be able to see what horror they've wrought on all us hapless souls."

Their conversation moved on to the more generalized topic of the San Francisco Bay area. They exchanged names of favorite places, seeking some in common. The getting-to-know-you process reminded her of one of her tavern girlfriends, relating the story of a first date with a new man. She'd summed it all up by saying, We have so much in common! We both *love* Chinese!

Kate laughed a little at the memory, but it served as a warning, too. They were checking each other out, measuring, probing, finding things to appreciate in each other. It would've been so easy to let go and be carried off by it all. He was personable and considerate, with a lively intellect. In a thousand different ways, his eyes and those magnificent eyebrows told her he appreciated her, and whenever their glances met and held in a moment's quick intake of breath, her heart raced like an engine on high idle. She had to keep a tight rein on it. She had to, it was too dangerous not to. She could've easily fallen off the edge of the evening into something that couldn't be. It simply couldn't be. And so she kept the light talk a mind's distance away from her heart.

At one point, he mentioned liking to go to simple places, do simple things, like shooting pool on a Sunday afternoon in a local tavern. Just something to get his mind off work.

"You shoot pool?" she asked.

"Hey, I'm deadly with a pool cue. Ask anyone. How about you? Do you play?"

She widened her eyes in innocence. "Maybe you could give me a lesson sometime."

His look was skeptical. "You don't shoot pool?"

"There's always more to learn."

"That's what I thought. A shark if I ever saw one. Where do you usually play?"

"Smokie Jo's in Kirkland. Nice place. Where do you go?"

"The Workshop in Redmond."

The name connected. She kept her voice casual. "The Workshop. Are you a regular there?"

"Pretty much so."

"Ever run into a man named Bob Wilson?"

"It doesn't sound familiar. Though there are a lot of Bobs there. Big Bob, Little Bob, and half a dozen other Bobs. Who is he?"

"Catherine Fletcher's ex-husband."

At the mention of Catherine's name, there was a flash of regret in his eyes before he retreated into the businessman persona he'd worn at the beginning of the evening. His lips tightened together and his voice turned precise, as if he were highly irritated, but controlling it. "Catherine Fletcher's ex-husband," he said flatly. Then he sighed. "All right. Let's bring it out into the open. What's happening, and how is the investigation coming along?"

"Slowly, as usual. We're still sorting out truth from fiction."

"What have you done so far?"

"Talked to a lot of people, gathered some background information, taken some formal statements. Except for yours, of course."

"And what have you learned so far?"

"Aren't I the one who's supposed to be asking the questions here?" Kate asked lightly.

"What have you learned?"

She grew serious. "That, if you'll forgive me for saying so, Catherine Fletcher left a lot to be desired as a human being."

"Why should I have to forgive that?"

"Because, according to her, the two of you were engaged." She gazed at him steadily and waited.

"Ah, yes," he said with a humorless smile. "Now we've come full circle. And how do I rank as a suspect?"

She kept up the steady look. "In my book, you're at the top."

"I see." His eyebrow moved skyward in some amusement. "Then you are a courageous lady, spending an evening in my company. Exactly what has propelled you to that conclusion?"

"First of all, you won't talk. You refuse to explain exactly what your relationship with Catherine was, and why it ended. If indeed it did end. Secondly, from what I've learned about Catherine's character, I wouldn't be surprised if she'd tried to pull something on you, one kind of scam or another. She specialized in that. And if she did, I don't think you'd take that lightly."

"That's very perceptive of you. I wouldn't. I can be ruthless when it comes to a betrayer of trust. However, I'm also quite cautious in awarding my trust. Not many people get in the position where they can betray me."

She thought about that. "You're implying, then, that she didn't fool you, so therefore she did no damage to you, therefore you'd have no motive for killing her."

"It might prevent you from going astray."

"You also could be trying to throw me off the track."

"That, too."

"So what you're saying is that you're innocent. You didn't do it, and I'd be wasting my time trying to connect you to the murder."

"That's what I'm saying, plain and simple. I didn't do it. To concentrate on me means the murderer walks free that much longer."

"Fine. Let's say I accept that. Then *why* won't you answer my questions about the breakup?"

"What month are we up to? The end of March? And you're looking all the way back at November." He counted back on his fingers. "That's four months ago. It's history. Ancient news. No more relevant to today's world than the fall of the Roman Empire." He reached across the table and took both her hands in his. "She wasn't important to me, Katie," he said softly. "Please believe me. Catherine Fletcher was not the kind of woman I like to spend time with, and so I quit seeing her. That's all there is to it."

She thought it over, studying him, then finally nodded slowly. "All right, I'll accept that. For now. If anything—if anything *at all*—surfaces that indicates differently, I'll be back on your doorstep to haunt you."

When they'd finished the last of their coffee, he walked her to her car and held the door for her. As she started to slide in behind the wheel, he placed a hand on her arm and stopped her. The parking-lot lights threw his face into shadow, but even through the darkness she could feel the intensity of his gaze. "I've enjoyed your company," he said softly. "It's probably against the law for a murder suspect to date the detective, isn't it."

A deep yearning, instinctive, almost irrepressible, swamped her. She struggled against it until it was boxed in and locked away again, where it was supposed to be. "I'm sure there's a law like that somewhere, yes."

"Too bad," he murmured. He lowered his lips to hers, pausing a hair away from touching them. "That's too damned bad," he whispered, his breath warm on her mouth. He gave her a gentle kiss, then pulled away. "In fact, it's a damned shame."

Eyes locked on his, she whispered, "A damned shame."

She turned on her heel and climbed into her car. When she

made the swing onto the street, she twisted to glance back at him. He was standing where she'd left him, watching her drive away, his face a patchwork of light and shadow.

She straightened forward in her seat and drove slowly away.

A damned shame.

At home, she went through her ritual—mail, robe and a final glass of wine, curled up on the couch, magazine again in her lap, and again unread as she slipped into memories of the evening.

It was late when the phone rang. She jumped for it, heart racing.

"So you're finally home." Sam's easy voice came over the wire. "Where've you been?"

Her heart slowed back to some semblance of normal. Of course it wouldn't have been Jack Turner. With an irritated shake of her head, she jerked herself firmly back to reality and carried the phone base to the end of its long cord and curled up by her wine again. Untouched, she noticed. She really had gone off into fantasyland. "What's up, Sam?"

"Oh, nothing much." His voice was overly casual and she knew it was big news. "The M.E. caught me as I was checking out for the night."

"And?"

"He wants to see us first thing in the morning. It looks like Catherine Fletcher might've committed suicide, Katie. It doesn't look like a murder case after all."

14

Kate's alarm went off before dawn. The M.E. had given Sam no specific information. He'd simply stated a time for them both to be at his office in Harborview Medical Center. She dressed in slacks and warm blazer, shouldered her gun, and headed out for the meeting.

With dawn just topping the Cascades in her rearview mirror, Kate drove across Lake Washington to Seattle. The 520 bridge was empty of traffic and the lake waters spread still and dark around her. As she swung up over the bridge's high-rise and onto Interstate 5, the rising sun's rays from behind her reflected a rosy pink ahead of her against the tower windows of Seattle's skyline. The first of the ferries was coming in from one of the several islands out in the Sound, looking from this distance like a fat white duck contentedly drifting through the still black waters. It was at moments like this that she loved the city passionately.

She took the exit that led to the Capitol Hill District, negotiated the steep city streets up to Ninth Avenue and parked easily in a half-empty lot. Sam pulled in behind her before she'd climbed out, and they walked down to the building together.

The M.E. had coffee waiting for them, and was bright and cheerful as he shoved stacks of file folders around to make room for them to pull a couple of side chairs up to his desk. "Nice time of day," he said, as he fussed over the coffee. "Night stiffs are in, day stiffs aren't dead yet. The in-between hour. Cream or sugar?"

Both detectives shook their heads.

"I take my energy where I can find it." He loaded his cup with both. That settled, he fussed then through still another pile of file folders, checking tab labels, until he pulled one free. "Knew it was here somewhere," he muttered. He adjusted his bifocals, scanned the sheets stapled to the top, nodding as he read. "Yes, yes, um-hum, um-hum, mmmm." Finally he peered up at them. "Yes, all right then. The Fletcher report. All done except the various toxicity tests that'll take a while yet." He began to grin. "Looks like our gal has caused you a lot of unnecessary work, Katie."

The two detectives had worked with him before. He'd been known to lash out and turn the toughest cops into mush if anyone had done more than lift a dead wrist to feel for a pulse. But once away from a body, he was a cheerful little man who got his kicks from coming up with the unexpected, then watching the reaction around him.

His grin broadened. "Catherine Fletcher was eaten alive with cancer."

Both detectives stared at him.

The M.E. nodded, his button eyes snapping with good humor. "Sad, but true. We found the first of it in the liver. Just a single spot. Then we went hunting. The primary site was the brain. Tumor as big as your fist. And nasty. Real nasty. That's the one that would've killed her."

Kate yanked her notebook from her purse, and took rapid notes as the M.E. talked.

"I'll skip the technical jargon for you," the M.E. said, "but the primary tumor was what you'd call a silent tumor. It was eating its way into the silent parts of the brain. It's a particularly virulent form of cancer. I'm sure you've heard of cases where someone complains about a headache and six weeks later they're dead. This kind is the cause. Once the first symptom sets in, it goes quick. Of course, that's a horrendous six weeks you put in until you do die. Not pleasant at all. Not at all."

Mentally, Kate measured this knowledge against some of the strange facts of the case. "Would she be aware of it? Had any of the symptoms set in yet?"

The M.E. leaned back in the chair and studied the ceiling for a moment. "Could be. Could be. There's a couple of ways she could've known. First, some people are more sensitive to their body than others. Often, you'll see people who are really sick but who keep slogging right along, not even realizing it. At the other extreme, you see people who take to their deathbeds every time they sneeze. Some people are just more sensitive to their systems being out of whack than others. There's no telling with the Fletcher woman, but she might've been experiencing an occasional bout of nausea from the cancer. So, *if* she was the kind to run to her doctor over every little thing, and *if* he was any good at his medical witchcraftery, and *if* there was some distinctive symptomatology to be seen, then he *might've* found it. Lots of ifs, there. That's the first way. The other would be a routine physical within the last few weeks. That might've shown it up, too."

"How?" Sam asked.

"Anomalies in the blood test. Pressure on the eyeballs. Stiffness or minor pain in the neck."

Kate turned to Sam. "The day we were quizzing the partners in the studio the day Catherine was found, didn't one of them say something about her complaining of a stiff neck?"

He nodded. "They blamed it on her arthritis. Or she had, and they were repeating it. I don't remember which."

"She had plenty of that, too," the M.E. said. "Most of her joints were involved. She was taking aspirin by the fistful for it—her blood's as thin as chicken broth and her stomach lining's as irritated as a bumped shark. But that would argue against her knowing about the cancer, since the aspirin would help mask any pain she might've had."

"Is there any way you can identify the symptoms the cancer would've caused?" Kate asked.

"If she'd lived, you mean? What she would've experienced? Well, the tumor was edging just around the outside perimeter of the pain center, so in the near future, she'd have started having headaches. Violent headaches. She'd have had some problems with balance, a lack of coordination, staggering, that sort of thing. There'd be nausea and vomiting, followed by dehydration, and finally, death. Which, by that time, she'd welcome."

"If it had been discovered before she died, what would the treatment have been? Chemo? Surgery? Radiation?"

"None of the above. Nothing. It was inoperable and untreatable. However, the medical profession never says never until the patient reaches my grisly little second home here, so they might've tried chemo or radiation, just to be doing something. And maybe, one chance in a million, it might've shrunk it a little. But if she was smart, she'd have skipped the treatments, made out her will and simply medicated the symptoms. But don't take my word for it," he warned. "I can only help so far. Oncology is a field where advances are reported almost daily now. So my knowledge of cures for cancer is from the Dark Ages. Hell, my knowledge of cures for *anything* is from the Dark Ages. They come to me after all else fails."

"If she did know, would suicide be indicated?"

"That depends upon her personality and temperament. Some people cling to life. Some welcome death. And by the way, one last detail, just to clean up the record. Your gal was a boozer. A heavy boozer. Which also would've helped mask her symptoms. Alcohol acts as a painkiller. So the bottom line is this: If the morphine hadn't gotten her, the cancer would've, and if the cancer hadn't gotten her, the booze would've. Lesion aside, the liver had about had it."

Kate's thoughts were still trying to fit the cancer into the overall picture. "You said if you'd have been the doctor, you'd have just treated her symptoms. What would you have given her?"

"Suppositories to suppress the vomiting, a stiff painkiller—"

"Morphine," Kate said.

"You got it. Morphine." He finished his coffee and stood up, not much taller standing than Kate sitting on his hard side chair. He bustled around, refilling their cups, his tubby little body moving with quick spurts of energy. "I can only tell you this. She had a particularly virulent form of cancer that's basically untreatable, but she actually died from a massive overdose of morphine."

"Yes," Kate said slowly, "but *did* she take it herself, or didn't she?"

"That seems to be the big question, isn't it?" the M.E. answered cheerfully.

Seattle was wide awake and hustling by the time they left Harborview. Cars poured off the ferries. Buses roared down Fourth Street. Trucks fought commuter clog to back into loading docks. Pedestrians thronged the sidewalks at full stride, coats tossed open to the early-morning sun streaming over Capitol Hill. Awnings were being lowered on some of the older shops. Even the winos were out and about.

Sam knew of a little café down on Western Avenue, across the street from a small park overlooking the waterfront one block below, and Kate followed him in her car for some breakfast. The place was jammed with workers dressed in three-piece suits headed for a long day at their personal coal mines, wolfing down homemade muffins and gulping down cups of gourmet coffee, and they had to wait their turn for an open spot. At last they were shown to a back booth and handed menus. Kate's favorite meal of the day was breakfast, and as she combed the columns of egg dishes and muffins and gourmet coffees listed, she groaned to Sam, "I'll take one of everything."

She finally chose scrambled eggs and cranberry muffins, but stuck with the house coffee. Gourmet was for lingering over, not wolfing down. After they'd placed their orders, she sat quietly for a while, idly stirring her coffee as she did some people-watching. Eventually, though, the bright colors and sounds of a city on the move faded into a background hum and her thoughts turned back to the case.

Finally she set her spoon down, sighed and settled more comfortably against the well-padded seat. "Well," she asked him, "what's your guess? Suicide or murder?"

Her questions drew his gaze off his own people-watching mission. "Suicide. Without a doubt."

"You sound so sure."

He nodded. "That's because you don't have all the information yet. I learned a lot about Catherine Fletcher yesterday. Just by examining bank accounts. The lady was swiping all the money she could get her hands on and was stockpiling it." He took out his pocket notebook and flipped through the pages until he had the one he wanted. "By my calculations, she helped herself to better than twelve grand from the business alone. Six checks. Two thousand each. One a week for the last six weeks. All in her own handwriting, and all co-signed by Ginger."

"Two thousand a *week?*" Kate stared at him. "*Twelve thousand dollars?* My God, Sam, their business couldn't afford that. Their whole first quarter net was only *four* thousand!"

"Well, afford it or not, that's what she took," Sam said. "And four of those six checks were out of numerical sequence. They came from the back of a checkbook refill the business hasn't started using yet. And it looks like they were never entered into the checkbook, either, because the company checkbook shows eight thousand more balance than the bank does. Worse, checks to printers and office-supply houses have started bouncing. They've already had four sent back in the last couple of days. It's my guess their bookkeeper paid bills last week thinking there were funds in the bank to cover them, not knowing she should subtract eight grand from the balance before she did so."

Kate was silent a moment, awe-struck. "I wonder whether those bounced checks had anything to do with the credit problems Boeing uncovered."

"Probably." Sam shoved the notebook over to make room for the plates of food the waitress brought. "Now here comes the *really* interesting part," he said when they were alone again. "From January on, Catherine Fletcher made no deposits to her personal account at all. She simply went to the business' bank and cashed each of the checks in person. Furthermore, she hasn't paid a single bill in the last ninety days. And she owes bunches. Rent, utilities, credit cards, department stores. Nothing's been paid since the first of January. She was due to lose heat and lights tomorrow, the phone's being cut off on Monday, and the property-management company's already served her with an eviction notice."

Kate chewed a mouthful of scrambled eggs while she mulled it over. "So we have a lady with a deadly illness who quit paying her bills and started saving every dime she could get her hands on. As if she knew she wasn't going to live long. Is that what you're saying?"

"Basically."

"But then how does the happy reconciliation with Vern Riley fit in?" Then it hit. "Uh-oh. Riley. My God, is *he* in a jam. She cleaned him out of all his money, too. It's bad enough for him being dead broke, but he thinks he's at least got a place to live."

"Not for long. He's going to end up out on the street come the weekend." Sam didn't look broken up about it.

"Some reconciliation." Kate shook her head in disbelief. "This lady never quits, does she? She even reaches backward from the grave to pull her dirty tricks." She turned to a fresh page in her own notebook. "Okay, let's add it up. Twelve thousand from the business and fifteen hundred from Riley. That's thirteen thousand, five hundred dollars. And all cash. Where did she stash it?"

Sam cleaned up the last of his pancakes and eggs and poured a refill of coffee for both of them from the carafe left on the table. "That's the other interesting part. Damned if I can find any of it. It appears she only had the one checking account, and that has less than four hundred dollars in it."

"Have you checked the inventory list to see if there's another bankbook among her things? Or a safety-deposit key? A brokerage account? Money-market fund? Anything that might point the way to the hidden loot?"

"Yep. Nothing there. Just the one checkbook that was in her purse. There weren't any papers—period. Not in her purse, not in her condo."

"Her files were cleaned out, too," Kate pointed out. "And her stock certificate's missing from the attorney's."

"She was planning to die," Sam said simply. "It's the only explanation that fits. She was planning to die. And she took the opportunity to settle a few old scores. She drains the business of cash, spreads rumors about credit problems to sabotage the Boeing contract, and not only cons Riley out of fifteen hundred bucks, but puts him in a position where he's going to be tossed out on his ear. She had planned it all to happen this week, the week she died."

Kate thought about it as she finished the last piece of bacon and sat back over the coffee. "But, Sam, why would she go to all the trouble of crushing morphine tablets and doctoring up the tea bags when she could just plunk a few tablets in the cup? And where *is* that morphine anyway?"

He considered it. "Well, we know she had a vengeful streak in her. Maybe she didn't *want* it to look like suicide. Maybe she wanted to bring the cops down on everyone's head. So she crushed what she needed, loaded up the tea bags, and tossed the rest out."

"Boy, I don't know, Sam, that sounds like a hell of a lot of trouble to go to when you're sick like that. Just to get even with somebody? Besides, the lab crew went through her trash when they were searching her condo. They didn't find a thing."

"Yes, but supposing she'd known about this a few weeks ago. She could've fixed up the tea bags and tossed the stuff then. They'd be buried in the garbage dump by now."

She considered it, then slowly shook her head. "I'd sure be a lot happier about all this if we just knew where the morphine came from. I think we ought to at least make an attempt to find the source before we call it a suicide and shut the file drawer on it."

"Sure, Katie, it would be handy to tie up all the loose ends like that. But it's impractical. The Captain's got to be told about this, and when he hears the M.E.'s report, he won't authorize any more manpower. He's going to accept it as suicide. Everything fits. Her temperament, her character, her illness, her actions, her motives. Hell, she could've gone to any doctor in the country, under any name she chose, and gotten a prescription for morphine, and we'd never track it down. No, the Cap's not going to waste any more time on this. Trust me, Katie, he won't."

He was right, she thought, draining the last of her coffee. It would be written up as a suicide. Suicide with a new twist, a mean, vicious twist. Well, at least that provided a single direction to follow. She wouldn't be roaming all over the compass, trying to focus in on some ephemeral killer that didn't exist. There were set things to do now. Inform the Captain. Organize the file for closure. It would have to be held open until the last of the lab and test results came in, but that was a mere formality. The case was over. Done. Finished. Her first one as D.I.C. had been drawn to a successful, if rather obvious, conclusion.

Suicide. It all fit, as Sam said.

Then why was she left with this small doubt nagging away at the back of her mind?

Sam was going to stop at the partners' attorney's office for one last stab at locating the stock certificates. After that, with suicide as the verdict, it would become a civilian matter, and it would be up to the heirs to trace any of Catherine Fletcher's assets. Kate drove back across the bridge, fully swamped by commuter traffic now. Cars were thick in both directions, and she wondered why people just didn't move to the same side of the lake where they worked, and save themselves all this daily frustration. Her car crawled across the bridge and she didn't break free until she reached her turn-off. The ramp was clear, she sped up, then was instantly stopped by gridlock. Her mind climbed up on its soapbox again and it detailed the entire range of injustices road designers had inflicted on her. Personally.

A packet from Nordstrom's was waiting for her when she finally arrived at her desk. She quickly checked through the copies they'd sent of the Riley account. At the time of Becky's pregnancy, Catherine had run up over three thousand dollars in charges. *None* of them made in the infant's or maternity-clothing departments. All the charges were for women's clothes and jewelry. Riley had been taken to the cleaners on that one. And so much for Catherine's claim about helping her daughter. The things it would never occur to me to do, Kate thought to herself.

Before taking the file in to talk to the Captain, she placed a call to Catherine's doctor. He was in with a patient and would have to call her back. But her call was a formality. On the drive back across the bridge, she'd decided that Sam was right in calling it a suicide. After all, the lady had quit paying bills in January. She had been stockpiling cash. She seemed to have lost interest in her own business. She'd invited Riley back to live with her again. All the actions of a woman who know's she's dying, knows she's going to need money, and knows she's going to need someone to care for her at the end. It was a hundred to one the lady knew she was fatally ill.

Kate's imagination ran on. The pain had started and Catherine had received some morphine for it, but it was more pain than she was willing to bear and she'd decided to end it all before it got worse. That was it. The wind-up. Case closed.

Kate sat back in her chair. Confirm it with the doctor, fill out the reports, and she'd be done. Suicide. It was official.

But when the doctor returned her call, he sent that neat and tidy conclusion skittering. No, Catherine had not had cancer. Arthritis, yes. Flu and colds, yes. But cancer? No.

He'd last seen Catherine during the first week in January for her arthritis. The winter dampness had increased her discomfort, her joints were more swollen than normal, and he'd prescribed aspirin with codeine for stronger relief. She hadn't been back since. He assumed the change in medicine had helped. No, he hadn't given her an extensive examination, and no, she hadn't complained about any other problems. No nausea, no headaches, no balance or coordination problems. Nothing suspicious. Just joint pain.

Kate took him over her medical history, but nothing pertinent turned up. Cancer had not been diagnosed, or even suspected. And no, no referral to another doctor had been made. And absolutely no, he had *not* given her a prescription for morphine!

She'd hung up, deflated. If Catherine didn't know she had cancer, why would she commit suicide?

She wouldn't.

Damn, thought Kate.

Her phone rang. "MacLean."

"George Leffick, Katie." The officer's voice boomed at her. "I'm out at that graphics studio in Bellevue. You'd better get on over here. We got another dead body on our hands."

15

Ginger's body was folded over her drawing board. Her cheek rested in the crook of her left arm. Her right hand lay opened flat next to her face. The long brown hair had fanned across one cheek and her legs hung slack from the high stool several inches above the floor. A sketching pencil had rolled off the board and lay next to the foot of the stool. She looked asleep. It was the concrete-white stillness that made it more.

Face grim, Kate nodded a silent greeting to Phyllis huddled in the chair at her desk, surveying the body for a long moment, then moved to Leffick's side.

He kept his voice low for a change. "She"—he indicated Phyllis—"says she came in, found her like this, and called the nine-one-one number. The aid car arrived the same time I did, took one look and called the M.E.'s office. She's been dead awhile, she's ice-cold."

"And the lab? They been called yet?"

"Yeah, right after I called you."

"Okay. Sam's out, but they're patching through to him. Chase the curious back into their offices, will you, George? They're lining the hallways downstairs."

Kate moved over to the body to examine it more closely. A clamp-on lamp arched high above the board and spilled light over the head below, creating red glints among the deeper brown of the hair. Edges of a sheet of sketching paper protruded all the way around the head like a paper doily, but the actual design she'd been working on was hidden by the face. A long narrow table next to the board held a variety of art supplies—brushes, pens, pencils, several widths of tape, X-acto knives, stylus, whetstone, glue stick and an assortment of erasers. Among the supplies, within easy reach of the artist, was a Coke-sized paper cup. A few drops of golden liquid remained. Kate leaned forward and sniffed. Ginger ale.

She straightened and turned to survey Phyllis. The woman hadn't moved from her huddled position. Her face was gray and old, her mouth pressed into a taut line, her eyes flat and glazed. They were fixed at a point on her own desktop, as if by not looking around she could will this all not to be.

Kate swung a chair into position across the desk from Phyllis. "Do you want some water?"

The answer was barely audible. "No." She answered without looking up.

Kate studied her a moment, gauging the amount of strength left in the woman. "Tell me about it," she said softly.

"She was like that when I came in."

"What time was that?"

"I don't know. I didn't notice."

"Can you take a guess?"

"A while ago." The answers were slow in coming, flat and lifeless when they finally arrived. Like the spaced-out sputter of a dying engine.

"Was the door locked when you got here?"

"Yes."

"Were the lights on?"

"Just hers."

"But they're on now. The overheads."

For the first time, Phyllis raised her head to look at Kate. She frowned. "I must've turned them on. I don't remember. They weren't on when I got here."

"How can you be so sure?"

"Because Gin—" She stumbled over the name, not wanting to say it. "It was like a spotlight on her. Her light."

Kate rose and switched off the overheads. The dawn's early promise of a clear day had failed and a thick cloud cover had moved into the area. With the heavy gray sky overhead and no ceiling lights on, the studio turned into a dusky cavern. The pool of light pouring from the clamp lamp spotlighted the dead girl's head and arm. Kate nodded, switched the overheads back on and returned to her chair. "Okay. When was the last time you saw her?"

"I don't know, I can't think . . ."

"Let me help. Yesterday you stopped by to see me . . ."

Phyllis nodded. "Yes. I spent the morning at Boeing, stopped to see you, then I went on home. No. I had lunch first, then I went home. I remember now. I was planning to come in here to work, but I suddenly felt exhausted at lunch. Just plain worn out all the way through. So I went home. You called and talked to me there."

"Right. Did you go out again?"

"No. I took a hot bath and curled up in my robe." Color was returning to her face and it was losing some of its frozen quality. Her voice was also regaining some expression, too, Kate noted with relief. A collapse seemed to have been averted for the moment.

"And this morning?"

"I had to stop by the bookkeeper's. She called me at home last night. A couple of our checks bounced. Checks to some printers."

"Did you find out why?"

"No. The bookkeeper had looked for an error, but couldn't find one. All the deposits tallied, and the addition and subtraction was correct. We should've had over a thousand dollars left in the account after those checks cleared, but the bank said no. So she wanted me to double-check her books. Which I did. Then we called the bank to order out a special statement and I came on here."

Kate debated a second whether to tell her about the checks Catherine had written from the back of a refill checkbook, then decided against it. "So you didn't see Ginger earlier today."

"No."

"Or anytime yesterday."

"No."

"The last time was the day before?"

"Yes. When we were all here . . . when Catherine . . . was found."
Suddenly she blinked and looked around, her cheeks flooding a
fierce red. "My God!" she whispered, "what the hell's going on
here anyway!"

Good, Kate thought. We need you angry and responsive.
"What project was Ginger working on, do you know?"

The color stayed high. Phyllis frowned, her mind working at
full speed again. "A brochure design, I think. At least, that was
next on her production schedule."

"And where did she get her drink? Ginger ale, wasn't it?"

"Yes. That's all she ever drank. Except for some coffee now and
then. She must've gotten it from the refrigerator."

Startled, Kate looked around the room. "What refrigerator?"

"The one downstairs."

Kate went cold. "What refrigerator downstairs?" she demanded.

"There's a lunchroom for the tenants at the back of the second
floor. There's a refrigerator there."

"And Ginger kept her ginger ale there?"

Phyllis nodded.

"Show me."

Phyllis led the way. In the hall, Kate paused at Leffick's side
and jerked her head toward the doorway. "No one in or out."

The two women clattered down two flights of uncarpeted
stairway. A large room at the rear of the second floor had been
converted into a shabby lunchroom, furnished with two cheap
dinette sets, a battered candy-vending machine, and a long
linoleum-covered counter set on top of scarred base cupboards.
The refrigerator was as old and beaten as the rest of the
furnishings; it was a discolored white, squat, with rounded
shoulders.

There wasn't a hope of getting any meaningful fingerprints,
but Kate grabbed a paper towel from a wall dispenser and used it
anyway to open the door. A couple of lunch bags were set on the
top shelf. An apple and an opened jar of sweet pickles were on

the next one down, and an assortment of canned drinks spread across the bottom. An inner freezer contained ice-cube trays and a single Eskimo Pie. The door shelves held a sixteen-ounce bottle of ginger ale, partially empty.

Kate backed away. "Without touching anything, tell me who owns what."

Phyllis leaned forward. She immediately pointed to the ginger-ale bottle. "That's Ginger's. The three cans of Pepsi on the bottom shelf are mine. The rest I don't know about. The pickles aren't ours. Neither is the apple or the lunch bags."

"Is there anything missing?"

She peered closer. "Just the wine. Suzie usually kept a bottle of white wine in here. She must've run out."

The cold that had grabbed Kate upstairs at the initial mention of the refrigerator turned to icy dread. With an effort, she kept her voice even. "Okay, here's what I want you to do. I want you to go to the foot of the stairs and call up to Officer Leffick and ask him to come down here immediately."

She walked to the doorway and watched as Phyllis followed orders. When Leffick came down, Kate beckoned him over, keeping Phyllis in view all the while. "Watch this room, George. Don't let anyone in until the lab boys can get to it." She moved to where Phyllis waited. "Let's go back up."

Her stomach was sick with fear as they climbed back up. Stomach, hell! Her whole body was sick with fear from head to toe, and it had settled over her soul like a cold cloak from the grave. "Does the conference room have a phone?"

Ahead of her on the stairs, Phyllis shook her head.

They had no choice then but to go back into the studio. Phyllis hung back at the doorway for a second, then she took a deep breath and entered, averting her gaze from the body slumped over the drawing board. Some of the earlier dullness was back as she took her seat at her desk once again. She obviously hadn't connected the missing wine with the deadly ginger ale yet.

Kate dug in her purse for her notebook, found Suzie's number and used one of the phones to place the call. She let it ring a dozen times or better before reluctantly disconnecting. She stared at the other woman, debating what to say. Where the hell was Sam anyway? Finally she sighed. "Suzie's married, isn't she?"

Phyllis nodded.

"What does her husband do?"

"He's a sales rep for a telecommunications company."

"How big's his territory? Does he travel a lot?"

"Every week. He's got the whole Pacific Northwest and Alaska."

"Today's Thursday. He would've left Monday?"

Phyllis nodded. "Why? What's he got to do . . . ?" Her fact went white. "No! You can't think Suzie's . . ."

"Let's not speculate just yet." Kate kept her face and voice calm. "Where do they live?"

"On Queen Anne Hill in Seattle."

"Let me have her address."

With panicky motions, Phyllis searched among papers on her desk and pulled out her address book. She found the page and turned it toward Kate.

"Now I need a Seattle phone book."

Wordlessly, Phyllis moved to a bookcase and returned with it.

Kate found the number of the Seattle Police Department and placed the call. She was put through to the commander in charge. She explained the situation as Phyllis' face went from white to gray, received assurances they'd act on it immediately and gave the studio's number to call as soon as they knew anything.

She replaced the receiver. "All we can do now is wait. How do I get this off the answering service?"

Phyllis punched in a number, then resumed her seat, her hands folded in her lap, her head bowed as if in prayer.

The building was silent around them. Tenants had been shooed back into their offices. George was on guard two floors below. The ambulance attendants were lounging outside, waiting for the M.E. to arrive and get through. Overhead, charcoal clouds thick with rain displaced the dull gray and the first drops splattered onto the skylights. But the studio was removed from it all, isolated and insulated, a cavern empty of sound. It was as if no life existed here, as if no life *could* exist here. It was as if the living were dead, too, taken forever from the everyday world around them and sequestered in an antechamber of death.

Then the technical personnel arrived and the spell was broken. Half of the lab crew went down to the lunchroom two floors below while the others began to work in the studio, and the room was suddenly filled with a quiet activity.

The M.E. arrived and examined the body. He pushed up one eyelid on the dead girl, took a look at the pupil shrunken to a pinpoint and nodded to Kate. The message was clear. Morphine, again. A photographer angled in on the drawing board.

When the M.E. finally ordered up the gurney, Kate took Phyllis into the small conference room while the body was taken away. Phyllis turned her head away as the black body bag was rolled through the echoing hallway.

The phone rang twice and each time a member of the lab crew took a business message for the studio. The third call was for Kate.

She guided Phyllis back to her desk, sat her down, moved across the room to an available phone and answered the call. She listened, asked a few quiet questions, and listened some more. She slowly replaced the receiver.

Heartsick, she looked over at Phyllis, who was staring once again at her desktop. Kate moved to the chair still across the desk from where the silent woman waited and sank down into it. "Phyllis?"

Slowly, Phyllis raised a face filled with dread.

"They found her," Kate said softly. "They found Suzie. Next to a glass of white wine. I'm sorry, Phyllis, but Suzie's dead, too."

A cheek muscle clenched, then Phyllis's face fell into pinched, bleak lines and terror edged into her eyes.

16

Sea-Tac Airport was south of Seattle and north of Tacoma, splitting the thirty miles or so of distance between the two cities. The terminal was well-designed, with the main building curving around the parking garage and two satellite concourses at the points, reached by underground shuttle. Sam and Kate stopped for a late supper at a coffee shop near the airport, then went to meet the first plane.

It was getting on toward the end of the evening, and the airport was quieting down as the flights for the day began to taper off. Ginger's husband would be the first of the two husbands coming in, and the agent for his airline showed them the room they would be using for their meeting. It was a small employees' lounge, quiet and well-removed from the main traffic areas, with a coffeepot and some overstuffed chairs. They approved it, then walked down the concourse to wait for the flight to land.

The waiting room had a few hardy souls spread around, some dozing, some reading, some just sitting, staring off into space. It seemed to be the only flight left to land on that concourse, and the stillness was noticeable. Only an occasional echo of footsteps broke the eerie silence of the empty waiting rooms around them. Kate wandered to a window, staring out at the mechanical service area gleaming beneath the strong airport lights. The concrete glistened a wet blackish-gray from the drizzle still falling, and somehow it reflected what she felt. She was tired, she knew, the day had been long, and airports at night were lonely places to be. But she was sinking fast into a depression and was doing what she could to stave it off, without much success.

She knew what it stemmed from. The last few hours had been filled with tension and unending battles. Her first battle had been with the media. When she'd finally gotten a top-to-bottom search of the office building organized, she'd discovered the parking lot was overrun by reporters.

Some were badgering the patrol cops for information. Others stood back, taking notes on the general scene. TV and radio stations had their mobile units there, and one TV reporter was already standing with her back to the building, talking to the camera, her raincoat belted around her waist and the collar standing up around her neck, looking like a spy in a trench coat.

Somehow they'd gotten Kate's name as the D.I.C. and when they saw her car and recognized her through the drizzle dribbling down the windshield, they deserted the patrol cops like a pack of greyhounds making a sudden U-turn in the middle of a racetrack. Face grim, she pressed the automatic door lock, then edged the car forward, keeping up a slow, unyielding pressure on the pack of them until finally the last body gave way and she broke free. She sped up and raced away.

The murders made the noon newscasts and all hell broke loose. Through the windshield of her car, a TV camera had caught a clear image of her and the car inching forward, lips pressed tight in a forbidding line in an effort to avoid running over a few reporters. But on air, it looked as if she were avoiding their questions, not their bodies. The voice-over increased that perception. It stated that the police were refusing to make any statements to the press. The news spot upset the brass beyond belief. She was ordered in no uncertain terms to funnel all media inquiries upstairs.

In addition to that, the press had gotten the victims' names from someone, and one station—just one, she thought, with disgust—had gone ahead and aired them both, not bothering to observe the time-honored practice of withholding names until the families had been notified. Suddenly she found herself racing against time to locate the husbands of the victims before they heard the news from an impersonal broadcast announcer.

Suzie's husband was tracked down in Wyoming by his company offices, and Ginger's husband was located at a dental conference in Phoenix. Kate had to break the news to them over the phone. Ginger's husband went dead silent on the line, then breathed out a single "God *damn* it!" Suzie's husband broke down and wept. Kate did what she could to answer their questions, but there wasn't much she could tell them. Death was such a random thief, stealing in and taking lives, turning worlds upside down for those left behind. Especially sudden death. Especially sudden death by murder. The sheer haphazardness of it made it even more difficult to accept. She did what she could for them, but it was woefully little. They would arrive at Sea-Tac late that night, about an hour apart, and she assured them that she'd meet them there to answer any further questions they might have. She then called the airlines and arranged for the private room to be set aside.

During the period she was trying to locate the husbands, Riley had gotten through to her between calls, demanding protection from "that fucking killer out to get us all." It had taken a good twenty minutes to calm him down.

She still had to detail teams to scour the backgrounds of the building owner and the janitor. They were the only two people, outside of the partners, who'd had keys to the graphics studio. It was a lead that wasn't promising, but couldn't be overlooked. Just on the off-chance . . .

And with the luck of the draw, she'd drawn her old partner, Goddard, as her backup team. He was barely civil toward her under the best of circumstances, and he turned sulky at having to take orders from her. His new partner, Fry, stood in the background, not saying a word, watching her from the shadows like a skulking Peeping Tom, as he always did. She kept her voice even, her gaze steady, as she calmly handed them their assignment, not allowing herself to be intimidated by Goddard's surly glances nor Fry's crafty manner.

After getting those two off her hands, she'd tracked Brillo down over in Narcotics, and asked him to do a snitch survey for a possible street source for the morphine. Something was going down in his world, and he was on a short fuse with everyone. But she held her ground and had finally just received his promise of help when she was called into the Captain's office.

The Captain had been ordered upstairs for a big brass conference, which meant that he had to summarize the case for them, which meant that she had to justify to him why she hadn't arrested Phyllis Walsh on the spot. He greeted each of her explanations with growing disbelief, which made her feel stupid and incompetent.

The first thing she had to defend was her decision to send Phyllis home in a squad car, the cop ordered to stay with her until her husband could get there. It was futile to tell him that the woman was in shock, on the edge of collapse, virtually unable to talk. That it would've been pointless to bring her in for a statement until she'd had time to recover some composure at least. That with a night's sleep, sedated or not, behind her, they stood a much better chance of getting more information and better cooperation from her in the morning.

On top of that, she had to tell him she hadn't had Phyllis' residence searched yet, though the paperwork for a search warrant was underway, thanks to Sam. The morphine had been planted in the wine and ginger ale at least twenty-four hours earlier. Plenty of time to get rid of any extra. Every dumpster in the Pacific Northwest was open to a quick drive-by and a casual toss of a hot prescription bottle. His disbelief reached new heights of incredulity.

And then she had to tell him that with the two new deaths, Phyllis was the sole surviving beneficiary of *three* life insurance policies totaling *three* hundred thousand dollars. That did it. A bitter feud with one well-insured victim, a business on the brink of failure, and the two other well-insured partners now dead?

His glower had deepened into pure blackness and he'd roared, *"That isn't enough motive for you?! Jesus Christ, Katie . . . !"*

He no sooner got the words out when an assistant D.A. showed up and involved *himself* in the mess. He was young, ambitious, cold and on the edge of rude. In front of the Captain, he grilled her again on her handling of the case, his raised eyebrows implicitly criticizing her for every aspect of the investigation, from the way she'd handled the taking of statements to the kind of questions she'd asked or not asked. When he learned of the business feud and the insurance moneys, he decided they had plenty of evidence to take Phyllis Walsh to arraignment and wanted a warrant for her arrest issued.

She kept telling him he was jumping too quick, that there was no hard evidence of Phyllis' guilt yet, but he wouldn't listen. She kept telling him that they needed the source of the morphine, but he wouldn't listen to that either. He interrupted her and argued with everything she said, belittled the importance of finding the "smoking gun" and ordered her to file charges.

Up until then, the Captain had sat back and watched the two of them battle. But when the prosecutor started pushing her around verbally, Hatch suddenly turned on him. "If *my* D.I.C. says the case isn't ready, the case isn't *ready!* And if *she* says we need to find the goddamned morphine, then we need to find the goddamned *morphine!* Now fuck off!" By then he was on his feet, looming over the slightly built prosecutor. His face was blood-red and his eyes blood-hot. *He* could ream his people out. But no one *else* had better damned well do it.

Hatch's look alone was enough to chase the prosecutor out of there. Never mind the words. When the door to his office slammed shut, Hatch plunked back down in his chair, dropped his head and peered up at Kate from beneath the shrubbery of his fierce eyebrows. "You just better be damned sure you know what you're doing," he'd growled.

The only good thing she could remember about the whole day was Sam's support of her. He'd handled the crime scene at Suzie's house with the Seattle Police for her. He'd backed her with the Captain. He'd started some of the paperwork in regards to the new murders. And in mid-afternoon, when he learned she hadn't had any lunch yet, he'd brought her a cheeseburger. He'd even remembered the raw onions.

Sighing, she leaned her forehead against the cold glass of the terminal windowpane, as she used to do as a kid peering out her bedroom window into the night. Her grown-up reflection stared back at her. She looked so composed, so calm, so in charge. But inside, she felt panicked and frightened and weak. What if the killer really *was* Phyllis Walsh? Was she condemning more people to death by holding off arresting Phyllis until the morphine source was located?

If only she knew what else the killer had in mind. There he was, standing back in the shadows, biding his time, knowing the cops were a step behind, and his next move already planned, she was sure. Possibly already set in motion. And the next and the next and the next? How many would be enough for him? How many dead bodies did it take to suffice? How many more before he'd fulfilled his perverted agenda?

A terrible sense of doom swept over her. She felt besieged and beleaguered, by a killer on the outside and the big cheese on the inside. How could she battle both?

And what if she was wrong?!

She focused back on her reflection and was startled to see a second head next to hers in the glass. Soundlessly, Sam had joined her and now stood beside her, his good, solid body a strong contrast to her slender one. For a moment, they stared at each other through their reflections. With a gentle hand, he reached out and smoothed a curl back from her shoulder. Just the touch was enough to give her comfort. For a moment, she was tempted to lean against the reliable strength of him. Instead, she patted the back of his hand resting on her shoulder, and gave him a sad, lonely smile. Then she turned around to face the too-bright lights on the concourse and the plane just drawing up to the gate.

Don Burklund was a tall, thin, mild-mannered man, and seemed calm and steady enough. As a dentist, he was used to dealing with people in pain, but he did appear baffled by the shift in roles, where now he was the one suffering. But the reality hadn't fully hit him yet, so there was a detachment to his grief that left him with some measure of composure.

When the detectives met him at the page desk and introduced themselves and offered the private room in which to talk, he glanced at his watch and refused, indicating a vacant waiting room off the concourse. "I need to get to the children as soon as I can. They don't know yet." He led them to a corner grouping of seats, very much in charge. Kate suspected that he'd done the leading in his marriage to Ginger, too.

When they were all seated, he still assumed charge. "Exactly how may I help you?"

Kate began with questions about his weekend.

He'd left early Friday morning for a dental conference in Phoenix. He displayed his airline ticket for them to see. His days and nights in Phoenix since landing had been involved with the conference, starting with early breakfast meetings and concluding with late-evening nightcaps. He provided them with a list of people he'd spent his time with. He was so detailed and exacting in accounting for his time, referring to his pocket secretary only once, that it was impossible to disbelieve him. His whereabouts, if confirmed—and Kate had no reason to suspect they wouldn't be—would eliminate him as a suspect.

Unless . . . There was only one outside chance he could be involved with the murders. He'd have had to return to Seattle after the last nightcap, with a turnaround time that would allow him to appear back in Phoenix in time for breakfast. Even with a chartered jet, the logistics of that seemed doubtful. He was a dentist, though, which gave him access to painkillers, and so Kate made a note to check out Friday-, Saturday- and Sunday-night charters.

When the questions veered toward his marriage to Ginger, he took his time, giving them thorough answers. He'd had a lot of mixed feelings about the setting up of the graphics studio. He'd been in favor of it when he'd originally given Ginger his permission to go into business with the other three women, but now, frankly, he wasn't satisfied with the manner in which the business was being run. Not in any way. From the remarks that Ginger made at home, there seemed to be a complete lack of any businesslike approach to corporate finances. Catherine Fletcher appeared to be manipulating his wife unmercifully, and as far as he was concerned, the business would've been better off without her. Suzie he dismissed as a lightweight, cute, but with no backbone. The only partner he seemed to have any confidence in at all was Phyllis Walsh, and even that confidence was tenuous, given the fact that after each confrontation, Catherine still did pretty much what she wanted to do. But he'd loved his wife dearly, and would've done anything—and did do anything, including fixing dinners most nights, he pointed out—to make her happy.

Kate made a note of his permission being needed, then underlined it in heavy black. The day she needed permission from a husband to do *anything* would be the day she'd serve a plateful of spaghetti dumped upside down in his lap and divorce papers slapped across his forehead. "Dr. Burklund, what kind of painkillers do you keep in your office?"

He listed the drugs, including samples garnered from pharmaceutical reps, automatically spelling each chemical name for her. No, he kept no morphine on hand, and he didn't think any of the drugs he did use contained it, though he couldn't be sure. She made a note to have Homer go over the list. He'd know.

Before she could frame her next question, he ended the interview by suddenly rising. "I'm sorry, that's all the time I can spare. I must get home to the children." He glanced at his watch, gave each of them a brief nod and walked off.

Amazed by his abrupt high-handedness, Kate sat back in the chair and watched him stride away. A controlling man. Very controlling.

Johnny Plummer was anything but controlled and in charge. A plumpish man, his round face was creased with lines of grief, and his eyes were reddened, watery and swollen. They led him to the private lounge where he sank onto the edge of a chair and sat motionless, legs apart, hands clasped and hanging limply between his knees. Numbly, he refused coffee and looked up at them, waiting for their questions like a school kid waiting for the teacher to begin.

Kate watched him carefully as she took him through his travel schedule and whereabouts of the past few days. As he talked, now and then his eyes teared up and his voice trailed off, and he'd forget what he was saying as a tragic disbelief washed over his face.

As grief-stricken as he appeared to be, though, his schedule left him on the list of possibles. He'd been home all weekend. He hadn't left to travel his territory until early Monday morning, which gave him Saturday and Sunday to plant the tea bags and spike the wine and ginger ale.

Except for the hours she'd worked on Saturday at the studio, the weekend had been spent with Suzie. They hadn't done anything special, a few ins and outs to run some domestic errands. No, they hadn't seen anyone— Oh, a couple of neighbors now and then, but nothing more than a back-fence visit— and they hadn't eaten out. Traveling as much as he did, he preferred staying in when he was home.

Kate made careful notes of the events and times he mentioned, then began probing into his relationship with the business partners. She asked the questions in every way she could think of, but could not establish any close contact between them and himself. He'd stayed completely out of the business, except for occasional counsel and advice when called upon by his wife. She moved on to the next area of questioning.

On the whole, he'd gotten through the questions up to that point fairly dry-eyed. But when she began to explore his marriage, he completely fell apart. They'd all been sitting on the edges of their chairs, leaning forward in a semicircle, and at the very first question of a personal nature his face crumpled, he laid his head down on a forearm spread on top of the arm of the chair and he wept. Kate was sitting across from him, facing him. She gave him a moment or two to bring himself under control, but when the weeping went on, he was so obviously lost that she couldn't stand it anymore. She moved to the chair next to him and patted the hunched-over shoulder, not knowing what else to do.

Twice he tried to stop. The weeping would slow, he'd gulp back the next few sobs, raise his head, tears cascading down his cheeks, and whisper a shameful apology. Before he could get the words out, though, a fresh wave of grief would overtake him, and he'd simply shake his head helplessly and weep some more. Kate kept rubbing her hand in gentle circles along the plump shoulder blades just to provide him with some human contact.

When Plummer finally ran dry and the sobs slowed of their own course, he pulled out an already dampened handkerchief and blew a honk a goose would envy. Shamefaced, he looked from one detective to the other, sniffing. "I'm sorry, I—I just don't know what I'm going to do, how I'm going to manage without her. . . She meant so much to me . . . We never had kids, you know . . . There's nothing left of her anywhere . . . and she was such a—a *joy* to me . . . Even when we weren't doing anything special, just *being* with her was—*privileged*, know what I mean . . . ?"

He stumbled on, trying to get out all the tumultuous thoughts and feelings welling up all at once. They came out in fragments, in word sketches, in memories that tumbled one into another until it was impossible to separate any of it into rational order. But they let him go on, listening closely, until the top layer of grief emptied out and he'd worn himself down. When he finally fell silent, he slumped back into the chair, exhausted.

There was no point in putting him through more. They'd learned all they were going to learn for now. Kate exchanged a quick glance with Sam, interpreted his slight nod as agreement, and finally released Plummer to go on his mournful way. Mopping his eyes dry with the handkerchief, he mumbled a final apology and left the room, his shoulders slumped, his footsteps slow and heavy, subdued by what lay ahead. He was like a balloon gone soft.

They followed him out onto the empty and silent concourse and stood watching him shuffle out of sight.

The 405 heading north wasn't bad at that time of night. With Sam driving, Kate stared sightlessly out at the black night whizzing past. The depression was mushrooming inside of her again and she was too tired to fight it any longer. They made the trip in silence.

They'd left her car at headquarters for the trip to the airport, and Sam pulled into an empty space next to it. She'd parked at the rear of the well-lit parking lot, in front of a grove of trees. It was isolated and quiet there, rather shadowy and private. After a moment's hesitation, he turned off the ignition and shifted in his seat to face her. The overhanging tree branches just leafing out patched his face with shadows. "You all right, Katie?"

She didn't answer him. Her hands were folded in her lap, and she stared down at them.

Slowly, he reached out and lifted her chin and swiveled her head gently his way. The intensity of his gaze forced her eyes to meet his. "Johnny Plummer?"

She gave a reluctant nod. "The pain . . . his pain . . . oh, God, Sam, three women dead. It's such a waste. Such a senseless, stupid waste." She turned away from him so he wouldn't see the tears that were suddenly overwhelming her.

He wouldn't let her hide from him. He turned her face back again and dried an escaping tear with a gentle forefinger.

She searched the darkened eyes for some hint of censure. There was none she could see. Only deep pools of warm brown set in deeper pools of shadow. Finally, she accepted his gesture as he meant it, not of censure, but as a form of comfort.

Her eyes held his a moment too long, though. Before she thought to break away, his head was bending toward hers.

She gave in to it. All the tensions, all the turmoil, all the uncertainties of the day rounded up inside her in one volcanic hump. She raised her lips up to meet his, slumping against his body, feeling the good hard strength of him. As their kiss grew deeper, she burrowed closer and his arms tightened around her. It felt so damned good to be held—to not always have to be strong.

At some point, she came to her senses. He was sealing her face with small, light kisses, whispering her name over and over again, his arms growing tighter around her. "No," she said softly. She used her hands to push against his chest to free herself.

Instantly his arms dropped and he let her go.

She slid over to the passenger side. When she opened the door to get out, the dome light came on and at last she could make out his features clearly. His face was stark with hunger and need.

It was too strong, too naked. She drew in a long, ragged breath.

As quickly as she'd seen it, the expression was gone, blinked away in a split second.

"Thank you for being kind," she said softly, putting the best face on it. "Good night, Sam."

He cocked one eyebrow and managed a crooked smile. "Good night, Kate."

There was nothing left to do but to get out. He waited until she'd climbed in her car and had the engine started, then waved and drove away. Sitting behind the wheel, her gear shift still in idle, she watched his car shrink in the distance until the twin points of his taillight had compressed into nothingness.

The condos along Lake Washington were dark. An occasional rectangle of yellow patched the charcoal night, but most of the town was bedded down, sleeping away the transition hours from one day to the next. A couple of cars were still parked on Central in front of Smokie Jo's. She'd intended stopping for a wind-down game of pool, but suddenly she didn't feel like being with anyone. She needed quiet. Her mind needed quiet, her nerves needed quiet, her soul needed quiet. She drove on, made the jog around the broad lakeside park and continued up Market Street.

Her neighborhood was asleep, too. One dark, silent house after another slid past, with only the occasional lit window to indicate life within. The street lamps broke the ribbons of darkness with their misty circles of soft gold, and she was moved from light into darkness into light again. The irony was not lost on her. Was that all life was in the end, stretches of black broken now and then by patches of brief illumination? Or was it more like the equinox, periods of clear daylight alternating with equal periods of dense shadows?

She drove into the garage and turned off the ignition key. Home. Her shoulders slumped with relief. The day was finally over. For better or worse, she could put it to bed as others along the lakefront had and be done with it.

Was this the way Suzie had felt when she'd poured her glass of wine and made herself comfortable, that at last the day was done and nothing more would happen—*could* happen—until the dawn arrived?

The thought drove Kate from her car. The drizzle had died away and there was just a thick mist saturating the chill night air. For a moment, she paused and looked at her cottage, softened by the charcoal darkness around her. There was a pitched roof with standing headroom in the attic. If she wanted to, she could add a couple of dormers, put in a window on either gabled end, then divide the space into a couple of large, airy bedrooms.

For children?

The thought startled her, but instantly, as if waiting in the wings for a cue, her mind produced a fully detailed stage scene. Blue wallpaper, white woodwork, sheer curtains billowing in a soft breeze and two children quietly at play, a brightly painted wooden toy box next to them. She'd be down in the kitchen, putting the last touches on dinner, the dining-room table already set. Background music would drift softly through the downstairs area. And as she cooked, one ear would be tuned into the noises upstairs, monitoring the children's play, and the other would be listening for the sound of the back door opening and the firm tread of male footsteps. A solid male body would appear in the doorway, and he'd stop, smiling, at the sight of her, an air of deep satisfaction and warm contentment evident on his face.

Who?

At that point, the vision snapped like a broken film strip, and coming to, she looked around to reground herself. The dark distant house of her neighbors, the fifty-year-old shrubbery grown head-high, the thick solid walls of her own house, the misty night around her. . . Slowly she regained her sense of time and place. My God, she thought. My God.

Deeply shaken, she followed the path around to the front door.

She dug the mail out of the box on the porch wall. Bills. As she was ready to pull open the screen door to unlock her front door, she glimpsed a florist's package in the corner of the porch. It was set in a small, deep box, a tall, slender arrangement wrapped in a green light plastic tissue, stapled at the top. She swung her shoulder bag back so that it was out of her way and bent down and carefully picked the box up. It wasn't heavy. She got the front door unlocked and carried everything in.

She dumped her purse and the mail on the dining-room table as she went past, and took the florist's box to the kitchen sink. The envelope was stapled to the top. She pulled it free, then opened the plastic sack. Inside was a small cut-glass bud vase.

She lifted it clear of the sack and set it on the counter. Rising from a nest of ferns was a single deep-pink rose. Her breath taken away by the simple beauty of the flower, she admired it for a long moment before tearing the envelope open.

The message was brief. "To mystique. And the promise it holds. Jack."

17

The night was a horror of half-formed dreams. Dead women, a weeping man, a shrouded killer, a kiss and a rose mingled in a hideous black procession through a restless sleep. At four, she gave it up, got dressed and headed for work.

At this hour, headquarters was like the deserted airport terminal, vast and ghostly silent, its lights illuminating only emptiness. The bars had closed and the drunks had come and gone, the junkies were playing their mental gigs in wired solitude, the hookers were bedded down for more than a quickie and the homeless had found the doorway to stuporville. An hour before dawn, the uneasy world dozed.

Even the night-duty sergeant was comatose, too somnambulistic to do more than nod Kate in. Behind him, a cluttered carpet of mostly empty desks spread throughout the bull pen, a few odd souls from the night shift laboring over their written reports. At her desk, Kate slung her purse over the back of her chair and slipped out of her raincoat and shoved some files over to make room for it on top of the filing cabinets.

She'd straightened up her desk before leaving for the airport with Sam the previous evening, and set precisely in the center of the cleared space were Goddard's reports. So he'd actually done them, she thought, with a vague surprise. She'd been half convinced he wouldn't, that he'd openly defy her command. She picked the stack up and riffled the edges. Page after page after page. Names, addresses, statements and summaries. It must've taken him half the night. And he *hated* doing reports. A wry smile crossed her face. He'd be a bear today. Especially when he found out what she had planned for him to do.

Then the smile turned into a frown as her gaze idly moved over her desktop. She'd never considered herself a neatnik—which she probably should reassess, if ninety percent of the desks around her were examples—but it seemed to her that things were not quite how she'd left them. The paper-clip cube was on the wrong side of the phone. The stapler wasn't quite straight. Pens were turned the wrong way about in the mug she used as a holder. Small things, but to her trained eyes, they added up. Probably it had been nothing more than a homeless bull using her desk for a quick phone call. Or someone had run out of desk supplies and used hers. It happened.

She'd have shrugged it off except for the files. She'd stacked the pile square with the desk corner, the edges impeccably aligned. She remembered distinctly doing it, for it had been that slack time between the day's work and the airport meetings ahead, and Sam had been tied up on the phone, so she'd kept her hands busy with idle chores while she waited for him to finish his call. She remembered her mind free-wheeling in easy loops, not concentrating on any one thing, and saw herself carefully organizing, piling, and aligning the stack of files and squaring them up with military precision. Sam had called over to her then, and she'd left without disturbing them again. Now the alignment was ragged.

She pulled the stack toward her and ran her eyes down the tabs. They dealt with the Fletcher case, and there were already several of them—including a miscellaneous file marked "Ideas/ Thoughts." That was the one that concerned her. It was nothing more than a conglomeration of thoughts, glimmerings, leads to follow, questions to be asked and methods for organizing the investigation. Though she considered it private, there really was no reason for anyone *not* to see it. There was no reason why anyone should, either. The idea of it gave her an uncomfortable, creepy feeling, as if her privacy had been invaded. Had Goddard gone through her files?

She left her desk as it was and wandered the cabinet maze over to Narcotics and put on the first pot of coffee for the day. While it brewed, she leaned her back against a file cabinet, still troubled by the snooping. If it was the Dynamic Duo, what had they hoped to gain? There was nothing hidden there. The daily reports she made up were circulated among the whole homicide division. That was S.O.P., in case someone working another case came across something that might be pertinent to someone else's. The things that *didn't* go in the daily report were her own thoughts and speculations. But what use would that be to anyone . . .

Her thoughts were interrupted by a voice from behind her. "Sleeping, or is this what passes for thinking these days?"

She whirled around. Brillo was peering over the file cabinet. He'd hunkered his body down and rested his chin on the metal top, so that his head appeared decapitated at the throat. He flashed white teeth at her in an evil leer. He looked like Eddie Murphy on a bad day.

After he got a smile out of her, he straightened up. "Thought I recognized the top of that head," he said, slapping his hand down hard on the cabinet. A metallic thud rang through the empty space. "Get pretty good at I.D.-ing folks with these mothers around. That coffee done yet?"

"Almost. Just a few more drips left."

He came around and lounged against a cabinet next to hers. "So what's all the heavy-duty brainwork about? Your gears are grinding so loud it sounds like a buzz saw on speed."

She studied him, wondering how much she could trust him. She made a quick decision. "Let me ask you, Brill, if you were running an op, and you had a couple of play-games types who considered themselves lone eagles, better than you, how would you handle them?"

The dark-brown eyes on her were sympathetic. "Yeah, I saw Goddard with resentment planted all over his puss. If he was mine, I'd kick his balls in and toss him in a dumpster till he wised up and came into line. But that's no help. You can't do that. So what you gotta do is outthink 'em. Outthink 'em and outwit 'em. For instance, Goddard's got a problem working for you? All you gotta do is figure out where you're gonna be and send him off in the opposite direction."

She nodded. "I'm burying him over at the courthouse today, tracing some real estate records for me. That I can do. What worries me, Brillo, is what else he's got planned that I don't know about yet."

"He really out to sink you on this?"

"I don't know," she said slowly. "My alarms are going off like a clock shop gone berserk."

"That's good enough for me. Always trust your instincts. You can't trust 'em, you don't belong here. So here's the to-do . . . Stand back and look at yourself like someone else would, and figure out where the weaknesses are—what Goddard can find to exploit— then figure out how *you'd* exploit them if you were him, then figure out how to counteract *that*. Take the steps before he acts, and he'll run into a brick wall."

She was silent a minute, then said slowly, "I think he read my files on the Fletcher case. He knows what my game plan is."

Brillo poured out a heavy sigh. "Look, Mother MacLean, you're a nice lady. You're instinctively nice. And instinctively honest and instinctively sincere. Along with being much too serious. You divide people into simple classifications—the good guys and the bad guys. Which makes you prime meat for a coyote like Goddard. 'Cause I'm here to tell you that not all the bad guys are walking the street." His voice hardened. "It's not a nice world out there, no, you got that right. But now and again, it's not a nice world in here either. We cover it up by what we euphemistically call civilization, but underneath, the jungle gets first call. And you always gotta be prepared for that. *Always!*" The last few words came out bitter and intense.

Startled at the sudden vehemence ending what had been a rather philosophical discourse, Kate roused herself out of her own concerns and frowned. "What're you doing here at this hour anyway? You coming or going?"

"Shit." He rolled sideways until he was back leaning against the file cabinet again, his head tilted back, his eyes staring up at the ceiling. At last he blinked, and without moving, said into the air, "We lost another one last night. Third fucker this year."

"Someone got killed? Who?"

"Not killed. Wish he had been." He dropped his head, swiped at the floor with a boot, then glared up at her. "That black shit ready yet?"

She led the way to the pot. She didn't ask any more questions. He wouldn't answer them if she had. But she could make a good guess. A cop had been turned. Rosie. You never saw one without the other. She handed him a Styrofoam cup along with a nod of sad acknowledgment at the jungle in here.

Goddard's report was so thorough she knew he hadn't written it; Bernie Fry had. The five *W*'s were all there, presented with easy-to-grasp clarity.

Building tenants. Questioned, searched and found clean. Goddard and Fry had even tried something she hadn't thought of. They'd tried every key they could rustle up from the tenants in the lock to the studio door, in case someone had something they'd shouldn't have had. But no match. And even the building manager and the janitor, the two known to have passkeys, came up clean. The building manager had just returned from a week in Southern California and the janitor had been out of town as well.

So much for the building. She switched reports. Neighborhoods.

Ginger. Don Burklund had not been seen over the weekend. If he'd been at home, he would've been, for, according to the neighbors, good weather or foul, he worked around the place every chance he got. Ginger hadn't been seen either, but when he was away, she tended to hibernate with her children and her sketch pad. Nice family. No public battles. No marital rifts that anyone could see. No squabbles, no yelling, no screaming fights. And no hanky-panky that anyone knew about. Just a nice quiet family.

Suzie. Neighbors said Johnny Plummer was home; they saw the car going in and out a few times with both of them in it. There were no known marital problems here either. They did errands together, spent all their time together, even *looked* happy together. Always holding hands and giggling between themselves. A close twosome. Christ, Kate thought with disgust, you'd think *one* of them would've beaned the other one with a soup bowl now and again.

Summary of the investigating detectives: No new suspects uncovered.

Conclusion of the investigating detectives: Phyllis Walsh was *It.*

Kate went over every detail of the reports again, looking for any discrepancy. She found only one. Goddard had cleared the janitor by reason of his camping trip out of town with his family. But it didn't clear him. He'd cleaned the offices Friday night before he left. He'd had time to plant the tea bag and wipe down the canister then. Or he could've made a furtive return visit on Monday night. Of course, there were no visible links between him and the three dead women, but maybe some could be found.

She made a note to check on him further.

That was it.

The vague possibility of the janitor, and Phyllis Walsh.

She closed the file and swung around in her chair to stare absently at the row of file cabinets. Phyllis Walsh.

Damn.

She stared off into space, letting her mind free-wheel. The dead women, Phyllis, business, morphine, money and cancer. She tried out one scenario after another, analyzing them, but each one of them came to a halt at one point or another. Except the one with Phyllis as the killer. Yet she was having trouble swallowing that. Her instincts said it didn't fit the lady's character. She wouldn't have committed a series of murders designed to leave herself as the sole suspect. That really was the bottom line, Kate acknowledged. She simply didn't see the woman doing it.

Brillo said to trust her instincts. All right, she'd trust them. Then what she needed was a new approach to the case that would carry her beyond the obvious figure of Phyllis Walsh standing so prominently in the foreground. One beyond the norm. But Brillo'd also said to spot her own weaknesses and cover them. The old CYA routine. Okay, looking at herself from the Wonder Boys' viewpoint, her weakness was her belief in Walsh's innocence. If they were out to smear egg on her face, that would be the area of attack. And it wouldn't take much to persuade the Captain to their point of view. Since he'd have a sensational murder case all neatly packaged and tied up to present to the Chief, the Captain would be more than willing to be persuaded that the lady was guilty.

So if that would be the area of attack, what was she *not* doing that she *would* be doing if she were seriously after Phyllis?

The answer came instantly. A search for the morphine in the Walshes' homestead and a deep investigation into their backgrounds. Just simple, good old usual police routine. She wrote out a series of instructions for both Sam and Goddard.

Sam was to investigate the Walshes' finances and credit ratings. Bank accounts, money-market accounts, stocks and bonds, retirement savings, the value of their house, any other properties they might own . . . He was to track down every asset of theirs he could. He also was to find out the extent of their liabilities. Credit-card charges, car loans, mortgage or mortgages, toys they might've bought on credit, like a boat or a camper. Even department-store charges. He was to explore anything in their background that might give rise to a need for money.

As for Goddard and Fry, she buried them so deep in record tracing that neither would see daylight until suppertime. In addition to tracking down the ownership of Catherine Fletcher's condo, she would have them investigate the background of the janitor. Maybe, just maybe, somewhere along the line, there'd be a connection. If not, at least it would keep the Dynamic Duo occupied for the day.

She locked her files in a bottom desk drawer and pocketed the key, then checked out a departmental car. She'd started to drive out to the Walsh house east of town when she realized that dawn was far too early to drop in unannounced. She wanted their cooperation, not antagonism. Food was called for, anyway. After a restless night, food would be all that would keep the tiredness at bay. She made a left turn and drove back to Denny's for breakfast.

The world was coming awake. A few cars were on the road, joined by a few more, and then a few more as a rosy dawn backlit the Cascades. The fading night sky to the deep west was clear of clouds, and the temperature was already climbing into the comfort zone. It was going to be a gorgeous spring day in Puget Sound, sunny, warm and fresh. She shivered as she wondered what fresh disaster this beautiful spring day would bring.

When Kate showed up at his door unannounced, Richard Walsh turned into one unhappy man. He was testy with his wife and he was rude to Kate. The fact that it was only slightly past eight in the morning might've had something to do with it. On the other hand, it could be the strain of the murder case. Or it could be that he was simply that kind of man. But whichever, he guarded the door like a bear guarding his winter den, and scowled. "What do you want?" he demanded after she'd identified herself.

Phyllis, overhearing Kate's name, appeared behind him in the doorway. "Richard, please," she said softly. She bobbed her head at Kate over the shoulder that blocked the doorway. "Detective MacLean. Please come in."

Walsh turned on his wife. "She has no right to harass you like this."

"Don't. Please don't make it worse than it is." She tugged at his arm until he reluctantly moved to one side and allowed Kate room enough to duck past.

Their home was a large, gracious tri-level, overlooking the Tam-O'Shanter Golf Course, built in the days when construction was sound and the lots as well as the houses were spacious. In the roomy living room to her right, a pair of quilted couches formed an ell in front of a traditional brick fireplace, with a couple of deep chairs at the end of the grouping. Phyllis led her to one of the chairs, then excused herself to bring in some coffee.

Left alone with the husband, Kate sized him up as he took a seat on one end of the sofa. His scowl had lightened to a frown, and his intense glare had eased up a bit. He wasn't a bad-looking man: tall, slight, with the lines of middle age just beginning to creep into his face and figure. He was dressed for work, in a suit and tie, but he seemed in no hurry. He sat back on the couch, not bothering to make polite conversation, staring at an original painting hung over the fireplace. A seven-day clock on the mantel ticked away the seconds.

Phyllis brought in a tray of coffee mugs with some cream and sugar, served them around, then sat across from her husband. Her cheeks were pale, her face lined with deep creases of tension and worry. She sweetened her coffee, taking her time, stirring it slowly. Finally she raised troubled eyes to Kate. "Everyone thinks I did it, don't they?"

Walsh let out a sound of disgust, set down his coffee cup and collapsed back against the sofa cushion, rubbing his forehead.

"I've seen people in better positions than yours," Kate responded cautiously.

Phyllis nodded. "What can I do to help? If I help you, I'll be helping me. What can I do?"

Walsh's eyes flew open at that. "Hire a goddamned lawyer," he snapped, "I've been telling you that since Catherine was killed."

Kate nodded to Phyllis. "That's probably not a bad idea, though I'm not sure it's necessary at this point. I do have a couple of things in mind that might strengthen your position a little. That's kind of why I came here this morning. I'll need you to go into the station later to give a formal statement, but I thought we could go over what you'll be saying on a more informal basis and see what we've got."

Walsh frowned at her. "Isn't that rather irregular?"

"Possibly. And it could turn out to be futile, too. But at least we'd have tried."

"I'm not buying that. Looks to me like the cops are going to need a scapegoat and sooner or later my wife's going to be it."

"Mr. Walsh, I'm not at a point where I intend Mirandizing your wife. Things are leaning a bit her way, yes. But I'm far from convinced that she had anything to do with it. What I'd like to do is to take her once again over her whereabouts for the last few days and what she knows about the murders. This would be off the record. Then I'll ask her to go in and repeat it for a stenographer and sign it."

"And the alternative?"

Kate shrugged. "We'll skip the informal part and do it by the book."

"*Throw* the book at her, you mean," he said bitterly.

Kate studied him. She could understand a certain frustration under the circumstances, a fear for his wife's welfare. After all, she was the only surviving partner. Would she, too, be killed? *Some*one out there was doing *some*thing—possibly even as they talked. But what she couldn't understand was the extreme bitterness he was displaying. It was almost as if he thought it was a foregone conclusion his wife would be charged with the murders. That no matter what they did or what they said, they could not prevent the wheels of justice from overrunning and destroying them. Then a thought struck. *God, he didn't think his wife actually had committed murder, did he?*

The mantel clock ticked on in the drawn-out silence.

Phyllis broke the silence. "What exactly do you need from me?"

"Let's start with your schedule, your whereabouts, from Friday night at suppertime on. I know you've given some of this to me, but let's go over it one more time."

She nodded, and without giving her husband a chance to interfere, Phyllis outlined her days from Friday on. She went through the weekend hours spent outside of the studio, turning to Walsh for confirmation when appropriate. He corrected her only once. They hadn't left the pizza house at nine-thirty on Friday night; it was nine forty-three. Otherwise, he confirmed everything. He confirmed everything he knew, that is. Unfortunately, there were gaps where Phyllis had been alone, doing this or that, running here or there. There was no getting around it, Kate thought. She had had plenty of opportunity to create some morphine cocktails.

Kate kept her expression carefully neutral and her voice encouraging. When Phyllis had finished her recitation, she let a tick of the clock go by, then leaned forward in her chair, her forearms resting on her lap. "Phyllis, I'm going to ask you straight out: Did you kill your partners?"

That roused the bear again. Walsh jumped forward, ready to do battle, but Phyllis motioned him to stillness. Her face had gone dead-white at the question, but her eyes never left Kate's. "No," she answered quietly. "I had nothing whatsoever to do with their deaths."

Kate drew in a soft breath. The woman spoke the truth. It was there in her steadfast gaze, it was in the firmness of her face, it was in the quietly measured tones of her voice. What she was hearing was unequivocal truth. She'd stake her life on it. She had one more question to go. "Do either of you have painkillers of any kind in the house?"

Husband and wife exchanged puzzled glances, then both began shaking their heads at once. "Just some Percocet from the dentist one time," Phyllis said. "And some aspirin."

"All right," Kate said softly, "I'd like to do something that might help your situation." Phyllis' look turned to curiosity. Richard Walsh's frown deepened. "I'd like you to give me permission to have a lab crew come in this morning and do a thorough search. And I mean, thorough. Not only thorough, but documented clear down to the last vitamin pill you've got hanging around."

"Whoa, now," Walsh said. "Search for what?"

"Morphine."

He shook his head. "No way," he said firmly. "No way."

For the first time, a little humor came into Phyllis' face, erasing some of the defeat written there. She swung her head toward her husband and, with the faintest of smiles, said, "Gee, honey, do you have some habits I don't know about?"

He started to react, then his look turned to one of total exasperation. "I suppose you're in favor of this."

She seemed surprised he asked. "Of course I'm in favor of it. If they can't find any morphine here, then that's one factor in my favor. And right now, it looks like I need every little thing I can get hold of. Damned right I'm in favor of it."

They stared at each other, a husband-and-wife stare that conveyed some silent marital messages. Wearily, he tossed up his hands in surrender. "Go ahead, then, and do what you want. Don't mind me. I'm just the husband around here."

Ignoring the bite in his voice, Phyllis led Kate to a phone in the kitchen, then worked quietly at the sink while the call for the lab crew was made. Walsh leaned against the doorjamb, watching them, not saying anything, his face disapproving.

Kate completed the arrangements and hung up. "They'll be here as soon as they can."

"How long will this take?" Phyllis asked.

"Most of the morning, I'm afraid."

Watching from the doorway, Walsh straightened. "Well, it's obvious I'm just excess baggage. I'll just go on into work. When you get this whole thing with the cops worked out, Phyllis, give me a call." He strode through the kitchen, stopping to give his wife a peck on the cheek, then, with a nod at Kate, he headed toward the door leading to the garage.

Kate hated to chance setting him off again, but there was no help for it. "I'm sorry, Mr. Walsh, but I'll have to ask you to wait."

He stopped and turned, scowling heavily. "What now?" he demanded.

"The lab crew will need to go over your car before you take it anywhere." She decided she wouldn't mention the body search yet. She'd skate through that bit of thin ice later. She smiled at him and indicated the kitchen table. "Shall we have some more coffee?"

The lab sent out four men, quiet, mild-mannered, inoffensive. The professional demeanor, Kate thought as she briefed them, designed not to rile. They were to look for morphine tablets, she instructed. Maybe in a prescription bottle, maybe not. They could be tucked whole into an aspirin bottle, mixed in with vitamin pills, or taped individually to the back of a picture frame. They could be ground up in something as simple as a letter-sized envelope or a plastic sandwich bag. She didn't know. They were also to take samples from every opened bottle of liquid in the house. Particularly, any soft drinks, wine or hard liquor. She also wanted samples from any opened tins of coffee or tea or hot chocolate or anything else to drink. "And no upheaval," she said. Then she left them alone to do their work.

They took one look at Phyllis in her robe and three of them headed for the master bedroom and bath to clear it first so she could get dressed. At Kate's request, the fourth went out into the garage to search the cars. The Walshes were confined to the small den off the kitchen under Kate's watchful eye. Phyllis sat in a wooden rocker, which she absently set in motion, comforting herself. Richard Walsh paced the room like a con in solitary, his long legs eating up carpet yards, first one way, then back again. He was dazed at this point, as if he couldn't yet believe this was really happening to him. The air crackled with the tension of his strain.

Kate brought them both fresh cups of coffee. Phyllis sipped hers with the same remote air she used in rocking. Walsh motioned his away with an impatient shake of the head and when Kate set the cup down on a table near his path of travel, he left it untouched.

The mildest of the mild men came to the doorway and conferred in low tones with Kate. The master bedroom and bath had come up empty. Richard Walsh and his briefcase were next. As if sensing he was the subject of the conversation, Walsh stopped his pacing and watched them intently from the far end of the room. The rocker went dead on its runners as Phyllis looked on.

"Mr. Walsh," Kate said calmly, "they need you back in the bedroom for a moment. Please follow this gentleman here."

Walsh's jaw firmed and his eyebrows dropped into a deep scowl. "What the hell is it now?" he demanded.

The lab man, about Walsh's age, of medium build, with gentle eyes, said mildly, "It's nothing serious, Mr. Walsh. We simply need you to turn out your pockets for us."

"My pockets," said Walsh dumbly, staring at him.

"Yes, sir." The lab man kept his eyes steady.

"My *suit* pockets? You mean *these?*" His hands swept along his jacket lapels.

"Yes, sir. It won't take a minute."

Walsh swung in Kate's direction, on the verge of rebellion. She forestalled it. "Just part of the routine," she said quietly. "If we're not thorough now, there could be uncomfortable questions later."

"Please, Richard," Phyllis pleaded. Her eyes were huge and dark.

He started to snap at her, then held up at the entreaty written all over her face. His jaw bulged with displeasure. "It damned well better be only a minute," he growled at the lab man. With a last pugnacious glance at his wife, he marched out.

Phyllis' eyes followed his rigid back out of sight. "He doesn't mean it," she murmured to Kate. "He doesn't mean to be difficult. This is all so hard for him . . ."

"I know, I understand completely. I'm sorry, Phyllis, but I need you to stand up."

Obediently, she rose without thinking why she was doing it. "Men don't cope with these things as well as women, do you think?" she said in a wistful tone of voice. "But they don't see that, do they. They mostly just see things from their own point of view. Don't you think?"

Kate thought of Sam. Did they? "Now, I'm going to have you remove your robe, but you can keep your nightgown on."

Then it dawned. Phyllis' face turned alabaster-white. "You're going to *search* me?" she whispered in horror.

"Yes." Kate made it a matter-of-fact statement. "We have to make sure."

Standing like a statue with her eyes closed and hands clenched by her side, Phyllis endured it. She said nothing, but her face was filled with revulsion.

As efficiently as she could, Kate patted her down. "Okay, Phyllis, just let me check over your robe . . ." She took it up, checked slash pockets, seams, sash and hem, then handed it back with a smile. "Now that wasn't so bad, was it?"

Phyllis grabbed her robe back and wrapped herself tightly in it. "It was horrible. This whole thing is horrible! Do you understand? It's *horrible!*" She backed up until she felt the rocker behind her, and sank into a shrunken huddle, her anger suddenly collapsing. "I'm so scared, Katie," she whispered, "I'm terrified all the time. I feel like I'm lost in a nightmare. They're going to get me for this, I know they are. Somehow they're going to prove I did it and—"

"*No, they're not!*" The male voice boomed from behind Kate. She whirled and Richard Walsh was standing in the doorway, his face florid with anger. "That's it! I've had it! So much for cooperating with you, Detective Mac—Whatever-your-name-is! I'm calling a halt to this right now! It's bad enough you come in here and tear my house apart. It's bad enough that you come in here and paw through every goddamned thing my wife and I own. But to paw us, too! Well, lady, that's it! That's as far as I go! You just call off those bloodhounds of yours and get the hell out! *Now!*"

Kate kept her eyes firmly on his. "I'm sorry, Mr. Walsh, but that's impossible," she said calmly. "I know it's a horrible thing to have to go through, but we can't stop now. And we really appreciate the cooperation you've given us so far."

He was having none of it. *"Out!"*

Slowly, Kate shook her head. "I'm afraid we can't do that. May I use your phone, please?"

His eyes narrowed. "Why?" he demanded.

"I'll have to call for a search warrant."

"You wouldn't," he declared flatly.

Kate shrugged. "I'm sorry, but I'd have to, yes."

In the rocker, Phyllis closed her eyes for a moment in pain. "No!" she said hoarsely. She looked from one to the other. "That would be the final indignity. No search warrant. Just finish it up as quickly as you can."

Walsh wheeled on her. "Goddamn it, Phyl—"

A flush of anger erased the dead pallor. "Goddamn it yourself, Richard, I'm in the middle of this! Can't you see that? Can't you understand that it's me out there all by myself? Can't you get it through that thick head of yours that I'm their sole and only suspect? For Christ's sakes, Richard, you're *not* a stupid man!" Her voice took on a tinge of hysteria. *"Can't you see any of what's happening to me?!"*

Walsh stared at his wife, openmouthed, brought to a halt by the tremendous anger being hurled his way. He stuttered, nonplussed. "Phyl—"

Phyllis' anger was gone as quickly as it had come. She slumped back against the hard spindles of the rocker back. "Just let it alone, please," she said tiredly. "Don't say anything more. Just let them do their job and get it over with. Just let them be gone." Then she closed her eyes and shut them both out of her sight.

Walsh stared helplessly at her. Kate moved to his side. "Let's leave her alone for a bit," she murmured. She placed a hand on his arm. "Let's have some coffee. She's fighting a terrible battle inside, and she needs to regain her balance."

He allowed himself to be led away.

It was a long morning and there were some other touch-and-go moments with Richard Walsh. Like when he found out they'd searched his briefcase. That set him off again briefly. But he never regained the ferocity of his earlier rage.

The lab crew finished up shortly after noon. Every inch of the house had been gone over. Attic, walls, floorboards, linoleum, house siding, window ledges, crawl space. All were minutely examined. Plumbing traps had been removed and scrapings taken, in case morphine crumbs had been washed away. The freezer had been emptied and any suspect packages like home-wrapped ground beef which could hide a packet of pills were packed up for laboratory testing. Countertops and table surfaces were carefully vacuumed in case they'd been used to crush any morphine tablets and a crumb or two might have escaped. The invasion was all-pervasive, absolutely nothing was missed.

There was no morphine anywhere.

Correction, Kate warned herself, there were no *visible* signs of morphine. It would be days before she got reports back on the frozen meat and plumbing traps.

She arranged for the Walshes to come in that afternoon for a formal statement, then drove back to the station house both pleased and troubled. She was pleased because the lack of morphine was one small factor in Phyllis Walsh's favor. But she was troubled because she realized how deeply now she believed in Phyllis' innocence.

But if it *wasn't* Phyllis, then who?

18

When she got back to the station house, Sam was still out. So were Goddard and Fry. She slung her purse over the back of her chair and checked her messages. Sam had left a note: "Lunch? Wait for me." There were three other messages. Vern Riley: "Urgent! Call immediately!" The Captain: "See me *now!*" And Saint Homer.

She glanced at the Captain's office. Door closed, blind down. He was tied up.

She returned Homer's call first. His cheerful voice boomed through the line. "Any luck locating a morphine tablet for us?"

"None," she admitted. "Isn't there any other way to identify the pharmaceutical company?"

"Nope. Like I told Sam a couple of days ago, morphine is morphine. What we were trying to trace were the different materials used to bind it into tablet form. They're different from company to company. But they're inert materials and don't react to chemical tests. If we had a whole tablet, the thing would be a snap."

"What about the crushed tablets in the tea bags? They'd contain the binding material, wouldn't they?"

"That's what I'm saying, Katie, we can't get them to react to anything. They're inert. Harmless. We've run every conceivable test here, and come up with zilch."

She cradled the phone tight against her ear and closed her eyes. "What do you suggest I do now?"

He sighed. "I'm loath to even mention it, but I think it's good old-fashioned shoe-leather time. You're going to have to call on the various pharmacies and see if you can track down the actual prescription—who ordered it, and who filled it. I don't see any other way out."

She directed a rueful look at the phone. "Want a job?"

"No, thanks, I've got one. If I do change, it'll be to something simple, like brain surgery."

"And there's *nothing* you can do to give us a steer in any one direction?"

"Nope. Wish I could. Well, I gotta run. I'm lunching today with a corpse." He paused, and when she refused to take the nibble, he added, "Well, next door to one, anyway. See you."

He hung up, leaving her wondering—a new restaurant next door to a funeral home?

She opened the Seattle and Eastside phone books and turned to the Yellow Pages, looking first under "Physicians," then under "Pharmacies." There were pages and pages of both. Disheartened, she closed them up. Could she safely eliminate Seattle from the hunt? The answer was instantaneous. No. If she'd been buying morphine, and wanted to hide it, Seattle would be the first place to go.

She sighed. Back to the damned morphine again. Always the morphine. If you don't know you're sick, and the doctor doesn't know you're sick, how do you get a prescription for it? And if you don't have a prescription, then you have to get it illegally, but Brillo had already checked his sources. Could his sources be wrong? Christ, what a nightmare. What now, MacLean? What miracles are you going to pull out this time?

None, at the moment, she decided. She picked up the slip with the number Riley had left, and placed the call. He was panicked, and on the attack, claiming someone was out to get him. At first, she thought he'd been assaulted, or had been handed a morphine cocktail, but she bit back that little nibble of panic and did some probing. Riley's concern was nothing more than a poor night's sleep. He'd spent the night brewing up phantoms and was now laying them on her doorstep, looking for salvation. "Don't drink anything from an opened bottle," she advised. "And watch out for tea bags." It was the best she could do for him. Her attention was focused elsewhere.

Out of the corner of her eye, she saw movement at the Captain's doorway. Brillo emerged, slouching as usual, his face deadpan as usual, but there was a deadness about him, a slogging quality to his motions quite unlike his usual quick litheness, as if he were wading uphill through a hip-high mud slope. The case of the cop gone bad, Kate deduced. This would not be the time to question him on the reliability of his sources. He drifted away and disappeared from sight.

The Captain, his large bulk framed in the doorway, watched Brillo disappear, his own face impassive, then glanced Kate's way. He beckoned and stood waiting for her. He was looking more intimidating than usual. His lips were pressed together in a tight downward curve, his jowls were more pronounced and his eyes were hard. He lumbered around behind his desk and motioned for her to close the door and take a chair, then sank heavily into the scarred, oversized wooden desk chair he'd personally provided himself. He swapped one stack of paper for another and hunched over the fresh pile a minute, shuffling through the top few pages.

She waited quietly. He'd left the blinds down. Very few noises from the bull pen penetrated the office when the door was closed, she noticed. Just the sound of phones ringing. And even they sounded muffled and faint, as if they were a long distance away. At least, the architects had done a good job here with the soundproofing. She could be yelled at and no one would ever know.

The swivel bearing of the chair creaked as finally he put the last sheet of paper down and leaned way back to stare at her. Brillo and his problems had been set aside for the moment, she knew, and his attention was focused purely on her now. She suddenly wished Sam was lounging comfortably in the chair next to her. Maybe she wouldn't be feeling quite so intimidated.

Hatch propped his elbows on the broad arms of the chair,

steepled his fingers, rested his chin on his fingertips and peered at her from beneath shrubby brows. "Goddard and Fry were in here this morning. They want me to yank you off the case and turn it over to them. Any reason why I shouldn't?"

Kate's heart clutched. "Any reason why you should?' She kept her voice as even as possible.

"They copied me on the reports they gave you—"

Bastards. That was strictly against the chain of command.

"—which were good, thorough, professional and well-reasoned." He halted, waiting for a response.

She nodded. "Yes, they were. Fry does a good report."

One of the shrubby brows quirked upward. "Why Fry?"

"He's the writer. Goddard's the talker."

He shrugged that off as irrelevant. "Anyway, by process of elimination, they've pretty much fingered the Walsh woman. They're claiming you're too emotionally involved to handle the case objectively, that there's more than enough to go to warrant on Murder One. Basically, they're claiming incompetence on your part, but in a polite way." He shut up again to see how she'd respond.

The only way to deal with this was head-on. "Exactly how am I being incompetent?" she asked calmly. "Simply because I feel it's too soon to jump on her?"

"That . . . plus the fact that you haven't ordered a search of her house—just in case there happened to be some morphine lazing around the place."

Kate kept her own face impassive. "Anything else?"

"So far no background check on the Walshes to see what kind of a welcome the three hundred grand would receive."

"And?"

"You haven't had her in yet for a formal statement since the last bodies were found, and that was over twenty-four hours ago."

"And what do they expect that formal statement to reveal? Something that would indicate her guilt? A clue for conviction, a confession maybe?"

His face took on a look of great innocence. "Hey, I'm just the messenger."

Yeah, she thought. Like Henry the Eighth was just the

messenger when he ordered his wives to be killed. "Anything else?"

"They claim you're wasting their time on shitwork, tracing real estate deeds, tracking some poor jerk of a janitor who has nothing to do with nothing clear back to his cradle."

"And have they done that?"

"Have they done what?"

"Have they done what I've asked them to, trace the deed and research the janitor?"

"I got the impression they were headed that way."

That would fit, she figured. The D.I.C. ran the case with the borrowed authority of the Captain. With four major crime divisions under his control, and empty lieutenant slots without the money to fill them, he couldn't call every shot on even one case, never mind all of them, so instructions from a D.I.C. carried the same weight as if they'd been issued from his office. Ignoring those instructions was skirting insubordination. Since she was the D.I.C., the Asshole Twins didn't dare *not* follow her orders, though obviously they felt they could go over her head to gripe about them. "Anything else?"

"They expressed concern about wasting departmental funds and manpower on a case that for all practical purposes is solved. They didn't say so outright, but they hinted that you may be trying to stretch out your day in the sun at the department's expense."

Uh-oh, that was the biggie. Especially in light of the request she'd have to make for men to comb the streets for the morphine. The timing was rotten. She bit back a sigh. "Anything else?"

"Nothing comes to mind, no."

"Why are you telling me this?"

He stared at her impassively. "Snitches bother me."

She nodded agreement. "Unpleasant critters, aren't they." Bull-like, she lowered her own head and stared at him from beneath her own not inconsiderable brows. "All right, what do you want me to do, what do you need from me? Tears, temper and tantrums? Something like stamping my foot and yelling, 'No, I *won't* let you take me off the case'? Or maybe you'd rather have me defend my case management and refute each and every misguided point they made, wasting your time, and mine. Or could it be you're merely conveying information about the low morale within my command, and you have full faith and belief in my ability to get the job done in spite of them. What do you want me to do, what do you need from me?"

A brief flicker of something flashed in his eyes. She couldn't have identified it if her life depended on it, it was gone too quickly. Anger? Disgust? His chair twanged as he straightened abruptly. "Okay, MacLean, it's your case, you run it. But Goddard and Fry did make one telling point. The budget. I ever hear of this case going one hour longer than necessary, I'll have your hide. Is that understood?"

"Yes, sir." She rose. "Thank you, Captain."

"Now about the rest of it, you gonna get the Walsh dame in for a statement?"

"She's scheduled at two."

He glowered. "What about the background check on the Walshes?"

"Sam's already started on that."

His glower deepened. "What about a search warrant? You gonna get the Walsh house checked out like the Wonder Boys seem to think you should?"

"Oh, we won't need a warrant," she said casually. "The Walshes agreed to a voluntary search this morning and the lab crew just finished up over there."

His glower turned mud-black, though there was a twitch of the mouth that might've been amusement. "And?" he grumped.

"No morphine." Resisting a smile, halo not only in place but polished to a fare-thee-well, she gave him time to absorb that. Maybe the issue of her competence had been put to rest. Thank you, Brillo.

Her small moment of triumph faded, though. She had to bring up the issue of the morphine hunt. "There is one new development that I'm going to need some help on. Homer just called in. For chemical reasons, the lab can't identify the pharmaceutical company just from the crumbs of morphine crushed in the tea bags. We can run some more house searches on the people involved—Burklund, Plummer, Riley, Wilson—but if that doesn't turn anything up, we'll have to start going door-to-door to all the pharmacies in the county. I'll need some more men to do that."

He stared at her with disbelief. "Weren't we just talking about man-hours?" he demanded.

"We'd have to do it even if Phyllis Walsh is the guilty one. The D.A.'s going to want the smoking pistol if we can get it. Otherwise, his case is pretty circumstantial, and that's iffier than he likes them."

He rubbed his chin a time or two until he had himself under control. "Does it have to be detective personnel? Can some patrol cars help?"

She thought about it, then nodded "They might be the best at it anyway. But we have to cover Seattle, too. Should I ask their P.D. for coverage, or should we just go for the courtesy permission and do the search ourselves?"

"Let's see how the manpower stretches. Get the duty sergeant to run up some schedules, then we'll see how it looks." His glower was back. "*Every* goddamned pharmacy and doctor's office?"

"I'm afraid so. Homer didn't know of any shortcut. Neither do I."

"What if a false name was used?"

She sighed. "Lord help us all. I guess we'd better use photos, too."

He didn't want to hear any more. "Do what you gotta do, MacLean, only get this thing wrapped, will you? *Jesus!*"

He was through with her. She managed to keep her backbone stiff enough to make it out of his office and get the door closed. then, knees weak and wobbly, she sagged against the unforgiving wood with relief. If he'd only known how panicked she'd felt.

Sam was at his desk, watching her with concern. Goddard and Fry had come in, too, and were also watching her. Without concern. The faint edges of a smirk played around Goddard's lips as she'd sought the support of the Captain's door. Nothing blatant. Just the slightest hint. Fry looked on in unblinking intensity. She straightened, nodded to them and walked to Sam's desk. "Five minutes?"

He smiled. "Five." His eyes were so deeply warm she could've drowned in them. And wanted to.

Deliberately staying as casual as she could, she ambled over to Goddard and Fry. She perched on the rear of Goddard's desk, facing both of them. "So, guys, what's up? How'd you make out this morning? Any lead on the condo ownership?"

Clearly, this wasn't what Goddard expected. There was a flicker of wariness that came and went like lightning, then he adjusted his face into sculpted lines of solemnity and played it straight. "It's a dead end, Katie. The condo's owned by a Delaware corporation, a real estate investment company."

"Who're the stockholders?"

He shook his head. "We didn't carry it any further. We figured no one in Delaware would be interested in knocking off a tenant and her business partners in Seattle."

He was right. On the surface, the connection seemed tenuous at best. "Better look into it, Goddard. What about the janitor? What've you found out about him?"

He shrugged. "Nothing. We spent the morning at the court-house. Like you asked."

Four hours to look up one deed? Hardly, Kate thought. A twenty-minute job at the most. Thirty, if the line at the counter was long. They'd had their little visit with the Captain, had done a quick and dirty check on the condo deed to cover their ass, then had probably gone on a three-hour coffee break to give her a chance to get back here first. By the time they'd waltzed in, they'd fully expected her to have been yanked off the case, and the janitor could go swinging in the wind for all they'd care then. Hadn't quite worked out for them, had it?

She nodded, as if accepting the explanation. "Okay, here's what we'll do. I'm going to split you two up. Fry, you've got a sharp mind for detail work. I could tell from the reports you wrote last night. They were pretty damned good. So you track down the stockholders of that Delaware company. If it's another corporation, trace that one back, too. Keep backtracking until you get some real names of real people. Then do a background bio on them. I want the info for my daily tonight, so you'll have to hump a bit to get it done. But let's get this bit of the puzzle put to bed today."

Fry blinked.

She took it as acceptance and concentrated on Goddard. "Goddard, I'm putting you in complete charge of the janitor. You trace him back to the hospital where he was born and the brand of diapers his mommy used. Grade school, high school, college, if any. Wives, kids, girlfriends, brothers, sisters, guys he hangs out with, the kind of car he drives, his bank balance, his credit rating, the whole banana. I want it all. By quitting time tonight."

Goddard wasn't a stupid man. He knew somehow his maneuver with the Captain hadn't worked. Otherwise, one Detective Kate MacLean would not be perched on the edge of his desk handing out orders like this. He also knew—or strongly suspected—that she'd been informed of his talk with the Captain, and this was her way of getting even. Divide and conquer, and hand out the shitwork while she was at it. But if she was still the D.I.C., short of faking illness or invoking a personal emergency necessitating his immediate attention, there was nothing he could do about it for now.

His face became a frozen mask of nothingness. "What'll you be doing?"

"Well," she drawled, "first, I'm gonna get some lunch. I'm ravenous." She inclined her head toward the Captain's office. "When I ate you guys up in there, I spit the pieces out."

Biting back a laugh, she pirouetted off the desk and went to where Sam was waiting. She loved a good exit line.

Her humor lasted only briefly. Riding next to Sam through the golden spring sunshine to Papa's Diner she sat silent, staring sightlessly out at the busy streets. The kiss of the night before hung in the air like the spring warmth. She couldn't quite meet his eyes and she didn't know what to say to him to make things between them easy once again. So she stayed silent. Men. Why did they have to confuse things so?

At Papa's, she buried herself in the food choices and settled for just a grilled cheese sandwich. The tension was affecting her

appetite. But not Sam's, though. He ordered a double cheeseburger and fries. The thought made her stomach turn.

Their cold drinks arrived. In honor of her knotted stomach,
she skipped the usual teaspoonful of sugar she put in her iced tea,
and took a long, slow sip of the straight brew instead. When the
food got there, she stared down at her sandwich, absolutely
revolted by the thought of eating.

Sam was watching her closely. "Tell me what the Captain had
to say. Your Dynamic Duo was closeted a long time with him this
morning. I hung around to see. They came our smirking."

She looked up at him. So that was how he was going to play
it. Act as though it never happened. Mentally she shrugged. All
right, she'd do it his way. She wasn't up to a long heart-to-heart
just now anyway. "I just bet they did," she said. "Basically,
Goddard and Fry had put together a thorough report on the case,
documenting why Phyllis Walsh was the only logical choice as
the guilty one."

Sam frowned. "How well documented?"

"Well done. They brought up a list of things that they felt
should've been done and hadn't been. They claimed I'd gone soft
on Walsh, that I'd lost my objectivity and the case was suffering
because of it—that's why these things *hadn't* been done. They
stated I should be dumped as D.I.C., that they should be put in
charge, and Walsh should be brought in and booked on Murder
One. Their most telling point as far as the Captain was concerned
was that I was wasting man-hours and budget by not bringing
the investigation to its natural conclusion. The Captain was *not*
pleased to hear that."

His eyes showed concern. "What did you say?"

"Mainly, I listened." She had to eat. She tried a bite of her
sandwich. Her stomach twisted a bit and she chewed slowly,
postponing the swallow as long as possible, then sipped some
iced tea to settle the lump that landed in the bottom of her
stomach. She dawdled, holding the sandwich, but not taking the
next bite. Sam was eating his with vigor, and as she watched
him, her stomach played volcano again.

He prompted her between chews. "And then?"

She gave up and set the sandwich down. "Well, I had an

inkling something was coming down, so I was a little bit prepared. I didn't try to defend myself, I just asked the Cap a series of questions about all the things Goddard had said, making a few pointed comments along the way, and sort of got the message across that maybe there was rhyme and reason to what I was doing. I think the Captain bought it. It seemed to work, anyway. But with the Captain, who really knows? He did say he'd skin me alive if I spent one man-hour more than necessary on the case. And that was before I told him about Homer's call."

"Hold it, one thing at a time. Stick with the Wonder Boys a minute. Did you say anything to them about all this when you came out? I saw you talking to them."

"Not directly, no. They fully expected me to be replaced and when I wasn't, they knew their strategy had backfired on them." She grinned. "Now they've got one pissed-off D.I.C. over them, with all kinds of evil powers and authority to make their work days pure hell."

"You'll have to watch out for them, Katie. They'll do whatever they can now to prove their point."

"You mean, uncover evidence that confirms Walsh's guilt, and not find any that would exonerate her? I thought of that. I've split them up and sent them off in different directions this afternoon where they can't do much harm. Unless the janitor did it. But enough about my morning. How was yours? What did you find out about the Walshes' finances?"

"That they're rich, basically. I don't have all the information in yet, of course, but I did manage to uncover some nice comfortable C.D.'s they've got moldering in the bank. And they appear to owe next to nothing. They've got a small mortgage on the house, less than fifty thousand, and that's it. He's a marketing V.P. for an up-and-coming high-tech company in Redmond, and is pulling down some pretty good money. And he's got all the perks, stock options, 401K, bonus plan, automatic savings deductions—I don't think they spend half of what he makes."

"So money's not the object with Phyllis."

"Not unless he's a tightwad and keeps it all under lock and key for himself. This is all preliminary, though. There'll be more info coming in on Monday. Fridays are good and bad for this kind of stuff. People don't want to be hassled, so they'll either give it to you when they probably shouldn't, or they'll put you off until next week. Anything to keep their Friday nights on the town pure and unsullied." He poised to bite off another hunk of sandwich. "What was your morning like?"

"Fifty-fifty. As usual, there's good news and bad news. The Walshes agreed to let the lab search for morphine. The good news is that none was found. At least outright. The lab's testing samples of everything else."

"So they were cooperative. That's a surprise."

"Well, maybe. Phyllis was okay about it, but her husband raised quite a fuss at first. She finally got him settled down. He's kind of a strange man, Sam, I can't quite figure him out. He's protective of Phyllis on the one hand, and testy with her on the other. It's almost as if this whole thing is causing him a lot of inconvenience and he's blaming her for ever having gone in business with the other three at all." She decided she wouldn't mention the wild notion that had careened through her mind that maybe he thought his wife really was guilty. Too many people were already too willing to put a noose around the lady's neck.

"Earlier you mentioned Homer. Has he found anything helpful yet?"

"Nope. That was the bad news. He was a major disappointment." She told him about the problems with tracing the pharmaceuticals. "Which means we hit the streets. I vote we rescind his honorary Saint title."

"Poor Homer. Fame is so fleeting." He grinned. "Tell me, did you bring this up with the Captain before or after the man-hour threats?"

"After," she said glumly.

"Brave lady."

"Not brave, foolhardy. The idea of those two rats going to him like that . . . I'm telling you, Sam, I'd like to use a little morphine on them myself."

"Katie, let me ask you, *are* you objective? *Are* you completely impartial as far as Phyllis Walsh is concerned?"

She didn't answer directly. She finally took another bite of sandwich and chewed it slowly, trying to figure out how to deal with both her stomach and his question. She managed a swallow, then set down her sandwich again and sipped some more iced tea.

"Let's pretend," she said slowly. "Sam, let's pretend Phyllis Walsh doesn't exist, that she's not involved with the case. That means you've only got three business partners, not four. And all three are dead. Killed exactly like they were, and in the same order. Two of the three have husbands. The third has an ex-husband, an estranged husband, and a repudiated child of legal age. How would you handle the case, and who would you look at?"

"Well, you'd look for the ways and means, opportunity and motive."

"Starting with the nearest and dearest."

"Exactly."

"Then let's do it. Let's check them out thoroughly. They can't have all led perfect lives. Let's turn the rocks over and find the slime."

Sam's eyes played over her face. "So you're *not* impartial," he said softly.

"Did I say that?"

He smiled. "She's really conned you into believing she's innocent, hasn't she."

"I don't think 'conned' is quite the right term for it," Kate said somewhat stiffly. "I simply haven't been persuaded that she *is* guilty. It's like mystery books. Don't believe the obvious." She shoved aside her plate and took out her notebook. "Okay. The easiest first. Don Burklund, Ginger's husband. At a dental conference in Phoenix. Check chartered jets for a quickie trip to town. Which I haven't done yet."

"Slothful, aren't you?"

"Next. Johnny Plummer, Suzie's spouse. Was around all weekend. But neighbors claim a perfect marriage, no fights, just a pair of cuddly lovebirds. We'll check that out. No marriage is *that* good."

"Cynical, too. My God, the things you don't know about a person . . ."

"We'll check their credit rating, bank accounts, his job, who he sees and why... Maybe we should question their families, too—just to see if a tiff didn't happen now and then. Next, Bob Wilson, Catherine's ex. We'll leave Becky Wilson out of it for the moment."

"What, skip over someone? Besides, poison's a woman's weapon."

Bent over her notebook, she glared up at him. "Your enthusiasm's underwhelming, Morrison. You got a problem with this?"

"Me? Far be it for me to question how you spend the Captain's budget."

"Wonderful," she muttered. "Be sure you memo him on it. He loves snitches." She went back to her notebook. "Okay, Bob Wilson. Same as for Johnny Plummer—bank accounts, credit ratings, work situation, friends..." She stopped, caught by an idea. "You know, Bob Wilson's probably never even had a girlfriend since the breakup of that marriage. He sure has one hell of a good motive for wanting Catherine dead. Look at all she cost him. Money, business, career, home... and love, too, I bet." She added a note. Check out romances.

"How do you tie in Ginger and Suzie with Wilson? They were past his time."

"Good question. I don't know yet. Maybe something will turn up if we look closer. Ah, and rounding the clubhouse turn, Vern Riley... You know, Sam, we've really slighted him. He's been so openly obnoxious, I just kind of chalked him off as a braggart with no unlit corners of his mind hiding in the shadows. But that's not right, is it? If he is half the con man he brags about being, then he could easily be conning us, too. He drags the little scams into the open and let's us walk away with our disgust intact and unsullied. But supposing it was a *calculated* openness. You confess to the graveyard robbery so no one will think you murdered the poor corpse to begin with."

Sam grinned at that. "A time-honored technique."

"Sure. And stop and think... What exactly is he living on, anyway? Now here's a guy who supposedly starts a new job on Monday, so has no money coming in, yet he has—or had—an apartment in Renton, keeps a car going and spends enough at the bars to end up taking a different bimbo home with him each night. And after all that, he still has enough money to hand a

bunch of it over to his estranged wife on Sunday. Where did he get it all?" Her eyes widened. "Sam, I've *got* it! *I've got the motive!* I *know* why those damned murders were committed! And I know *why* we can't find any of Catherine's money! And I know *why* she's been taking it from the business! God, it's so *simple!* *Why* didn't I think of it before?"

He grinned. "Am I ready for this?"

"Listen up, flapjaw. Catherine has been supporting him all along. The estrangement, if there was one, was a phony. *That's* why she needed money all the time. She couldn't afford to support him just on what she made. That's why the money never showed up in her bank accounts, and that's why we never found the fifteen hundred dollars he supposedly gave her. Because he didn't give her any money. *She* gave it to *him!* *Not* the other way round, like he'd have us believe."

"Okay, I'll play salmon and bite. Why?"

She frowned slightly. "We'll have to find that out."

"Okay, next question. How does that make him the murderer? If *she* was giving *him* money, then why would *he* want to kill *her?* That's killing the golden goose, isn't it?"

Her frown dissolved and a beatific feeling filled her. She glowed. "The insurance."

"The insurance. He doesn't *get* the insurance."

"Oh, yes, he does. He's named as second beneficiary on Catherine's life insurance policy."

"That doesn't help him now."

The beatific feeling grew and spread. "Ah, but Sam, if Phyllis Walsh is convicted of those murders, she can't benefit from the crime. So who *does* get all the insurance money?"

It hit him then. "The secondary beneficiaries."

"Right. There'd be no other business partner left to inherit the whole bundle. Each policy then becomes simply a personal one, and each one has been left to the individual husbands in the number-two slot."

Her appetite had returned in full force. Hard to believe what a sense of supreme well-being could do for the gastric muscles. She polished off the rest of her sandwich, then reached over and helped herself to a handful of Sam's french fries. He was too de

in thought to notice. She munched happily away. Hot damn, she had it!

"I hate to cloud up your sunshine, Mother Nature, but that motive would fit all the husbands. Except Bob Wilson and Richard Walsh. Kill the three business partners and frame the fourth, and you're home free with a nice hundred grand to keep you warm at night."

Suddenly the French fry turned into a greasy wad of potato mush in her mouth as doubt set in. He *couldn't* be right. Could he?

Damn.

19

Schreiber and Rice were the old men of homicide. Both in their early fifties, both dedicated family men, they'd paired up early in their detecting careers and were now only a couple of years from retirement. Dennis Schreiber was tall and thin, a taciturn man, Gary Cooper style, well-organized and detail-oriented, with an accountant's love for making tidy columns of figures add up to the proper total. Charlie Rice was less cerebral, more outgoing. Short, plump and bald, he had a kindly Santa Claus look that people instinctively trusted. They'd tell him things they wouldn't tell their shrinks. They were probably the most respected team in the division. Even the young smart-mouths like Goddard and Fry comported themselves with more dignity around them.

When Kate and Sam returned from lunch, the Schreiber-Rice team had just wound up the final paperwork on a shooting and were free for reassignment. As soon as she learned of it, Kate grabbed them to take charge of the search for the morphine. Rice would run the foot soldiers while Schreiber coordinated the results back at his desk. She explained what she wanted and the information she was looking for. When she left them, they were already absorbed over a map of King County, quartering both sides of Lake Washington into search sectors. Between them, nothing would be missed.

Kate then turned her attention to the husbands' statements she and Sam would be taking that afternoon. She had one fierce objective. Discrepancies. Times that didn't jibe. Events that didn't quite happen the way they'd been described. The slightest change in stories from one statement to the next. *Anything* that might provide a fresh lead to follow.

Johnny Plummer was the first. His eyes were glazed and empty. His face was slack with grief, the fleshy mounds of his cheeks melting into dewlaps hanging from his jawbone. Numbed by tranquilizers, he was slow to respond to their questions. When he finally did, his voice was dead, devoid of any expression.

His story was the same one he'd told the night before. He and Suzie had spent the weekend at home, only running out for grocery shopping and other domestic errands, then he'd flown early Monday morning to Bozeman, where he'd picked up a rental car to make his swing through his Montana-Wyoming territory. When questioned, he knew of no reason why anyone would want all three partners dead. Catherine, maybe. But certainly not his wife. He was sorry, he said in a listless voice, but he knew nothing about the murders that could help them. He couldn't even make a guess as to why.

Kate sat across from him at the interrogation table, with the recorder positioned at the end of the table. Sam sat off to the side, watching Plummer intently, making his own notes. Kate probed and probed, taking him over and over his marriage, his relationship with the business, his weekend schedule. No matter how many times and in how many ways she asked the same thing, Plummer didn't seem to notice. He answered each question as if it were brand-new, always with a time gap before he spoke. It was as if the synapses in his brain had gone on vacation, she thought. He was too traumatized to think. With his deadness, he managed to get through their questions without breaking down as he had at the airport the night before, though his eyes had teared up a time or two.

At last she gave up. When she finally released him, he followed her like an obedient dog to a waiting area and sat politely in his chair, staring down at his hands folded in his lap, until his statement was ready to be signed. When she escorted him to the front of the building, she watched him leave. Stuporous, he trudged out onto the sidewalk with a slow and heavy gait, as if there were no place special he needed to be, nothing special left to strive for, no one special left to care about. He struck her as the loneliest man on earth. Reluctantly, she crossed him off her list of possibles. His grief was too real, too vivid.

Burklund was next. He came in with the same brisk high-handedness he'd shown at the airport, nodded at Sam and Kate, then took note of the recorder at the end of the table. Without being asked, he rattled off names, days and times of his schedule in Phoenix, directing his list toward the tape, not Kate. He spelled each name fully for the record, even Jones and Smith, of which there were two of the former and one of the latter. He was meticulous in his times, stating the exact minute an activity or meeting began, and the exact minute it ended. He was a busy man, his manner implied, with many, many demands on his time, and only a carefully coordinated schedule timed to the second would allow those demands to be met. He was intolerant of delay, impatient with slowness, unintentionally self-absorbed. He—his life, his world—was the centerpiece of his existence. He would bury his wife, Kate predicted, observe a proper, closely timed period of mourning, then set about with surgical efficiency to find a wife to replace the one he'd lost.

Yet in some ways, that was unfair to Don Burklund. She had seen grief take many forms. Johnny Plummer's was probably the most common— the complete breakdown and an overwhelming sense of betrayal by God or fate or whatever. But some people simply were too controlled to let themselves go that way. Rigid discipline was too ingrained in their lives. So they lost themselves in schedules—clocks and calendars—keeping every minute of the day and every day of the week filled to hold the abhorrent at bay. They appeared cold and heartless on the surface, indifferent to the loss of human life, yet inside the volcano smoldered, tightly suppressed, until one day, months down the way, the surface fissures appeared and spread, the minor quakes began, then the major eruption occurred, shocking themselves as much as the people around them. And so she was as gentle, though unyielding, in her questions to him as she had been with Johnny Plummer.

Asked about the murders, he claimed he knew no one who'd want to harm his wife. Or Suzie. His theory was the killer was after Catherine, and had not known she'd exclusively drunk tea and so had spiked the wine and ginger ale to make sure she got her dose.

It was a new thought, Kate acknowledged. But if the killer didn't know she drank only tea, then out of all the items placed in the communal refrigerator by everyone in the building, how'd the killer know that only the wine and ginger ale belonged to the partners?

He simply shrugged with impatience. That was her job, not his. That pronouncement out of the way, he stood, ending the interview. He had to get home to the children. He did condescend to stay until his statement was ready for signing. His signature was an impatient scribble, not much more than a strong line with a slight hump in the middle, then he strode briskly out of the building, a schedule to keep.

As she watched him forced to stop for traffic, it occurred to her that he was too impatient to use poison. If he killed anyone, it would have to be with immediate results. None of the plant-now-and-die-later stuff for him. She felt kind of sorry for his patients. He probably was a brilliant dentist, with instant diagnosis and instant cure, but would he have the patience to wait until the Novocain took effect before drilling for the gold?

Turning away, she sighed. At any rate, if his schedule in Phoenix proved out, he was eliminated from contention. Two down, only Riley to go.

In spite of the cold water Sam had thrown on her revelations at lunch, she was still enamored with her theory and had asked Riley to come back in to make another statement. He'd been in a foul mood when she'd called. He'd argued, wrangled and cursed, then almost immediately switched topics and came out with what was really bothering him. He'd just learned that no insurance moneys were going to be paid out until the murderer was found. That left him with a three-thousand-dollar funeral to pay for and—supposedly—no money to do it with. And the funeral home was not inclined to extend any credit. Just how the hell was he supposed to bury Catherine without money or credit?

After listening to him and soothing him, she finally got him to agree to a repeat visit to the station by pointing out it was in his own best interests to cooperate with them as much as he could. Possibly—just possibly, she warned—he might have that one nugget of information that might crack the case for them. And the sooner they cracked the case, the sooner the insurance company would release the policy benefits.

So in he came. He sat at the interrogation table and jerked and twitched and tapped and crossed his legs and uncrossed his legs until she wanted to clamp a hand down on him and roar, *Sit still!* All the while, his mouth ran on with a blatant, uncaring stream of vulgarity that made her stomach turn. Whenever he made one of his off-color remarks, he'd aim a grin at Kate, watching to see the effect. Sam kept his head bent over his notebook, glancing up at Kate now and then with hidden amusement. Kate refused to play Riley's game, merely waiting each time until he'd had his little fun, then asking the next question in a calm voice, her unsmiling gaze fixed on him.

Asked specifically about money, what he lived on, how long he'd been out of work, how he made his car and rent payments without money coming in, Kate received a new education in bureaucratic chicanery. Riley had actually quit his last job at a used-car lot, but he knew enough about the mileage being set back that he blackmailed his boss into telling the state he'd been laid off. So he was able to collect unemployment while he looked around for an opportunity more suitable to his talents. The unemployment check covered basic apartment and car expenses. As far as food went, you went out at happy hour, ran up a tab for drinks, and filled up on free hors d'oeuvres. Simple. Then, well after the dinner hour—so's you wouldn't be stuck for the price of a meal, he explained—you made a move on the best-looking babe still hanging around, one who seemed to have a lot of money to spend. Then you schmoozed her up a little, got her to pay the tab and then you took her home with you. Free drinks, free food, and free nooky. You just had to know how to work the system.

Then, grinning the whole time, tapping out a speedy rhythm

on the table edge with his forefingers, he proceeded on with Kate's education. Didn't she know that men were a prized commodity, much in demand? That there were ten times—a *hundred* times!—more single women then men out there? And hey, if a babe wouldn't stand for a few drinks, what the hell was she worth anyway? A tightwad with money would be a tightwad in bed, so why bother? There were too many broads waiting to be laid to waste time with the ones who wouldn't ante up a little dough now and then. There wasn't anything that couldn't be worked right, if you only used a bit of brainpower. Hadn't she figured that out yet?

After a while, Kate's nerves were rubbed raw. Both by the rapid-fire vulgarity of the man, and by his constant twitching and tapping and jerking and all other manner of hyperactive fidgeting. Finally, when it looked as if her tutoring in the fine art of getting laid would continue on, she caught Sam's eye. "I need to make that phone call now. Could you finish up for me?"

Sam's face stayed expressionless, but she saw the humor come into his eyes. There was no phone call, and he knew it. His look said, I'll get you later for this, but he nodded and she escaped.

Worn down and drained, she walked straight past the homicide division to the coffeepot over in Narcotics. It was quiet this afternoon. Three men were grouped around a distant desk, conversing in low voices. Another was on a phone nearby. A fifth had his head down over a stack of paperwork higher than hers. Brillo was nowhere in sight.

She filled a Styrofoam cup with the strong, bitter brew, then leaned back against the same filing cabinet she'd been using when Brillo had found her there early that morning. God, was it still only Friday? She glanced at her watch. Still Friday and only three-thirty. Phyllis Walsh had called in at lunchtime and postponed her appointment until four. That gave her half an hour of relatively free time to try and regain some calm and tranquillity.

She was so damned disappointed with the interview with Riley. It was difficult to believe he was hiding *anything,* never mind any guilty knowledge of a triple murder. He certainly seemed to have no sense of guilt or wrongdoing at the scams he'd pulled. The world was peopled with suckers waiting to have their pockets picked, and he'd made it a lifetime career to accommodate them. He was just another flimflam man. He'd lie, cheat, steal—and yes, probably kill, if it was part of the scam. But not this time. If he'd planted any poison, there'd be areas of questioning where his eyes would turn blankly innocent and a flood of misdirection and misinformation would pour forth. A direct questions would *not* be answered in a direct manner. He really was what he appeared to be, and nothing more. And it shot her lunchtime theory all to hell. She was back where she'd started. With Phyllis.

She found a more comfortable position for her shoulder blades against the metal cabinets and took a swallow of the coffee, closed her eyes and tried to summon up a sinister figure. What was he thinking, this killer of hers? What was he after, what was his goal? Why would he want three women dead? Not just one. Three. Or was he not through yet? Were there more to come? If so, was Phyllis Walsh next on the list? Or would it be a perfect stranger, someone not involved with the case yet? What about the janitor? Was there *any* possibility there?

"Is this a private think tank, or can anyone join?"

She opened her eyes. Sam stood at the coffeepot, fixing himself some coffee. His face was drawn and his eyes looked tired. Three days and they were already wearing down. She was going to have to see to it they paced themselves a little better. Her tendency was to go until she dropped, grab some sleep, then go again. That wouldn't do for the long haul. Detectives were salaried, not hourly. Overtime was paid in comp time, not dollars. And from previous cases, she'd already built up enough comp hours to take a month off if she wanted to. She'd have to watch carefully to see another month's worth didn't pile up in the next few days.

Without straightening up from the filing cabinet, which was quickly becoming an old familiar friend, she held her cup out for a refill. "Riley done?"

"He's waiting for the statement to be typed." He topped off her cup.

She stared at the muddy liquid. "Sorry I walked out on you like that."

Sam took the cabinet next to hers, leaning against it sideways so he faced her. "You owe me big-time now. It got so bad in there I thought I was going to need an up-chuck bag. And I'm not even a member of the female sex."

She shuddered. "Sex. Don't even mention it. He's enough to make me want to take vows at a convent. Did you think to ask Riley if he's kept his apartment in Renton?"

"Yep. And yes, he did." He grinned. "Since you don't want me mentioning sex, I won't go into all the whys and wherefores. Suffice it to say that faithfulness to Catherine was not uppermost in his mind."

"What about searching it?"

His grin broadened. "That, too. He not only gave us permission, he suggested I take you there to supervise the search personally. He indicated he had some unusual toys that we might be interested in."

Kate simply shook her head. "The man's amazing. Disgustingly amazing."

"Maybe that's part of his charm. You think I should try his technique and see if it'll get me anywhere?"

"It'll get you a cold bed, is what it'll get you." She sighed. "I guess I have to take my gorgeous theories about him and Catherine and money and insurance and trash them all. Reluctantly, mind you. I'd love to see him swinging from a rope—"

"He'd probably choose lethal injection."

"Okay, then, swinging from the end of a needle. I don't care. I'd even push the plunger down." She straightened up, emptied her cup and tossed it into the trash can. "Okay, Morrison, ever onward and upward. Walsh is next. Maybe *she* can persuade me she did it. Everyone else seems to think she did. Maybe I'm wrong, after all."

"Perish the thought."

His face was impassive when she looked at him.

Phyllis Walsh came in with her husband. She was dressed in a beautifully-cut blue tweed suit, with a pale-blue blouse ruffled at the neck, her usual professional and competent look. But she was wan and pale, and obviously shaky on her feet, clinging tightly to her husband's arm for support. Richard Walsh seemed much calmer since the morning, much more composed and in command. He even managed a civilized nod of greeting toward Kate.

"How are you feeling?" Kate asked her when she went to the security gate to meet them.

"Dreadful. The doctor's given me some medication and it's left me feeling sluggish. My head feels like it's lost in a cloud bank somewhere, my brain feels like cooked spaghetti, and when I go to move, I'm never sure my legs will hold me up." She gave a wan smile. "Other than that, I'm in great shape."

Kate smiled back sympathetically. "That'll wear off. Come on back, Phyllis, we have a few questions for you. Mr. Walsh, we have a small waiting area where you can make yourself comfortable. I can bring you some coffee if you'd like."

He was shaking his head even before she finished talking, his gaze intent on hers, his jaw firm. "You won't be taking Phyllis anywhere. We have a lawyer meeting us here in a few minutes."

He'd caught her by surprise. "I beg your pardon?"

"We have a lawyer due to meet us here, now," he said patiently.

"Who?"

"Ralph Remington. Our family attorney recommended him. Supposedly he's very good." Walsh shrugged. "I've never heard of him."

Kate had, and she stared at Walsh with dismay. Ralph Remington was one of the state's premier defense attorneys, working only the most sensational murder cases, and he'd successfully acquitted clients from Spokane to Forks. The few—the very few—who had been convicted had still been spared the death sentence. He was tough, ruthless and notorious. He also was flamingly gifted with the media. He played the press like a violin virtuoso and they loved him. He was always outstanding copy. And with a full head of flowing white hair and courtly Old World manners and charm, he received more than his share of television air time. She wondered that Richard Walsh had never heard of him.

But worse, when the Chief heard about this, it would cinch his conviction that Phyllis was the killer. In his eyes, only the guilty hired Remington. There'd be no stopping him then. He'd go straight for the warrant. What a mess. She cleared her throat, seeking some way of undoing the damage that was bound to occur if Remington was brought in on the case at this point. "We need to talk," she said, keeping her voice calm. "Let's go where we can be private, just the three of us."

Walsh looked uncertain. "I don't think we're supposed to do that. I don't think we're supposed to talk to you at all."

She nodded grimly. "That's about the case. About the details, answering questions. What I want to talk to you about is how the world really works. Please follow me."

Without waiting for a response, she swung around on her heels and led them to the interrogation room she'd been using. She waved Sam back as he started to follow. "Later," she muttered as she led the Walshes past him.

Once in the interrogation room, with the door firmly closed, she sat the two of them together on one side of the table while she took the opposite side. She wasted no time. If Remington was due any minute, he'd yank them from her grasp as soon as he arrived.

She leaned forward. "Let me sketch out for you our situation here, and what's liable to happen if Ralph Remington enters the case at this point. I'm not going to bat words around in an effort to be diplomatic, Phyllis. If you polled the station house today, every damned person in the place would vote you guilty. Including the Captain, whom I report to, and the Chief upstairs, whom the Captain reports to. The only thing keeping you on the street is my insistence that we explore every possible lead in the case before we jump on you. Now, that's the plain and bald truth. I'm it between you and jail."

Shocked, Phyllis stared at her. Richard started to react, but Kate shut him down with an impatient gesture.

"Let me explain my job a second here," she continued on. "My brief as D.I.C. is to produce an airtight case for the prosecutor to try in court. With no loopholes, no cracks, no sloppy casework. To do that, I have to keep an open mind until all the facts are in and the evidence clearly points to the guilty party. To uncover the evidence, we explore and question and probe and analyze a whole range of people involved in the case and track down whatever physical evidence exists that can help pinpoint the murderer. The one thing I have to be damned careful about is not jumping to quick conclusions until the evidence warrants it. In this particular case, we're still missing a key bit of information which I feel is going to be critical to successfully solving the murders. And until that information is in, I really don't want to make a move. Not on you, not on anyone."

Both Walshes were listening intently, emotions forgotten.

Kate took a deep breath. "Now let me describe Remington to you. He's the Lee Bailey of Washington State. He takes on seemingly indefensible cases and blows holes in them big enough for his clients to walk through. And walk they do. He has something like a ninety-eight percent record of acquittals. As you can imagine, he's as popular as the plague with the D.A.'s and cops around the state. They hate his guts. They're convinced that he's set all manner of evil beings free to roam the streets and kill again. And unfortunately he has, more often than we like to think about."

Richard Walsh had skimmed ahead and anticipated her. "What you're saying is that by hiring someone with Remington's reputation, Phyllis is going to look guilty as hell to the D.A."

"Exactly. *If* you are charged with the murders, Phyllis—and I stress the *if* you could do no better than to get Remington. But I'm afraid of the conclusions that'll be drawn if he shows up at this point in the case."

"But only this morning you yourself agreed we needed legal advice," Walsh pointed out.

"I guess I had in mind someone cautious and conservative who wouldn't let you place yourself in a bad position legally. But someone—uh, a little less flamboyant, a quieter personality who wouldn't push things to a forced conclusion."

He was shaking his head before she'd even finished. "I'm not going to buy that. We've got a system of justice in this country that's based on justice for all. And one of the rights we're guaranteed is legal representation. I can't believe it's going to make a difference one way or the other who we hire. Except in the matter of competence. The more competent the man, the better our position. Because my wife didn't do this. She didn't do any of this. And I want her out from under suspicion as quickly as possible. And you don't do that by retaining someone less competent than the top."

"We're talking people here, Mr. Walsh. Not justice. People and personalities, actions and reactions. We can never really know what goes on in another person's mind. To a certain extent, we all have to judge on appearances. You do it, Phyllis does it, cops do it. And the D.A.'s office does it. I'm just trying to persuade you to *not* give the wrong impression."

"Miss MacLean, my wife has insisted that you're a fair person, that you've treated her decently. But you *are* a cop, and we can only trust you so far before we begin to hurt ourselves. I'm not so damned convinced my wife should've been as open as she has been with you. But that's neither here nor there at the moment. What *I'm* hearing you say is that we've got a bunch of asses running the police department and the D.A.'s office, so we shouldn't do anything to upset them. And that's—if you'll forgive the crudeness—plain bullshit. We need legal advice, and I'm getting the best available, and that's the end of it. If the Chief or your Captain or the D.A.'s office has a problem with that, then it's their problem, not ours."

"But that's what I'm trying to tell you, Mr. Walsh," Kate said softly. "It *will* be your problem. If your wife is arrested for murder in the first degree, you're going to have one *whale* of a problem."

She almost had him. Listening, at least. Thinking, anyway, if not completely persuaded yet.

Then Phyllis stepped in. During the exchange, her face had slowly whitened as her position became ever clearer, and now her composure deserted her. "Richard, maybe we should listen," she said desperately. "Maybe she knows what she's talking about." Her eyes were huge, fastened onto his in mute appeal.

That did it. Any chance of consideration was gone. Walsh's face turned hard and his jaw stuck out like a window ledge. "She's a cop. She's on their side." All of his pugnaciousness was back now. He knew what he knew, and he wasn't going to be talked out of it.

Kate sighed. To continue arguing with him would be fruitless.

She wouldn't be able to budge him now. Which meant Remington would be entering the case. What would be, would be. *Que será será.* Acknowledging the inevitability of it all now, she reached across the table and gave Phyllis' hand a reassuring pat, then rose. "Let me get you some coffee while you're waiting."

There wasn't much of anything else left to say.

20

When Ralph Remington entered the building, his timing couldn't have been worse. He was so damned noticeable, and there were so damned many people there to notice.

The bull pen was full of cops—plain-clothed cops, uniformed cops, on-duty cops, off-duty cops—brought in by Schreiber and Rice to pick up their pharmacy assignments. As they became aware of the elegant, slightly-stooped figure standing patiently at the security gate, talk died away and the bull pen fell completely silent for a moment except for one lonely phone ringing its head off.

Goddard and Fry were back, too—coming in together, Kate noticed, as she walked forward to greet the lawyer—and Goddard's lips pursed in a silent whistle. Never a slow thinker, he glanced from her to Remington and back again, made a shrewd guess, and began to grin. She could've smacked him one. Any thought Kate had of slipping Remington unnoticed in and out of the station house fled.

She reached the security gate and nodded. "Mr. Remington," she said evenly.

"Detective MacLean?" He was on the downward side of sixty, with a long, flowing mane of white hair. As he greeted her, he gave a courtly half-bow that was totally in keeping with his elegance, the white locks falling forward slightly on either side of his neck. His smile was gentle and his blue eyes were benign. He looked more like a revered symphony conductor than a lawyer. "I'm Ralph Remington, and this is a pleasure, I assure you."

He knew how to appreciate a woman visually. As his eyes moved slowly over her face, his appreciation at what he found visibly grew and grew. By the time he was finished with the minute examination, he'd taken a thorough reading of her character and temperament while making her feel like the most attractive and appealing woman he'd ever met. A powerful and heady feeling for any woman. But it was all done with such a grave, gentlemanly air, it was impossible to take offense. No wonder prosecutors all over the state went nuts trying to keep women off the juries when he was in court, Kate thought.

To her own amazement, she found herself smiling back at him. When she realized it, she stopped and turned instantly serious.

He'd seen and accurately read her initial reaction, though, and a slight twinkle entered his eye. "A pleasure indeed." The courtesies over, he, too, grew solemn. "I believe we have a client of mine here?" His voice was rich with inflection, a baritone with undertones to the undertones. An orator's voice. "Phyllis Walsh?"

Kate nodded. "Please follow me."

Up to that moment, in spite of the onlookers in the bull pen, things had been calm and under control. But as she led Remington back to the interrogation room where the Walshes waited, the Captain chose that moment to emerge from his office.

He stopped dead at the sight of the elegant attorney. Like Goddard, he, too, took it all in with one glance. Well aware of the stir he was creating, Remington twinkled and gave him a courtly nod as he passed. The Captain's eyes went dark and muddy and he turned the full force of his glare onto Kate. With only a slightly rueful smile, she ushered the attorney past him into the interrogation room, made the introductions, then left Remington alone to confer with his clients.

The Captain was waiting for her, of course, his thick body blocking her path like a hulking semi blocking a motor scooter.

He nodded toward the closed door behind her and snapped, "Tell me Phyllis Walsh isn't in there!" His fury glued her into place.

She said quietly, "I can't."

Hatch stared at her in disbelief, then drew in a breath so long and so deep that when he exhaled it came out in one loud whoosh. He gave one menacing beckon aimed her way, turned on his heel and marched straight into his office. Taking her own deep breath to maintain her calm, Kate followed him.

He'd sunk into his huge swivel chair by the time she entered. He didn't motion her to sit, so she stood. The blinds were still down. It had been that kind of day.

His eyes were dark and unreadable, his face an icy mask. "I want every note, a transcript of every interview and every scrap of anything else you've got on that woman. I want to know why the hell the woman felt so compelled to hire Remington that she did so before she was ever charged!"

"It won't do the case any good to jump to conclusions," she said as calmly as she could manage.

"It doesn't appear that *I'm* the one jumping to conclusions!" he snorted.

"We don't have a case built against any one person yet. There isn't one shred of physical evidence to point in any direction. No eyewitnesses, no fingerprints, and no morphine."

Hatch snorted. "The hell with that! You don't always need the smoking pistol to know who pulled the trigger!"

"We could be open to an harassment charge if we aren't careful."

"Only the guilty hire Remington. It's as good as a confession!"

Kate matched him with stubbornness. "We need the morphine link."

"We've got everything else. Motive and opportunity. We can go with that."

"It's not enough."

Hatch's voice now was the same pure ice of his eyes. "Not enough? Three hundred grand in insurance, not enough? Sole ownership of a wealthy little business instead of quarter owner of a starving one, not enough? A bitter feud with one partner, a second partner who'd sign checks for anyone who wanted them, that's not enough? I wish we'd had that much in all the other cases we've handled. They'd have been a cakewalk."

A pulse in her head began pounding. "And the third partner, Captain? What about Suzie? What's the reason for Walsh killing her? They were the best of friends."

"She was silenced because she knew Walsh had done it."

"And how did she know that?" Kate snapped.

"She knew she herself was innocent. Ergo, it had to be Walsh."

"So Phyllis kills her so that she's the only partner left, and now the whole world knows she did it instead of just Suzie?" Kate shook her head at the reasoning. "Remington'll make hash out of that. He'll blow more holes in our case than a pistol at a firing range. He'll confuse the jury to the point where reasonable doubt not only exists, it'll be as clear and real to them as the chairs they sit on. Then Phyllis Walsh will walk. All because we jumped too soon."

"All right, supposing *you* tell *me* what's coming down." The Captain squeaked his chair back and steepled his fingers, supporting his chin, as he watched her intently.

Uninvited, she sank onto the edge of a chair. "As far as the morphine goes, the search is underway. I managed to snag Schreiber and Rice to head it up, and they've got men pounding the pavements now. I've ordered them to canvas every pharmacy within King County and get the names, addresses and prescribing doctors for every grain of morphine sold since the first of the year. We'll take those names and find out why the morphine was bought. In most cases, I suspect, it'll turn out to be for some kind of a terminal disease, like cancer or AIDS. But whatever the reason, I intend to have every purchase of the morphine explained to me by the time we're through with the search."

He lowered his fingers a second to ask, "And if there's some that can't be explained?"

"Then we're going to zero in on those people who bought it for no valid reason and look for a connection to the dead women."

The fingers steepled again. "Go on."

"If we could prove access to the morphine, I'm positive we'd have our killer. Or at least a bloody arrow pointing his way. But it'll take a few days for leads to start getting back to us."

"You got *any* other ideas going for you at all?"

She hesitated. She did have one, half-formed. Could she put it into words? If so, was this the time? Well, she thought ruefully, things couldn't get much worse. What the hell . . . She edged a little bit further forward in her chair. "Supposing Phyllis Walsh really *didn't* do it . . . That means the whole thing's being set up to make it look like she did. So the question is, who'd want her to take the fall? Catherine Fletcher would be my main candidate, but she's dead, too. The only other person who could possibly benefit would be Phyllis' husband. He and Phyllis have a lot of assets. They've managed to salt away a nice tidy nest egg. Supposing, for some reason, he wants out of the marriage, but doesn't want to give up what a divorce would cost him. He kills her partners, frames her, then, when she's convicted, he gets his divorce *and* all the assets, and he's free as a robin in the spring."

"If he wants out so badly, why wouldn't he simply kill her instead? Why go to all the time and trouble to be so indirect about it?"

"Because if he killed her, he knows we'd be all over him like fur on a dog. Unless he committed a perfect crime. And they're as rare as sunshine in Seattle. So this was his substitute."

"Isn't this stretching credibility a bit thin here?"

"Maybe," she answered slowly. "There's only two possibilities, though. Either Phyllis Walsh did it, or Phyllis Walsh didn't do it. There are no other choices. If she did it, that's that. But if she *didn't,* then *someone* has gone to a lot of trouble to make it look like she did. It's a theory worth following up."

"And tell me, clearly and succinctly, why you're so convinced Walsh is innocent."

She chose her words carefully. "First, her character doesn't fit the profile of the killer. We're looking for a cold-blooded intellect with the patience to plant the killing seeds and sit back and watch them flower. Phyllis is not that kind of person. She'd have to be powerfully enraged to kill someone. Even then, it would be on the spur of the moment, a case of picking up a handy pistol and pulling the trigger. But we're not dealing with anything like that here. These murders have been coldly calculated, planned and executed. They're not crimes of passion; they're crimes of the intellect. Secondly, it's a gimme. It's too easy, too blatant. There's no free lunch in a murder case, Captain, but someone's trying to hand us one."

He brooded on it, his chin resting heavily on his fingertips, his dark eyes staring sightlessly at his desktop piled with stacks of folders. "Jesus," he muttered finally, "you're one stubborn broad . . . You get something stuck in your craw, and you don't budge, do you." He passed a hand over his face, drawing his muscles down, then releasing them. His chair came alive with an abrupt screech. He sat up at his desk and peered at her from under the shrubby brows. "All right. My ass is on the line on this. And that means *your* ass is on the line on this. If you expect me to back you up, you better come up with something more concrete than just the pabulum you've been feeding me. In the meantime, I'll tell them upstairs that the investigation is not conclusive yet, that there's still a theory or two left to check out. I can make them give us a bit more time. But not much. Not with Remington on the case. You do what you can on Richard Walsh, and see what the morphine hunt turns up. But if you don't find anything—or if anything else happens that implicates her further—you go for the warrant on her. And without any prompting from me! Hear?"

She rose. "Yes, sir."

Swamped with relief, she left him. He was going to back her up. By God, he really was going to do it! Knees weak, Kate found her desk and sank gratefully into her chair and buried her head in her hands.

Sam came over and sat on the edge of her desk. "What's going on?"

Kate peered up at him through her fingers. "The Walshes felt the need for some legal advice. They've hired Ralph Remington."

"Jesus."

Kate nodded tiredly. "That's what the Captain said. Along with a few other choice words."

Sam's face turned thoughtful. "The brass going to bring in the D.A. now?"

She shook her head glumly. "Not quite yet. The Captain's going to get me a bit more time. Not much, but some." Her phone rang just then. With a look of apology toward Sam, she picked it up. "MacLean."

"Good news, Katie, my love." Her brain was still sludge from the encounter with the Captain and it took a moment to recognize the chipper voice booming in her ear. Homer. "All the samples from the Walsh house have come up clean. No morphine anywhere. They can drink coffee, tea or whatever, and know they'll wake up to see another day."

"What about the sink traps? Any traces there?"

"I'll let you know soon as they're tested. I cleared the things that might do them in first. Hi-de-ho, it's off to work I go . . ." He hung up.

"That was Homer," she said to Sam. "No sign of morphine at the Walshes so far." She glanced over to where Schreiber and Rice were handing out assignments. "I need to see Dennis and Charlie and tell them we're on a tight deadline. That morphine has got to be found."

When she rose from the chair she was surprised to find her legs still a bit shaky. The Captain had terrified her. Literally terrified her. And her adrenaline had gushed out in the old fight-or-flight surge. Now she was left feeling drained and physically weak.

Sam's sharp gaze caught the slight stagger she gave leaving her chair. "Are you all right?"

She walked around, taking deep breaths, gaining strength. "Yeah, just a bit of a reaction to a terrorist is all." Once her legs were reliable, she moved off toward Schreiber and Rice.

Goddard ambled forward on a path designed to intercept hers. The faint tinge of righteousness in his look set her teeth on edge, but she merely nodded to him. "How'd you make out with the janitor?" she asked.

"There's nothing there, trust me." Goddard looked smug, making no effort to hide an I-told-you-so smile. "He's buying an old junker of a car, on time. He's buying a ten-year-old piece of fishing shit, also on time. He's got three kids and doctor bills up his ass. His credit cards are maxed out, and his Sears bill is outta sight. And every now and then, he bounces a check to try and keep it all together. Just your average working jerk. Robbery he might attempt, but murder? Nope? Not when he doesn't gain anything."

"What about Fry? He have any luck on the condo records?"

Goddard shook his head, looking pleased. "Dead end. Owned by a holding company owned by another holding company owned by an off-shore corporation. We don't have the clout to penetrate that curtain."

"What about the feds? Would they have any information on the off-shore corporation?"

"Fry says no. Looks like you're stuck with the Walsh broad." He grinned, enjoying her disappointment. "Kind of blows your game plan, hunh."

Bastard. "Not really," she said calmly. "We just work harder is all," and she moved on.

She pulled Schreiber and Rice far enough to the side where they could talk without being overheard. "We're running out of time, fellas. This is what I want. It's Friday night, a lot of the pharmacies will be staying open late tonight. Have your men cover all of those, then finish up the others tomorrow. By tomorrow night, I want the name and address of everyone who bought morphine in King County since the first of the year. Also the name of the prescribing doctor. And none of this confidentiality crap. Pharmacists are not doctors. They should be willing to help. Then Sunday, we'll start tracking the customers down."

She was asking the near impossible. Even under the best of circumstances, it wouldn't go that smoothly. But neither man bothered to point it out to her. She received nods of agreements, not arguments, bless them both. "By the way," she added, "Goddard's free to help now, too. Fry, too. Go ahead and use them both. Liberally." Rice's sympathetic grin plainly said her problems with the Wonder Boys had made the bull pen circuit. Well, so be it. She had enough wasps loose from their nest without worrying any further about those two.

The bull pen gradually emptied as the teams received their assignments and moved out. A measure of early-evening calm descended. The welcome stillness should have allowed Kate to concentrate on her work, but she found herself watching Schreiber and Rice instead. The first report back hadn't even come in yet, and she was already waiting for the bloody arrow to hone in on the bull's-eye. It was irrational, she knew, and she fought the urge to watch them, but discovered after a moment or two that she'd be back at it again. She finally chalked it up to tiredness. Her day had started fifteen hours ago and lunch was a childhood memory. She stretched her legs and looked over at Sam. "Let's go eat."

When they walked out to the parking lot, day was already dwindling into dusk. The sun was just going down behind the Olympic Mountain Range and the western sky shimmered in a shroud of pinks and oranges and crimsons. She stopped to watch. The colors deepened as the sun hung on the horizon for a long moment before sliding down out of sight. Slowly the blush died away and the black night sky took over.

The new night's chill had deleted the last lingering warmth of the day. Shivering, she followed Sam to his car. She'd missed it, she thought, with a pang of regret. She'd missed a perfect spring day in Puget Sound. The kind of day to comb deserted beaches for driftwood and seashells, to hike the mountain ranges through hillsides of spring wildflowers, to explore the islands of the Sound and ride bikes through their deserted lanes curving around meadow and forest. The kind of day to run away and play.

They made a quick stop for the evening newspapers and went to a hole-in-the-wall for Mexican. After they'd ordered their food, Kate sat back in the booth and eyed Sam speculatively. "We're becoming workaholics, you and I," she said to him. "You know that?"

"What brought this on?"

"The sunset. Do you realize I have a month of Sundays coming to me, and today was a gorgeous day, and I could've taken one of my Sundays and gone and done something fun with it? Kicked up my heels a little? Been just plain unthinking and irresponsible?" She gestured extravagantly. "We're surrounded by green forests and snow-capped mountains and white boats on blue water. And what do I spend my day looking at? Dung-colored walls. Now that's sad, Sam, it really is. I might as well be

working New York City for all the good living here does me."
She looked at him. "And you, too. You're no better than I am.
We have to change our life-style, Sam. We have to do things
differently."

"I agree. So we'll start tonight. I hereby invite you aboard my
private yacht, the Bremerton ferry. A majestic round-trip cruise,
coupled with wine and moonlight and the tang of salt air. As
well as other paying passengers, of course. But what the hell,
right?"

The idea captured her imagination. She could picture them
aboard the ferry heading out into the night darkness of the
Sound, the skyscrapers of Seattle rising like bejeweled giants
clustered on the hillsides behind them. Heavy laden freighters
from the Orient would glide on past the rail, headed for port,
and in the distance, the islands would rise like low, dark shrouds
out of the black waters surrounding them. She could see it all,
and she hungered for it.

She sighed. "You see what I mean?"

"Do I see what?"

"I can't go," she said ruefully. "I have to work tonight."

He grinned. Point made.

"Someday . . ."

They spread the newspapers out on the table between them
where they could both read the front page. The headline said it
all. REMINGTON HIRED IN MORPHINE MURDERS! There was a three-
column shot of him emerging with a wan Phyllis Walsh on his
arm. He was bent over her protectively, his hand covering hers,
the slight stoop and the white waving hair increasing the sense of
indignation he portrayed. Next to him, Phyllis Walsh looked
thin and fragile. And terribly, terribly vulnerable. Richard Walsh
was a vague background figure, barely seen standing behind
them.

His client was innocent, Remington proclaimed to the world,
and he was going to do what the police had failed to do . . . He
would bring the full powers of his office to bear on these crimes,
to get them solved and his client cleared of all suspicion. Par for
the course, Kate thought.

Inside the front section, though, there was a coy little editorial that pointed out that Phyllis Walsh was the only surviving partner of a four-member partnership, that she'd already hired the premier defense attorney in the state *before* being accused, and exactly *when* were the police going to bring some charges in the case?

"Ouch," Sam said.

Kate nodded. "They're thinking what everyone else is thinking . . . that she's guilty as hell."

Their orders of food arrived and they tossed the newspapers aside. While they ate, Kate told Sam about her meeting with the Captain. As she outlined her theory about Richard Walsh's setting his wife up, his chewing slowed and his eyes grew concerned. "I hate to pop all your champagne bubbles," he said when she finally finished her tale, "but it's nine to one she's guilty."

She shook her head. "Uh-uh. It's too obvious. She's being set up."

"By her husband." He gave an exasperated sigh. "All right, why? Just tell me that much—why?"

She didn't answer for a moment. His reaction surprised her. He sounded on the verge of real anger. "Sam, we investigated Richard Walsh's money, but we never dug into *him*. Look, this sounds wacky, I know—"

"So what's new?" he murmured.

She tossed him a dirty look. "What if Richard Walsh wants out of the marriage. But he wants out with his money and all his comforts intact. But he's also smart enough to know he can't get away with murdering his wife. We'd be on him like stink on shit if he tried. So he sets it up so the three *partners* die and his wife gets hung for the crime. That frees him up and saves his assets, in one fell swoop."

"Katie . . ."

"No, listen to me, Sam. Maybe he has another romance going. He's met someone, maybe at work. He's in the high-tech industry, isn't he? Aren't they notorious for life in the fast lane, for all the fun and games? Anyway, he's met this chick at work—"

"Katie."

"All right, maybe it's at a bar. Maybe he stops in for an after-work drink and somehow or another they fall in together . . ."

"Kate, goddamn it!"

"*What?!*" She lowered her fork and confronted him, chin stuck out with stubbornness. "Goddamn it *what?!*"

"You're doing it again! You're making up reasons why Phyllis Walsh can't be guilty! Now, goddamn it, cut it out, will you?"

"It's a perfectly valid theory and you know it. In any kind of murder, you look to the nearest and dearest first. You know that, Sam! You're the one who taught me, for Christ's sake!"

"Obviously, I left some parts of your education out!"

They were glaring at each other. Finally Kate sighed. "You think I'm chasing fireflies, don't you." Her voice had a tinge of sadness. "You think that I'm following up every wink and blink that comes my way in an effort to prove Phyllis Walsh didn't do it. That I've gone off half-cocked after a bunch of fireflies that won't even survive the night."

The drop of his gaze was his answer.

Disappointed, she finished the last of the coffee and tossed her napkin on the table. Never ask a question if you don't want to hear the honest answer, she thought. She picked up her purse to ante up her half of the check and tip. "We'd better get back. Maybe Schreiber's getting some reports in by now."

He rose. "Katie . . ."

She looked at him sadly. "No, that's all right, Sam. I understand. Maybe if you were running the case and our beliefs were reversed, I'd think you were crazy, too." She rose and placed her half of the tip on the table. "But I'll tell you this, Sam, that woman's innocent. She's being framed. And I'm going to prove it to you—To you, and the Captain, and the whole damned world. She didn't do it, Sam—*she simply didn't do it!*"

They rode back to the station house in silence. As she climbed out of Sam's car, in spite of the work that was waiting for her, she made a sudden decision to call it a day. Schreiber and Rice were doing what they could, and they didn't need her peering over their shoulder at every phone call. And Sam . . . well, she'd had enough. She'd had enough of cops for one day. All cops.

Including the Captain. Including herself. "I'm going on home, Sam," she said abruptly.

Sighing, he turned her way. "Katie . . ."

She raised a hand to stop him. "It's okay, Sam, honest. We'll talk about it in the morning when we're both not so tired."

"Sure you don't want to go for a ferry-boat ride and talk about it?"

"I'm sure. It's teddy-bear time for me. Good night, Sam."

As she backed her car out of its parking stall, the headlights swept over his figure standing there, watching her. His face wore a look of absolute dejection. Good, she thought, suffer a little. And she roared through the parking lot and turned toward Kirkland.

She thought briefly of a game of pool, but she didn't feel like it. She was feeling bereft and lonely. Always before, she'd been able to depend upon Sam. Always before, they'd worked as a team, using each other's strengths to form a solid whole. But this time, she had this hollow feeling inside that she was on her own. And the trivial chitchat of a tavern would increase the lonesome void inside, not ease it. She passed Smokie Jo's without a glance and headed home.

After retrieving her mail, she scoured the front porch for a florist's package. There was none. Her disappointment was sharp, instant and extreme. With a slight shock, she realized she'd been half hoping . . .

Her depression—if that's what it was—deepened. Standing on her porch, she reconsidered the idea of some pool. Maybe, after all, she did need people around her. Plain, ordinary people simply out to have a bit of fun. Non-cops type of people. But her body rebelled. She ached from head to toe from fatigue. It was bed for her.

She didn't even bother with her usual routine of some quiet reading and a glass of wine before bedtime. She pushed her shoulder holster out of sight in its place on the closet shelf, showered, slipped into her nightgown and fell into bed.

Instantly, she sank into a heavy, deep sleep that grabbed her and wouldn't let her go. Her dreams that night were of a tall and slender dark-haired woman, eyes filled with bleak despair, with shoulders too fragile for the burden they carried. She was being stalked by a blackened, heavy-footed creature that looked like a charred corpse. She stirred in her sleep, trying to escape the intense sense of doom that colored the dream. But it captured her and held her fast. She couldn't seem to break out of it. It was actually a relief when the phone slowly brought her out of the whole rotten morass.

She clicked on the bedside lamp and glanced at the clock. Four A.M. She picked up the receiver and mumbled, "MacLean."

Sleep fled and she jerked upright from her pillows as she listened to the droning voice on the other end. Richard Walsh had been found dead at home, and Phyllis Walsh had been the one to find him.

"Oh, God," she whispered into thin air. "Oh, *damn* it, God."

21

The body of Richard Walsh lay on the couch in the lower-level family room. He was still dressed in the suit slacks and shirt he'd worn that day, his jacket pulled off and tossed over the arm of a nearby chair, his tie loosened and his collar button open. His head was cushioned by a couple of loose sofa pillows. One arm dangled to the floor. The back of his hand rested on the rug, open and loose. An empty glass lay on its side inches away from his fingertips, a puddle of liquid darkening the rug near its mouth. His face had the same peaceful look of sleep that the other victims had had. And there was that same odious stillness of death.

The M.E. was already there, bent over the body. He straightened up and looked at Kate. "Looks the same as the others," he said in a gruff tone. "Pupils are contracted to a pencil point. My guess is it was in there." He pointed to two bottles of Scotch on the coffee table, one empty, the other half empty.

"Morphine?"

"Almost a given," the M.E. said.

"How long ago?" Kate asked.

"Death? Oh, a couple of hours, more or less. I'll know better when I take the temperature of the body."

Kate took in the scene one last time. A man, drinking alone.

Not reading, not watching television, not listening to music, just drinking. She made her way up a level to the living room at the front of the house, pausing in the archway.

Phyllis Walsh, in pink robe and slippers, sat huddled, crying, on the couch by the fireplace, her legs drawn up and her feet tucked beneath one hip. The last of her reserves had gone and she wept the way a child weeps; head bowed, hands folded loosely in her lap, tears sheeting her cheeks. There was no effort made to stop them, nor to prevent them from dripping onto the front of her robe. An ever-spreading wet spot was darkening the pink. She hadn't seen Kate yet.

A beat cop standing guard came over to Kate. "She's been this way since we got here," he said in an undertone.

"Okay. Let me talk to her. You stay close and witness." She moved so she stood directly in front of the woman. "Phyllis?" she said softly.

Slowly, Phyllis raised her head. Her eyes were swimming with tears and her wet cheeks glistened brightly in the soft lamplight. "Oh, Katie . . . Richard is . . . is . . ." She couldn't get it out.

"I know."

"I didn't do it. Katie, I didn't do it! You've got to believe me! I didn't do it, not any of it!" A fresh burst of weeping broke out and her head dropped again.

"Phyllis." Kate kept her voice soft and waited for the woman to raise her head again. "I have to read you your rights. You understand that?" She waited for the nod. Kate repeated the memorized ritual, then asked, "Do you understand what I've just said?"

"Yes." Phyllis' voice was ragged, hoarse from the weeping.

Kate looked meaningfully at the cop. He nodded. She mimed writing in a notebook and he took out a small pocket pad and a pen. When he was ready, she asked Phyllis, "I'm going to ask you a few questions now. You don't have to answer them if you don't want, but it would help if you would. Can you tell me what happened?"

Fresh tears welled up and overflowed. "I don't know. I came down and—found him. That's all I know."

"You'd been asleep?"

Phyllis nodded.

"What woke you up?"

"I haven't been sleeping well. I'm up and down all night long. Ever since . . ." She faded out, the meaning clear.

"When were you up last before this time?"

"About ten. I took a sleeping pill."

"What time did you go to bed after that?"

"About ten-thirty."

"And you woke up when?"

"About three-thirty."

"Had your husband been to bed at all?"

Fresh tears poured out. "No," she whispered.

"He didn't go to bed with you?"

"No. He hasn't been." There was almost shame in the admission.

"I saw the bottles of Scotch. Has he been drinking a lot?"

Phyllis nodded. "Ever since Catherine was killed. He knew everyone thought I'd done it. I mean, *he* didn't think that. But he knew everyone else did, and it got to him. But I didn't, Katie. I didn't do any of them . . . And now, Richard . . ." She caved in again, buried her head in her hands and wept anew.

Kate gave her time to regain some control, then asked, "When you came downstairs, did you find him right away?"

Phyllis shook her head, tears still streaming. "No. I went to the kitchen for a glass of iced water. I saw the light on below in the family room, but I didn't hear anything, so I thought he was just asleep."

"Then what did you do?"

"I sat at the kitchen table, drinking the iced water. And then, when I was ready to go back up to bed, I went down to wake him . . ." Her voice broke and the tears started again. "Oh, God . . . if only I hadn't sat there. If only I'd gone to wake him sooner . . ."

"Phyllis, just a few more questions." Kate waited patiently again until Phyllis looked up again, the tears back under some control. "Did you drink any of the Scotch?"

She shook her head. "I don't like the taste."

"What do you usually drink?"

"Vodka. Always vodka and something."

"Did you have any vodka tonight? Any liquor at all? Wine, or anything?"

"No, I've been too upset to drink. All I had was the water. Oh, God, Katie, if only I hadn't . . . if only I hadn't thought he was asleep. If I'd just said something to him, gone to him, skipped the water. . ." She was back out of control again, the tears drowning out her speech.

Kate squatted in front of her, taking her hands in hers, by the sheer intensity of her look forcing the other woman to meet her eyes. "Phyllis, listen to me. From what the M.E. said, he was already dead before you ever woke up. You could've skipped fifty glasses of iced water and it wouldn't have made any difference. Don't do this to yourself. You'll drive yourself crazy if you do."

"I can't stop thinking about it . . ." Phyllis held on to Kate's hands like a life raft. "Katie," she whispered, "please help me. Help me, Katie . . . I don't know what's happening anymore . . . Please help me . . ."

"I'll do what I can, Phyllis, I promise. But you'll have to help me, too. Is there *anyone* you can think of who wants to harm you like this? *Anyone*, no matter how absurd or remote the possibility? Anyone at all?"

Her tears worn out for the moment, Phyllis shook her head slowly. "Catherine," she said hoarsely. "She's the only one I can think of. But she's dead, too, isn't she." She looked lost and hopeless. "There's no one else. There's simply no one else, is there."

There wasn't any answer to that one. Kate didn't even try.

Sam was just arriving when she reached the station, Phyllis seated next to her and the beat cop in the back seat, and they pulled in next to each other. He came over and opened the driver's door for her, peering quickly over at Phyllis, then back to Kate. "What's going on?"

"Someone got to Richard Walsh," she said, wearily climbing out. "He's dead. Morphine in the Scotch. At least that's what the M.E. thinks."

If he noted the use of the vague "someone," he let it pass. He watched Phyllis climb out with the help of the beat cop. Her face was dead-white and skeletal, her cheeks sunken in, her eye sockets ringed with black. She looked like someone suffering the ravages of a terminal illness. There was no trace of the competent professional woman whom Sam had first met four days ago. With a tilt of his head, he asked in an undertone, "Is she all right?"

"She's better than she was. She's gone numb. Shock, I think. But to answer your questions, no, she's in bad shape. Emotionally, physically—and every other way." As she watched the cop guide Phyllis into the building, she leaned back against the car fender, hugging herself for warmth. Dawn had broken, but the night dampness still clung in the air.

"What exactly happened?"

"Evidently Richard Walsh has been hitting the bottle pretty steadily all week . . . ever since Catherine died, according to what Phyllis said. So she went to bed alone around ten-thirty and slept until three-thirty. When she went downstairs, she thought he was just asleep on the couch. She was thirsty, so she had some iced water, then went to wake him up. Only he wasn't asleep."

Sam shook his head in empathy. "Tough one, that. Are you going to book her?"

"I guess I have to."

"It's pretty well airtight now, isn't it? A husband and three partners?"

"There's still no morphine, Sam."

"But who else would have a chance to spike Walsh's liquor?"

She stared down at the ground and swung a toe at a pebble. Then she peered up at him. "I know," she said glumly. "I know what it looks like. I know the pattern's crystal-clear and everyone can see it except me." She stared into the distance. "I keep remembering her face, Sam. How she looked when I told her Suzie was dead. She'd been shocked by the other two murders. But Suzie's absolutely devastated her. And tonight—you should've seen her, Sam. The total collapse—there was nothing of her left. It was as if she'd been turned inside out and the contents dumped . . . There was just nothing left."

"So she's a good actress."

"Or maybe she really *is* innocent."

"And maybe there is a Santa Claus."

She gave up. Nothing she'd say would persuade him. Nor the Captain either, she realized. Forces had been set in motion that were out of her control now, and there was no way to prevent them from rushing on. Like the hole in the dike, she thought. A finger can hold the water back just so long before the dam crumbled around it anyway. When it happened, you gave in to the inevitable.

The cop had seated Phyllis in the waiting area and was standing at ease nearby. Phyllis slumped back in the chair, staring at nothing. Kate ordered up a policewoman from the holding cells to release the beat cop back to patrol, saw that Phyllis had some coffee, then headed to her desk. The Captain was next. She glanced at her watch. It wasn't even five-thirty yet. She'd be waking him up. Would that help or hurt? She picked up the phone and dialed.

At her news, his sleep-thickened voice cleared to a growl instantly. "I'll be right down. Don't do *anything* until I get there, you hear?"

"I won't," she said quietly, and hung up.

The bull pen filled up with first arrivals for the day shift. With the morphine hunt on full-bore, the weekend had been canceled. Why cop marriages fail, she thought. She watched the others as they milled around, forming and reforming groups like amoebas under a microscope. The news, she knew, was making the rounds, and there'd be speculation about whether or not the search would be continued. If it was called off, there'd be momentary hopes raised for a weekend being rescued after all. Dream on, she thought. That search will be canceled over my dead body.

Schreiber and Rice, the first in, had their heads bent, coordinating lists. Goddard and Fry were nowhere in sight yet. They'd been assigned to cover pharmacies in the boonies, she knew, which they wouldn't like, and they'd stall coming in until the last possible moment. Hopefully, they'd be in and back out before Ralph Remington appeared.

Remington. So far, Phyllis had shown no indication of wanting to call him in. That had been Richard's idea to begin with, and now Richard was dead and Phyllis seemed ready to let the idea of legal protection die with him. So far, she had done nothing to hurt herself. Unless she was lying, in which case all bets were off, Kate thought. But at some point, the woman was going to tire of the whole process. She was going to be put through one questioning session after another, and eventually it would dawn on her that, innocent though she might be, Remington was needed simply to stop the process. Booked or not, Phyllis Walsh was looking at one long, exhausting day.

When he arrived, instead of heading straight for his office, the Captain detoured to her desk. "Where is she?"

"She's in room three."

"You booked her yet?"

"No. I'm going to get a voluntary statement next if I can."

He nodded, his jowls bobbling with his motions. "Come in," he said, indicating his office. He turned to Sam's desk. "You, too."

Kate's heart sank. She knew what was going to happen next. They'd have another argument about charging Phyllis, the Captain would sit back and listen to her, then he'd turn to Sam for his opinion. And Sam would give it. Sam had the seniority. Sam had the experience. She was D.I.C., but only because in the beginning it had been a nice ladylike murder. Now it wasn't so nice. The Captain would have more confidence in Sam's opinion than in her own. Damn. She picked up her notebook and followed the two men in.

In the privacy of his office, she'd expected the Captain to be bull-headed and angry, impatient with the new murder and ready to climb all over her because Phyllis hadn't been booked yet. But he seemed calm, almost sympathetic, as he took his seat in the over-large chair and motioned them to chairs in front of his desk. "Tell me what happened," he said to Kate. Then he leaned back and steepled his fingers in his normal listening posture.

Kate gave a brief recounting of the facts, much as she had with

Sam. The Captain heard her out, then sat and thought about it for a couple of minutes. His brow creased into a frown—not his normal scowl—just a thoughtful frown, as if he were intent on solving a puzzle in his own mind. Finally he said to Kate, "What do you think?"

"It's pretty hard to know what to think, exactly. I haven't questioned her closely yet. She was so distraught out at her place that it made more sense to get her moving and calmed down and out of there than to put her through a comprehensive interrogation on the spot. I have read her her rights, though. Anything we get from here on out can be used in court, without question."

The near-black eyes never left her face. "But what do you *think?*" he asked again.

"It's looking bad," she finally admitted. "Damned bad."

"Are you persuaded she did it yet?"

"I should be, I guess."

"That isn't what I asked. Are you *persuaded* she did it?"

Trapped by the question and her own honesty, she slowly shook her head. "No. But I can't explain it either. I can't even *begin* to come up with an explanation. I was hoping a thorough questioning might produce something new—a fresh lead or some kind of a breakthrough."

The Captain switched his gaze to Sam. "And you? What's your thinking?"

I knew it! Kate thought. She dropped her gaze to her lap and kept her face expressionless, but her thoughts were roiling like an angry sea. Goddammit, anyway!

Sam was quiet so long that she finally stole a glance his way. He was staring off into space. Finally he spoke in a thoughtful tone. "On the surface, Phyllis looks as guilty as hell. But I know that Katie has some serious doubts. Some instinct is goading her on. In the past, those instincts have always been good. So I guess if I had to choose between what the case *looks* like, and what Katie *thinks* is going on, then I'd have to go with Katie."

In spite of her control, Kate drew in a deeper breath than she should've. He'd come through for her. By God, he'd come through for her! She raised her eyes now and looked directly at the Captain.

He was nodding, his jowls bobbing, his face as thoughtful as Sam's voice. "All right, let's put our little Miss Muffet through some questioning and see what's what. Katie, you handle it. I want it tough, and I want it pointed. I also want to sit in on it." He shoved his chair back. "Let's go."

22

In the interrogation room, Phyllis was sitting lifeless in a chair, shoulders slumped, an untouched cup of coffee in front of her. The policewoman was seated across from her. At the end of the table, the stenographer's equipment was all set up. Kate wanted more than a tape recorder for this session. Though that, too, would be running. From the doorway, she beckoned the officer to her. "Would you have the desk sergeant send in the stenographer, please? Interrogation room three. And please wait, we might need you later."

The policewoman nodded and left.

Kate went around the table and stood behind a chair across from Phyllis. She was shocked at the change in the woman. Her initial reaction had passed and now all emotion was gone. Her shoulders were slumped, her expression vacant. Her eyes were glazed over and her mouth was slack. She looked like a corpse.

Alarmed, Kate bent close to get her attention. "Phyllis." When there was no response, she said more sharply, "Phyllis!" Slowly the eyes raised to Kate's. "Phyllis, drink some of your coffee." She made it an order.

Obediently, like a child, Phyllis picked up her cup and took a swallow. Then her eyes met Kate's again, waiting for the next command. Her mind simply wasn't there.

The two men were standing off to one side of the room. Feeling helpless, Kate looked over to the Captain, still unnoticed by Phyllis. With a single nod acknowledging the situation, he moved to Kate's side and leaned across the table, taking Phyllis' hand in his grasp. "Mrs. Walsh, I'm Captain Hatch. I understand you've been having some problems lately." His voice was sharp and probing, insistent, demanding a response.

Phyllis blinked. After a moment she nodded. Once.

"We want to help you. Do you understand?"

There was another slow taking-in, another blink and finally another nod.

"We're going to ask you a few questions. We need you to answer them. Can you help us?"

Slowly, some intelligence came into her expression. She nodded again, more alert this time.

"All right, then. As soon as the stenographer arrives, Detective MacLean will begin." Satisfied, the Captain released her hands and eased into the background again.

While they waited, Kate kept her eyes on Phyllis. She seemed all right, still a bit numbed, but back in the present at least. Kate did what she could to keep her there. "Phyllis, do you have any family in the area?"

Her voice was soft and vague. "No."

"No one at all?"

Phyllis frowned. "Just my parents in Portland." She was beginning to think now, Kate thought with some relief.

"When we're through here, would you like me to call them for you?"

Slowly Phyllis nodded. "I guess so. They probably should know."

"Right. Will do."

The door was pushed open and the stenographer came in. Kate took the chair across from Phyllis, Sam two seats down, the stenographer at the head of the table by his equipment. The Captain leaned against one wall, out of Phyllis' direct line of sight, but where he had a clear view of her face.

Just to make sure of Phyllis' competency, Kate asked her to state her name and address for the record, as well as the date and time. Then she read her her rights again, and insisted Phyllis state them back to her in her own words. Only then did she take her over the events of the night.

Phyllis told her story, her voice faltering in the beginning, words escaping her now and then so that she had to search for the ones she wanted. But as she talked, her mind seemed once again to function. As she gathered some inner support, her voice strengthened and the story flowed more fluently. By the time she was through, she was fully alert and in control.

The details didn't change. She'd taken a sleeping pill at ten and had gone to bed at ten-thirty. Her husband was on the couch, already at work on the first of the Scotch. She'd woken up at three-thirty, gone downstairs, sat at the kitchen table drinking iced water, thinking her husband was just asleep. At that point, her eyes teared up a little, but she blinked them back, and with only a small break in her voice, went on to tell of finding him, then calling nine-one-one for help.

Kate listened, letting her tell it in her own way, watching her closely to make sure her mind was functioning all right. It seemed to be, and when Phyllis was finished, Kate led her into the next stage of questioning.

She began by backing up in time to a point that needed clearing up—the couple who'd been guests at the Walshes' the previous Saturday night. But nothing suspicious turned up there. They'd been merely some former neighbors who'd come for dinner and to play some bridge. Richard had set up a bar on a library table set in a secluded corner of the living room and had handled all the bartending duties. At no point during the evening had anyone other than Richard been near the table.

So much for that possibility, Kate thought.

She then questioned Phyllis about any other visitors they might've had. Neighbors dropping by for coffee or a drink, a friend stopping in for a casual chat. There was no one. The Walshes, like many working couples, had little time for unplanned socializing with drop-in guests.

Next Kate concentrated on access to the house. "Do you lock your doors at night?"

Yes, Phyllis explained, they kept their doors locked at all

times. Except when they were working out in the yard. And no, they didn't keep a key buried in a flowerpot.

"Does anyone have a key to your house? A cleaning lady, anyone?"

Phyllis shook her head. "No."

"What about deliveries? Your neighbors keep an eye out for deliveries for you? Let the guys into your house, maybe? Like a serviceman or anyone?"

Phyllis shook her head. "No. We either arranged it for weekends, or vacations, or one of us would stay home."

"Any break-ins, robberies, anyone hanging around, any strangers at all in the neighborhood, anyone who didn't belong?"

"No."

"Where do you keep your house key?"

"With my car keys. On a key ring."

"Have you lost or misplaced your key ring at any point?" Kate asked. "Have you lost a wallet, have you been mugged, has your purse been snatched?"

"No."

"Could any of your partners, anyone coming into the office have borrowed your keys?"

"No."

"No one? At any time?"

Phyllis shook her head. "I always kept my key ring in my purse."

"Where did you keep your purse?"

"In my desk. Bottom drawer."

"What about quick trips out of the room? Rest room, lunchroom?"

"My purse went with me."

"Conference room?"

Phyllis thought a minute, then reluctantly shook her head. "I never met clients there."

Kate studied her. "What about Richard? Did he lose his keys or misplace them at all?"

"Not that I know of."

"So no one had a key to your house except you and Richard."

Phyllis could see what she was after, and she tried to come up with an answer. Finally she shook her head, her eyes filled with misery. "No, no one else had a key."

Kate asked the same questions again and again, mixing up the order of them, phrasing them one way, then another. Sam and the Captain looked on. The stenographer kept pace. The answers came up the same. Only two people had keys to the Walsh house—Richard and Phyllis Walsh. And only two people had access to Richard Walsh's Scotch. Richard and Phyllis Walsh.

Kate moved onto the subject of the marriage now.

Richard put in long hours at his job, depending upon the company's needs, Phyllis explained. No, she said, she didn't mind. Those nights he worked late or was out of town traveling allowed her a chance for a quiet dinner and evening on her own. When they were together, they enjoyed each other's company all the more. No, there were seldom any arguments. Those few that did happen occurred when they were both too tired to cope with running a household as well as a job, and centered on who'd do the cooking and who had to do the clean-up. That was one reason they were looking for recreational property. As an escape hatch from the pressures of the work week. They'd been looking for a couple of years now, and hadn't found just the right parcel of land yet.

Up until now, Kate had worked at establishing an easy, rhythmic flow of questions and answers. So easy, in fact, that Phyllis directed her answers to both detectives, her gaze switching back and forth between Kate and Sam, including him in.

Now Kate rose from her chair, walked around behind it and gripped the top of it. Her voice hardened. "So your marriage was good."

Phyllis frowned at the abrupt change in tone of voice. "Yes, I'd say so."

"You'd say so. That doesn't sound real positive."

The frown deepened. "Yes. It was a good marriage."

"A happy marriage."

"A happy marriage," Phyllis echoed.

"Everything was lovey-dovey between you."

"Yes."

Kate dealt the zinger then. "So when did he stop sleeping with you?"

The frown gave way to a flush of anger. "He didn't, sexually, if that's what you mean."

"But you told me he did."

"I meant he's stopped coming to bed at night."

"Isn't that the same thing?"

"Of course not. I meant *literally* sleeping. Closing your eyes and going to sleep. That kind of sleeping with me."

"That doesn't sound like a happily married man to me."

"But it wasn't me," Phyllis protested. "It wasn't our relationship bothering him. It was the situation with Catherine that disturbed him so much."

"What situation with Catherine?"

"First, the money she was taking out of the business. That bothered him."

"Why would it bother him? It wasn't *his* business."

"Richard was very much a take-charge kind of guy. But with Catherine, there seemed to be no way to take charge. You'd think you'd have her tamed down and cornered, and you'd find she'd slithered out from under control and would be pulling some other rotten deal. That's what bothered Richard."

"But I still don't understand. It was *your* business, not his. Why would *he* stay awake worrying about it instead of you?"

"It wasn't the business keeping him awake. It was all those murders."

"Oh, I see." Kate arched an eyebrow in disbelief. "The *murders* were keeping him awake. Why, Phyllis? Why would the *murders* keep him awake?"

"Because he knew what it looked like. It looked like maybe I had something to do with it. Then, when Suzie and Ginger— Well, *everything* pointed to me then. He could barely stand it after that."

"Oh. And *that's* when he started drinking heavily?"

Phyllis was growing deeply angry now. Angry with the questions, angry with the implications, angry with the tone of voice and the intense gaze that wouldn't allow her any breathing space. "That's not really fair. I wouldn't call it drinking heavily. He was having trouble sleeping, is all. And he had a few drinks to help make him sleepy. No, he didn't drink heavily. That's not a fair judgment at all."

"Then you bought the new bottle of Scotch for him yesterday?"

"What new bottle of Scotch?"

"The lethal one he drank from tonight. The bottle of Scotch that wasn't there when we searched your place yesterday morning. *That* bottle of Scotch."

Phyllis was totally confused. "I don't know what you're talking about."

"It's rather simple, Phyllis," Kate said coldly. "A bottle of Scotch shows up at your house, your husband opens and drinks it, and promptly dies. Now I'm asking how it got there, when it *wasn't* there yesterday morning."

Phyllis stared at her numbly. "I guess Richard bought it then."

"If he wasn't drinking heavily, why would he buy it? Obviously he still had some left in the other bottle. If he wasn't drinking heavily, how did he happen to have a new bottle on hand?"

"Richard's organized. He'd always pick up a new bottle as soon as an open one got down toward empty. Like filling the gas tank. He always filled it when it reached the halfway mark."

"Was he mean to you when he was drinking like this?"

"Of course not! Richard wasn't a mean man."

"Well, he certainly seemed testy with you every time I was around the two of you. Abrupt. Impatient."

"But don't you see, that was on my behalf? Because things *really* got out of control then. Like when you showed up at our door to search the house. Suddenly, the police had taken over our world, and there wasn't anything we could do to stop it. *That's* what got to him. *That's* what made him act that way. The idea that there was *nothing* he could do to stop you! Don't you see? He wasn't in control any longer! It wasn't *me* he was upset with, it was *you*. But he was powerless to do anything about it, and so he snapped at me instead!"

Their eyes were locked on each other in fierce battle, the others in the room forgotten. Phyllis' face was red from hairline to jawbone with anger. Kate's was full of determination. "And you're telling me you didn't mind?"

"What do you mean?"

"If someone snapped at me like he snapped at you," Kate said flatly, "I'd have kicked his face in."

"It didn't happen often enough to worry about. And when it did, I've learned through the years that there was something going on outside of the marriage. Pressures at work, usually."

"So you say." Kate made her disbelief obvious. "I don't know, Phyllis. Here you had a serious ongoing feud with one business partner. She's dead. Two other partners carried hefty life insurance policies on them. They're dead. I don't know what your husband was worth, but now he's dead. You're the sole, common denominator among all four. Seems to me you're the only one who gains out of all this."

"I gain?" Phyllis stared at her. "I *gain?* I've lost my husband, I've lost my two best friends, and I *gain?!*"

"Certainly you gain. You gain a business, and you gain all the money. Of course you gain."

"You think a business and some *money* can ever replace these people?"

"Oh, come on, Phyllis, let's be honest here. Money doesn't *really* hurt, does it."

"Money can be *earned,* for God's sakes! Businesses can be *bought!* They're bought and sold every damned day of the week! You can't buy and sell friendship! You can't buy and sell love! I've lost more with their deaths than I'll *ever* find again in my lifetime."

"Yet," Kate said softly, trapping Phyllis' gaze with the intensity of her own, "Richard was *so* worried you committed the murders he couldn't sleep at night."

"*No!* You're twisting my words. He knew that it *looked* like I did. But he *knew* I didn't."

"How did he *know* that?" Palms flat on the table, Kate leaned toward Phyllis. "How did he *know* you didn't do them?"

"Because I *didn't* do them!" she exploded. "I *didn't* do *any* of them!"

"Well, someone laced his Scotch."

"It wasn't *me!*" Phyllis cried out.

"Then *who,* Phyllis?" Kate's glare was relentless. "*Who? Who would set you up like this?*"

In her extreme anger, Phyllis sought an answer. But there was none. Her fury collapsed and she suddenly slumped back in her chair, her face bleached to a bleak white. "I don't know," she whispered. "I simply don't know."

At noon, they left Phyllis under the care of the policewoman again and congregated in the hallway outside the interrogation room. Kate leaned against a wall, looked up at Hatch and said, "Well?"

His eyes were narrowed in thought. "The facts tell one story, and the personality another." He looked halfway angry. "Christ. That gal is either the slickest schizoid I've ever met, or she didn't do it."

"So what're we going to do?" Kate felt tired, dispirited, drained and discouraged. They'd kept up the questions throughout the morning, but nothing new had emerged.

"*Do?*" he said in disbelief. "We're gonna kick it upstairs. That's what we're gonna *do!*" The anger turned on full volume now. He glared at Kate as if it were all her fault. "You drew a big zip in there as far any new leads goes. What else you got in that bag of magic tricks?"

"The morphine. Other than that, I'm fresh out. When it was just the three partners, there were other theories that might've worked. But three partners and a husband? Who'd go after that combination, and why? Sam? Have we missed anything else, anything at all we should be following up on?"

Frowning, Sam was lost in thought, as disturbed as the Captain. At her question, he came to and shook his head. "Not that I can think of."

The Captain grunted. "Well, I'll ponder on it a bit. The Chief and the D.A. are going to want a recommendation. Which they may or may not take. All I can do is play apostle to their God."

Kate stopped him before he could move away. "There is one thing . . . My feeling is the killings are done. Whether Phyllis did them or not, either way, the killer's done."

The Captain stared down at her. "How do you figure?"

"If she did them, she's through. Everyone close to her or involved with her in some way is dead. If she didn't do them, the frame's complete. There's no one left to kill that could logically be blamed on her."

"Yeah, so?"

"That means even if she is guilty and walks the street for a while, she's not a danger to anyone else. The damage has all been done."

"So that'd be your recommendation, let 'er walk." The Captain shook his head. "The Chief isn't going to buy that reasoning. He wants a solution, not a stall."

"No," Kate agreed, "he won't want to wait. But the D.A. might."

His expression turned into one of pure wonderment. "You live in a world of high idealism, don't you, MacLean?" he growled before stalking off to his office.

Kate watched him as he disappeared, then turned to follow Sam to their desks. As she entered the bullpen, she glanced over at Schreiber, bent low over his work. She hesitated, then swallowed back the desperation that made her want to go over and plead with him to find *something, anything!* and went to her desk instead to call Phyllis' parents.

It was not a pleasant call. How do you tell someone's parents that their daughter's husband had been murdered and their daughter was the number one suspect and don't bother driving to the house, the daughter was being held for questioning at the police station. Especially when the mother sounded like a sweet little-old-lady type. She did the best she could, dealt with the shock the news caused with as much comfort as possible, and received their assurances they'd be on their way as soon as they could toss an overnight bag in the car.

As she hung up the phone, she caught sight of the Captain lumbering out of his office, trudging down the hall and toward the stairs. A few minutes later the D.A. strode into the station and disappeared upstairs, too. Outside, the media, dogging the D.A.'s footsteps, milled around in front of the station, waiting for a break in the case.

Around her, the bull pen stretched out in calm silence. The few people who were there worked quietly at their desks. A pseudo sense of calm and order prevailed in contrast to the chaos she was feeling inside.

God, she needed help. Some break somewhere in the logjam. Something to show a direction other than the well-tromped path to Phyllis' door. If only a new suspect would appear, someone from Phyllis' past who'd take extreme pleasure from setting her up like this. If only someone not connected with Phyllis had been fed a morphine cocktail. If only there'd been a fifth business partner to inherit . . . if only, if only, if only . . . Unable to stop herself, she glanced in Schreiber's direction once more. *If only he'd find the goddamned morphine!*

Kate stared off into space. There had to be an answer. Somewhere out there in that Forest of Answers, there was an answer-tree waiting to be felled, one that fit just this case. But where was it, and what was it?

From the corner of her eye, she saw the Captain trudge back down the stairs. He made his way directly to Kate's desk. Eyebrows drawn down into a fierce, black vee, he glowered down at her. "Book her. Four counts of Murder One." He turned on his heel and walked away.

She spent the next few days winding up the case. She ordered the Walsh residence searched once more. But this time, no longer having to worry about the sensibilities of the residents, the crime lab really tossed the place. Even to the point of taking up carpeting to search for loose floorboards, to probing walls for hidden cavities and to examining the gardens and foundation plantings for disturbed earth. Everything, it seemed, except the shingles of the roof, were felt, poked, and pried up, and even they were given a thorough going over, along with the fireplace chimney and the rain gutters.

No morphine.

On Wednesday, the pharmacy search withered and died a natural death. Though Schreiber and Rice fought valiantly through the reams of data to try and find something out of the ordinary, every purchase of morphine they could uncover was properly accounted for. No names surfaced that didn't match real people with legitimate prescriptions, and no person with a legitimate prescription matched the photos of any of the people involved in the case. The D.A. accepted the news with near disinterest. He had a strong enough case without it.

Kate refused to accept the failed search as the end. She hammered on everyone she could think of to come up with something else. *Anything* else. She made a dozen phone calls to Homer as one wacky idea after another came to her. But try as he could, he couldn't help her. There'd been no tampering with the seal on the lethal bottle of Scotch that he could detect. Once the seal had been broken, there'd been no effort to try and repair it. The bottle had simply been opened and used. And no, no one had inserted a syringe full of morphine through the unopened cap and pushed the plunger. The morphine had to have been inserted after the bottle was opened.

This last was said with serious sympathy but with just as serious firmness, and Kate hung up the phone knowing at last she'd been defeated. The case was as dead as the murder victims. She was out of leads. There were no more trails to follow. Even her files were in impeccable order, all the paperwork done, thanks to two nights of almost no sleep, poring over every single note, looking for that one contradiction that would lead to a different conclusion.

She glanced at her watch. It was almost five o'clock. Wearily, she pushed her chair back from her desk and gave Sam a wan smile as she grabbed her purse and headed for the ladies room up one flight, on the steno floor. The last-minute, mass makeup repair before quitting time hadn't started yet, and she had the place to herself. It was a horrible room—clean, yes, but sterile. All cold tile and harsh lighting, filled with cubicles and bare sinks and metal shelves below a bunch of small mirrors. There wasn't even a comfortable chair where she could just curl up and think for a while. Planned, of course, by those inspired architects who gave Homicide a coffeepot in the Narcotics division and no one a coatrack anywhere. What else did she expect?

She removed her makeup things from her purse and stared at herself objectively in the mirror. Her eyelashes were naturally dark, so were her brows, fierce and strong. The only ravages from the day were the lipstick she'd chewed off and the wan paleness of her face. A touch of pink in both places fixed that, and a comb settled her hair into place. She looked composed, and in charge.

She snapped her purse closed and gave one last check. Aside from the slight cast of depression deepening the splay of tiny lines at the corner of her eyes, she looked as she always looked. Detective Kate MacLean, master of her own fate, always in control, always in charge. God, if people only knew.

Back at her desk, she arranged her files in alphabetical order, dug out some hanging file folders and made out the tabs. Then she pulled open a half-empty file drawer in one particular cabinet marked "Trial Pending." She inserted first the holders, and then the files, and then she shoved the drawer home. It clanged shut like the steel doors on a prison cell.

When she returned to her desk, Sam nodded at her, acknowledging the symbolism of the clang. His face was seamed with weariness, too. He'd stayed with her through the long days and nights, matching her minute for minute. Now he glanced at his watch, then shoved the last of his own paperwork aside. "Mexican tonight?"

Kate shrugged. "Why not?"

They gathered their coats from the top of the filing cabinets and turned their backs on the bull pen and walked out into the cold, raw night.

23

March stormed to an end and spring resurrected itself one more time. Almost before the new calendar page had time to settle into place, the wind died down, the rain clouds moved on and the sun came out to warm and dry the earth. The hillsides took on a hundred shades of new green, the daffodils, tulips and early rhododendrons burst into bloom, and Lake Washington was twenty miles of glistening blue waters. Drab winter clothes were exchanged for bright spring ones; pale bodies stretched out in lakeside parks to seek the first of the season's tanning rays; joggers and bikers took to the streets; boats took to the water. It was Puget Sound living at its best.

Kate took some of the time coming to her. She cleaned her house during the first morning off and spent the afternoon attacking the first of the spring garden work. There was comfort in working the spade and trowel, in turning over the rich soil. She dug up old plants and separated them, then splurged on a beautiful deep-pink rhododendron that she planted at the corner of the porch as the showpiece of the foundation landscaping.

What Sam did with his time off she didn't know. He didn't call her and she didn't call him. Unusual between the two of them. But she was content to leave the work world behind and did what she could not to think about her job, or Phyllis Walsh, or the murders.

After a few hours of yard work, when her muscles cried enough and the misty chill of dusk had permeated her body, she fixed herself an omelet, then showered and changed and headed for Smokie Jo's for some pool and a good visit with Pearl. The street in front of the tavern was mostly empty, only a couple of cars were parked near the tavern. One of them was Jack Turner's. She recognized it instantly. Years of memorizing makes, models and license numbers had gone on automatic in her brain. Her feet slowed. Her heart sped up.

He was making himself at home at the bar, across a cribbage board from Pearl. The after-work regulars were long gone, and it was too early for the mid-evening crowd yet. The two had the place to themselves. His eyes found her the minute she walked through the tavern door, and his lean face creased into a mischievous smile at her entrance and he looked exceedingly pleased with himself.

Pearl saw her the second after Jack did, and with her usual good humor, she waved Kate over. "Hey, stranger, I thought you'd died and gone to heaven without telling me. Meet a new friend of mine."

At Kate's approach, Jack slid off the barstool and stood waiting, his eyes intent on hers.

"Katie MacLean," Pearl said, "meet Jack Turner. Jack Turner, meet Katie MacLean."

Jack bowed low. "You are," he said softly, "the most incredibly beautiful woman . . ." His voice was low; the blue eyes were deep with warmth.

Caught by his nearness, trapped by the intense gaze, she came to a halt and simply stood and absorbed the physical presence of him. Her heart was skipping rope with her veins. "You are," she said at last, just as softly, "the most incredibly nearsighted man . . ."

Eyes locked, they burst into spontaneous laughter while Pearl watched them as if they'd both taken loco pills. Then her confusion cleared. "This is either the quickest love at first sight on record," she said suddenly, "or you two know each other, right?" Grinning, she laid a card down on the stack, then set down her hand. "I can't beat him at pool," she explained to Kate, "so I thought I'd try at cards. Wrong again. What're you going to have, Katie?"

Kate slid onto the stool next to Jack's. "A glass of rosé."

Jack pushed his glass toward Pearl. "And a fresh Henry's for me." He was still wearing the broad grin he'd shown when she first walked in.

"You look pleased with yourself," Kate said to him.

"I knew if I sat here long enough, sooner or later you'd show up. Pearl's threatening to charge me rent for the stool, however, so I'm glad you finally made it in."

"Sounds like you've been here for days."

"Well, don't let the fact that I've got my jammies tucked into my back pocket create a misimpression."

She laughed softly and accepted her wine from Pearl. He still stood by her shoulder and his nearness was more intoxicating than the liquor. She could feel the small hairs on the nape of her neck come alive, alert to the incredible nearness of him. She suddenly imagined him rubbing them lightly, back and forth, back and forth, around in slow circles, then back and forth again . . .

With a jerk, she brought herself back to pragmatic reality and searched for something light to say. "So. You beat this lady at pool? You must be pretty good. She usually has all the good sticks begging for mercy after a game or two."

"I just got lucky."

From her seat across the bar, Pearl snorted. "The hell you did. All I did was give him one tiny slice of an opening and he ran the whole damned table on me. Now he's doing it to me in crib. Lay-down a card, fella, we're gonna keep going till I win a game."

Kate sipped her wine while they finished the cribbage game. Jack won with a skunk. In disgust, Pearl put the board away. "So I'll stretch it out over a couple of decades, like house payments." She poured herself some coffee and brought it over. "Now tell me the truth, you two—you knew each other before, right?"

"This lady is a total stranger to me," Jack said. "For instance, she told me she doesn't know much about playing pool, and so, of course, I believe her."

Kate directed a smile to Pearl. "Smart man."

He didn't quite snort. "Okay, Miss MacLean, let's just see what kind of game you shoot. Since I own the table, put your quarter in and rack 'em up." The strong blue eyes were dancing with amusement. "You *do* know how to rack, don't you?"

"Oh, I've watched now and then." She dug the coin out of her purse and slid off the stool.

After racking, she selected her stick from the house rack. Jack had his own cue, she noticed. One sign of a good shooter. He chalked up, lined up his break shot, and with an even, strong stroke, sent the cue ball careening down the green to the triangle of balls tucked tightly together. The cue hit just off the tip of the triangle and the balls exploded in all directions. The eight ball broke free and rolled to the corner pocket, where it slowed and held up on the very edge. A single breath more, and it'd have dropped. Sinking the eight on the break was an automatic win. After that, sinking it out of turn was an automatic loss. Nothing else had gone in. The table was open. And dangerous.

She had clear shots at both sets of balls, stripes and solids, but chose the stripes since most of them were at the opposite end of the table from the eight ball. She ran the first five balls, easy shots all, then paused to figure out her next move. Her last two balls were both near the eight. Her fifteen was totally blocked by it. There was no way to sink the one without nicking in the other, too.

But there was just enough angle to the thirteen to make it slide along the rail, nudge the eight out of danger, and drop in. *If* she got exactly the right angle on the cue ball. But there was a lot of green between the cue ball and the thirteen, and the angle had to be precise, otherwise the thirteen would bounce off the rail instead of running along it, and would bop the eight in instead of knocking it out of the way. And that would be the game. Her only other choice was to play safe and leave the whole mess alone.

Jack was watching her, his grin broad. He was as aware of her position as she was.

She chalked up, took careful aim, then hit the cue ball easy, using some low right-hand English to keep the thirteen snug against the rail. The ball rolled, bumped the eight out of the way and dropped in.

The cue ball rebounded back toward the center of the table. With the eight ball out of the way now, she had a clear alley for the fifteen. She made her shot, waited for the cue ball to return to center, called the corner pocket and sank the eight. She'd run the table her first turn up. From behind the bar, Pearl clapped and cheered.

"Beginner, huh?" Jack fished a quarter from his pocket. "I must be a masochist." He racked up a fresh game.

They played in dedicated silence. Their skills were about equal and they took turns beating each other. Kate led, 5 to 4, and Jack had just evened the score, when another pool player arrived and challenged the table. As the loser of the previous game, Kate was through and she went to sit at the bar with Pearl. The tavern was beginning to fill up with the mid-evening regulars. Greetings, news of the day and small talk were exchanged as newcomers made the rounds, pausing to visit with each person. Pearl was kept hopping with orders and Kate had a chance to watch Jack unobserved.

He'd held the table through several games now. As other regulars added their quarters to the table, he smiled a greeting and continued shooting. As an outsider, he didn't push his way in, but just relaxed and made a few light comments during each game. The regulars accepted him as a pleasant, easygoing stranger, about the most he could expect during his first few nights there. He seemed content with that. He had a nice way about him, Kate mused. No overriding ego, a nice wiry grace to his movements, and the easy confidence of a man very much in control.

"Nice man," Pearl said quietly. With a slack between orders, she'd taken her stool inside the bar once again.

With a dreamy half-smile, Kate nodded. "That's just what I was thinking."

"How long have you known him?"

"We've been out to dinner exactly once. And that was business."

"Katie, you're a cop. What kind of business could you have with Jack Turner? Didn't he say he was in bearings or something?"

"Yes, he is. He owns his own company."

"So? My question still stands. What kind of business could you two have in common that would require a dinner together? Or even meeting each other to begin with?"

"Nosy, aren't you."

"My middle name," Pearl said promptly. "Come on, Katie, tell Mama all."

Kate began to grin. "Have I mentioned my new rhodie yet? It's called Britannia, and it's this gorgeous shade of deep pink, mixed in with corals and reds—"

"No, you haven't mentioned your new rhodie yet," Pearl interrupted. "But now that you have, let's move on to more important things. Just exactly how did you meet this guy to begin with? What'd he do, swipe the damned bearings?"

"You're relentless, you know that, Pearl?"

"Good. Now that we've established that . . ."

Kate and Pearl bantered back and forth as the hour grew late and the tavern gradually emptied. Jack, Kate noticed, had lost only one game and he'd immediately placed a quarter back up and rotated back in, holding the table this time until the last player quit for the night. So, she thought, losing just makes him try harder. Interesting. She dug up another quarter and went over to his side. "This is for ownership of the city of Kirkland."

Jack had started unscrewing his stick to put it in its case, but he twisted it back together, grinning. "I've always wanted to have my own town."

"We'll see."

He broke, ran six balls and missed his last one. She ran six and missed her seventh, too. But she'd buried the cue ball behind the eight, leaving him no shot at his own ball of any kind. "Your turn," she said with a grin.

"Do me a favor," he growled as he studied the table, "stay out of the bearing business. I wouldn't want you for a competitor."

They played a tight defensive game the next dozen turns, each leaving no clear shot for the other. Then Kate misjudged a bounce and scratched. Able to place the cue ball anywhere he liked, he gave himself an easy shot and quickly finished the game off.

The tavern empty now, Pearl busy with side work, they carried fresh drinks over to one of the high tables angled out from the wall.

"Good games," he said. "I needed that. You can't concentrate on pool and worry about business at the same time. Like sex, it's all angles and concentration."

She laughed. "But one's a bit more acceptable in public. Are you worried about business?"

His eyes lightened with humor. "Well, we've got this little bearing problem spread all over the countryside of Montana. The cows are definitely unhappy. They're on the verge of writing to their congressman. In milk, of course, with a high fat content. Only suitable." He raised his beer glass. "Down with all cows and politicians."

Amused, she clinked her wineglass in toast. "Amen."

They drank, silent a moment, then he set his glass down and reached a hand across the table and covered hers. She resisted the urge to pull it away. "I haven't called you," he said softly, "because I've just returned from a business trip on the East Coast. But I caught up with the news that you've arrested Phyllis Walsh. I'm assuming that means you've wound up your case."

"I have. Yes."

"Does that mean I can ask you out now for a date, a real date? Like dinner tomorrow night? *Miss Saigon*'s also in town. I could get tickets for Saturday night. Then on Sunday, we could wander the San Juans . . . maybe take the ferry over for the day. Or no, I've got a better idea. We'll take the hydrofoil up to Vancouver Island and explore Victoria . . ."

Laughing now, she held up a palm to slow him down. "Hey, not so fast. Let's take it one at a time. Dinner tomorrow night? Yes, I'd love to. If you're sure your cows can spare you."

"I'll force them to moo without me for an evening."

"In that case, I accept. Then, after the evening's over, if you'd like to, you can invite me out again. And when that evening's done, if you still want to, you can ask me out for the next time. See how it goes? Slow and easy."

"Not about to be swept off your feet, eh?" He grinned. "Okay, one day at a time. And did you receive a little florist's gift a few nights ago?"

Instant chagrin overcame her. "Yes," she exclaimed. "And I intended thanking you when I first saw you in here tonight. It was perfect. Both the bud and the meaning behind it."

"I did think about sending you the whole greenhouse, but I figured that'd be overdoing it a little."

"Just a tad." She found herself lost once again beneath those wonderful blue eyes, filled with a ready humor always waiting just off-stage. Not only was he nice, he was fun.

"Seven o'clock tomorrow night then?"

She nodded, biting back a sudden yawn, and began to gather her things together. The day's fresh air and hard physical labor began to catch up with her. Sensitive to her tiredness, he paid the tab, said good night to Pearl and walked her to her car. "What about Pearl? She's alone in there now. Will she be all right, or should I hang around and see her safely to her car?"

That concern touched her more than all the flattering comments he'd made about her during the evening. Flattery was bullshit, when you came right down to it. Concern for someone else's welfare showed a real caring quality that she liked. "She'll be all right," she assured him. "She closes up five nights a week on her own. Besides, if anyone tried to fool with her, she'd crack their skull open with a pool cue. She's a tough little broad."

He accepted that and held her car door open for her. When she was behind the wheel, he closed it and motioned for her to roll down the window. When she stuck her head out to see what he wanted, he leaned down and stole a quick kiss, then, laughing, backed up out of arm's reach. "Good night." He looked exceedingly pleased with himself.

She laughed softly, then drew in a sudden deep breath. Take it slow, Katie, old girl, she warned herself while driving home. Slow, and cautious, with feet firmly glued to the ground. All you are is in the Gee, we both love Chinese, isn't that amazing? stage.

But she couldn't help herself, she fell asleep with a schoolgirl smile of happiness on her face.

*   *   *

Jack spent every moment he could spare from his business with
Kate. They took advantage of the warm weather and explored the
city. They roamed Pike's Place Market, the Aquarium, the zoo
and the Pacific Science Center. They wandered the piers and rode
the trolley back and forth along the waterfront. They ate seafood
at Quinn's, Stewart's, Pantley's, Hiram's, Salty's and Anthony's
Home Port. They had quiet late-night drinks at the top of the
Camlin. They combed deserted beaches for driftwood and shells,
picnicked in lonely isolated coves and browsed through small
villages and secondhand shops over on the Peninsula.

She memorized small ways he had: the way his eyes crinkled
with natural humor at the corners; the way his mouth was always
in a slight upward curve, ready to break out into a grin or a
laugh; the way he'd sometimes stop in mid-sentence and stare at
her with such wonder on his face that she'd end up blushing; the
way he'd automatically turn to her in a crowd to keep her close,
or the way he'd casually take her hand in his, or place his arm
around her shoulders. He had a hundred different mannerisms
that she found beguiling.

At first, their talk was all light and gay, a period of discovery
where compatibility rested on the exalted discovery that they both
loved trolley rides. And she kept it that way for a long while.
She'd seen too much rottenness in life to buy the Cinderella story
first lick out of the box. So she kept their talk at arm's distance
from her heart, learning a little more about him each time,
letting the quiet moments between them slowly deepen.

Little by little, though, encouraged by his gentle probing, she
opened up and began to share her thoughts and feelings with
him. She told him a little about San Francisco. Not as much as
she'd told Sam, but enough so that he understood why she'd left.
He sat quietly listening, his entire attention focused on her, his
hand reaching over and taking hers when she reached the tough
parts of the stories.

Another time, taking his turn, he told her about the dozens of
bright idea men he'd helped found and start their own businesses.
How he'd helped get their companies up and running for them,
and how, once they were stabilized and on sound financial

footing, he'd sell back his interest at an arrangement agreeable to all and move on to the next one. Then he told her how he'd rescued the bearing company from near-oblivion, and the things he'd done to bring it up to a healthy, functioning organization. She knew next to nothing about the business world, had always thought it rather dreary and mundane, a cruel and ruthless realm that vied with her own. Her perception was that the bottom line seemed to govern everything and everyone, no matter the cost in human terms.

But Jack disabused that notion. His philosophy was more in line with the Japanese way of viewing business—as a lifetime home for every employee. "You make them feel worthwhile, they're happier, more productive employees. So in the end, everyone benefits."

"That's an unusual attitude," she said.

And he grinned that wonderful grin again, and said, "I'm an unusual man."

She'd laughed. "And modest, too, I can see."

The one change that came through loud and clear in his attitude toward the buying and selling of businesses was the desire to settle down. "I've passed the big four-oh, Katie, and time doth march on." His tone was light, but his eyes were dead serious. "What I'm discovering is that while the high-tech industry is exciting, and volatile, with a new challenge every single day, and sometimes by the hour, it's a young person's game. Look at Bill Gates What is he, thirty-six? And the richest man in the United States. Or is it the world? One of these days he's going to want family and children around him, and Microsoft will simply have to manage without him a few hours less each day. Well, that's about where I am."

It was late at night when he said that, and they'd been talking in a quiet windowed corner of Latitude 47 over a nightcap, with Lake Union and its houseboats twinkling against a backdrop of city lights climbing the hills beyond. Now he twisted his glass, staring down at the wet ring left on the cocktail napkin. "I hadn't planned on getting into bearings. It seemed as exciting as watching paint dry. I simply bought the company because I saw a challenge there. But now that I'm in it, I'm finding it—I don't know, it's hard to put into words—challenging, yes. But it's more than that. It's become meaningful to me in a way I would never have predicted. I'm really enjoying the people I'm dealing with. And I'm filling a real need with it. Every time an aircraft takes off, there's a good chance it has our bearings in it. Do you see what I mean? It's a good, solid business, and strangely enough I'm not only liking it, it suits me somehow. And it's a great base for a family life."

He seemed almost shamefaced by his words, as if he were confessing to some deep need within him that he wasn't sure should be there. Her heart was touched by the nakedness he'd just displayed and it was her turn to reach out and clasp his hand in hers.

Over the next few outings, they'd begun talking—theoretically, of course—about what a good marriage should be: a partnership, with both helping out in equal shares, a private world filled with kindness, respect, love and laughter. They talked about how many children made up the ideal family: three, two boys and a girl; where would be a perfect place to raise them: on a lake somewhere; about things parents should do with their children: camping, hiking, swimming, picnicking, and reading to them; about how parents should emphasize education at home and how they should agree on discipline. They talked about fidelity and honesty and trust in relationships. And they talked about money. Specifically, his money.

While she sprang for an occasional beer or a hot dog or an ice-cream cone now and then, she really couldn't compete with his wealth. Even to try would be ludicrous. So he picked up the check wherever they went. But aside from the single rosebud that showed up on her porch each evening, and an occasional steak he'd bring to broil at her house, he didn't swamp her with gifts or try to impress her with his money.

On her part, she dipped into her meager savings and bought herself some new spring clothes, then dipped in a little more and purchased an inexpensive auto-focus 35 mm. camera. With the camera, she came up with a beauty of a shot of him. In it, he was laughing into the lens, his dark hair blowing wild in a strong breeze, his eyes and features pinpoint-sharp, with the ever-ready humor glinting through.

As a gift, she had an eight-by-ten reprinted for him, and a wallet size made for herself, which she carried in her purse, along with the first floral card he'd sent: *To mystique—and the promise it holds.* There was just something about the shot that seemed to capture the essence of the man. And gradually, as her trust in him built, she began to relax and to luxuriate in the attention he paid her.

It had been years since she'd felt this way about a man, and the wonder of it caught at her breath several times a day. It was a glorious, heady feeling. And her world was damned near perfect.

Near.

For none of her euphoria was lost on Sam, of course.

The easy relationship between the two of them was gone. He was closed and uncommunicative, his face tight and morose. There were no more after-work pizzas or marathon tournaments of pool. They met at the station each morning as polite strangers, put in their hours, and parted at quitting time. It was as if Jack Turner were riding shotgun with them as a third partner and it deadened their relationship.

Kate, acutely aware of the change, kept her newly discovered feelings under solid control around Sam. Still, at odd moments, they'd slink out from the rigid hold she imposed on them and she'd be filled with such an overriding feeling of benevolent goodwill that a soft laugh would escape her lips in spite of the best of her efforts.

At such times, Sam's jaw would clench even tighter, his mouth would press into a thin line, his eyes would darken and he'd be curt and impatient with her. "Look alive, Kate," he'd say sharply. He no longer called her Katie. Or even Mother MacLean. "Come out of your dreamworld; look alive here!"

She never drifted away on duty. Never. And she resented the implication that she was doing less than her best. For she wasn't. She was doing her job as she always did. The Morphine Murders, as the media had dubbed them, had faded from the front pages, eclipsed by more current goings-on in the world at large, and weekdays now drifted past in a string of humdrum homicides, straightforward slayings by knife, gun and fists, that kept them busy while still allowing for a regular workweek.

Her feelings toward Sam were a Halloween bag of oddments: pity, because she had found someone interesting and he hadn't; kindness, because she found someone interesting and he hadn't; sympathy, because she had found someone interesting and he hadn't. It all added up to a casual cruelty that she tried to mitigate with as much compassion and empathy as she could. There were times when she wanted to open her arms and heart to him, to take him in and share with him all the joy that she was feeling. But that, she knew, would be cruelest of all. And so she bit back her resentment at his acid comments as she bit back the happiness coursing through her, in order not to worsen a rapidly deteriorating situation.

But the situation had to end, of course, and he was the one who ended it. He'd stayed on past quitting time one night in April, and the next morning, a Friday, there was a message on her desk to seek the Captain immediately.

The Captain was in one his glowering moods and he ordered her to shut the door, pull the blinds and take a seat.

A faint alarm bell chimed in her soul. Pulling the blinds was serious stuff. Fighting the sense of intimidation she always felt in the Captain's presence, she perched on the edge of the seat and asked pertly, "What's up?" It was pure facade. Inside she trembled with fear. Was she to be fired?

Hatch leaned back in his old swivel chair and steepled his fingers, his eyes hard on hers. "We got some new rookies coming on board. Got to make some room for them. I'm reassigning you to Charlie Rice. Schreiber's retiring and Rice needs a new partner. Starting Monday, you'll be working with him."

Stunned, Kate simply stared at him.

He swiveled slightly. "I need Sam to take on one of the greenhorns and train him up."

Another silence, then Kate found her voice at last. "You *never* do that," she burst out. "You *never* split up a good working team. Why can't Rice take a rookie and you leave Sam and me alone!"

"Yeah, well, this time I'm doing it different." He glowered at her. "You'll get along just fine with Rice. He's a couple of years away from his own retirement, and by that time you'll have enough experience to head up your own team. It'll be good for you."

"But Captain, I don't *want* to head up my own team. I don't *want* to leave Sam—"

Hatch creaked his chair upright and held up an impatient hand. "Decision's done. That's it. Final. You got complaints about the way I run things, you take 'em upstairs. Work your shift with Morrison, take the weekend off and report back in to Rice on Monday. That's all." He picked up some papers from a stack in front of him and bent his head low over them. All Kate could see was the pink of his scalp showing through the thinning gray fringe.

Dazed, she got up and walked to the door. Hand on the doorknob, she paused and turned back, mouth open to protest once more.

Hatch was waiting for her to do just that. His eyes were already on hers, a fierce look in his eyes. "Out."

She went.

Carefully, she closed the door behind her and paused to catch her breath and slow her whirling thoughts. When she felt calm enough, she walked over to Sam's desk. "See you a minute?" She motioned toward the interrogation rooms.

Wordlessly, he got up and followed her into an empty one. She held the door for him, closed it gently, then walked around the table to face him. She leaned forward on both hands laid flat on the table. "The Captain's just told me about my reassignment. This was your idea, Sam, wasn't it. You did this."

He leaned against the opposite wall, arms folded, face inscrutable. "You'll have your own team in a couple of years, Kate."

"Don't bullshit a bullshitter, Sam. You wanted me gone and you went to the Captain and you made him do it. You made this happen. Why, Sam? Why the power play? We made a good team and you know it."

He shrugged, eyes cold. "Them's the breaks, Kate." He straightened. "Now if you're through emoting, we have a shift to finish out." Without another word, he strode from the room.

Appalled, she sank into a chair. Her mind replayed a hundred images of the two of them together. The shared laughter. The quiet times. The comfort he gave her at the airport waiting for the dead women's husbands. The pool, the pizzas, the quiet late-night drinks after a particularly tough day. The kiss. The way he'd looked at her.

Then the image of a lean face with dancing blue eyes and a shock of black hair tumbling over a bony forehead came into her mind and her blood turned electric. So, she thought, this was the payback. This was the penalty for meeting a man who could turn out to be someone pretty special in her life. This was the punishment for simply feeling like a normal woman felt, and doing the things a normal woman did. This was the punishment being meted out to her for her great sin. Crime and punishment. Wasn't that what law enforcement was all about, really? Crime and punishment? Her crime had been meeting someone special, and her punishment was the end of a partnership. No, more than a partnership. The end of a friendship.

Well, then, so be it. Rice, she thought, you've just got yourself a new partner, and you're going to have the best goddamned partner this fucking station has ever seen.

Determined, she rose and strode out of the interrogation room and went up to Sam's desk. "Ready when you are, Sam." Her eyes were ice. She swung away on one heel and went to collect her jacket and purse.

They finished the rest of the shift without talking.

At the end of the day, she did her paperwork, then got ready to leave. Swinging the purse strap up on one shoulder, she went up to Sam's desk. "Thanks for everything, Sam," she said coldly.

His rough-hewn, swarthy face was carved from stone. He simply nodded.

She turned her back on him and walked out.

The next day, a Saturday, Jack had another outing planned for them. She was still smarting a bit from the treatment by Sam, but she pulled on a blouse, a pair of jeans and tennis shoes, tossed a sweatshirt around her shoulders and greeted Jack with a huge smile that belied the sadness locked away inside.

They breakfasted at a little waterfront café in Edmonds, then ferried across the Sound to Kingston and began driving up the Olympic Peninsula. She played navigator and directed him to a remote beach peopled only by seagulls and shore birds. They parked the car and strolled hand in hand along the deserted beach. The water was absolutely still, a summer-blue mirror reflecting sky and coloring-book clouds and seagulls circling overhead. They walked in a companionable silence, and gradually the beauty, the solitude and the sun's warmth on Kate's back accomplished their healing miracle and thoughts of Sam faded into the background.

On impulse, she broke away from Jack and chose some prime flat pebbles from the rocky shore. Bending low, she skipped the first one across the surface of the water. It took three hops before it sank. She laughed with delight and tried again. Three hops. Another. Only two, this time. She was losing it. With her last pebble, she bent much lower, took more careful aim and swung her arm in a sideways pitch. Four! She turned to where Jack stood, watching her. "Did you see that?" she crowed with triumph.

"A championship toss. The Mariners need you badly." Suddenly, he crossed the span of beach and took both her hands in his. "You're enchanting," he murmured. He stared down at her in unblinking intensity for a long moment, then he pulled her into his arms and bent his head to hers.

After a breath tick of hesitation, she leaned against him, slid her arms around his neck and gave herself up to the kiss. Their bodies meshed perfectly. Both tall and slender, both long-legged, they melded like two sculptures carved from one piece of clay. By the time the kiss eased and they broke apart to stare at each other in wonder, she knew she'd come to the edge of a very high cliff.

With her eyes, she traced out every small line, every curve of his face, the shape of his mouth, the hard, flat planes of his cheeks, the lightly arching eyebrows—and the eyes, those incredible electric blue eyes that could darken with warmth or lighten with humor.

He was examining her with the same intensity. His fingers traced the high cheekbones, sought out her lips, smoothed a lock of curl, leaving a trail of tingling warmth behind. "My God, I love you," he whispered. He kissed her again. And again. And again.

When he finally let her go, his smile broadened and broadened until it broke into a grin of pure delight. He grabbed both her hands and swung her around on the beach at arm's length. "I love you!" His voice spilling laughter, he shouted out at the top of his voice, *"I love this woman, God, you hear?!"*

A seagull swirled and swooped overhead, mimicking their dance of love on the beach, crying out his own delight. Around them, the deserted headlands stretched on and on in empty stillness. The last of Kate's reserves disintegrated. Trusting that his arms would be there to catch her, she finally allowed herself to fall.

Back at work on Monday, she reported to Rice as ordered. The sadness as she did so was quickly submerged by the overriding happiness she felt. She looked at the world with fresh eyes filled with a new-found love for everything and everyone. She found herself laughing for no reason. She doodled "JT" on napkins, scratch pads and solemn memos. She even teased the hell out of Goddard, who recoiled with aversion, which increased her good humor even more. Such a prick, she thought. But she thought it with something close to affection.

Sometimes she found Rice a bit slow to work with, but she curbed her natural impatience and they worked okay together. Not great. Just okay.

But when she was honest with herself, it was obvious that her interest in work had slackened off since the old Sam-Katie days. In the first place, Rice was marking time until retirement. He had no interest in playing Sherlock Holmes any longer and knew by now he'd never save the world from its sins. In his personal life, his marriage had been one of the few that had survived a career as a cop, and after thirty-odd years of perfect wedded bliss—to hear him tell it—his conversation revolved around his wife, Hilda, and his seven grandchildren. That was whenever he spoke. He was mostly quiet during their shift, content to let his days pass in an easy flow of the hours so he could cross off another box on the calendar page.

Kate found herself adopting some of his attitudes, idling back on duty, not anxious to do anything that would tie up her time as the Fletcher/Walsh case had. Rice had enough pull with the duty sergeant to catch the safe squeals, and most of their assignments were elderly people who'd died in their own beds. A pillow-killer had prowled through the elderly community the previous year, and since then, whenever an older person died at home, homicide was always called in as a precaution. So Rice worked his magic and got those cases assigned to them, and after a while Kate gave grateful thanks that they were pretty much working an uncomplicated, straight eight-hour shift.

She was aware that a couple of exciting cases were going on around her that she was excluded from, but she accepted that as a small price to pay for a relatively normal life. Sam continued to avoid her as much as possible, and she accepted that, too. When he was forced into contact with her, he treated her like a stranger, with politeness and no great interest. She accepted that as well.

More and more, her world revolved around Jack Turner. He was in and out of town often on business, but when he was in town, he spent every moment he could spare with her. His business demanded long hours, and sometimes their evenings consisted only of a quick dinner together before he returned to the office to put in another late night. But she admired him for his drive and quickly adapted to his routine, and spent her own free time visiting with Pearl at Smokie Jo's, playing a little pool, or simply curling up in her slippers and robe in front of her fireplace, dreaming into the flames.

Slowly, the sadness of losing Sam was replaced by a calm serenity that permeated her entire world. She loved and was loved back. Life was good. She was a happy lady.

And then Homer called.

24

A week of drenching rains had chased the April sunshine away when Homer called. "I can't stand this weather anymore," he complained to Kate. "I'm heading out to the land of warmth and sunshine where you don't need hip-waders every time you step out the door."

She groaned. "So you just had to call and tell me, so I can shrink to nothing with envy."

"Nope. Well, not just that. A little envy's not out of line here. But I'm calling 'cause I'm clearing up odds and ends of this and that, and wondered if you can spare a few minutes the next couple of days?"

"Sure. How about an early breakfast tomorrow?"

"Great. When and where?"

She named a small coffee shop near him. "Six o'clock?"

"See you there."

She arrived first, got a booth in the front section and waved him over when he entered. He was tall, skinny, intense, with a head of loose black curls that tumbled forward over a high forehead. A heavy pair of squared-off glasses covered sharp blue eyes. He was all bony shoulders and pointed elbows which even his best suit jacket couldn't hide. He looked like an adolescent in the gawky stage of growth, which drove him crazy because, as he would tell anyone who'd listen, he was horny as hell and all he ever got was mothering. He also was the brightest of the lab boys, and in spite of his often-heard mutterings that he should've joined the Rand Think Tank, he loved his work. The nicest part was the bureaucracy hadn't gotten to him yet. He basically ignored it.

They ordered breakfast, then he pulled a notebook out. "You've got a couple of problems left over from the Morphine Murders, Katie. Remember when you kept calling me a while back, badgering me to come up with something, anything to get a fresh perspective on the case? Well, the whole time I was fighting you off, I kept thinking there was something I should be noticing, a connection I should be making."

She kept silent. She didn't dare hope.

"Well, I've been playing around with this notion ever since, and the other night I finally triggered onto exactly what it was, so I ran a bunch of tests, then I talked to the M.E., and one thing led to another, and here I am. I'm not sure what it means, but he and I both agreed you need to know, 'cause for sure it'll come out in court. I'm sure you recall, Katie, that when Richard Walsh's body was found, there were *two* bottles of Scotch by his side, one empty, the other half empty. The implication was that he'd emptied the first, opened the second and drank it halfway down before the morphine sent him off to bye-bye land. And that's where I went wrong. I bought the implication. I shouldn't have. It was Elementary Deduction 101 all over again. There was too much morphine in the Scotch for anyone to have drunk half a bottle of it. He'd be asleep after the second glass. If not before."

Kate simply stared at him.

"So I called the M.E. Blood alcohol levels indicate that he'd taken in less than four drinks, all told. Assuming there was only one drink left in the old bottle, that still made only three that should be missing from the new one. That's a lot of Scotch unaccounted for."

Her mind finally clicked into gear. "But you tested all the open bottles the morning he was killed and they came up clean."

"Yep."

"How many samples of Scotch did you test?"

He grinned, proud of her. "I checked back on my notes. Only one."

"So you're saying that second bottle of Scotch wasn't there in the morning, and too much of it was gone that night when Walsh died."

"Yep."

"So either he dumped some of it out, or he wasn't drinking alone."

"You catch on real fast." He paused while their breakfasts were served, then used the salt and pepper enthusiastically. "That's only your first problem."

"Wonderful. What's the second?"

"The brand. Scotch drinkers are unlike any other drinkers. They have one brand, and one brand only. Unless they get stuck at a bar where they have to settle for something else. But when buying their own? Never."

"Let me guess. The morphined Scotch was a different brand."

"Johnny Walker. Now for your third problem. Like a lot of people, the Walshes stored their liquor in the cupboard above their refrigerator. And like a lot of people, they probably cleaned out that cupboard once a year. If at all. Some people don't do it until they move."

Kate was ahead of him. "Fingerprints," she said with dismay.

He nodded. "All the bottles except the Johnny Walker were lousy with prints. Most of which we couldn't identify. Obviously, the person who stocked the shelves at the store, the person who checked it out at the cash register, the person who bagged it, et cetera. And Richard Walsh. All of them had his prints on them. In several places, right where they should be—for unloading bottles from a bag, putting them away in a cupboard, taking them down, pouring a drink, putting them back. Mr. Walsh obviously bought, stored and served the drinks at his house."

"Phyllis Walsh's prints weren't on any of them?"

"Only one. She drank vodka. But even then, they were sparse compared to Walsh's. He fixed most of her drinks, too."

"And the morphined Scotch?"

"Wiped clean. Shiny, spotless clean. Except for a couple of sets of Walsh's, for opening and pouring however much he did drink that night." He fell silent to let her think about it and attacked the rest of his food.

"So," she said slowly, her fork stilled, "what you're saying is that you think someone other than Richard Walsh provided the second bottle of Scotch."

"That's what I'm saying."

"You're also saying that you think whoever provided it didn't *know* what brand of Scotch he drank."

"I'm saying that, too. You see the problem?"

"So our murderer erred," Kate said dreamily. "He—or she—finally made a mistake."

"Yep."

"This would all come out in court, wouldn't it?"

"You can bet on it. Even if I didn't present the evidence in full, I've been cross-examined by Remington before. He's thorough. You can bet I'll be taken over every test I've made. And all the fingerprints found there. And it won't take him a full second's thought to pick up on the amount of Scotch missing, or the difference in brands. Yeah, I'd say it's all going to come out in court. All it takes is a reasonable doubt, and your lady walks free forever."

She nodded. "If it turns out that someone other than Phyllis killed Richard, the case goes to pieces. No jury's going to believe that Phyllis knocked off her three business partners while *coincidentially* someone else was knocking off her husband. The whole thing's gone. Unless she actually bought the Scotch herself, doctored it at home, wiped the bottle clean, and . . ." She fell silent.

"And left it on the counter for her husband to drink? Well, it's farfetched, but maybe. Seems to me, though, most wives would know what brand of Scotch their husbands drank. But maybe she'd think of that, and purposely buy the wrong brand so that's what the cops would think."

"Maybe." Kate pushed her half-finished breakfast back. "It's that morphine again, damn it. If we could just track it down!"

"You still trying?"

"No. The D.A. decided to go with what they had, and the Captain needed me on other cases."

"It's all circumstantial, isn't it?"

"That was my argument. But they felt it was strong enough,

given the motive and the opportunity. The only thing all four victims had in common was Phyllis Walsh. At least, that we've been able to find."

"I'd start digging further, if I were you." He glanced at his watch. "I've gotta keep moving if I'm going to make that plane Saturday morning."

"Where are you headed?"

"Hawaii. I'll be that ninety-pound white shark watching the rest of the tanned brutes score."

Kate laughed. "You'll have better luck than that."

"Maybe. At night. In a dim light. Fully clothed." He shook his head, curls tumbling back and forth, his big glasses losing ground on his nose by degrees. "And I've got such a pretty face, too," he mourned.

"Well, thanks, Homer. You've pulled off a miracle again. I'll talk to the Captain this morning."

He made a face. "Lots of luck."

She thought of the Captain's intimidating glower. "Yeah," she said glumly.

For once, the traffic slowdowns didn't bother her. As she inched along, she mulled over the information from Homer. How had Richard Walsh come to have half a bottle of Johnny Walker at night that hadn't been there in the morning? The neighborhood liquor store might sell Scotch, but Scotch lethally laced with morphine? Hardly. Yet there'd been no visitor to the Walsh household that night.

That Phyllis knew about!

She saw a break in the traffic slowdown ahead and beat out a BMW for the open slot and raced away.

She didn't even bother taking off her jacket before placing the call. She caught the M.E. just as he was headed toward his first autopsy of the morning. She named the sleeping medication and dosage Phyllis Walsh had taken the night her husband died, and asked, "Would that have put her in a deep-enough sleep so that she wouldn't have heard a visitor come to the door?"

"Sure, that'd do it. She could have a circus trooping through and wouldn't know a thing about it. That's strong stuff she's taking."

"And would she have stayed asleep if the visitor stayed awhile, talking?"

"Until morning. That stuff's designed to get you to sleep and keep you there. Like I said, that's mighty strong medicine."

A new worry set in. "But she claims she only slept five hours," she said slowly. "She took the pill at ten, went to bed at ten-thirty, and woke back up at three-thirty."

"Phyllis Walsh, you say? Isn't she the one charged with the murders?"

"Yes."

"Well, that's easily explained. Generally, those pills at that dosage will keep you asleep until morning. But if the person's under a severe strain, then after the first half of a night's sleep, when the body's had a bit of a rest, the tension will counteract the drug and she very easily could've woken up then."

Relief swept through Kate. Phyllis was all right. So far. "But during that first half of the night, the pill would keep her asleep soundly enough so she wouldn't hear anyone coming in to visit awhile?"

"Right."

Satisfied, Kate hung up. Now for the Captain.

Kate cornered him as soon as he arrived, not allowing him to put her off. When she was through outlining the problems and the implications, he sat back and considered it. "What action are you suggesting we take, Katie?" he asked finally.

"That we reopen the case."

"You've admitted the Walsh woman could've bought the Scotch, spiked the bottle, wiped it clean and left it for her husband to drink."

"Homer and I both agree that's a possibility. But wouldn't she at least have made sure it was the right brand of Scotch? And after he was dead, would she have left it sitting out like that and drawn attention to it? And why would she dump some of it out? We know she didn't drink Scotch. She didn't like it and wouldn't touch the stuff."

"She could've dumped some to purposely throw suspicion off herself."

"That's true. But the other two points? The brand? And

drawing attention to it? After all, it's fairly conclusive he's the one who kept their liquor cabinet stocked. Now suddenly she produces a new bottle of Scotch at home? Wouldn't that have struck him as odd? Why not just wipe it clean and put it away?"

"Okay, those are points to be considered. But they're not fatal to our case."

"That depends upon the defense attorney. And Remington's too good. This won't get past him." She leaned forward in her chair. "But most important, what if she's *really innocent?* What if we *do* have the wrong person?"

He sighed. "Okay, I'll take it up to the brass and see what they think."

Kate hesitated. "They've been after Phyllis from the beginning. Maybe we should go after that morphine source first."

He made an impatient gesture. "Katie, that's a dead horse you're beating there. Your men covered every drugstore from Everett to Tacoma. Schreiber and Rice checked through thousands of computer printouts. Everything short of ransacking the White House has been done, and nothing's turned up. It works that way sometimes. It just works that way. And you've got to learn to accept it. As far as the brass goes, I'm in charge here. At least on the organizational charts—for whatever that's worth. If I decide to reopen the case, I'll reopen it. But I am going to bring the brass and legal into this and hear what they have to say."

It was the best she was going to get; she had to make do with it. Back at her desk, she tried to involve herself in some of the current work going on. But it was run-of-the-mill stuff and it took only a small part of her attention to handle it.

She waited out the morning, but the Captain had no answer for her yet. She waited through the noon hour. Nothing. Finally, she poked her head around the Captain's door when he returned from lunch.

He raised his eyes from his paperwork. "I'm seeing them at four," he growled.

She ducked back out and put in another long afternoon. He caught her as she was cleaning her desk off for the night.

"They said to thank you for bringing it to their attention. They don't see where it makes that much difference. They feel that these are minor points and can be handled on direct testimony. If necessary, they'll do some redirect."

"Even if it convicts the wrong person," she said flatly.

"They don't think it's the wrong person. Phyllis Walsh is the only one involved with all four victims. She's the only person with a motive."

She made one last effort. "Captain, I just feel it's wrong. That they're wrong. That we're reading the whole thing wrong. It's a gut feeling I've got, and you've always said to follow your gut."

He shook his head. "Sounds more like an obsession to me. Sorry, Katie, but that's it. No more." He walked away.

She was very careful in closing her desk drawer that it didn't slam shut. She calmly picked up her shoulder bag, gently pulled her suit jacket from the back of her chair and quietly walked out. But she was muttering under her breath all the way to her car, and her eyes blazed with fire.

She'd had enough. Enough of her own brooding, enough of the worry of having the wrong person under arrest, enough of wondering whether every person she passed during the course of a day was The One, the killer. She simply was sick of it all.

She stopped for a quick dinner, then drove straight home and went to bed, setting her alarm for three. When it went off, she dressed for another workday, grabbed an old, unused briefcase and made her way down to the station house. "Paperwork," she growled at the desk sergeant's surprised look. She removed the Walsh file from the "Solved" bin and headed toward the copy machine. An hour later, the file replaced in the filing cabinet, she left the station, growling "Breakfast" at the sergeant, a complete copy of the file safely stashed in her case. She locked it in her trunk, had something to eat and reported back in at her proper starting time.

She put in her shift, then arranged to take some of her comp time off and drove home. After canceling a planned weekend with Jack, she unplugged her phone and settled in.

She started in from the beginning. She studied, sifted, probed and picked at every detail. By Sunday night she had a list of questions that hadn't been answered, starting with why, if Phyllis Walsh *was* guilty, had she killed her husband? What could he have done or known? The last question was: Where had the bottle of Johnny Walker and the morphine come from?

An idea came to her, and back at work on Monday, she took one deep breath and headed for the Captain's office.

He took his own deep breath when he saw her face. "I'm not going to like what I hear, am I. I'm not going to like it when you tell me you've been off working those murders again, am I. And I'm sure as hell not going to like it when I find out you've gone against my direct orders to forget it."

Kate grinned. "You're going to like it from me a whole lot better than from some wise-ass defense attorney in front of a jury."

He tossed his pen down in disgust. "This better be worth the ass-chewing you're headed for."

"I've come up with a way to maybe, just maybe, trace that morphine. But I need your approval."

He sat back and sighed. "Well, spit it out."

"Check back to the doctors on the original prescriptions. We didn't go any further back than the pharmacies."

He stared at her. "You're out of your mind! You must be talking hundreds of doctors!"

She nodded. "Maybe more. But I'll just start with the ones closest in and work outward."

"You're talking months! Months of being tied up on one case we've already solved!"

"Well, weeks at least. That's why I need your approval. Rice can handle what I've been doing, you can assign a floater to him while I'm gone. What he does is all pretty routine."

He sat back in his chair, studying her, his eyes muddy and unreadable.

"And you know," she continued on, "I've been thinking, too, we really needn't bother the brass or the D.A. with this. The trial date's not even set yet. It will be fall at the earliest. So we needn't bother them with this at all."

"You really expect me to swallow that line of bullshit? You just don't want them knowing what you're up to. They'd have your balls for breakfast."

"I don't have any."

"You've got more than anyone else around this place."

"It's just that I hate wasting all my time in arguments, that's all."

He snorted again, then his face grew thoughtful. "If I thought there was the slightest chance you'd succeed . . . Your theory is that someone hornswoggled a morphine prescription out of some jerk of a doctor. . ."

"It's the rock we've left unturned."

"Let me chew on it awhile." He held up his hand to stop any questions. "No, this time I won't go to the D.A. Missing Scotch is not enough. Phyllis Walsh has a sink and knows how to use it. But let me think about going to the docs."

She was back to waiting again, but there was a happy singing in her veins. She knew—she *knew!*—he'd agree. She dived into the mess on her desk, organized each current case, made notes on what still needed doing and readied everything to pass to Rice. Sam was in, watching her from the corner of his eye. They still were avoiding each other, so she kept her head bent low over her work.

At five, the Captain beckoned her into his office. "Okay. Under two conditions. You're the one that's got to get Rice to agree that he'll release you and take on a floater in your place for a while. Second, this stays between you and me. Nothing to anyone. Understand?"

"You've got it! Thanks!"

Rice was an easy sell. With Sam, something like this would've cost her an oceanful of margaritas, a dozen dinners out and twenty thrown games of pool before he'd agree. But Rice simply listened to her explanation of being assigned to a special project and readily nodded.

Her sobering up, both literally and spirit-wise, came later that afternoon when Jack called her to ask her out. "I can't. The Captain's put me on a special job."

He chuckled. "Well, I'm excited for you, I think. Whatever it is. You sound more like yourself than you have in weeks. I was on the point of buying a detective agency for you to run just to see you perk up."

God, she thought wistfully, have I really been that bad?

She had to admit that she probably had been.

* * *

That night, she attacked the piles of pharmaceutical data collected by Schreiber and Rice.

There were computer printouts of morphine users from the large drugstore chains, along with laboriously handwritten lists from the Mom-and-Pop pharmacies. Theorizing that the murderer would've stayed away from the small neighborhood pharmacies where customers were more likely to be known personally, she set those lists aside along with a note to herself to check in case some small pharmacy or another had been overlooked. She didn't think it likely, the search had been too thorough, but still, it had to be done. She pulled over the whole pile of computer printouts and began an overview.

Pay 'N Save, Bartell's, Payless, K Mart, Fred Meyer's, Osco . . . The chains were all there. Though the printouts varied somewhat in format, they all contained the same information: patient, doctor, medication, strength, usage and number of refills left. They were all in chronological order, beginning at the first of the year.

She pored over sheet after sheet, but, organized by dates as they were, about the only pattern she could spot was refills. Some patients appeared only once; presumably they'd gotten better. Other patients started off at one tablet every four hours, then worked themselves up to "Take as needed." Two or three refills of that and their names would disappear from the list. Presumably they had gone into the hospital. Or died.

Death notices, she thought suddenly. She could eliminate dozens of people through correlating their prescriptions with death notices. Which could eliminate some of the doctors. She called County Records, wove her way up the ladder of bureaucratic indifference until she reached the higher echelons where humanity existed and was promised a list of all deaths in the county occurring from the first of the year through the present.

"Two sets," she said into the phone, pushing her luck. "One chronological, and the second alphabetical."

They weren't sure about the alphabetical, but they'd try.

She pulled over a fresh yellow pad and started listing the doctors. The flaw in the information provided by the printouts showed up instantly. No first names were given. In the case of

Kozarek, how many doctors could there be? But in the case of a Smith, Brown or Jones, the problem was a major one. Damn, she thought, how am I going to overcome that without visiting every drugstore listed to look at the prescription blanks?

She sat back and exhaled sharply, overwhelmed by the enormity of the job she'd cut out for herself. Could the F.D.A. help? She guessed not. They probably just dealt in overall statistics, not individual prescriptions. Besides, the Captain'd have her head if she went to the feds. What she needed was Homer and his weird and wonderful approach to things, but he was still on vacation. Sam? Her chin jutted out. Absolutely not. Was there any other way?

She looked at the yellow pad. Unfortunately, no. She picked up a pen and began to work.

It took the better part of the three days. The lists from County Records helped. More than half the people taking morphine the first part of January had died within weeks. She eliminated those names. She also could eliminate those who'd only used their prescriptions once. The prescriptions were too weak to cause death from an overdose in four different people. Eliminating some patients also eliminated some doctors.

When she had the remaining doctors listed, she had another inspiration and called in a pharmaceutical rep. His help was priceless. From years of detailing doctors' offices in the area, he knew exactly which doctors were which. He pulled out his account book and supplied first names and addresses. He also provided her with impressions gleaned from years of observations. He knew which doctors pushed him for as many samples as they could get to hand out to impoverished patients, and which ones pushed for the samples to manage their own addiction problems. "If they only want the uppers or downers and care less about the antibiotics," he told Kate, "you pretty well know why." He also knew who prescribed painkillers liberally, and who made their patients tough it out.

Headquarters was operating with less chaos than usual that day, and she had managed to secure an interrogation room for their meeting. The rep, a man named Erickson— "Lars, not Lief, thank God"—was nearing forty, sandy-haired and tall, with a sturdy Scandinavian build. He was clear-eyed, quiet-spoken, a calm, steady person, and he studied Kate a moment before saying, "It would help if I knew what you were looking for."

She hesitated. He already knew of the murders, so that wasn't the problem. The problem was exactly how much to tell him of the reasons behind the current search. "We still haven't come up with the source of the morphine," she said finally. "It's a loose end that could unravel on us."

"Why not off the street?" he asked. "It may not be as available as coke or crack, but it's out there."

"To date we haven't found any link between the people involved and the drug scene. From the background checks we've run, they all seem to be clean."

"So what you think you're looking for is a doctor naive enough to be hoodwinked into giving someone a morphine prescription. A refillable one." He shook his head. "That's tough. You're going to be looking either for someone who keeps the junkies going, or a softy who'd believe any story he heard. Let's see your list. I can probably pick out the most likely in both groups for you." He hesitated, his hand poised over the list. "This is unofficial. I won't put myself in the position of fingering anyone for prosecution later."

"You got it. I promise. In fact, let me make some copies of my list first, then we'll only mark one up. And I'll destroy it when I'm through. Or return it to you, if you'd prefer."

An hour later, she had a list of twenty-two names and addresses written down on fresh paper.

Things were underway at last. With only twenty-two doctors to call on, she was sure she'd know something in a day or two. With that comforting thought in mind, she slept well that night. Her sleep was dreamless.

What she had naively thought would take a day or two ate up the better part of two weeks. Armed with the group photo of the four women and a list of patient names, she waited among flu sufferers, broken limbs, and a variety of sneezers and coughers and the aged and infirm in waiting rooms throughout the county. The few doctors who had been marked as serving the upscale junkie trade saw her as soon as she identified herself as a police detective and got rid of her quickly. But for the most part, she cooled her heels until the doctors could work her into one overbooked schedule after another.

Nothing turned up. Most of the doctors had long-term relationships with their patients, many of whom were hospitalized in the terminal stage of their illnesses. And every patient being dosed with morphine was verified as being legitimately ill. No doctor recognized any of the four women.

Kate came away having learned two things: that morphine was generally not prescribed until the very last stages of cancer, when all other milder forms of painkiller had been exhausted; and that doctors subscribed to boring magazines.

After seeing the last doctor on her list, she called Lars Erickson in again.

"Okay," he said, studying the printouts. "Let's try a new profile. Eliminate all those doctors with research centers, teaching-hospital connections and full-service clinics. They'd insist on doing their own diagnostic tests before they'd even prescribe an aspirin. Let's look for the G.P., the old country-doctor type." He started marking names. When he was through, he twinkled at her as he handed it over, "Nothing incriminating here. You can keep this set."

She ended up with a list of twenty-five names scattered all to hell and gone. This time she made appointments. They ended up not being in any rational geographic order, but driving back and forth throughout the county was quicker than cooling her heels in a series of waiting rooms. At least, she'd be seeing four or five doctors a day, instead of two.

Filled with a renewed hope, armed with her photos and her list of patient names, she set out to find out where the damned morphine had come from.

25

She found him in Carnation.

Dr. Earnest B. Schofield was straight out of a Norman Rockwell painting. He was a short, plump man, with a cherubic, beaming round face, a fringe of white hair and twinkling blue eyes. The kind of doctor who'd announce the birth of a baby while rubbing his hands with glee—a hairless Santa Claus delivering another present.

"We're checking out a death involving morphine," Kate explained, after showing him her credentials, "and I'm following up every prescription of morphine that was given since the first of the year. You prescribed morphine for a man named Saunders? Robert Saunders?"

"Yes."

"Why?"

"He had cancer of the liver."

"Had? We show him as still alive."

"He died last night."

"I'm sorry," she said automatically.

Schofield gave a pious nod.

"How long had he been ill?"

"Since October. And bedridden since February. It goes fast with liver."

"Yes, I guess it would." That did it. Saunders was the only morphine patient on Schofield's list. "Well, I'm sorry to have troubled you. I don't see how he could've been involved."

"No, I don't either. And the only other patient I've got on morphine is still alive."

In the midst of gathering herself together to leave, Kate paused. "Who would that be?"

"Alice Regan."

"Regan? Alice Regan?"

"Yep. Wonderful woman. Simply wonderful." He beamed at her.

"Why is she taking morphine?"

"Brain cancer."

Kate's heart did a sudden leap. "Tell me about her."

Ethics and patient confidentiality didn't slow him down at all. He pressed his intercom. "Bring me the Alice Regan file, Margaret, please."

A plump, motherly, gray-haired woman delivered the requested file to him, then left, quietly closing the door after herself.

"Ah, yes," Schofield said as he read it over. "Mmmmm. Uh-huh. Ah, yes, yes . . . Well, let's see now—Alice first came to me in the early part of February. She brought in a set of skull X-rays for a second opinion. They showed a tumor the size of a fist eating up half her brain. No possibility of surgery. The thing had tentacles everywhere. She said the doctor who'd diagnosed it wanted to cut out what he could, then load her up with radiation treatments and chemotherapy. But she felt it was useless, that it was just going to make her sicker and not accomplish much. I had to agree. The tumor she had was pretty deadly. Nothing much was going to slow it down. About all you could do was make her comfortable. She was already having plenty of pain and nausea. So I gave her a few prescriptions to help her out. Morphine, suppositories to control the vomiting—"

"Wasn't that unusual?" Kate interrupted. "Loading a patient up with medicine and narcotics all at once that way?"

"The whole situation was unusual. In fact, Alice Regan was a phony name and I asked to see some I.D. before I prescribed anything."

"What made you think it was phony?"

"The name on the X-rays was different, that's why. But she showed me her driver's license, and the name there matched the X-ray, and the picture matched her. It was the same person, all right. No question about it." He was unutterably pleased with himself.

She kept the excitement out of her voice. "Where were the X-rays done, do you remember?"

"The Virginia Mason Clinic in Seattle."

"Do you have a date? A doctor's name?"

He shook his head. "If they were on the X-rays, I don't remember them. And she kept those."

"Why would this woman use a fictitious name?" she asked softly.

"Ah, that was the question, of course. Fascinating situation. Utterly fascinating." He settled into his chair. "She was divorced, with one child, a little girl, and her ex-husband spent all his time lurking about her, looking for any excuse to gain custody. Now that she'd been handed the death blow, so to speak, all she wanted to do was to spend whatever time was left to her with her daughter, in as comfortable a way as she could. She cried when she said that. You could see it was real important to her. Anyway, she'd used her middle name, Alice, and her maiden name, Regan, with me to keep the ex from finding out about the cancer. She didn't feel she had the strength to fight him and the cancer, too. Poor lady." He shook his head in sad admiration. "Strong lady, though. Took one heck of a knock on the chin from the diagnosis of terminal cancer, yet all she was concerned about was her daughter. Admirable. She asked me for help." He looked at Kate with his cherubic goodwill. "How could I refuse?"

She didn't respond. She didn't *trust* herself to respond.

"Of course," he continued, "I had to point out one problem she might run into doing all this. Morphine's a dangerous drug. Some pharmacists will make you show identification. And she didn't have any for Alice Regan. So to help her out, I called our local druggist here in town and smoothed the way for her. Told him I had a patient I was sending in with some prescriptions, but she'd left her driver's license at home, and anything he could do to help her out would be a favor to me. No harm to fib once in a while, is there?" He chuckled. "Especially in a case like this."

A Carnation pharmacy, Kate thought. Within the search area. Why hadn't the Regan name surfaced? "Did she follow your advice and have them filled in town here?"

"Of course, why wouldn't she?"

"You said you saw her the first time in February. Did you see her again?"

"About three weeks later. The old tumor was moving like a railroad train through her brain. Already, one tablet of morphine wasn't enough. So I doubled her prescription. The suppositories were working, though, and her nausea and vomiting had eased, so she was managing to maintain her weight. That was important to her. Her ex-husband mustn't have any reason to suspect she was sick. And she did look perfectly normal. To look at her, you wouldn't think she had anything the matter with her at all. That's the horror—or blessing, I guess—of tumors like hers."

"Did you see her a third time?"

"Yep. Along about the second week in March. I'd only given her two refills on her morphine, and she was running low. But except for the pain, she seemed to be holding her own. That's the way that thing operates. Eats away here, eats away there, the patient seems to stabilize, then wham! It's all over."

"What did you do about the morphine prescription this time?"

"I strengthened the tablets, then ordered some liquid for her. She was reaching the point in her illness where a morphine cocktail would soon be required to conquer the pain."

Kate bit back a sigh. "How did she come to you, Dr. Schofield?"

"Good question. Never thought to ask." He reached for the buzzer again and Margaret bustled right in. "How did Alice Regan come to us? Did she say?"

The grandmotherly face dimpled up. "Now, I remember that call like it was yesterday. She called and said she needed a second opinion. That she had X-rays of a brain tumor, but if it was hopeless as it seemed, she wanted to be told the truth, and then simply made as comfortable as possible until it was all over. Poor thing, I felt so sorry for her. Well, I told her, you just come on in here, Dr. Schofield is the kindest, most compassionate doctor she could find in a whole week of Sundays."

"But why did she call you at all?" Kate asked her.

"Now, I never asked that directly. Not outright like that. I had the feeling she was just going down the yellow pages until she found someone to help. Took her all the way to the S's, poor thing. All these modern doctors and their modern machines and their tubes and wires and little sharp knives . . . Well, being a good doctor's a lot more than that, I can tell you."

Dr. Schofield had let her go on, listening with pleasure, beaming agreement. "Thank you, Margaret."

"Just a moment, please." Kate stopped Margaret from leaving. "What exactly was Alice Regan's attitude throughout all of this?"

Margaret answered before the doctor could. "Oh, that's simple. She was just plain mad at first. Downright furious. Furious with God, furious with doctors, furious that her own body would do this to her. Said she had too many things left to do in life to be cut down like this. Oh, she was mad, all right. Perfectly understandable."

The doctor listened, musing a bit. "But she was determined, too," he added when Margaret had finished. "She was determined to live as much as she could in the time left to her. To be with her little girl every single minute she could. My, she loved that little girl. More than anything in the world. She was an admirable lady. Admirable. Very brave."

"And later? What was her mood then?"

"More—serene, I guess I'd describe it. More at peace. She said she'd worked out a plan of the things she could accomplish in the time she had left, and she was truly grateful for all my help in keeping her going like I was. She made it a pure joy to help her, but she didn't seem to be aware of that. She was so humble about it all. Admirable lady, purely admirable."

Kate pulled out the group picture of the four business partners. "Do yo recognize any of them?" she asked Margaret.

"Sure, that's her." She pointed to one. "That's Alice Regan."

"And you, Doctor?" She carried the photo over as Margaret left.

He pointed to the same woman. "That one."

"And the name on the X-rays and driver's license?"

"Catherine Fletcher."

Of course.

The pharmacist, a mild-looking man with bifocals, was working behind his high counter. Kate showed him the group photo of the four women and he identified Catherine Fletcher as Alice Regan. When she explained the circumstances, he provided her with copies of all the prescriptions he'd filled for Regan.

Intent on the murders now, it was almost as a by the way that she asked him why Alice Regan's name hadn't been given to the police detective who'd called on him, checking on recent morphine sales.

"Detective?" he said in his mild-mannered way. "What detective?"

"Never mind," she said quietly, then asked him to calculate the total amount of morphine the filled prescriptions had contained.

The amount caused her to raise an eyebrow. The good-hearted doctor had handed Catherine Fletcher enough morphine to wipe out a twelve-story office building.

The pharmacist had nothing with Alice Regan's signature on it, and she returned to the doctor's office. Margaret confirmed that Alice Regan had signed a medical release form, dug it out of the file and went to make a copy of it.

As Kate waited, Dr. Schofield escorted a stooped old man to the door, caught sight of Kate and beckoned her into his office once more. His beam was obscured by a frown. "I should have asked you this before. Why exactly are the police interested in Alice Regan?"

"Catherine Fletcher, you mean? We're investigating her death."

"Oh, she died? I'm sorry."

"I'm surprised you didn't know. It was in the headlines for a week or more. With her picture. Even if you knew her as Alice Regan, you'd have surely recognized her photo. I just wonder why you didn't come forward with your information to help straighten things out."

"When exactly did she die?"

"The third week in March. The week after you saw her for the last time."

He waved a plump hand. "That's easy to explain. Margaret and I—Margaret's really my wife. We just don't let everyone know at the office here. Married forty years now. Anyway, we always spend the last half of March in Hawaii. For our anniversary, you know. Been doing it now ever since we could first put the money together to go."

"Was Catherine Fletcher aware that you'd be out of town?"

"Of course. I have to let all my patients know. They have to deal with a covering physician in case of emergency. Particularly in a case like hers."

Of course, Kate thought. So Catherine knew the one person who could help clear up her death would be out of town. Wearily, she rose to leave.

She might have left the doctor with his innocence intact if he hadn't caught her at the door with one last remark.

"I assume, since the police are involved, that she committed suicide." Before she could answer, he folded his hands piously over his plump belly and continued on. "Some people should be allowed to arrange their deaths as they choose, you know. Especially when death is so near anyway, with the promise of being a particularly unpleasant one."

Kate paused, one hand on the door handle. She was filled with a sudden intense distaste for this beaming, kindly man. He displayed all the symptoms of a benevolent God, she thought, the power and the control and the megalomania. The supreme power over another human, the authority to control another's actions, the ability to affect their future, it was all there in his beaming face. A dangerous man.

Her voice cool, she pricked his little bubble of all-knowing piety. "Let me correct a few pieces of misinformation you might have, Dr. Schofield. First, her 'little girl' is a grown-up woman with a child of her own, and Catherine hasn't spoken to her in years. She just cut her out of her life like a wart when the girl got herself into trouble in high school. Secondly, Dr. Schofield, this woman you find so 'wonderful' and 'admirable' not only appears to have taken her own life, but to have taken three other people with her. In a word, Dr. Schofield, she committed murder, and framed someone else for them. And she did it all with the morphine *you* prescribed."

His face went from a cheerful pink to a pasty white as she pulled the door open and closed it behind her.

The murder solution was as clear to her now as the sidewalk beneath her feet, she thought, walking to her car. Especially given Catherine's character. Take one amoral woman, hand her a death sentence with no hope of a pardon, add a soul full of good old-fashioned evil, mix with a handful of morphine prescriptions, set to rise a few days and watch the mayhem result.

She started the car and drove over the river and made the turn back toward Redmond. The timing. *That's* what should have tipped them off. They'd *known* that the ginger ale and wine had been doped *before* Catherine's death. The fact that she'd died first had thrown them off. They'd looked at her as the first *victim,* not the *killer!*

But what about the Scotch that had been given to Dick Walsh the day of his death? Could Catherine have given it to him at another time and he'd just *brought* it home then? But why would she give him Scotch? And why would he accept it from her?

The answer came as such a blinding shock she almost drove off the road. She jerked the wheel back, her veins singing with discovery. The cruelest, most hurtful thing one woman could do to another was to seduce her husband. Richard Walsh had accepted a bottle of Scotch from Catherine because they were lovers!

Someplace, somewhere, they'd shared a bottle of Scotch. When they were through with the drinking, Catherine had laced it with morphine, wiped it clean, then handed it to Walsh to take home with him. Probably done during that last weekend, just before the reconciliation with Riley.

Walsh, not wanting to bring a strange bottle of Scotch in the house for Phyllis to see, had stashed it somewhere. Probably at his office. Then the day of his death, knowing he was about out of Scotch at home, he had brought it back from the office, waited until his wife was asleep, then brought it out and took his last drink ever.

The picture was so clear. And all the facts fit. It fit with Catherine's character, with her temperament. She had the motive, the opportunity, and the means. It all fit, and all Kate's doubts, the terrible sense that something was wrong, were gone.

And all to get at one woman, Kate thought with awe, as she retraced her route through downtown Redmond and turned onto the 520 back to Bellevue. All designed to "get" Phyllis Walsh.

The ruthlessness of it was staggering. The complete disregard for human life. If I can't have it, baby, you can't have it either. No matter that Ginger and Suzie and Dick Walsh had full lives ahead of them. No matter that these people had their own dreams and destinies to fulfil. None of that mattered. Not to Catherine Fletcher. God's done this to me, so if I'm going to be cheated of life, so are you. My God, it was *appalling!*

Kate pulled into the station parking lot. She was keeping this news to herself until every last fact was checked out. Her first priority was to build up the evidence that would indict Catherine Fletcher and free Phyllis Walsh. To get her free and let her start rebuilding her life . . . whatever was left of it. The way to do that was to gather up the last of the evidence. Track down the doctor at Virginia Mason Clinic and get his statement. Then confirm Catherine's signature as Alice Regan on Dr. Schofield's medical release. *Then* hand it all to the Captain. Now *there* would be a *pleasure!*

Homer was back from vacation, thank heavens. By messenger, she sent him the signed form for handwriting comparison, marked "Most urgent!" Knowing him, she'd have those results by morning.

The Virginia Mason records department was next. They called up the Catherine Fletcher file on the computer and gave her the name of the primary doctor treating her. The doctor's secretary set her up to see him at the end of the day when they could talk without being rushed.

The appointment would make her late for a dinner date with Jack, and she'd just picked the phone up to call him when his call was put through to her.

"Listen, my love, a snag's developed with the new contract I'm trying to land and I'm taking the red-eye special to D.C. tonight to handle it. Much as I hate to, I've got to cancel our dinner date."

"No problem. I was just calling you to tell you the same. How long will you be gone?"

"A few days, maybe a week. I'll let you know as soon as I know." He paused. "Why were you going to cancel?"

"You know that special project I've been working on? Well, the case broke wide open today. And I've got a lot of work to do in connection with it."

"Good. That'll keep you out of the pool halls for a while."

Laughing, she hung up.

The world looked sweet.

Dr. Stanley Kubrachek of the Virginia Mason Clinic was young, amiable and open. He seated Kate in a chair in an examining room, taking a low stool on wheels for himself. The murmur of an ending day sounded distantly outside the door, otherwise they were totally private.

He was surprised to hear of Catherine Fletcher's death.

"Were you in town in March?" Kate asked him.

He grinned. "Does anyone stay in town in March?"

"Evidently not. Hawaii?"

"The Caribbean. Aruba. Best snorkeling in the world. Of course the Cayman fans will argue that, but what do they know, right? Now, how can I help?"

"I need to know how she discovered she had the tumor in the first place. Exactly what her symptoms were that drove her here."

"Be right back." He bounced up and disappeared for a minute. When he swung back in, he said, "I've sent for her chart so I can give you exact dates. It'll only take a minute or two to get here. Now, about Catherine. She had a fairly severe case of arthritis and I suggested a research program we've got going here. But she didn't want any part of it. Wasn't about to be used as a guinea pig. All I could do was to treat her in standard fashion. Medication to ease the pain, exercises to keep the joints as mobile as possible. And I got my share of treating her for flu, as well, though I think she saw a doctor over on the Eastside for that."

Kate nodded agreement.

"Which she had quite often. The flu, I mean. Very suscepti-
ble. She wasn't what I'd term a particularly healthy lady. She
never struck me as a bouncy person, full of energy. She always
seemed to drag in here, even when she was feeling fine and I just
needed to check her over. So that's the background. Low energy,
susceptibility to flu, and severe arthritis.

"Now, as for the cancer, around the middle or the end of
January—we'll get the exact dates when her file arrives—but
somewhere in that time period she came in complaining of
stiffness in her neck. She'd assumed the arthritis had struck the
top of her spine and was afraid of it crippling her. But when I
checked her over, there wasn't any sign of arthritis up there. But
a lot of times, a virus will attack the muscles and create an
uncommon amount of pain, so I gave her a thorough going-over.
One look into her eyes and I immediately sent her up to
neurology. There was a lot of pressure on the eyeballs. A *lot* of
pressure," he emphasized. "The next day they ran a full skull and
body scan on her. She was full of cancer. The primary site was the
brain and it was spreading from there. It had already involved the
lymphatic system, and there was a spot on her liver and another
on her lungs. Bad case, bad case.

"Be right back." He bounced out again and returned with a
file and a sheet of paper. He pulled his stool up close to Kate's
chair and showed a pen-and-ink drawing of the brain. "The
tumor was here, located in what we call the silent part of the
brain. No noise, no symptoms, just evil, virulent growth. It's a
particularly malicious form of tumor, fast-growing and deadly.
We usually don't catch them until the headaches—or any of
another half dozen symptoms—set in. Once the symptoms mani-
fest themselves, it's all over in a few weeks."

He wheeled his stool to the small desk area. "Some of the
research being done shows promise, but right now we're fairly
helpless against it. Especially when it's metastasized—spread—
like this one had. Surgery was out of the question. Radiation
therapy was considered. I don't recall a final decision being made
on that. And there was chemotherapy that could've been used, to
try and shrink the tumor—or slow it down, at least. But she was
terminal, definitely. Nothing would've helped her much. And

there's lots of vicious side effects to radiation and chemotherapy. Swelling of the tissue, loss of hair, nausea, vomiting, extreme weakness . . . It can be a brutal regime."

"And you explained all this to Catherine?"

"Yep. We have a philosophy here at Virginia Mason of involving the patient as much as possible in his or her medical care. We lay out all the facts, keeping it as simple and nontechnical as we can, then outline the options available. We also encourage second opinions outside of the clinic. Catherine came in the day after the CAT scans, and as her primary doctor, I laid it all out for her."

"How did she react to the news?"

"She didn't take it well. No one ever does. But her reaction was more extreme then most. She fell into a rage. She raged at me, raged at the results, and raged at God. She was furious that she couldn't just take a pill and make it go away. Usually, that kind of anger comes further on down the road. But she cut through all the earlier stages of emotional reactions and went straight into a bitter, red rage."

"How did you handle that?"

"I let her wear it out. Not much else you can do. Besides, I understood. I wouldn't like to be told what I'd just told her. No way. And I told her that, too. That calmed her a little bit. Enough so she began thinking, at least. She quizzed me extensively on various treatments, what exactly would be happening and when, and exactly what was in store for her. While I didn't linger on the horrors ahead for her, I didn't minimize them, either. She said she had a kid to think about—a little girl, I think she said—and she had to know my best guesses as to what would happen when. So I laid it out for her pretty plainly. I also emphasized that, as bad as it seemed, we had plenty of help to offer her. It's our job not to make anyone suffer more than he has to. There were all kinds of medications available to help with the symptoms. Anti-nausea drugs, suppositories for vomiting, pain medications from mild ones to the real heavy-duty kind. Even tranquilizers and anti-depressants to help her get through this if she needed them. In a terminal case, you don't worry much about addiction."

"Did she ask questions about the pain medications?"

"Yep. I kept it pretty general, though. One of the more severe problems she'd face at the end would be dehydration. For that, we'd have to hospitalize her. And that would be before she'd need any of the heavy-duty stuff. We just don't like turning patients loose with a handful of life-and-death like some of those medications are."

"Was morphine mentioned at all?"

"She asked a couple of questions about it. What did it do, was it available other than by injection. Said a friend of hers had had it at the end, and it had to be injected each time. I just reiterated the fact that she'd be under our full-time care well before that point."

"Did you tell her what the first symptoms she'd notice would be?"

"One of three. Headaches. I mean pain, real pain. Not just an ache. Or loss of balance. The primary tumor was already putting pressure on her neck. It wasn't going to be long before it started on the inner ear. That would affect her balance. And also cause a lot of nausea. Which was the third symptom I mentioned. That one would be the most prevalent."

"Did she ask about time frames? How long she had?"

"Sure. I gave her three to six months, max."

"And that was late in January."

He checked the file. "January twenty-first, twenty-second and twenty-third. The first date was my exam; the second, the CAT scan and the MRI; the last was for my report to her of the results."

Kate did some calculations. "And approximately seven weeks later, what would you guess her symptoms would've been?"

He closed the file and thought a minute. "Headaches, most likely. Some staggering. Possibly nausea. Not to the vomiting stage yet, I should think."

"And once they set in . . ."

"Rapid deterioration."

Kate stood up. "You've been very helpful. Thank you." She was at the door when another question occurred. "How did she come to have possession of the X-rays of her skull?"

"We release X-rays to patients all the time for second opinions."

"And she wanted a second opinion?"

"Oh, yes. She was in such a livid rage at the bad news that I'd expect she'd shop around for someone who could promise her a cure."

"Shop around anyplace in particular?"

"She asked about Stanford in California. And I mentioned Sloan-Kettering in New York."

"Weren't you surprised not to see her again?"

"Nope." He shook his head in sorrow. "The messenger is often the one slain."

Still paused at the doorway, she studied him a moment. "Aren't you curious about what killed her?"

He was surprised. "Was it something other than the cancer?"

"An overdose of morphine."

"Ah, suicide." He nodded. "That's why I don't turn my patients loose with that kind of stuff."

"Well," Kate said slowly, "that could be argued either way. A case could be made against continuing life under some circumstances. In her case, however, there is no argument. She took three other people with her."

"Murder?" He whistled. "She *was* angry, wasn't she."

"And a bit vengeful, yes."

"Where'd she get the morphine?"

"She did like you said she'd do, she shopped around."

26

The next morning she awoke with a great sense of peace. The case was broken and she experienced a tremendous feeling of relaxation. She had slept deeply and well, and for the first time in weeks felt truly rested. She took a lazy shower, blow-dried her hair into soft dark waves that fell to her shoulders, then headed toward the living room to check the western sky for weather in order to decide how to dress.

On the coffee table a dozen roses splayed from a cut-crystal vase, a gift from Jack she'd found on her doorstep when she returned home the night before. Every time she passed them, she marveled that he'd taken the time to actually do this on his way to the airport. Or to even think of it, especially in the midst of some kind of business crisis. And the handwritten card that had accompanied the vase and bouquet had sent her already soaring spirits clear up to the stratosphere. "We need to talk seriously about us and our future. I love you. Jack." She laughed softly to herself as she paused a moment to enjoy the roses' fragrance.

Even the day was cooperating with her mood. The sky was a pure crystalline blue, with the snow-capped Olympics glistening in the distant west. Sunshine, the fresh tang of the marine air, the occasional whiff of pine trees—one of Seattle's picture-perfect days that made living there so wonderful. She returned to the bedroom to choose a bright-colored outfit to match her spirits. Before she left the house, she picked up the card from Jack and tucked it into her purse. She wanted it close by her today. She wanted *him* close by her today.

She must've been radiating happiness everywhere because Brillo gave a whistle when he passed her signing in. "Not bad, MacLean. You're rather gorgeous-looking this morning."

She laughed. "Thank you. So are you!"

As she passed Sam's desk, he gave her a startled glance. She gave him a huge smile and felt his eyes on her as she moved past.

Even the old bull of a Captain, on his way from the coffeepot to his office, paused when he saw her, and his melancholy eyes seemed to soften a bit. She sang out a good-morning to him, then followed him in. "Have I got news for you!"

He settled behind his desk and leaned back in the old scarred chair. "I haven't seen you around much these past few days. I assume you haven't been spending all your time lazing around this beach or that. What've you got this time?"

She grinned. "You're gorgeous. Have I told you that? What an opening. What a straight line."

"I guess this means you have."

"Oh, I just cracked the Fletcher case is all," she said with assumed modesty, playing Ms. Cool. "And Phyllis Walsh came up as innocent as the proverbial newborn." She couldn't contain herself, though, and pounded her fist on his desk with delight. "I *knew* it! I *knew* she hadn't done it, and by God, she *didn't!*"

He glowered. "*If* you can control yourself long enough to make some sense, I'd surely appreciate it. I'd hate to have to go to the D.A. and ask him to drop four counts of Murder One because the D.I.C. came in and pounded a fist on my desk."

"Okay, okay, I'll tell you." Laughing, she calmed down and took the visitor's chair. "But it just feels so *damned* good, you know? And I've got it all, Cap. The morphine, the buyer, the killer. It's all there, as solid as a brick."

"Okay, I'm convinced. Now let's hear it."

"You remember the M.E.'s report of Catherine Fletcher? The brain tumor? Well, she *knew* she was sick. She *knew* her number was up weeks ahead of her actual death. And she *knew* there was no way out for her. She was dying and no one could make her well again. No one could stop it." Serious now, she carried him through the story chronologically, beginning with Virginia Mason and ending up with the doctor in Carnation and the morphine prescriptions.

Fingers steepled beneath his chin, he heard her out. When she'd finished the story, he leaned farther back so he could stare at the ceiling without unsteepling his fingers. Then he lowered his head to glare at her. "Why didn't Fletcher's buying the morphine show up in the Schreiber-Rice report?"

She was cautious in her answer. She had a couple of things to check out there. "Catherine used a phony name. Alice Regan. I've sent a copy of her signature over to Homer for confirmation. I expect him to let me know this morning."

"But you're sure it was Fletcher who bought it?"

"I got a positive photo I.D. from the good doctor. *And* his nurse. *And* the pharmacist. Catherine Fletcher was Alice Regan, no question about it. She's the killer. She spiked the ginger ale, Suzie's wine, and gave the lethal Scotch to Walsh. When everything was done and the timing was right, she doctored her tea bag and said *adiós!* to the world. It's so simple. I should've gotten it a lot sooner. Once you realize the timing's the key, it all comes together and there it is, like a road map. It fits Catherine's character, the bitter hatred she had for Phyllis, her desire for revenge."

"Okay, so Catherine bought the morphine. What was to prevent Phyllis Walsh from swiping one of those bottles of pills? Maybe filching them from Fletcher's purse while she's off answering a call of nature."

"Nothing. But she'd have to get her hand on more than one bottle. The first prescription was too weak to knock off four people. And that would've made Catherine suspicious, wouldn't it? One bottle you can maybe misplace. But two? That's if she carried them in her purse at all."

"Who else would have access to those bottles?"

"Vern Riley. He moved back in with her on that Sunday, two days before her death. But supposedly he didn't know she was sick at all, so he wouldn't have known about the pills."

"He might've found them sitting around, though."

"True. But then you've got the time element involved. He moved back in on Sunday night, and from Monday morning on, the office was occupied by one of the four partners at all times, clear until forty-thirty the next morning. So when would he have time to dope the ginger ale and wine? And switch the tea bags? And he'd have to know what each of the women drank, and where they kept the stuff, and which bottles in the building refrigerator were theirs—I don't think so. It's not likely he'd coincidentally learn all that stuff at the same time he coincidentally stumbled onto the pills."

"But you didn't find any morphine bottles or tablets or liquid when you had Catherine Fletcher's condo searched, did you?"

"Nope. But if *I* were going to commit murder and suicide, and make it look like someone else did it, after I'd spiked everything around, I'd make sure I'd dump the leftovers in a dumpster someplace. I wouldn't leave them lying around for the cops to find."

He nodded. "Okay. It looks like you've got Catherine Fletcher fenced in. What's left to do?"

"The handwriting analysis on the medical form. Then get the charges against Phyllis dropped and get her out of there."

He frowned. "Are there *any* unanswered questions this time that could unravel the whole thing on us?"

"Nope," she said, her happiness soaring once again. "Absolutely nothing." Her grin broadened. "It's picture-perfect."

One last detail and the case could be closed. She placed a call to both Sloan-Kettering in New York City and Stanford Hospital in Palo Alto, California. Stanford came up winners. They'd received a call from Catherine Fletcher late on Friday afternoon, January 23. She was admitted on Sunday, January 25, for tests the next two days, and was dismissed on Wednesday, January 28. The supervising doctor was an oncologist, a Dr. Althea Swanson.

Kate had the call transferred from records to the doctor's office. After a wait of several minutes, Dr. Swanson came on the phone. As soon as Kate identified herself and explained the call was about Catherine Fletcher, Dr. Swanson's pleasant voice turned cool and formal. She was sorry, but she couldn't give out any patient information.

"It's all right," Kate assured her. "It won't go any further than us. We're a local police force in the Seattle area—"

"But I don't know that for certain, do I."

"I'll let you have our switchboard number and you can return my call, asking for me."

"That wouldn't mean anything. There are ways of setting things like that up, aren't there." Her voice was implacable.

Kate took a deep breath. Lord, what kind of people was she used to dealing with anyway? The cop was supposed to be the cynical one, not the doctor, for God's sakes. "Dr. Swanson," she said as soothingly as she could, "your patient is deceased and we're running an investigation up here and all we're looking for is confirmation of Catherine Fletcher's state of mind. We *have* all the medical information already, so we're not asking you to violate any confidentiality ethics that may be involved. I need to ask just a few questions and it'll only take a moment."

"The time it'll take is hardly the point. We don't release patient information except under a court order, or a signed release from the patient."

"But your patient is dead."

"In that case, the family's permission would be needed, preferably her husband's."

"She didn't have a husband."

The doctor's voice sharpened. "Of course she did. I met him."

Kate rubbed her forehead in frustration. "Yes, I understand she had a husband. Vern Riley. But they were separated and divorced last year." She purposely left out the fact that the final papers had never been picked up, which made Riley still legally her husband.

"That may be. I didn't meet any man named Riley. But she and Mr. Fletcher were here in my office, and he claimed to be her husband. He signed the financial responsibility form for her."

Kate frowned, confused now. "As Mr. Fletcher."

"Yes. They're right here in her file."

"I'd like to have a copy of that, if I may."

"I'm sorry, we—"

"I know, I know. Patient confidentiality. Dr. Swanson, would you accept a court order from a Washington State judge?"

"Certainly. But I would have to hand over the information in person to some officer legally assigned to receive it."

"We can set up some reciprocity with other police agencies in California. Wouldn't they suffice?"

"On a Washington State court order? No, that would not do at all." There was a finality to the voice that made further appeal useless.

Kate gritted her teeth. "If," she said slowly and distinctly, "I come down there with a Washington State court order, then (a) would you have the courtesy of seeing me; and (b) would you allow me access to the information I need?"

"Well, of course, Miss MacLean." The voice took on a slight lilt of humor. "We're not ferocious dragons down here. It's just that I cannot break patient confidentiality except under certain conditions."

"Thank you, Dr. Swanson, I'll get back to you."

So much for the notion that Californians were easygoing and mellowed out, she muttered to herself as she hung up. They had more rigid rules than the Pentagon.

But she still was confused. A husband? A man named Fletcher? What was going on here?

On a hunch, she picked up the phone and called Virginia Mason. Dr. Kubrachek's answer was brief. No, there was no husband. Not to his knowledge.

"Just what I thought," she said to him. "Thank you, Doctor."

Just to be sure, she called Dr. Schofield's office in Carnation and asked her question of Margaret.

"Oh, no, Miss MacLean. Mrs. Fletcher put down 'divorced' on her form. I know she was single, that was part of the problem that she was facing. The ex-husband, remember? Are you sure you don't mean the man who was with her?"

"What man?"

"The one that drove her here that first day she came to us. He stayed out in the car, so perhaps the doctor didn't know. Or didn't think to mention him."

"Can you describe him to me?"

"Just his hair. That's all I saw. It was through the front

window here. He drove the car up to pick her up, and leaned across to push the door open for her and I saw the top of his head. He had dark hair. That's all I saw."

"Lots of it? Curly? Straight? Balding? Thick? Black? Brown?"

"Dark-brown, I think. I don't know, it was pretty shadowed." Vern Riley.

"There seemed to be a goodly amount. He certainly wasn't balding."

That fit. Riley had a full head of hair. So he'd lied about not knowing anything about her illness. Or not having seen Catherine for months. He'd lied all the way through. What did that do to her case? Hunched over the phone, she buried her head in her hand, suddenly depressed. "The car, Mrs. Schofield. Can you describe the car for me?"

"Oh, goodness, no. I don't know about such things. I don't know one from another."

"Would you recognize a picture of the man?"

"I don't see how I could. I didn't see anything more than just a wee bit of the top of his head. Really, that's all."

"But you're sure it was a man."

"Oh, yes. His hand and wrist had little hairs on them. Like men's hands do."

"Did you see him on her other visits there?"

"No, just the first one."

"Who signed the financial responsibility forms for her?"

"She did. But she paid in cash, anyway."

"And you're sure you don't remember anything about the car at all? The color, or anything?"

Mrs. Schofield gave a hearty laugh. "I'm such a terrible dummy about things like that. Why, I can barely find my own car in a two-car garage."

Hilarious woman, Kate thought, hanging up. Simply hilarious.

As a last resort, she called the family doctor who'd said Catherine was in perfect health except for the arthritis. No husband in the picture there. The doctor had known about Vern Riley, but stated Catherine had separated from him the previous summer. She'd come in for a mild tranquilizer to get through that period. No, she'd never asked for a refill.

Totally at a loss, Kate hung up the phone.

Suddenly, there was a husband in the case at Stanford. A Mr. Fletcher.

And now, a second man who'd driven Catherine to Carnation.

Were they the same man? Were they two different men, one playing the husband and the other acting as the chauffeur?

She'd assumed Catherine had worked alone in planning her big frame. Did this change anything? Had there been an accomplice in the murders?

The luster of the gorgeous day faded. The simple, crystal-clear case had clouded over again. Why the hell hadn't she closed the goddamned file *before* calling Stanford? But oh, no, not Miss Fusspot here. She had to dot every goddamned *i* and cross every goddamned *t* before she could be satisfied. What a nitpicking perfectionist of an asshole *you* turned out to be, Kate MacLean. *Jeez,* would she *never* learn!

She shoved her chair back and rose. There was only one thing to do: go find these people and ask. She grabbed the addresses she needed and ran.

By nighttime she was tired, disgruntled, frustrated and out of sorts. She paced her cottage like a restless dog.

She'd tracked down the on-site manager of the condo complex and he'd stonewalled her. He didn't know nothing, he didn't see nothing. All he knew was the former tenant's name, Catherine Fletcher. What she paid for rent, he didn't know. What other units rented for, he didn't know. What hours she kept, and her comings and goings, he didn't know. If she had visitors or a husband, he didn't know. He didn't know nothing, he kept saying again and again.

He did know the name of the property management company who handled the rental of that particular unit, though, and she drove back into downtown Bellevue and questioned the general manager in his luxurious suite of corner offices. He stonewalled her, too. Three hundred and fifty a month. That was the rent, he insisted. For that luxurious waterfront condo? she said with disbelief. Yes, that was the rent Catherine Fletcher had paid. Why? Because that was the arrangement she'd made with the investment company who owned it. Who owned the investment company? Another company. Who owned that? Damned if he knew. Their checks went to the Delaware corporation. That's all he needed to know. When Kate asked if *she* could rent the waterfront condo for that, he glowered and said it was off the market now.

Rent figure aside, she'd gotten nowhere.

That left her with the doctor at Stanford. To accomplish anything there, she'd need a court order. The only problem with that was she'd have to work through the Captain to get it. And the only problem with that was that she hadn't broken the news to him yet about her picture-perfect case turning ragged at the edges. She squirmed with embarrassment at her triumphant crowing just that morning. It would not be a happy scene when he found out.

And if she had to hand-carry the damned warrant to California, he was going to be even less happy. Not in this day and age of budget cutbacks and taxpayer watchdogs. Well, if it came to that, she had some money in the bank, and most of her comp time left. She could make the trip on her own.

But what about the court order?

She stopped her pacing, struck by an idea. *Or a release of information signed by a family member.* Becky Wilson. Becky certainly qualified as a family member. And they had releases for everything down at headquarters. She looked at her watch. Eight o'clock. Not so late if she moved on it right away.

It was done by ten. A uniformed officer baby-sat a sleeping Mark while Kate took Becky down to the station to sign the forms and have her signature notarized. Before she took the girl home, she packed her briefcase with the forms, a copy of Catherine Fletcher's death certificate and a supply of photos, then left a note for the Captain stating she'd be out of the station for the next two days.

Her spirits were a bit higher as she drove home. The case may have clouded over, but the trip would clear up a lot of it. It really wasn't that serious, she told herself. Just another small glitch. The kind that cops run into a zillion times a day. It really wasn't all that serious. Was it?

* * *

The flight to San Francisco took only a couple of hours. As the plane circled and banked for landing, the Bay Area spread out below the wing tips in a dazzling array of mountains, city and water. The plane dipped into its last bank, then there was the heart-stopping moment of just barely clearing the bay's white caps as they came in on the final approach to SFI. A sudden blur of concrete runway and they were down.

Kate picked up a rental car, caught the Bayshore Freeway heading south and turned off at Palo Alto. The mid-morning sun was already strong, traffic was light—or as light as it ever got there—and her trip a quick one. Within an hour, she was inside the Palo Alto police station for a courtesy call. Cooperation was applied for and quickly granted, and she drove directly to the Stanford University Medical Center complex.

There was an hour's wait, then a nurse led her back to a pleasant office with a broad window that overlooked the rolling green grounds with their spreading oaks. A pastoral painting a world apart from pain and sickness.

Dr. Althea Swanson was a short slender brown-haired woman in her forties who exuded an air of professional competence. In spite of the cool, remote tone she'd used on the phone with Kate, there was a hint of compassion and softness in her face. "Detective MacLean?" Her handshake was strong and firm. "I apologize for keeping you waiting, but I had to check your release with the legal department. It wasn't on one of our regular hospital forms, you know." She raised a hand to forestall the alarm rising in Kate. "No, there's no problem. Since Catherine Fletcher has died, there seems to be no reason not to cooperate. Please have a seat." She sat behind her desk. "What is it you need to know?"

They spent the next few minutes going over the medical information. Catherine had been put through an exhaustive series of tests on the last Monday in January, and Virginia Mason's diagnosis and prognosis had been confirmed. Surgery was out. Radiation therapy was not indicated. Stanford had recommended a course of chemotherapy in hopes of slowing the growth, but that's all they could do. The cancer was terminal.

"And this was explained to Catherine Fletcher?" Kate asked.

"Yes. We went into it thoroughly with her and her husband."

"What was her emotional state?"

"Rage. She was a very angry lady. She accused us—all of us, not just Stanford, but the whole medical profession—of medieval practices. We'd wanted to start chemotherapy immediately. She wouldn't hear of it.'

"'Did she ask about painkillers at all?"

"Yes. We're making great strides against the pain that cancer creates. As a matter of fact, Virginia Mason Hospital up your way has a pain clinic that is producing excellent results. We referred her there."

"What was her response?"

"She said she'd handle it herself. A very angry lady, as I said."

"About her husband—can you describe him to me?"

Dr. Swanson stared into the distance, a light frown between her brows, then shook her head. "No, I'm sorry. I remember Mrs. Fletcher clearly. But I deal with too many people to remember him. No image comes to mind. Though he did seem to be concerned for her. I remember getting a strong feeling of caring on his part. But that's all. I'm sorry."

"If I showed you pictures of some men, would you be able to pick out the husband if he was among them?"

"Probably. I'm sure I could. As soon as I saw him, I'd know him. I just can't conjure him up out of thin air."

Kate pulled out one of the photos she'd brought. Richard Walsh.

Dr. Swanson studied it, then shook her head.

Kate took it back and exchanged it for the rest of the group—Vern Riley, Johnny Plummer, Don Burklund and Bob Wilson.

Dr. Swanson examined each picture as carefully as she had the first, then shook her head again. "I'm sorry. None of them. Maybe I wouldn't remember after all."

Kate's hope for a quick and simple solution to the new puzzle collapsed. "None of them?" she asked, more out of habit than hope. "Do any of them seem familiar at all?"

"No. I'm sorry. He's just not there."

Kate took the time she needed to try and think it through. Dr. Swanson was silent, watching her not without some sympathy, evidently recognizing that this left some kind of a problem that had to be struggled with and conquered. She was used to watching patients struggle with bad medical news; a stretch of silence was not unusual. Kate appreciated the tact.

She went down the list again. There were only five men in the case. One ex-husband, an almost-ex-husband, and the three partners' husbands, one of whom was dead. There was no one else. Unless . . .

She hesitated, then set her jaw firm, pulled her wallet from her purse and extracted a picture from the glassine window, a picture of a black-haired man with deep-blue eyes laughing into the camera. She held the snapshot out to the woman.

The doctor took the picture and immediately nodded. "Yes, that's the man." She handed it back, and with a shrewd look at the wallet, said gently, "You know him, too?"

Kate was silent a moment. "Yes, I know him." She had to speak over a sudden thick lump in her throat. "He's a man named Jack Turner."

27

The diner was on a back street of town where gentrification hadn't struck yet. A single row of booths lined a long wall opposite the lunch counter. It was still well before noon, and the place was nearly empty. Kate took a booth, and in spite of the day's heat ordered a cup of coffee. When it arrived, she stared down into it, not drinking it.

At one point the waitress came around, coffeepot in hand, took one look at the full cup and the blank-eyed woman, and said with rough sympathy, "You look like you got trouble, honey."

Kate's gaze moved slowly up and she finally comprehended what the woman had said. She nodded. "Yes. I think I do. Yes, I think I've got trouble."

She stayed another hour before reaching a decision. Once it was made, she returned to the present. She noticed the coffee, took one sip and grimaced at the cold, stale taste of it, and left a dollar bill to cover the check and the tip.

First she went back to the precinct station, where some phone calls paved the way for her, then she spent the afternoon at Hewlett-Packard. She started in the Director of Personnel's office, then talked to the half dozen people the director had recommended before finding one who could give her a name. By the end of the afternoon, she had the address and phone number. She called the man, was given an appointment for seven, and wrote down the complicated directions to his home. Then she went to another restaurant and stared at a plate of untouched food until it was time to leave.

Walter Marks lived in Sunnyvale, on the wrong side of the freeway. When the subdivision had been built, it hadn't been anything more than a cheap imitation of an Eichler tract, with flat gravel-and-tar roofs, cheap plywood siding and cement slabs for floor. The thirty years that had followed had not been kind. Yards were run down, either overgrown or filled with sparse scrub grass. Junk vehicles filled driveways and lined streets, many of them on blocks rusting into permanent sculptures.

The light was fading fast from the soft California evening by the time she found Marks' house. His yard was no better or worse than its neighbors. The lawn had died years ago, trim paint was cracked and peeling, and the few shrubs that had survived grew in unchecked freedom, covering windows and walkways. She picked her way around branches that owned the front walk and bypassed a rusted doorbell to knock instead.

A thickset man opened the door, peered suspiciously at her, and insisted on being handed her I.D. before letting her enter.

Walter Marks was nearing fifty, she judged, with heavy dark features, balding head and thin wire-framed glasses at least a decade out of style. His face wore a fussy, petulant look, that of a child interrupted at play to finish chores, and his tone bordered on the surly as he'd asked to see her identification. He carried it to a nearby floor lamp and pored over it under the direct light of the bulb. He looked from her to the I.D. twice, then harrumphed and handed it back. "I guess you are who you say you are," he said in cross tones. "Come in the other room. I hope you won't take long, I've got a lot of work to do."

Beyond the two-sided fireplace of the shabby, cluttered living room was a kitchen, breakfast bar and eating area. A week's worth of dirty dishes and pans were confined to the stove, sink and a stretch of counter between the two. The breakfast bar was reserved for stacks of file folders, technical schematics and loose notebook pages piled in messy heaps.

The dining area was jammed with wooden tables and workbenches. Enough electronic equipment to stock a factory was piled up in heaps all over the work surfaces, the floor and on a series of shelving climbing the walls. One narrow aisle carved through the maze allowed access. A cheap unpainted wooden stool sat in front of one workbench that was the only cleared area in the place.

Marks swept off a pile of folders onto the floor to uncover a second stool in a corner and indicated it for Kate, then he threaded his way through the maze and perched in front of his work area. His face was glowering. He made no attempt to disguise his extreme displeasure at her intrusion as he sat there and waited for her to begin.

"I'm really sorry to have to take your time like this," she began. She paused to see if he would soften at all.

Nothing. He was still the sulking child who had no intention of giving up his act.

"This isn't easy for me either!" she said sharply. Then she stopped again, surprised at herself. She hadn't realized her nerves were that close to the surface. She'd thought she had herself under better control than that. She sighed. "I'm sorry. This really isn't easy for me. And I sense it's not going to be for you, either. And I'm sorry to have to put both of us through it, but there's no alternative. It's about Jack Turner."

The changes were instantaneous. From initial truculence, to surprise at her apology, then a quick veer into bitter hatred. "That bastard," he spit out with venom. "You're a cop, so you must've caught up with him at last. I hope you put him away for the rest of his life."

"You were his business partner?"

"Victim, you mean. You want the story, that what you want? The story? Because I'll sign anything that'll put that bastard away."

"Yes, I want the story."

"Then first you've got to understand me." He glowered. "I'm a simple man. When I work, I work. I don't answer phones, I don't drink coffee, I don't talk to people, I don't run a business. I work. And he used it against me. He knew that about me, and he used it against me."

She glanced around the incredible mess everywhere and nodded, though she didn't quite understand.

He was still glowering, this time into the distance. "He and I—we met at H-P. Hewlett-Packard. He was bright enough, all right, but he was always behind. You know what I mean? The difference between the kid being taught at the teacher's pace, and the kid light-years beyond." There was no doubt he considered himself the kid light-years beyond. "By the time he had an idea, it was already in the works by someone else. Usually me. But he had one thing I didn't—he knew the rules of the game. Street rules. I didn't. So he kept watching me turn over one patent after another to H-P, and after a while he suggested we form our own business and make the money on my ideas ourselves instead of always for someone else. He'd take care of the financing, the marketing, the contracts, the business, everything. All I'd have to do was create and design. No more company bullshit with requisitions and purchase orders and departmental approvals and all that crap. He'd take care of everything and I'd be free to just do my work. Like I said, when I work, I work.

"Shit. It was leading a lamb to slaughter, I was so goddamned simpleminded. We set up this company, fifty-fifty. All I had to do was sign stuff now and then as a partner. Partner-kind of stuff. So I'd be working and he'd come in with stacks of papers and checks and I'd sign. He'd show me a line and I'd sign. Eight, ten, twelve times, I'd sign. Then he'd disappear and I'd be left alone again to work until the next batch had to be signed. He took care of everything, and I just signed. I got money every week, and freedom to work, and that's all I cared about. He'd drag me out to give me a progress report every once in a while. I'd say great, fine, wonderful, let me go back to work now. That's all I cared about. I was turning out ideas faster than I could develop them. And everything was great, fine, wonderful. Right up until the morning he didn't show up for work."

Marks shrugged. "I didn't think much of it. Neither did our office girl. Jack traveled all over, all the time, meeting manufacturers, getting contracts, setting up royalty arrangements for my designs. We figured he was on another of those trips of his. Until the end of the week, when the gal wanted to be paid. Christ, I didn't even know where the checkbook was, or how much was in it. I hadn't paid any attention. So I told her Jack'd have to be back soon, lent her some money and she worked a second week. We had suppliers and vendors and creditors calling for him all week long. She tried to find out where the hell he was, but couldn't. Then along around Thursday, we went to the shop that morning and the IRS had padlocked it shut.

"I can't remember the exact order that things happened in after that, but the upshot of the whole thing was, there was this Delaware corporation. And it turned out that some of those papers I'd signed sold some of my designs and patents to them outright. All the contracts and royalties were going to them. In return, they'd funded the company I was a partner in, and that had kept us going. One day, the funding had stopped. They quit paying us, so my company had quit paying anyone else. Jack Turner owned that Delaware corporation, lock, stock and barrel. I'd also signed, it seemed, a dissolution of our partnership, which released him from all obligation and responsibility for the company. I owned it all, lock, stock and barrel. Including all the debts. Supposedly we had split the patents evenly, according to the papers I'd signed. At least the his-column and the my-column of assets were equal length. I got half and he got half. All legal and aboveboard. Except my half held the unworkable patents, the ones no one wanted. He got the good ones that made him millions. These papers giving me ownership of the company were dated early in the partnership, before any contracts came through. From that day on, Jack never wrote another check for our company. They were typed and I'd signed them all. Every one of them sons of bitches. From every standpoint, it looked like I ran the company. He'd even drawn up a consulting contract with his Delaware corporation to explain any checks drawn to him, and to explain his presence in our company offices. Then, when I ended up in bankruptcy court, the son of a bitch even filed a claim against me, stating that I still owed his company over a hundred grand in back payments on the consulting contract. There was no way to touch him. None. He was clean, and I was on the hook."

He glanced up at Kate from underneath the murderous eyes. "Did you know that you cannot eliminate IRS debts in bankruptcy court? And did you know that interest and penalties over the years can exceed the original amount owed? I'm still not clear of those bastards yet. Over twelve years, and I owe them more than I did then. I can't have a bank account, own a house, collect a paycheck or have my own business. I have to peddle all my own designs for cash, and let the buyer take out all the patents and receive the royalties. IBM alone used seventeen of my designs in just *one* of their divisions. Do you know how rich I'd be? Instead of living like a mole in this trash dump!" He lowered his head and blazed at her like a bull taunted by a red cape.

They sat half a room apart, separated by the maze of clutter. The dim light cast his eye sockets into deep shadow, but there was no mistaking the bitter rage. It was the timeless rage of the elements, the ominous sky, the towering black thunderheads, the crashing explosions of reverberating sound, the hailstorm of winds. The momentary stillness was filled with the rage, like air heavy and thick with mist. Outside, the night pressed blackly against the windowpane, locking the two of them into the present. No future, no past, just the now.

At last Kate found her voice. "Couldn't a good attorney help?" she asked softly.

"What could they do, even if they believed me? There's not one shred of paper to back anything up with. Every single thing points to one story: we formed a partnership; shortly afterward, we dissolved that partnership, splitting all the assets evenly; then he went on to make his new company rich; I didn't. And on top of that, he can prove through checks and the consulting contract that he even tried to help *me*, his good old partner. He comes out looking like the good guy; I look like the fool. Lead the lamb to slaughter?" He gave a harsh bray of laughter. "Shit, I handed him the goddamned knife, then rolled over and bared my stomach for the gutting."

She checked him out, of course. She left a message for the Captain that she'd be gone a few days longer than expected, then she went to the IRS and the bankruptcy court. Once that was verified, with the help of Walter Marks she followed the trail that led up through the years. One name led to the next. Out of twelve people, she talked to eight. The details differed from one to another, but the story was the same. Jack Turner had swindled each and every one of them out of their businesses.

She finished the final interview late on the fourth evening. She'd missed the last flight of the night to Seattle and had checked in at an airport motel. She knew she wouldn't be able to sleep, so in spite of the late hour, she drove through San Francisco and across the Golden Gate to Sausalito. She parked and walked along the waterfront. The houseboats had new generations of residents since she'd lived there, and naturalness had given way to fancy architecture. Gingerbread chalets and modern cubicles topped the old barges now and she envisioned a mass of three-piece business suits and Gucci briefcases being disgorged each morning as they left their waterlogged suburbia on the way to the fast lane of the city. The simple life had been suburbanized into just another upscale housing development with foundations of water. She thought about Nick, her artist lover, and wondered if he was one of those three-piece-suited figures now.

In her car, she wound through the darkened narrow streets up to the hotel spread high on the hillside. The dining room was closed for the night, but a sympathetic night clerk allowed her to sit on the bluff-edge terrace and brought her a cup of coffee from his own private supply. Sausalito and the bay spread out below her, and the lights of the town edged the water like a collar of rhinestones. The night air picked up the damp of the sea and she shrugged deeper into her suit jacket for warmth.

The perfect crime, Kate thought, her gaze wandering over the sleeping houseboats below. But was it a crime, though? Against any ethical and moral standards, yes. But was what Jack Turner had done a crime legally? She doubted it. Probably just a fact of life. Some won. Some lost. And if you lost, you either picked yourself back up, learned the rules and returned to the fray, or you hid yourself off in the dark breeding ground of bitterness where no one could ever hurt you again. Like Walter Marks.

Her thoughts moved from Marks to Jack Turner. The facade of his life was gone, torn apart like so much fluff. She could've— maybe—excused him for the lie about not being involved with Catherine Fletcher. People lied for all sorts of strange reasons. His motive could've been nothing more sinister than simply having washed his hands of her when he learned that she was terminally ill, then later feeling shame or guilt over having let her down when she really needed someone. Sometimes you had to let someone down like that once in your lifetime to learn that you can't live with yourself for doing it, and so you'd never do it again. At least, there were grounds for doubt about that lie.

But Marks' story had finished him. She wasn't dealing with a decent person who'd given in to a momentary expedient impulse. She was dealing with a cold-blooded, methodical, thorough, ruthless, win-at-any-cost opportunist who made Catherine Fletcher and Vern Riley look like amateurs in the Swindle Game of Life.

Now the murders had to be looked at from the viewpoint of the new evidence—Jack Turner's real character. Had Catherine really planned and executed such a murderously contrived scheme all by herself? Or had she and Jack worked together to figure out the exact whos, wheres, hows and whens? But if they had, where was the proof of his involvement? Or was he going to get off scot-free, as he had with Walter Marks?

So far, there were two links to Jack. The first was the nebulous "dark-haired man" seen by the doctor's wife in Carnation. He was safe there; she hadn't seen enough of him to make a firm identification. Not one that would hold up in court.

The second link was firm; he'd been identified as the "Mr. Fletcher" accompanying Catherine to Stanford. And Dr. Althea Swanson's competent, quiet manner would make her testimony unshakable even by the most highly skilled defense attorney.

But then what? Any half-witted defense attorney could make hash out of both. The world was full of dark-headed men. And where is the crime in holding a sick woman's hand while she is being handed a death sentence, Ladies and Gentlemen of the Jury? Are you *actually* telling this court that you are going to *convict* a man for *compassion?!* Since when, Ladies and Gentlemen of the Jury, is it *a crime to help another human being? Especially a sick human being, a human being in pain, for God's sakes!*

The defense attorney would continue: Supposition, Ladies and Gentlemen, sheer supposition. And from such flimsy evidence the prosecution's going to ask you to convict this man of *murder?*

Now I ask you . . . And with a wave of a disbelieving hand, the state's case would vanish.

No, they had nothing. No fingerprints, no link to any of the victims except the one to Catherine, no provable access to the morphine. If he was involved, he'd committed the perfect crime. But why? Why had he done it at all?

Her thoughts and emotions tumbled through a vast void inside of her with the sharp, painful brilliance of a lightning jag shooting through a night sky. She stayed out in the cool night air until they'd worn themselves out. Finally ready to leave, she cast one look around the sparkling scene spread out below. The passage of years had erased any turmoil she'd experienced there and her memories of Sausalito were good ones. It was temptation to want to return there now. But Sausalito, and that time, for her were gone. She was as stuck in the present as Walter Marks was, and stuck in a situation that had to be dealt with now. But she had no answers anymore.

Dear God, she thought in a mind-whisper, help me.

The next morning, she flew back to Seattle.

She wanted to go to Sam for help, but her pride wouldn't let her. She'd been *so* wrong that there seemed no way to redeem herself in his eyes. Over the next few days, she steered a course well wide of him, and when a meeting or even just a casual pass-by couldn't be avoided, she made sure her face reflected the bright perkiness that had become so natural in the weeks gone past. She found his gaze on her often, but his expression was unreadable, and she simply chalked it up to his habit of observing every little thing in the world around him, like a tourist at a zoo. And she was the perfect exhibit, she thought ruefully. A fool's monkey.

She did go to Brillo, however. She caught up with him during her first morning back. He took one look at her and waltzed her into an empty interrogation room and sat her down. Then he leaned against a wall across from her and said, "What's up, Mother MacLean?"

She told him the whole story, starting with the death of Catherine Fletcher and ending with the involvement of Jack Turner. She laid the evidence out before him, and not sparing herself, explained abut the personal relationship going on between Jack and herself. She took her time and told him in detail the trip to San Francisco.

He listened to her without interruption, not allowing her gaze to leave his. Since Rosie had "tendered his resignation" from the force, Brillo's face had aged. Deep lines creased each side of his mouth and his skin looked like milk chocolate poured over two fistfuls of wrinkled paper and allowed to set. Now, as he listened, his face grew even more seamed as the word picture she presented became first clear, then conclusive.

When she had finished, he allowed a silence to stretch out, then he closed his eyes and whispered, "Son of a bitch."

Diminished sounds from the central room outside filtered like dust through the closed doors. She was acutely aware of them, automatically cataloging them and filing them into familiar compartments. As the minutes stretched on and the man stood motionless, she found herself listening for the sound of each of his indrawn breaths. There was that kind of awful stillness about the slump of the shoulders and the forward droop of his head.

When he finally looked up at her, though, his face was composed. "There's been some discussion around here about how rough you are, Mother MacLean. Well, now we'll see, won't we." Without allowing her to respond, he took her by the arm and guided her out to his car.

It was after noontime, and he stopped to pick up a bag of burgers and Cokes, then drove her to a small, remote state park on Holmes Point on the north end of the lake. On a workday like this, they had it to themselves. They sat on a fallen log by the lake's edge and ate. Clumps of clouds alternately covered, then cleared, the sun. The world was patched in living black and white.

When they'd had enough of the burgers, he picked up all their wrappings and crumpled them back into the bag. Then he got off the log and walked the length of the park along the water's edge. He stood for a long while at the far end, then lumbered slowly back to the log where she sat. Then he began to talk.

He talked about their world—the city, the streets, the gutters. He talked about guilt and innocence and justice and injustice. He talked about cases that he'd seen in the past. He talked about victims who died and killers who walked. But mostly, he talked about the system and the way it *really* worked. Then he talked about what had to be done.

As he spoke, the blood drained from her face. She realized she'd been waiting for a rescue. Someone or something to pull her from the swamp mire of her nightmare. And it wasn't going to happen. She swallowed against a dry throat. It simply wasn't going to happen.

He spoke on and on. Inside, she fought, rejected, resisted. At times, she shivered when the clouds covered the sun. At times, she shivered when the sun baked her back. At times, she thought she was just going to shiver to death.

When he was finally through, she sat still a long time, staring at the buildings of Sandpoint rising from the earth across the lake. They stood stolid in the sun, impenetrable monoliths, not giving her any of the help she needed. Her gaze moved to the Olympics in the distance, looming up over the earth as impassive as the buildings across the way. No help there. Then into the sky beyond. No, no help there either. Win or lose, it was her struggle. There was no escape.

In the end, she merely nodded.

That night, at two o'clock in the morning, she reported a prowler. The beat cops who responded to her call found no one there, but dutifully made a report on the call. As planned.

The next day she purchased a small-caliber revolver, loaded it and placed it behind a sofa seat cushion. As planned.

And when Jack returned to town from his business trip, she insisted on cooking him dinner at her place as a welcome home. As planned.

The final design was underway.

As planned.

28

Late-afternoon sun warmed the dining room of her cottage as she set the table for two. Deep green place mats, white china, pink candles and a yellow-pink floral centerpiece. She pulled the chain for the soft lights on the slow, lazy ceiling fan overhead then stepped back to check the table and nodded. It would do.

She moved to the bank of windows. A few filmy streaks of clouds above the Olympics in the west promised a spectacular sunset. She lost herself in the view for a moment, only vaguely aware of the gentle stir of air around her created by the easy turn of the fan. What would the night bring? She shuddered at the possibilities.

She turned away from the lure of the sunset's beauty. The steaks were marinating. The salad makings were crisping in the refrigerator, ready to assemble. A filled ice bucket and an assortment of liquor sat out on a side table in the living room. The gun was behind a cushion on the couch. Everything was ready. She headed for the shower.

She'd planned to wear a long, colorful hostess gown, but at the last minute switched to a dressy but comfortable jumpsuit, with a lot of fullness at the waist and hips that carried down into the loose-fitting pant legs. Brillo had wrangled from some agency he knew a MIRACLE—Micro-Integrated-Random-Access-Controlled-

Liaison-Equipment—in the form of a garnet dinner ring that transmitted sounds to a remote recorder, its tiny wire antenna built in as part of the filigreed setting. She slipped it onto her third finger, right hand. A simple gold pendant at the V-neck of her jumpsuit and open-backed sandals completed her outfit. She checked herself in the mirror.

The dark chestnut hair spilling over her shoulders framed a face too white and too thin. Makeup had softened the circles around each eye, but they still looked sunken and tense, much too large and serious. She tried on a smile, but it came out grotesque. She would just have to plead overwork and tiredness and hope for the best.

The doorbell chimed as she gave her hair a last flick of the brush. She drew in one long, deep breath to still the stomach flutters before heading toward the door.

Jack was hidden behind an armload of packages. "See what happens when we're apart for a week?" he grinned. "I needed a semi just to haul all this stuff here."

"I love it," she said, forcing a light tone. She led him into the kitchen to unload.

He began opening bags, holding up each item for her inspection. "Wine, of course. Candy. Cheese from the cheese factory. Summer sausages from the summer sausage factory. And roses from the rose factory." He held another brown bag at the bottom and turned the top down to unveil the label. "And Bailey's Irish Cream from—guess where? Of course! The Irish Cream factory!" He rolled the top back up and set the bag over on a far counter, out of their way. His eyes warmed as he turned to her. "But you put all my gifts to shame. You look absolutely stunning this evening."

"Courtesy of the stunning factory," she said lightly. She buried her head among the roses and took a deep smell before going for a vase. "Thank you for everything. It's almost overwhelming." She smiled at him. "How about playing bartender while I get the bouquet in water, please? The mixings are in the living room."

He caught her as she passed and pulled her close. "Do you have any idea how much I've missed you?" he whispered, holding her tight. He tilted her chin to force her lips up to his.

She gave herself up to his kiss for a long moment before

pulling back to laugh breathlessly. "If one week's absence does this to you . . . whew! Now about those drinks . . ."

"On their way." He disappeared.

As she arranged the bouquet in a tall vase at the kitchen sink, she listened to the sounds drifting in from the living room. The clink of ice cubes into glasses. The thud of the ice bucket lid being replaced. Bottles hitting the rim of glasses as their drinks were poured. By the time he reappeared, her heart was thumping hard. Was there just liquor and mix in her glass?

She set the bouquet on the sideboard in the dining room, then began slicing the cheese he'd brought. He set her drink beside her, then sat on a snack-bar stool while she worked. "I really have missed you, Katie," he said. It sounded sincere. "What did you think of the note I left you?"

She started to keep her eyes firmly fastened on the cheese, and instantly realized it would be the wrong thing to do. She raised her gaze to meet his. "About a future together?" She smiled as best she could. "Well, now, I do have some thoughts on that, but I'd like to save them until after dinner. Do you mind?"

Smiling, he shook his head. "Nope. I figure you'll just be more agreeable after a couple of dozen bottles of wine."

"*A couple of dozen!*" She burst out with a real laugh. "Two glasses and I slur my words!"

"See? You'll slur them into an easy yes."

"Dream on, sport. Okay, let's hear about your trip. Everything that happened."

"I'd rather hear about your week. And about this special case you've broken."

"Nope. I'm going to talk all evening. My latest case is a fascinating story and I want your full attention on it. So you'd better grab your opportunity now."

She moved the plate of cheese and crackers in front of him and began tearing apart lettuce for the salad. He settled himself more comfortably on the stool and began to describe his week-long trip. At first, she listened intently, trying to decipher the real Jack Turner beneath the surface lightness of his chatter. But there was nothing different or alien in him that she could detect. A strong instinct for fair play made her want to warn him to be careful tonight. To not say or do anything incriminating. To tell him that all he had to do was to do nothing, and he'd be safe. An hour for dinner, a couple of hours after dinner, and he could leave and be safe forever. She tore the lettuce leaves apart with a vengeance.

Suddenly she became aware of his silence and glanced up. "Is something wrong?" she asked.

"That's what I was wondering." He was watching her, his head tilted to one side in sharp curiosity.

She gave a light laugh. "I guess my mind *was* wandering a bit. I'm sorry." She moved to the broiler to slip the steaks in. With difficulty she scraped up the echo of the last sentence he'd spoken and jogged him onward. "And so the patent office had fouled up again . . ."

But his story had been spoiled. "Yes, nothing exciting," he said shortly, "just another boring human error." He stared down into his drink.

The last of the sun's rays poured through the kitchen window and bathed one side of his face in a soft, yellow glow. The physical perfection of him made her catch her breath. The shock of black hair tumbling over the high bony forehead. The electric-blue eyes that could so disarmingly appeal. The thin aquiline nose; the strong, lean planes of his cheeks; the enticing gentle curve of his mouth; the air of charm he wore as easily as his clothes—

He glanced up and caught her examining him. "What are you thinking?" he asked softly.

"I was thinking how truly attractive-looking you are," she said honestly. "If you wouldn't be insulted, I'd call you beautiful."

He broke into an easy grin. "You certainly know the way to a man's heart." He slid off his stool and began carrying food into the dining room for her.

By diverting the conversation into innocuous chatter, she kept the dinner talk light. She pointed out the changes in color of the sunset from the first pale pink to the final deep scarlets. When darkness extinguished the light show, she went into lengthy detail about the garden she was planning for the summer. Through it all, she watched his reactions. He did a masterful job of showing interest that only cracked a time or two. Nothing more than a slight hiccup in the facade. If she hadn't been looking for it, she never would've suspected anything. She wondered how many other times she'd bored the hell out of him.

He insisted upon clearing away their dinner plates and bringing in the coffee. The noises from the kitchen sounded right, but when the cup was in front of her, she stared down at the black liquid, suddenly afraid. Was it all right, or wasn't it? Her hands trembling slightly, she held the cup firmly to her bottom lip and took a small sip. Strong and bitter. But it tasted like coffee. She set the cup down and tried to smile at him.

"Okay," he said with his crooked half-grin that she'd found so charming. "Enough suspense. Let's have the story of this new case you've broken."

She dropped her gaze. "It wasn't exactly a new case. I finally figured out the mystery of the Morphine Murders. Or the Catherine Fletcher case, if you will."

He gave her a sharp look and raised an eyebrow. "I thought you had that one solved a long time ago."

She glanced up at him. "It appeared that way, didn't it. But it looks like Phyllis Walsh is innocent after all."

His eyebrow climbed higher, but he said nothing. He sat silent, waiting for her to continue.

Her mind went over the scene the way Brillo had rehearsed her a dozen times. She was supposed to play the innocent. She was supposed to tell the story of the murders with Catherine Fletcher cast as the warped but brilliant killer who decided to knock off two partners and frame the third, before committing suicide in a way that made her look like still another murder victim. She was supposed to toss the story out on the table as casually as a used dinner napkin and see what the response would be. And it was right at this point that she should be launching into the fictional tale.

But Jack was eyeing her as if there wasn't a thing in the world wrong. There wasn't even a twitch of a facial muscle or a flicker of his gaze to indicate anything other than casual interest in what she might have to say. What had seemed logical at the time now seemed artificial, futile in the face of his playacting, and the whole scheme suddenly collapsed in her mind.

Without knowing she was going to do so, she said sadly, "I've been down to Stanford, Jack. I know about your involvement with Catherine Fletcher."

"Stanford?" His tone was easy, almost innocent, as if he were puzzled by the reference.

"Dr. Swanson identified your picture as the man posing as Catherine Fletcher's husband."

His eyes went instantly neutral. "Ah, yes, I see." He gave a slightly crooked smile. "That damned camera you bought." Amused, he shook his head at his own folly in allowing that to happen.

She kept the pain she was feeling out of her voice. "I guess you'd better tell me everything," she said evenly. "Before I go to the Captain with the story."

His eyes narrowed slightly. "You haven't told him yet?"

She shook her head. She hadn't. The Captain had no idea what was coming down tonight. Thus she was able to meet his gaze fully and honestly. "No. I wanted to give you a chance to explain first."

He relaxed. "Explain what? What do you think my trip to Stanford means?"

"I think it means you're involved with Catherine and these murders clear up to your neck."

"I see." He quirked a quizzical eyebrow. "Do I detect a little female jealousy operating here?"

The suggestion was so outrageous that she simply stared at him openmouthed. Then she realized that was exactly the reaction he'd intended to provoke. Oh, Kate, you *are* swimming with the sharks tonight. She closed her gaping mouth, smiled coolly and said softly, "No, that's not what you're detecting. What you're detecting is a professional at work."

Suddenly she took her own words to heart. If she was going to claim to be the professional, then goddammit, she'd damned well better start acting like one. She was so far off the script now that there was no hope of getting back. But that didn't mean the cause was lost. A glimmer of a new path began to materialize in the far corner of her mind.

First she had to get through to this man. "By the way," she

said casually, "I saw an old friend of yours while I was in California. Walter Marks. Remember him?"

She'd finally shocked him. A surge of momentary emotion got past his mask before he managed to slip it back in place. Anger, hatred, confusion, calculation—all flashed in their turn. Then it was gone and he was once again the pleasant and charming man the world saw every day.

Taking advantage of that moment of shock, she took control. "Let's cut the bullshit, Jack. I know what you are. I've talked to Marks and eight other people you've swindled. I've talked to the doctors. Dr. Kubrachek at Virginia Mason, Dr. Schofield in Carnation, Dr. Swanson in Stanford. I've also talked to the resident manager of Catherine's condo, as well as the head honcho of the property-management company. I've spent weeks tracking your life history down"—an exaggeration, but at this point, who cared?—"and it all tells one story: you're a con man from the word go. But there are some things I want to know. Like what happened to all the money Catherine stole from the business. Like how Phyllis Walsh got saddled with four counts of Murder One. Like how Richard Walsh got the spiked Scotch. Like a lot of things. So let's just cut out the lies and the fairy tales and get right down to the guts of the matter. Exactly *how* did you and Catherine come to plan those murders?"

He'd hidden behind his carefully donned neutrality once more and sat staring down at his cup. She left him to his thinking while she sipped more coffee. The world beyond the French doors had blackened and all that could be seen now were their own reflections in the pane. A good-looking man lost in thought, and a not-too-unattractive woman, calmly watching. With the table settings, the low lights, the coffee cups at hand, it looked like a romantic setting. But her spine was stiff as a broom handle.

Finally he frowned up at her. "You could be taping all of this."

"I could be," she answered calmly. "You're free to search the room. Walls, ceiling, doorjambs, electrical outlets . . ." With a half-smile, she indicated the bouquet he'd brought that sat on the sideboard. ". . . the flowers . . . me. I can show you what to look for, if you'd like."

He gave an answering half-smile of his own. "Never con a con man, Kate," he said with high amusement. "If you think your casual assurances are going to allay my concerns, I assure you I'm not that simpleminded." He set down his napkin and began to explore the room.

He was thorough. Baseboards, switch plates, rug, table legs, chairs—he explored every inch of the whole dining room while she sat calmly drinking her coffee, her dinner ring sparkling beneath the lights of the ceiling fan. And he even took a chair, climbed up on it, and examined *that,* she noted with amusement. Then he gave her body as thorough an examination as any doctor's—and more impersonal—running his hands over her rib cage, back, waist, hips and legs for any taped-on wire. He even checked the cleavage between her breasts. He didn't glance twice at her ring.

When he was fully satisfied the room and Kate were clean, he resumed his seat and relaxed back. "All right, nothing hidden that I can see. Besides, you're much too honest and sincere to lie," he added in a mocking tone. "Aren't you, my dear."

So. That was his real opinion of her. Contempt. She really had been the fool. She smiled back at him. "Much."

"Well, I must admit, you've done better than I would have given you credit for. That really was an amazing piece of detective work." The smile faded as he stared off into the distance. "Yes, the condo. I knew that was a weak point. I was pretty sure you couldn't penetrate the corporate curtain I'd set up to prove actual ownership, but I was afraid that a pair of weak lips would let the cat out of the bag. At the time I let Catherine move in with me, I didn't realize how critical hiding the fact that we lived together would become. Well, I'll have to see to that loose end." Ever the businessman, he seemed to add a note to his mental to-do list before he focused back on her.

"The murders?" she prompted.

"The murders." The soft smile was back. "Ah, yes, the murders. But before we get into that, may I suggest a bit of an after-dinner drink to lubricate the voice box? The tale is long, I fear, but not boring. Hopefully not boring. Nothing drains the color out of life like boring, right, my love?" He rose and picked up their coffee cups. "Sit still," he said gently, "I'll see to this." He disappeared into the kitchen.

She listened to the kitchen noises. The thud of glasses being placed on the counter. A carbonated hiss as a cap was opened.

A carbonated hiss? She straightened. For a liqueur? A quick glug-glug as some liquid was poured into the glasses. Then a pouring of more liquid. Then a moment of silence. It was broken after a bit by the clink of an ice cube against the lip of the glass. A spoon tinkled a merry rhythm as it stirred the drinks. The script called for her to drink whatever he offered. Which had sounded reasonable in theory. But now her heart thudded with fear.

When he returned and placed a glass in front of her, she stared at it. "An old-fashioned tumbler for an after-dinner drink?" she said. "I do have liqueur glasses."

"Don't be rude to your elders, my dear," he said lightly. "This is a Jack Turner special. A bit of soda water to cut the sweetness, but not so much as to make it bitter. And tradition has it that you chug-a-lug the first one straight down."

She took a sip and made a face. "But it is bitter."

He nodded wisely. "Too much soda water. Drink it down a bit and I'll add more Bailey's."

Grimacing, she took two more swallows, then handed it to him. It was a quarter down. He returned it to her full, and it tasted better. Delicious, in fact. Decidedly delicious, as a matter of fact. She sent a brief prayer heavenward. When he resumed his seat, she prompted him once more. "The murders."

"Ah, yes, the murders. Well, it was fascinating how that all evolved. You see, Catherine and I actually met in the summertime, not in November, as I'd first indicated. She and her husband, Vern Riley, had gone out for dinner at Mia Roma's, a small Italian restaurant up in Bothell. After dinner they settled at the bar, where Riley proceeded to drink himself into idiocy. He began pawing the women at the bar, making lewd comments, telling filthy jokes, that sort of thing. Basically acting like the real low-class jerk he was. Well, Catherine got upset with him and they had a fight and he ended up stomping off into the night. With their car. Leaving her stranded. I happened to be there by myself, and, well, how could I leave a beautiful woman like her abandoned like that?" He smiled, splaying his hands wide to illustrate his helplessness. "I bought her a drink to calm her

down a little, then offered her a ride home. But she didn't want
to go home. Riley would be there, and she was tired of dealing
with him. After a second drink, I suggested she take the extra
bedroom at my condo for the night. That was much more to her
liking, and so I took her home."

He drifted off into memory. "You know, you can really tell a
person's character when they're confronted by obvious signs of
real money. You've seen my condo. Or Catherine's condo, as you
know it. It's top of the line. Even some of the Seahawks live in
the complex, using it for housing during the playing season.
Really top-drawer. Well, when Catherine saw it, her eyeballs
spun like a winning slot machine, and you could see her toting
up my net worth. It was amusing to watch it happen. The
greed . . ." He smiled with affection at the memory. ". . . the pure
greed that flickered there. Oh, just for a second, understand. She
was pretty good at concealing her true feelings. I'm sure any
other person watching her wouldn't have noticed. But you see,
Katie, I've trained myself to watch for the hidden areas in people.
The dark places in their soul, if that doesn't sound too dramatic,
where greed and lust and all the other human passions reside.
You need to know what makes them tick if you're going to have
control over them."

He refocused on her. "Like you, my dear. I knew that first
moment you walked into my office that here was a nice, sincere,
pretty little girl, who still believes in fairy tales and wants the
world to make nice-nice at all times. Motherhood, apple pie and
Chevrolet, as the old commercial used to go. Anyway, I read you
clear through, right down to the husband and children you
secretly want so badly." His gaze sharpened as he saw her glass.
He interrupted his discourse to lean forward. "Drink up, my
love," he said gently. "Chug-a-lug. Remember?" He raised his
own drink and swallowed the contents down, watching her over
the top rim of the glass, his eyes filled with amusement.

Reluctantly, she took another sip.

He nodded his approval. "That's the girl. Now, where was I?
Oh, yes, Catherine. Anyway, I could see Catherine toting up my
net worth, and I watched her as she turned on this wonderful,
warm charm. I let her seduce me that night, and the next day I

let her move out of the squalid little apartment she shared with Riley and move in with me.

"Of course I didn't trust her worth a damn. But that didn't matter. She wasn't the kind of woman you keep around because you trust them. I really thought I'd found my soul mate. Here was an utterly beautiful, conniving, ruthless woman who believed in taking what she wanted, whenever she wanted it, and for no better reason than the fact that she wanted it. But a few character flaws emerged over the next few months. Nothing serious, really. A bit too much love for her wine. A touch of laziness. And a tendency to think small. To be honest—which we are being, right, my love? Totally honest?—To be honest about Catherine, she was rather a stupid woman. Cold, calculating, ruthless, yes. But stupid. Still, she wasn't the kind of woman you kept around because of her intellect, either.

"And then she was diagnosed with cancer. Ah, my dear, she did carry on so about it." His tone was light, edged with contempt. "It was most unattractive. But she did do one practical thing. She decided that if she were going to die, she was going to make a few others suffer first, and she began to set little goals for herself. The one thing she wanted to do more than anything else was to get even with Phyllis Walsh. I could understand that. Phyllis was another of those boringly sincere people who make life such a chore to get through. The second thing she wanted to do was to ruin the business, to leave the partners with nothing more than a horrifying mess on their hands. That was a respectable want, too. Why should they be happy if she couldn't even live, for God's sakes, was her thinking. I agreed. Why should they? And her last wish was to repay Vern Riley for all the misery and unhappiness he'd caused her. That one was the simplest of all to understand.

"But this is where the small thinking comes in." He sighed his disappointment. "Catherine's idea of revenge for Phyllis Walsh was to seduce her husband, causing her all kinds of emotional pain and agony. Now, seducing Richard Walsh wasn't a completely bad idea. Phyllis was certainly bound to have found out, and the ruckus it would've caused would've been a joy to watch. Especially since approaching death made Catherine somewhat invincible against any retaliation. But really, Kate, my dear, there was no finesse there. No thought or intelligence given to other possibilities. No subtlety to it at all.

"The same with her idea for ruining the business. Her thought was to bleed it dry. But bleeding it dry meant nothing. I've seen businesses resurrected from grave sites so deep you'd have thought they'd gone clear down to hell. And yet they survived. So why not destroy it totally? Why not destroy it so completely that it could never be resurrected again? But that didn't occur to Catherine. You see? Small thinking again.

"Now, to give her her due, when it came to Vern Riley, she didn't do quite so badly. Her plan was to invite him back into her life when the time came that she needed someone to take care of her during the final stages of her illness. I had already made it quite clear that I would not undertake such a job. But since he was her husband, not only would he be stuck with some distasteful duties during that final stage of dying, he'd also be stuck for all the medical bills. Now that revenge seemed fitting. He was such a damned loser anyway. There were appealing elements in it that simply tickled the imagination. But the others? Catherine got all wrapped up in her petty little retributions and ignored the larger potential of the situation.

"Because, you see, here was the opportunity of the century," he said with emphasis, stressing its importance. "Here's a woman, terminally ill, with no hope of remission. The doctors—*all* the doctors—had made that quite clear. There was no hope for Catherine. There was no saving her. I thought long and hard about what could be done under such dire circumstances. I'd always been curious about murder. How it feels to commit murder. How it feels to watch someone's life ebb away in front of you, knowing that you—Not God, but you—a lowly mortal, have caused this person to stop existing."

He leaned toward Kate, his eyes glittering beneath the crystalline light of the chandelier. "You see, Katie, my love, death is irrevocable. You can't snatch a person back and say, That's enough now. You can't change your mind and say, No, no, I didn't mean it, come back now. No, you can't do any of those things. It isn't at all like folding a company and reopening it the next morning. It's so *final*, you see. And now, fate, or God, or whatever you want to call it, had thrown a rather unique opportunity my way. It was a temptation I couldn't resist, and I conceived the idea of committing the perfect murder. That's the utmost challenge, isn't it, the ultimate game? To commit the perfect murder? To take a human life and not get caught?

"But I didn't want just some plain, drab, sordid kind of murder, and I liked the concept Catherine had of getting even with Phyllis Walsh. Personally, she meant nothing to me. I didn't even know the woman. I could've cared less whether she lived or died. And I did think at first of having Phyllis Walsh herself as the murder victim. But where was the retribution there? She'd be dead and out of it.

"So I played around with some ideas until I came up with one that tickled my sense of the macabre. I would select victims *other* than Phyllis, and eliminate them in such a way that it appeared she had committed the murders. She'd be accused, tried and found guilty, and she'd be spending the rest of her life in prison for a crime she didn't commit."

He smiled at Kate. "And you know what the beautiful part of it was, the truly exquisite little touch was? She'd be spending the rest of her life *knowing* she hadn't committed the crime, but being helpless to prove her innocence. Now *that* to me was real revenge. Subtle, appealing, delightful. Now you can see that this was a far greater concept than Catherine's pitiful little plans.

"But still, what Catherine wanted to do wasn't going to interfere with anything I was planning, so where was the harm? I went ahead and let her do what she wanted. It kept her amused. Like taking money out of the business. That was fun. She liked that. She enjoyed bilking the ladies out of their hard-earned dollars while she slept in till noon every day. And she thoroughly enjoyed watching the trouble it caused.

"As for the affair with Richard Walsh, she played him easy and cautious, like you do a wily old fish. She got him to agree to meet her for a drink, playing on his ego. The excuse she used was that she needed his marketing expertise and feedback for an idea she had for the business. An idea *I* provided for her, of course. She persuaded him to hold off saying anything about the meeting to Phyllis until she knew whether the idea was workable or not." The fond smile of memory was back again. "Once he agreed to the first meeting, she had him. I watched, of course, from a dim corner of the lounge where they met. Even from there, I could tell his ego was monstrous, and it's easy to land a fish like that. You just tell him what he already knows—he's the best and the brightest. Which Catherine did, of course. Then it was a simple move for her to start draping a careless arm over his, to brush accidentally against his thigh, to find reasons to touch his hand gently while asking a wide-eyed question—all the things you do to activate the sexual buttons. Richard was easy once his ego was stroked, and all Catherine had to do was to let nature take its course. Poor man. He really thought he'd found the garden of Eden when he started the affair with Catherine."

He laughed softly, shaking his head at the folly of such simplistic thinking. Then his gaze sharpened as he left his memories and focused back on Kate. "It was really no different than the technique I used with you, my dear," he said softly. "You needed to be told you were pretty, made to feel you were desirable, made to feel wanted. All people want to be loved and admired, isn't that true? All people want to believe they're attractive and desirable. Well, then, you simply give them what they want. Isn't that true, my dear? The words may differ from person to person, but the music's the same. And that's what I did with you. I made you believe."

Kate simply stared at him. Yes, she'd believed. She'd been ready to believe and she had gone ahead and allowed herself to believe, and it had all been false, all a fake, all a sham. The shame of it washed over her like a torrent of dirty water, and she wanted to close her eyes to get away from it. But he was too full of pride over what he'd accomplished to linger over the small matter of her humiliation, and she had to put aside her self-contempt to listen.

"While Catherine was busy putting her little schemes into action, I began to work on mine. I outlined my program step-by-step, like any good business plan. The first thing, of course, was to choose the victims. They had to be people Phyllis knew, that Phyllis—and *only* Phyllis—would have a reason for wanting out of the way. Her business partners were obvious. And so there could be no doubt as to Phyllis' guilt, I tossed in her husband." He preened a little here at his own cleverness. "A unique combination, I rather thought. Don't you agree, Katie? A combination of victims that no other person on earth could remotely have a reason for killing. Only Phyllis."

He nodded, well-pleased with himself. Then his businessman's mind took over again and he continued on down his list. "Once I had the victims chosen, then it was time to select the means for the murders. It should be by remote control, I decided, my first time out. I didn't want to appear on the scene, involved in any part of it. After reviewing various options, morphine seemed the answer. It's so closely connected with terminal cancer that it seemed a natural. Second decision made.

"Next decision—how to acquire the drug. Buying it off the local street corner was out. I wanted no one else in on this. Particularly some petty little crook who might overreach himself with a bit of blackmail. No, that wasn't for me. Not at all. Instead, I would use Catherine, and her cancer, to acquire the drug. She was terrified of pain, and terrified of the agony she'd be going through, and it was exceedingly simple to persuade her to get some morphine well ahead of time, so she'd have it on hand when the pain began. At my suggestion, she called around and found a doctor who'd fall for any sob story that sounded reasonable, and suddenly we had as much morphine as we could ever want. Then I simply helped myself." He smiled. "She didn't even notice. She was always careless about things. For instance, she was missing her office key ring for a day while I had duplicates made, and she didn't notice that either. Poor Catherine. She did have her little flaws."

He shook his head in mock sadness and went on with his tale. "Now I had plenty of morphine on hand. And I had a key to the studio. The only thing left was to figure out a way to administer the drug to my chosen victims. I couldn't exactly walk in and have them pop a pill, could I?" His eyes gleamed with vast amusement at the thought. "So one weekend when no one was there, I had Catherine take me on a private tour of the studio. Catherine, as we all know, was the only tea drinker. That set up her demise. But the others were a little trickier. Everyone, it seemed, drank coffee, including stray visitors, so that was out. It wasn't narrowly targeted enough to suit me. But when I asked about a soda pop machine, she took me down to that drab little lunchroom and showed me the refrigerator shelves. White wine for Suzie, ginger ale for Ginger, and cans of Pepsi for Phyllis. It was on the honor system, of course, since other tenants used the refrigerator too. But I wasn't worried about that. If someone helped themselves to Suzie's wine, then they'd simply suffer the consequences, and it would be one more murder charge against Phyllis.

"Once I had the method, I began working out the timing. By now, the first of Catherine's spiteful little retaliations were in progress. She was taking more and more money out of the business. At the same time, the affair with Richard Walsh was going red-hot. Now it was time to set up Vern Riley.

"Ah, yes, poor Vern." His face took on a dreamy quality. "I had, of course, already parted company with Catherine. I'd rented a small apartment for myself and moved my personal belongings out, so there was no trace of my presence left at the condo. It looked as if she lived there alone. She called him that final Sunday, sang him a sweet song about being sorry they'd broken up, and suggested they try a reconciliation again. He couldn't grab the offer fast enough. Later that evening, while Catherine was in bed with him at my condo, convincing him that he was in for a long and happy married life, I slipped into the graphics studio and did what needed to be done. I'd already crushed the morphine tablets into powder and prepared the tea bags at my apartment. All I had to do at the studio was to clean out the top layer of tea bags in the canister and place the doctored tea bags on top of the second layer, where they'd be used first. As for the wine and ginger ale, I merely divided some extra tablets I'd crushed among them and swirled the bottles around until they'd dissolved. I used gloves, of course, for everything. Then I walked out. I simply walked out. It was all so simple, really." His voice died away, and he was lost among his memories again. "It was all so simple," he said slowly.

For a moment, the silence stretched out between them. Finally he shook his head and sighed. "In the end, it was too simple, though," he said softly. "Once the planning was done, and once the deed was done, it became all preordained. All I could do was to sit back and wait. The challenge was over." His face reflected his disappointment. His gaze drifted off into space and his voice died away again.

Throughout the tale, Kate had sat, still and silent, caught up in the story, listening intently. Now, in the silence of the room, she became aware of the small night sounds that surrounded her. The refrigerator humming quietly away in the kitchen. The slight creaks and groans of the house as the warmth of the day turned into the chill of the moonless dark. An occasional car driving past the house. A night bird singing in the shrubbery somewhere in the neighborhood.

She'd long since finished the drink he'd given her, and shadows were gathering at the periphery of her vision. Her spine was no longer the rigid broom handle it had been. Her eyelids felt heavy and she had a terrible desire to lay her head down on the table and go to sleep. She had to keep swallowing back a tendency to yawn. Finally, one escaped.

It caught his attention instantly, and he was filled with contrite concern. "Oh, I'm sorry, my love," he said in a gentle, caring tone. "How thoughtless of me. You're getting sleepy, I should've noticed. We'll just move you into the other room now. You need to stretch out on the couch for a while."

He moved around the table and helped her stand. Her knees were weak, reluctant to hold her up. She gained some steadiness, and, leaning heavily on his arm, made it into the other room and over to the couch. She flopped down on the cushions like a drunk seeking support for a too-soggy body.

Satisfaction evident in his face, he stared down at her a moment, then smiled. "I'll be right back. I'm just going to freshen our drinks a little."

As she fought to keep her eyes open, he vanished from her line of sight. She waited a few seconds and then, when she was sure he was out of the room, she struggled up to a sitting position. The arm of the couch provided her lower spine the support needed in keeping her upper trunk upright.

He was busy in the kitchen now. She could hear him. She forced her right hand down behind the cushion. The gun felt cold and hard to her fingers. She pulled it free and laid it next to her leg, in handy reach. The fullness of her jumpsuit hid it from sight. She eyed the effect critically. It would do. Still upright, she laid one cheek against the back of the couch and waited.

He reappeared and handed her the fresh refill. Totally relaxed now, he sat on the other end of the couch, near her feet, his eyes lazy on hers.

She stifled another yawn and curled up deeper in her corner. "Pardon me," she said in apology. "It's just that I'm feeling so sleepy."

"Actually, that's just the liquor hitting your system. I really loaded up those drinks. I would think there's a few minutes yet before the other stuff begins to affect you."

"Other stuff?" she asked innocently. "What do you mean, what other stuff?"

He laughed and reached out to pat her knee. "You are such a delight at times, Katie, my love. Such total trust and naiveté. It was intriguing trying to be what you wanted me to be, in matching your little middle-class standards with little middle-class standards on my own." His eyes gleamed like a cat's from the glow of the nearby table lamp. "I knew exactly what you wanted to hear from me and gave it to you, word by word, line by line. 'Yes, my darling Kate,' " he mimicked himself. " 'I, too, seek companionship for my old age. And grandchildren on my knee. And a love to keep me warm . . .' Oh, God, the platitudes I mouthed. It was a real challenge not betraying the total boredom I felt thirty seconds after meeting you. You were about as exciting and interesting as a bag of sand."

Kate wanted nothing more than to close her eyes to escape the mocking cruelty that clothed the man's face. But she didn't dare. If she closed her eyes, it would be too easy to drift into eternity. A great blackness was creeping in from all sides. She wasn't sure how much longer she could stay awake. Had she left it too long? She struggled to regain an inch of upright. As long as she sat up, she'd be all right. As long as she sat up . . . She kept her eyes fixed on his, using the cruel amusement she found there to fuel her waning strength.

"Still," he went on, "there was some small redeeming thrill at being so close to the murder investigation that I myself created. Even if it was after the fact. At times it was hard not to laugh, as you told me how you muddled along one trail after another. Ah, Kate, you tried every which way you could think of to avoid charging Phyllis Walsh with those crimes, but fight as you would, you finally had to accept her as the villain. And do you know the marvelous part now, the ironic part of this whole evening we're spending in quiet discourse? Nothing changes that. Nothing changes a thing. Not tonight. Not your death. Not anything. Phyllis Walsh will *still* be convicted of the first four murders. And now yours will be included. Five, altogether. Amazing, isn't it?" He laughed softly and patted her knee again. He was enjoying this hugely, she could see through her failing vision. He was loving it. His moment in the sun.

He basked a minute longer, then a sudden energy swept over him. "All right now! There's a lot to do." He rose and took her half-empty glass from her limp hand. "I'm going to start cleaning away this stuff. By the time anyone finds you, your kitchen will be immaculate, and all there'll be is your glass sitting next to the bottle of Bailey's. With Phyllis' fingerprints on it."

She froze. Hands, heart, blood. She froze. She had to have him in the room. She couldn't follow him. She couldn't *move* to follow him. Did she have it all yet? No. Dear God, *no!* "Phyllis' fingerprints?" she whispered. "How?"

"Ah, yes. Phyllis' fingerprints." He moved around the coffee table and sat on the edge of the wing chair across the room, facing her, her glass in his hand. He swirled the small amount of Bailey's left in it absently. "That was a rather simple exercise. Once I'd conceived of the original plan, with all signs pointing directly to Phyllis, I didn't think it would hurt to have a bit of insurance to back it up. For the unforeseen, you know. So I bought the Irish Cream a few days ahead of the murders and left the unwrapped bottle on Phyllis' desk one night where she'd be forced to move it. I knew she wouldn't take it home with her. Sincere people don't steal. The next night, I simply made another visit and reclaimed it. With gloves on, of course, so as not to smudge her fingerprints."

He looked exceedingly pleased with himself. "Now, when I

leave tonight, all traces of our little dinner here will be cleared away. I'll do a little post-mortem pressing of your fingers against the Bailey's bottle, on top of Phyllis', of course, and the story will be clear. To the police, it'll seem like Phyllis gave the Bailey's to you as a gift at some point in the investigation, already spiked, and you brought it home with you and only just now got around to drinking some. So you see, there'll be a direct link from Phyllis to you. That bottle will be her death warrant."

She stared at him. "Then you came here tonight *planning* to kill me?"

"Kill?" He seemed surprised at her comment and mulled the word over. "That's a rather strong term, isn't it? A hunter's term. Just a simple bang-bang. It lacks a certain subtlety, don't you think? But still, I suppose technically it's accurate. Yes, I did have your elimination in mind. After all, the murder investigation was finished. At least, I'd thought so. Everyone seemed satisfied with Phyllis Walsh being named the culprit. And there wasn't a whole lot further to go in our romance. I *certainly* had no intentions of marrying you. That was just for my own amusement, to see how far I could actually get you to go. But you were so easy, I rapidly lost interest. And my tolerance for boredom is fairly low. So, yes, this little conversation aside, I was planning to kill you tonight anyway." He smiled.

She was beyond being hurt any more. If you're stabbed ninety-nine times, does the hundredth really hurt?

Besides, she was floating now, gliding along like a seagull soaring on a gentle current of air. It was a pleasant feeling, like being adrift in a warm and buoyant sea. She wanted to close her eyes and simply drift away.

His voice was becoming fainter and fainter in her ear. She forced back the blackness awaiting at the horizon of her vision and tried to concentrate. *Now.* Did she have it all now? No. Just a bit more. "The money," she murmured. "The money Catherine took from the business. And her stock certificate. And her missing files. And the rest of the morphine. What happened to them all?"

"The files were destroyed. Just another little nuisance she dreamed up for her beloved business partners. The money and the stock certificate? She gave them both to me for safekeeping. She didn't want Riley finding them lying around. After she was dead, I simply went on keeping the money. You can never have too much, can you." Then he gave a broad grin of delight. "And the stock certificate . . . Ah, I had fun with that. 'Catherine,' I said to her just before we parted, 'your intent is to drive your company into the ground making that certificate worthless. Humor me, my love,' I told her, 'endorse it over to me.'" He grinned happily at Kate. "And of course she did. What she'd overlooked was the insurance. Three partners dead, the fourth convicted of murder. Which leaves me now as sole surviving partner, and recipient of all that lovely cash, three hundred thousand dollars' worth. As I said, you can never have too much, can you."

"And the morphine?"

"Safely tucked away in a safe deposit box. Except, of course, for the tablets I've used tonight."

Another question. Would they never stop? she wondered. "And Richard Walsh? How did you manage his death?"

"A midnight visit. Poor Richard. He was suffering so. His mistress dead, his wife the major suspect. He was full of little worries. Did Phyllis know of his affair with Catherine, or didn't she? Was that the reason she killed her, or wasn't it? I knew what he'd be thinking, you see, and so I posed as a friend of Catherine's and called him earlier that day. I told him I had a small gift that Catherine had bought for him—as well as a personal message from Catherine, and that I needed to meet with him in total privacy. He was so hungry for some word of Catherine, he didn't question any of it. When I insisted we had to talk privately, at his house, when Phyllis wouldn't be around, he set it for late that night, assuring me the sleeping pills Phyllis was taking would keep her knocked out while I was there. And they did. We had a completely undisturbed visit."

"And the Scotch?" The question came out a hoarse whisper. Her throat muscles wanted to go off duty. She was also having trouble with her breathing. Her chest was almost too heavy for her lungs to lift so they could fill with air.

"Catherine's gift for Richard, of course," he said with a grand gesture of generosity. "Undoctored, at first. I spiked his drinks individually. Then after he was dead, I dumped the rest of the morphine in the bottle to make it look like Phyllis had done it. Of course, I washed and wiped my glass before I slipped away. No trace of my presence at all."

He grew reflective. "I sat and watched him die, you know. It should've been exciting. It should've been an exhilarating moment. And I suppose it was, when he finally did take his last breath. But really, it ranks right up there with watching grass grow. Next time I plan something like this, it must be more direct, I think. And without mistakes, of course." He cocked his head at her. "But then, when I met Catherine, I didn't know this opportunity would come along. Next time, I'll make my own opportunity. I'll plan it from the beginning. Plot it all out." He nodded. "Yes. Next time, it will be mistake-free." And then he gave his appealing crooked grin. "You see? A new challenge. For perfection."

He had such an attractive surface, she thought. And it covered such evil depths. Like a rich blue ocean with brilliant sparkles of sunlight dancing over the smooth surface, hiding the warped and twisted black deeps below.

Did she have it all *now?*

Yes!

The urge to slide down into blackness was becoming overwhelming. Her eyes were narrowed into slits to keep them from closing completely. Casually, as if to help maintain her balance, she slid her hand under the material of the jumpsuit. She gripped the gun tightly.

Grinning, he watched her struggle. "You're almost asleep now, my love," he said softly. "You have only minutes left to go. Your breathing is already slow, erratic. And you don't have to fight it so. It's going to be painless, Katie, I promise you. Just a nice soft sinking into oblivion."

He cocked that remarkable eyebrow at her, his electric blue eyes dancing with curiosity. "How does it feel, knowing you're going to die? Knowing that from this time on, you will never exist again? I've always been curious about that, wondering what it felt like to know your time on earth is up. Are you afraid? Are you afraid it's all blackness out there, waiting for you? Is that what you think it's like, Kate?"

Then a new thought occurred and he looked at her with a sudden intense amusement. "Or worse—do you believe in hell? Are all your sins running through your mind at this moment, wondering if you'll be consigned to the fires of hell for all of eternity, one of the damned? I've always wanted to know. Tell me, Katie." His voice was hypnotically insistent. "Share it with me, Katie. Tell me what you feel."

"I'm going to cheat you," she whispered. "I'm not going to die." Her throat muscles closed and she barely got the words out past her tongue. "You're under arrest . . ."

Her voice was too low to hear and he had to lip-read her command. "Oh, really?" He gave a soft laugh. "How? You can't move. You can't even talk." He relaxed back in the chair, his face filled with high humor.

"I'm wired," she said hoarsely. "Everything you've said . . . has been taped . . ."

He simply shook his head at that. "Nice try, Katie. But you forget, I searched you myself."

"My ring," she whispered.

The false garnet caught the rays of the table lamp by her elbow, and it glittered in the cone of light like a third entity, filled with a self-sustaining power of its own.

For a brief second, shock kept him frozen to his chair.

She raised the gun clear of her jumpsuit. Her wrist was weak and the small revolver wavered in lyrical circles. She supported her right wrist with her other hand and aimed more or less for his chest. She forced all of her strength into her right hand and the gun steadied. "You're under arrest," she croaked again.

Belief struck then and he lunged

She pulled the trigger once. Then she pulled it twice more.

And then she closed her eyes and drifted away into the waiting blackness.

Epilogue

After weeks of cold and gray drizzle, the weather finally caught up with the calendar and June arrived warm and sunny. Kate worked in her garden when she could. When the weather became too bad, she escaped into a stack of suspense books she'd checked out from the library. She'd been pulled off active duty until the Internal Affairs investigation was complete. That was fine with her. She wasn't ready to hit the streets yet. Desk time gave her a chance to catch up with herself, to gain some detachment and emotional equilibrium and get life somewhat back under control.

She'd woken up in intensive care two days after Jack Turner was killed. Internal Affairs had barely waited until she was transferred to a private room before starting in on her. There were two of them, one short and stolid, the other tall and stolid. They both had a similar air of serious authority and quiet disbelief etched in their eyes. The shorter one asked the questions and watched her every expression and reaction as she answered. The other one took notes. They also had a tape recorder going.

As Brillo had coached, she kept it simple.

They'd suspected Jack Turner had done the killings, but there wasn't proof strong enough to take to court. Their hope had been to tape Turner's story, which would then lead to stronger evidence they could use. That was the whole justification for the dinner at her house.

No, she definitely had not anticipated killing him. The gun? Two nights before, she'd had a prowler and had reported it to the police. They could check the records if they wanted to; there would be a report of her complaint. The prowler was gone before she or the beat cops could do anything. But the next day she'd gotten a permit and purchased a small revolver she could keep by her side. Sure, she had her service weapon, but she kept that in her bedroom along with the other stuff she wore for work. The revolver she bought was much smaller, small enough to hide out of sight in the couch, since she usually curled up there in the evening to read. So she'd tucked it behind a cushion, near at hand, just in case . . .

Of course she'd suspected that Turner had put the morphine in her drink, but he would only talk if he was convinced that she wouldn't live to tell his tale. So she'd had to drink some of it to allay his concerns. When she had all the information she needed, she'd pulled the gun out to hold him in place until Brillo could get through the door. But when he saw the pistol and learned the conversation had been taped, Turner had lunged at her and she'd shot him in self-defense. The morphine had blurred her vision somewhat by then, and she wasn't sure the first shot had stopped him . . . or even hit him . . . It just seemed as if he kept coming and kept coming and kept coming . . . and she fired again, twice. Then she passed out.

That was all she knew.

They questioned her again and again. In the hospital, at her home after she'd been discharged, at the station when she'd finally received medical clearance to return to her desk. They took her over the story again and again, in a dozen different ways. But that was all she knew.

They questioned Sam and Brillo, too. That didn't get them anywhere, either. Sam wasn't even supposed to have been in on the action that night. But he'd sensed something coming down, had wormed the story out of Brillo just ahead of time and had simply included himself in. He'd helped man the electronic van they'd parked in her neighbor's driveway, and when the first of the shots sounded through their earphones, he'd been the first one to explode through her front door.

No, he and Brillo had not deliberately waited until Jack Turner was dead. The signal they'd set up with Kate were the words, "You're under arrest." Yes, they'd had to wait for her signal. She was the D.I.C. Only she would know when all the questions had been answered. And yes, they had known that the morphine would slowly shut down her respiratory system. That's why they'd had the doctor and an ambulance standing by. But what they hadn't known was that it would affect her ability to speak as it was doing so. And so they never heard the words. Even electronically amplified and enhanced afterward, her whispers were barely decipherable.

What Sam didn't tell them was about his own personal vigil. He'd ridden in the ambulance with her to the hospital and had stayed in the intensive-care room around the clock until she'd turned the corner and he knew she was going to make it. He'd been at her side when she finally woke up. His was the first face she saw, and without saying a word, he carved a path through all the tubes surrounding her, pulled her close and held her tight as the hard armadillo shell around her soul finally dissolved and she wept away some of the pain that was clotted there.

The Captain, of course, was livid. He reamed Brillo and Sam royally for running an unauthorized undercover op, especially a cross-divisional undercover op, and on his own, busted them back to their desks for a couple of weeks. Though he came to see Kate often in the hospital, as soon as she was off the critical list he took his shots at her, right in the hospital room. And he even saw to it that Sam and Brillo were there, in case they'd missed anything he'd had to say the first time around. It was hard to tell which had enraged him the most—the three of them taking off on their own as they had, or the danger they'd placed her in. But she couldn't help noticing that there was more bark than bite to the dressing-down he gave them, and there was something in his eye that she couldn't quite name, but the word respect came to mind.

Kate kept herself busy that spring and summer. While IAD ran their investigation, and in between her gardening and her reading, she made it a point to spend some time with Phyllis Walsh. As the weeks passed and she began the first tentative steps in rebuilding a life for herself, Phyllis slowly regained some of the weight she'd lost, and the terrible haunted look that she'd worn even after her release from jail began to fade. Her first day back in her graphics studio convinced her it was not the place to be, and she closed the business down. She also got rid of her house in Tam O'Shanter and moved into a rented place in Kirkland, half a dozen blocks from Kate's. To keep herself busy, she took a clerical job at an engineering firm in town.

In July, Kate took some of her comp time off and pulled some money out of savings and flew to California. It took her three days to find one, but she ended up with a top-notch licensing attorney in a prestigious San Francisco firm. When all the arrangements had been worked out, she drove down the peninsula to the dark little house in Sunnyvale. She corralled the crabby, unshaven man, coerced him into climbing into her rental car and drove him back to San Francisco. The meetings and negotiations lasted for two days. In the end, the attorney and the IRS reached an agreement, the attorney and Walter Marks signed a management contract, and Marks assigned a small percentage of his net to Kate in return for her help. Then he emerged under a cobalt-blue sky, free of the tax collector's chase, with the prospect of a hefty income ahead for anything he designed. He was still unsmiling, without so much as a thank-you as she paid their hotel bill and meal charges. He did deign to shake her hand before he left her car to clump up the overgrown walkway back to his cramped, dark world. She simply shook her head with wry amusement as she drove to the airport, turned the rental car back in and caught the next flight home.

She had one more small chore to clean up. She checked back over Schreiber's and Rice's notes and found the names of the detectives who'd been assigned to cover the Carnation area during the morphine search. Then, armed with the necessary information and documents, she'd gotten signed statements from the Carnation pharmacist and his employees, stating that none of them had been interviewed by any police detective other than herself. She combed other pharmacies in the assigned territory and turned up another handful of overlooked pharmacists. When all the statements were collected and properly signed and witnessed, she made copies of them, then deposited the originals in her safety-deposit box, along with Schreiber's handwritten assignment list giving Goddard and Fry the territory. Early one morning, before the Wonder Boys left on their tour of duty for the day, she walked up and dumped copies of all the documents on the desk midway between them. A little Post-it note, one of the cute kind she'd found just for this use, was stuck on top of the stack. It proclaimed in happy type: Your ass is *mine!* Without saying a word, she turned on her heel and walked off. It was just one of those nice moments in life.

But for the most part, sunshine and rain, the summer days moved slowly past in a grim march of time. After weeks of probing, sifting and analyzing, IAD finally concluded that while the three detectives had shown poor judgment, the shooting had been an act of self-defense, and Kate was reinstated to active cases and partnered back with Sam. August was long, dry and hot for Seattle. Violence increased and so did their work load. Their shifts were filled with the usual summertime assortment of stabbings, shootings and beer-bottle slicings.

She thought seriously of resigning, but couldn't seem to find the time to really think it through. She'd done what she could to repair the damage Jack Turner had caused. She'd dotted every *i* and crossed every *t*, as it was in her nature to do. There was no reason to hang around any longer. In fact, Ralph Remington, Phyllis' lawyer, had stopped by her hospital room to thank her for breaking the case, and had mentioned his office could always use another top-notch investigator. She'd thanked the white-haired legal impresario graciously and tucked the offer into a back corner of her mind. But still, she couldn't find it in herself to make a move. She simply didn't know what she wanted to do.

She often found herself staring at the eastern hills, following in her mind the highway that led over the Cascades, straight across Washington and Northern Idaho, and on into Montana. There, she knew, would be the wide-open ranges where the air was pure and clear, where the sound of traffic was a lone horse galloping by, where an eagle could soar high and undisturbed in the unbroken quiet of the open sky, and no one could sidle up on your blind side. The pull of the vision was almost irresistible.

Yeah, Kate, it is, she told herself again and again. Just like it had been in San Francisco. There'd been a road there, too, that had led up the coast through Oregon to Washington. So you can go to Montana, sure. But where after that? And after that?

And she'd turn her back on the hills and slog through another day of dealing with the human traffic that passed through the station door.

Then she discovered one day that Labor Day had come and gone, and the first touch of fall had cooled the air and the rain clouds had moved in. Winter was approaching and it promised to be as grim and unbearable as the summer. She just couldn't seem to shake her underlying depression.

Until one day in the early fall, late in the afternoon, Lars Erickson, the pharmaceutical rep who'd helped her track down the doctor in Carnation, called to invite her out for dinner that evening. He was hesitant about his invitation, almost shy, saying that he hadn't been able to get her out of his mind.

Surprised, she thought a minute. He'd seemed nice enough. And he'd certainly gone out of his way to help her when she needed it. She glanced Sam's way. His head was bent over the usual stack of paperwork. Holding on to the phone, she stared at his profile. He sensed her glance on him and raised his head up to give her a questioning look, his brown eyes warm on hers, the old family mutt. Someplace deep inside she felt something stir. "No," she said quietly into the phone. "Thank you, Mr. Erickson, but I'm sorry. I'm not available at this time."